The case was going nowhere...

Ever since Carly Stevenson had turned up in the detective squad room with her kids, Jackie had been floundering through some kind of quicksand, getting sucked deeper and deeper into personalities and irrelevancies.

A deliberate walkaway was the hardest kind of case to solve. The fact that Stevenson had apparently murdered someone a week after his disappearance didn't help at all. It only made the homicide doubly difficult to work on.

They couldn't even count on the man being drawn back into his old life because of his kids. If anything, he seemed more bent on harming his children than sneaking in to visit them.

Maybe someday in the future—if John Stevenson used a personal identification number somewhere to get a job or rent an apartment—it would ring a bell in some FBI computer and the cops would be able to get him.

But if the man had already managed to obtain some fake ID, he was gone forever.

"Margot Dalton's a writer who always delivers: probing characterization, ingenious plotting, riveting pace and impeccable craft."
> —Award-winning author Bethany Campbell

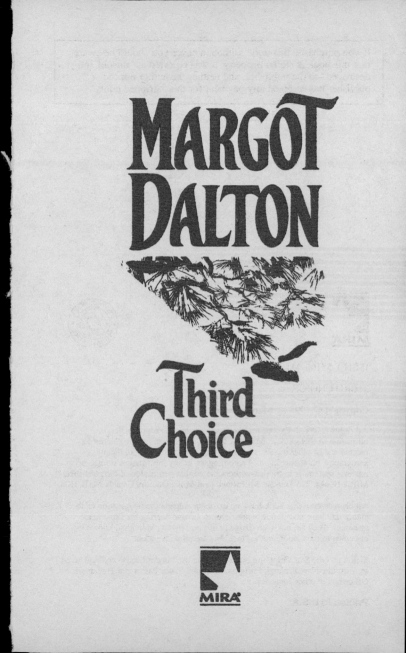

MARGOT DALTON

Third Choice

MIRA

ISBN 1-55166-441-0

THIRD CHOICE

Copyright © 1998 by Margot Dalton.

All rights reserved. Except for use in any review, the reproduction or
utilization of this work in whole or in part in any form by any electronic,
mechanical or other means, now known or hereafter invented, including
xerography, photocopying and recording, or in any information storage or
retrieval system, is forbidden without the written permission of the publisher,
MIRA Books, 225 Duncan Mill Road, Don Mills, Ontario, Canada M3B 3K9.

All characters in this book have no existence outside the imagination of the
author and have no relation whatsoever to anyone bearing the same name
or names. They are not even distantly inspired by any individual known or
unknown to the author, and all incidents are pure invention.

MIRA and the Star Colophon are trademarks used under license and registered
in Australia, New Zealand, Philippines, United States Patent and Trademark
Office and in other countries.

Printed in U.S.A.

Many thanks to Sergeant James Earle of the Spokane Police Department, and to Sergeant L. K. Eddy (retired) of the RCMP for their generous assistance. Any errors or discrepancies in this work are not theirs, but the author's.

Prologue

The child bent, puffing, to heave a ball of snow almost as large as herself. The snow was slightly sticky, heavy and dense, just right for building a snowman.

And it was fun to be outside in the darkness, exciting and a little scary.

Her house stood nearby, big and comforting, glistening with Christmas lights. As she stood erect to tug at one of her damp woolen mittens, the door opened and her father appeared in the glow of the entrance, holding a newspaper.

"Angel, are you okay?" he called into the darkness.

"I'm fine, Daddy. I got the whole bottom of my snowman finished and now I'm making his tummy."

"Well, you can't stay out much longer, sweetheart," he said. "It's almost time for bed."

"*No!*" she yelled passionately. "Not yet, I have to finish my snowman!"

He yielded as she knew he would. "All right," he said. "Just a few more minutes, then. And don't go past the fence."

"Okay, Daddy," she said contentedly, watching him vanish inside the lighted bulk of the house. She lifted a second ball onto the big one, then stood back to admire the effect.

Perfect, she thought.

Now she needed to add the smallest snowball for the head. In a plastic pail next to the fence, she already had a carrot to make the nose, one of her father's old slouch hats and a lot of...

She looked up, startled. The headlights of a car were bearing down on her, coming closer and closer, so near that their glow almost blinded her.

But that wasn't right, she thought in confusion. The cars were supposed to be on the street driving back and forth. Not here in her yard close to her house, where she was always safe.

Not here...

Belatedly she screamed and tried to jump aside. The car's tires screeched in the ice and a fender grazed the metal fence, then hit her body with a heavy, sickening impact.

She felt the car striking her, felt herself lift and fly through the air like a rag doll to land on the snow in a crumpled heap.

The car's red taillights vanished into the night and the pain began to blossom inside her body. She whimpered and tried to call her father, but her mouth was filled with salty blood and the words wouldn't come.

Gradually the world began to change, as if she were swimming underwater from sunlight into darkness. The windows of the house, the glistening Christmas decorations, the street lamps along the walk, all blurred to a single dazzle of color.

Then, slowly, the colors faded to blackness.

1

Beyond the window, snow drifted past the street lamp in big soft flakes, settling onto masses of cedar and juniper starred with lights. Each bulb cast a pool of color over the snow, pink and pale blue, green and gold, shimmering in the darkness.

Jackie Kaminsky curled up on the leather couch, hugging her knees. She looked through the window at the falling snow and the glimmer of lights, feeling a wave of melancholy. Finally she stretched out full length again, picked up a magazine and rested her stocking feet on the arm of the sofa.

"I'm always surprised that you go to all this trouble," she said.

Adrienne Calder crossed the room with a tray of cookies and eggnog, bending to place them on the coffee table.

"What trouble?" she asked.

Jackie waved a hand at the big Scotch pine covered with plaid bows and golden angels, the wreaths of shining holly and the mounds of cedar boughs adorning the fireplace.

"All this Christmas stuff. Somehow it doesn't seem like your style."

Adrienne poured a tumbler of eggnog and studied

her guest with raised eyebrows. "What do you mean, not my style?"

"I don't know." Jackie shrugged and flipped a page in the magazine. "For such a tough, cynical broad, you get really mushy and sentimental about Christmas."

"No kidding." Adrienne glanced ruefully at the big tree next to the fireplace. She was a slender, dark-haired woman in her mid-thirties, with an air of in-souciance and wry humor. "Actually, it's Harlan who likes to fuss over Christmas," she said. "I just go along with it to make him happy."

"Oh, sure." Jackie leaned over to help herself to a decorated sugar cookie. "Look at this place. Christmas is almost a month away and it already looks like Santa's workshop around here."

Adrienne seated herself in a leather armchair and crossed her legs gracefully. "So don't you believe in Christmas?" she asked. "I suppose all you hard-boiled cops just treat it like any other day?"

"Christmas is okay," Jackie said after a moment. "But Paul and I aren't making a big deal out of it this year."

"Are you putting up a tree?"

Jackie swallowed a bite of the cookie and shook her head. "Paul's out at the ranch all the time. It doesn't make much sense for me to bother with a tree for myself in my apartment."

"So why don't you go out there this weekend with a nice tree and some lights and decorate the ranch house for him?" Adrienne asked.

"I'm too busy right now to spend much time out there. A bunch of lights and dancing Santas would just make him more lonely."

Adrienne shook her head in disapproval. "You two need to get your act together," she said. "You really do."

"I know. It's just so damn..." Jackie frowned at a picture in the magazine. "How about this one?" she asked. "Can you see me in something like this?"

She held up the magazine. Adrienne leaned forward to peer at a model in an empire-style wedding gown of pale beige silk.

"I don't know," she said at last, studying the magazine thoughtfully. "You're pretty tall to wear a high waist like that. But the cream shade would be nice with your coloring."

A pretty, blond teenager came into the room, wearing black tights and a long white T-shirt. Alex Gerard, Adrienne's foster daughter, settled cross-legged on the floor next to Jackie and rested her head against the couch to look at the picture.

"I wish I had dark hair and a complexion like yours," she sighed. "Jackie, you're so gorgeous."

Jackie laughed in genuine amusement and patted the girl's head fondly. "Yeah, *right*," she scoffed. "I just chose my ancestors well, honey. Nothing like a dash of African, Cherokee and West Russian to give a girl some interesting coloring."

"I think you should wear a silk suit like that one," Alex said, indicating another picture. "It's more your style than a long gown."

Jackie examined the picture of a red-haired woman in a white fitted skirt and a short matching jacket crusted with seed pearls.

"You're probably right," she said. "I'd only feel moderately ridiculous in something like this, not absolutely idiotic."

"You know what else?" Alex leaned forward to help herself to a tumbler of eggnog and a cookie. "I think you and Paul should have a Christmas wedding. It'd be so pretty to have the whole place decorated with pine boughs and lights and stuff."

Adrienne looked at the girl with sudden interest. "Sweetie, that's a terrific idea! We could do a winter theme, and use a lot of—"

"Hey," Jackie interrupted. "Hold on there. Christmas is only a few weeks away, guys. Hardly enough time to organize a wedding."

Adrienne made a gesture of dismissal. "It wouldn't take any time to organize. Why don't you think about it, Jackie? You and Paul could even get married on Christmas Eve, and then every year your anniversary would be so romantic."

Jackie looked at their excited faces and felt a rising tide of uneasiness. "We couldn't possibly be ready that soon," she said. "Besides, it'd be impossible to get any kind of reservations. Everything in town's been booked for months."

"Oh, I could get a reservation," Adrienne said with the air of confidence that Jackie always found so endearing.

Adrienne Calder had grown up here in Spokane, Washington, the child of one of the state's leading families, in a world of wealth and power. She'd never known any other kind of life. Barely out of her teens, Adrienne had married a corporate lawyer fifteen years her senior, and she and Harlan continued to move in the city's upper social circles.

But in many ways, Adrienne's childhood, though lavishly privileged, had been just as lonely and un-supervised as Jackie's own careless upbringing in the slums of Los Angeles. Their common experience was one of the things that helped to cement their friendship.

"Even if you could get reservations," Jackie said at last, "I don't know if Paul and I are ready to do this right now. Maybe in a few months."

"Oh, that's really smart," Adrienne said scornfully. "Three or four more months of being miserable, living here in your apartment while Paul's out there all alone at the ranch. Dithering and keeping both your lives on hold, driving back and forth every weekend, worrying yourself sick about him falling under a tractor or something. That makes a whole lot of sense."

Alex was gazing dreamily at the fireplace. "We could tie white satin bows and sprigs of holly in the church, and have pine boughs all over the hall with little lights wound through them, and Jackie could carry a nice Christmas bouquet..."

"Honey, I don't think we want to get married in a church. I've never gone to church in my life. I don't think Paul has, either."

"Then you can have the ceremony right here in our living room," Adrienne said. "Or how about Mother's house?" she added. "That would be perfect. There's all kinds of space, and Alex and I could help with the decorating."

Jackie grimaced, thinking about the monstrous, elegant mansion where Adrienne had grown up.

"Sweet of you to offer," she told Adrienne, "but I don't think so."

"Why not, for God's sake?" Adrienne said impatiently. "My mother's house would be ideal for a wedding ceremony. And she'd love to do it for you, Jackie. You know she would.''

Jackie leafed through the pages of the magazine. She was becoming increasingly nervous at the direction the conversation was taking.

"Come on," Adrienne urged, leaning forward. "Why not consider the idea, at least?"

"Because we have to think about the reality of the whole thing. If I had a wedding like that, I'd have to invite my family. Can you really imagine Gram, to say nothing of Joey and Carmelo, rubbing elbows with your mother and her friends? Eating hors d'oeuvres in the drawing room?"

"We're not such terrible snobs, you know," Adrienne said. "And it's high time I met your grandmother. She sounds like an interesting person."

"Yeah, sure, if she's sober," Jackie said, looking at the shimmering tree. "But when she's drinking, she's mean as hell."

Adrienne was silent, watching her thoughtfully. Jackie paged through the bridal magazine without seeing the pictures.

She'd been abandoned by her mother, who'd been a child herself at the time of Jackie's birth, and raised by her grandmother along with a crew of assorted cousins. Jackie's troubled young mother had died of a drug overdose a few years after Jackie was born, and she'd never known her father.

Irene Kaminsky, her grandmother, had been both harsh and careless. Jackie suffered through a poverty-stricken, difficult childhood and had landed herself a two-year term in juvenile detention when she was just about the same age as Alex was now.

Soon after she got out of detention she joined the

police force, determined to turn her life around. And she'd succeeded. Jackie spent a few years with the LAPD, then moved to Spokane, logged the required service time with the Spokane Police Department and passed the detective examination on her first try.

She'd been a detective for almost four years, and in a lot of ways she'd traveled a huge distance from that tenement in west L.A.

But sometimes, especially lately, there were days when she wondered if she'd come very far at all...

"Jackie?" Adrienne was saying. "Won't you at least think about it?"

"Okay, I'll think about it," Jackie said reluctantly and then changed the subject. "So, Alex, what's up with you these days? Still playing your flute in the school orchestra?"

Alex nodded. "We're going out to seniors' residences two afternoons a week from now till Christmas," she said. "We do a program of carols for them. It's really neat," she added, munching on a cookie. "They're all so happy to see us."

Jackie picked up the girl's long braid and stroked it absently. "You're a pretty good kid, Alex," she said. "Did you know that?"

The phone rang and Alex sprang to her feet. "That's for me!" she called over her shoulder, vanishing into the hallway.

Adrienne and Jackie exchanged an amused glance, listening to the girl's feet running up the stairs to her room.

"She's doing really well, isn't she?" Jackie said.

Adrienne sighed and sipped her eggnog. "It's wonderful. She's got so many friends, and she's loving high school. It's been a world of difference between ninth and tenth grade."

They were both silent for a moment. Jackie thought about the kind of misery the girl had suffered, and the nightmare that Alex's life had been less than two years earlier.

"If I hadn't found her on that street corner and brought her to you..."

Adrienne shuddered. "God, Jackie, don't even talk about it." She looked down at the glass in her hands. "Her mother phoned here again last week," she said in a low voice.

Jackie glanced up from the magazine. "Really? You didn't tell me that."

"I was waiting till Alex went upstairs. The call upset her quite a bit."

"The poor kid," Jackie said with feeling. "What did her mother say this time?"

At fourteen, Alexandra Gerard had been sexually assaulted by her wealthy stepfather. When her mother discovered what had happened, she'd accused Alex of seducing her husband. The girl had run away from her home in Seattle. Soon afterward Jackie found her soliciting on a gritty Spokane street corner to get enough money to eat, and brought her to Adrienne and Harlan Calder when she couldn't find anywhere else for the girl to live.

"She wanted..." Adrienne clutched the glass tightly and paused. "She wanted Alex to go home for Christmas."

"Is the woman still married to that same son of a bitch?"

"Yes," Adrienne said. "But she claims things are different now. She wants to try again."

Jackie sat up and hugged her knees, resting her chin on them. "What did Alex say?"

Adrienne gave her a brief smile. "Alex said she's already home, and she didn't want to go away at Christmastime."

"Good for her," Jackie said. "But it still bothered her?"

"Yes." Adrienne ran her thumb over the etched crystal of her glass. "I feel sorry for her mother, too," she said at last. "It's such an awful situation. But I can't help being glad that Alex wants to stay with us."

"She'll go back and resolve issues with her mother eventually," Jackie said. "But she doesn't need to do it now when she's just settled in, starting to adjust and make friends at school."

"That's what Harlan says."

"Well, there you go." Jackie returned to her magazine. "Harlan's a pretty smart guy, you know."

"Jackie..."

"Hmm?"

"Is something going on here?" Adrienne asked. "About your wedding plans, I mean?"

Jackie frowned at the bright pictures. "What do you mean?"

"Is there some reason you don't want to get married? Because this isn't just about your family problems and the complication of booking a reception. I think it's more than that."

"So what do you think it is?"

"I don't know. That why I'm asking. Are you getting cold feet?"

Jackie shook her head. "I love Paul. I really do. But sometimes I feel a little..."

She fell silent abruptly and flipped through the pages of the magazine.

"When I met Harlan," Adrienne said after a moment, "I was twenty and he was thirty-five. He tried for months to talk me into marrying him. I kept refusing, mistreating him, going out with other guys to discourage him. I was a complete idiot."

"Why?" Jackie asked in surprise.

"I don't know. I guess..." Adrienne leaned over and set her glass on the coffee table. "I didn't have much of a home life," she said. "And you know how my mother treated me while I was growing up. I never really believed anybody could love me enough to stay faithful to me. He had a hell of a time convincing me I had nothing to fear."

"But if you hadn't married him, it would have been the biggest mistake of your life."

"I know," Adrienne said. "That's what I'm telling you."

Jackie put the magazine down and looked at the dying flames on the hearth. "Paul tells me we have two choices," she said at last. "And the current situation—living in two separate places and getting together only on weekends—isn't one of them."

"What are the options?"

"Number one. We could have a big wedding, invite all our friends, fly Gram and the boys up from L.A., to hell with the consequences."

"Well, that would be fun. So what's the other option?"

"Second choice, we could settle in at the ranch, get rid of my apartment and live together without being married at all."

"I'll bet Paul doesn't like that idea."

Jackie shook her head gloomily. "Not much. He says it's better than being alone, but he really wants to get married."

"And you don't?"

"I just wish there was some kind of third choice. Like, if we could put the whole thing off for a while, maybe live apart but still be..." Jackie paused awkwardly. "Don't get mad at me, Rennie. I hate having to make decisions about my life. Especially ones that can't be reversed. It's so scary."

"Believe me, sweetie, I know how that feels."

Jackie flipped aimlessly through the magazine again, then tossed it on the coffee table. "I don't know what's wrong with me," she said at last. "Everybody's pairing up, and they all seem happy. It's been more than a year since Carmen married Tony. Every time I see her, she's glowing. And Brian and Chris are disgustingly happy."

"They're a cute couple, those two."

Jackie grinned, thinking about her detective partner and his new girlfriend. "Brian's like the poster child for happy relationships now. And he used to be so bitter, kept saying he was finished with women after what Sarah put him through."

"Lucky Brian, after all the misery of that awful divorce. Now he's got a nice girlfriend, and a built-in family when he decides to take the plunge."

"He's a pretty contented guy," Jackie agreed. "And there's you and Harlan," she added, returning to her previous line of thought. "You're so happily married, you make it look easy. But I don't know if..."

"What?" Adrienne prompted.

Jackie moved restlessly on the couch, still looking

at the fire. "I don't know if I can do it. Nothing in my childhood gave me any confidence in family life or permanent relationships."

"Come on, Jackie. You're almost thirty-four years old. You have to move past that childhood sometime."

"I know you're right. And I love Paul, but I still wonder if it's ever possible to…"

Jackie got up, took a wrought-iron poker from its stand and prodded the crumbling logs, sending a bright shiver of flame leaping upward.

"I wonder if it's even possible to trust somebody that much," Jackie said. "No matter how much you love a man, can you really put your life into his hands and count on him to stay with you forever, not hurt or abandon you?"

"At some point, you've got to start trusting someone," Adrienne said quietly, "or you'll be alone all your life."

"I know, I know." Jackie replaced the poker and glanced at her watch. "Look at the time. I have to go." She went out to the hall to get her jacket from the oak clothes tree.

Adrienne crossed the room to stand in the open doorway. "Well, give some thought to Paul's choices," she said as Jackie laced up her winter boots. "He's a pretty smart guy too, you know."

Jackie smiled and reached for the doorknob. "Don't worry about me," she said to Adrienne. "I'll be fine."

"Of course you will." Adrienne hugged her, then watched as Jackie started down the walk. "Drive carefully," she said. "It's snowing hard and those streets are really icy."

"Hey," Jackie called, brushing snow from her windshield. "I'm a cop, remember? Don't tell me how to drive."

But her smile faded and sadness washed over her again as she drove across the city to her own home.

She'd always liked her apartment, enjoyed its spartan furnishings and the security of having her own belongings around her. Nowadays, though, when Paul was at the ranch and she was eating and sleeping alone, she felt restless and incomplete, as if some vital part of her had been misplaced.

She wandered around the place for a while, then stood looking out the window at the Christmas lights on the opposite building, wondering if she should get a tree and decorate it before Paul came back for the weekend.

Putting the thoughts aside, she picked up her flute, settled cross-legged on the ottoman and tried to practice. But the notes were rusty and harsh, and she couldn't smooth them out.

It was just a little past ten o'clock but Jackie felt almost unbearably weary. She put the flute away, turned on her stereo and lay on the couch, covered herself with one of Gram's old knitted afghans and battled a sudden, wholly irrational desire to burst into tears.

2

The city of Spokane lay near the eastern edge of Washington State, in a fertile agricultural valley bounded by the Rockies and the Bitterroot Mountains to the east and the Cascades to the west. Just a hundred miles north was the Canadian border.

In her early twenties as a young policewoman, tired of the violence in Los Angeles and equally sick of her own family troubles, Jackie had started looking for a better place to live and work. She finally chose Spokane because it was one of the few major cities in the Northwest without a ballooning crime rate, and because the Spokane Police Department had a reputation for effective community service and a minimum of internal strife.

Generally speaking, after nine years with the SPD, she hadn't regretted her choice. The one thing she hadn't yet fully gotten used to was the weather.

The climate here was nothing like Los Angeles's. Spokane was battered from October till April by blizzards, ice storms, mountainous dumps of snow and sudden inexplicable rises in temperature that brought massive flooding in their wake. At such times, police and emergency services were stretched perilously thin.

But there were also breaks in the weather when a

January afternoon could feel as balmy and fragrant as a day in June, and long spells during the summer when the place was absolute heaven.

Besides, we don't get earthquakes, Jackie thought as she drove to her job at the northwest substation. It was Tuesday, the morning after her visit with Adrienne, and the streets were piled and rutted with fresh snow.

A city plow crawled down the avenue next to the police station, sending curtains of snow upward to drop in mounds along the curb.

Jackie waited for the cumbersome vehicle to pass, then looked at the three-foot drifts blocking entry to the staff parking lot.

"Oh, *hell,*" she muttered, pulling around the block to the front of the building and parking in one of the public spaces.

She hauled her briefcase and notebook from the back seat, bundled them up along with her shoulder bag and climbed out of the car. Then she hurried to the front door of the police station, her breath coming in frosty clouds as she ran.

The vestibule was a small bare room no more than eight feet square, with two hard-backed wooden chairs standing against one wall. Ginny Clarke, the receptionist, perched behind a long wooden counter topped with bullet-proof glass, and typed entries into a computer.

"Hey, Jackie," she called through her communicating window as Jackie set her burden on one of the chairs and bent to unlace her boots. "Come here for a minute. Have a brownie."

Jackie took a pair of loafers from her bag and

slipped them on, then approached the receptionist and peered over the barrier.

"You've got brownies in there, Ginny? Oh, my Lord," she added, seeing the array of unwrapped Christmas treats spread out along the top of the file cabinet.

"They're mostly from the Police Wives Club," Ginny said, her mouth full. She reached for the keys at her belt. "I'll let you in and you can take your pick."

Jackie stepped hastily back from the glass cubicle. "No thanks. I'm planning to ignore Christmas this year. At least food-wise," she said, thinking about Adrienne's disapproving remarks. "I really don't want to gain ten pounds."

"G'wan," Ginny said, looking envious. "You never gain an ounce no matter what you do."

"That's because I come here early three mornings a week to work out downstairs in the gym. To say nothing of being too busy to eat on most days. Ginny…"

She paused abruptly with her hand on the door leading to the squad room, and looked at the young receptionist.

"What?" Ginny glanced down quickly at a box of caramel popcorn tied with a red bow.

"Were you going to tell me something just now?"

Jackie thought she saw a flash of guilt and apology on the girl's cheerful face.

Ginny hesitated, then shook her head. "I couldn't help it," she said at last. "I'm really sorry, Jackie."

Jackie took a step back into the room. "You couldn't help what?"

The door to the squad room opened. Alice Polson,

senior administrative assistant for the detective and
sergeant ranks, thrust her neat gray head into the vestibule.

"Oh, Jackie, I'm glad you're here," she said.
"There are some people to see you."

"Where are they?" Jackie shrugged out of her coat
and draped it over one arm.

"At your desk."

Jackie stopped short. "I'm not supposed to be doing interviews at my desk in the squad room before
I've even had a chance to hang up my coat. Besides,
morning briefings are going on. Couldn't you have
put these people somewhere else for a few minutes?"

"Just wait until you see them," Ginny said cryp-
tically. "We had no choice."

Alice nodded agreement, then vanished into her
own office at the end of the hall.

Sighing, Jackie carried her mound of belongings
into the squad room, which vibrated with early-
morning conversation, the clatter of keyboards and
ringing telephones. As soon as she entered the room
she could feel a buzz in the air, the kind of tension
that crackles through a police station when something
major has just happened.

Whatever it was, the story hadn't been carried on
the morning news. And it was clear that Jackie wasn't
going to learn anything new for a while, because she
apparently had a situation of her own to deal with.

Near her desk a young woman sat huddled on a
chair, holding a baby wrapped in a shawl. Two small
children stood by the woman's chair, one with a
thumb stuffed into its mouth, looking around gravely
at the uniformed officers and detectives in shirtsleeves
with leather holsters strapped under their arms.

Immediately Jackie's impatience with Alice and Ginny vanished.

The two women were right, they'd had no choice. Where else in the substation could you put a young mother and three little kids? Especially when there were briefings and morning patrol meetings going on in all of the sergeants' offices...

As she put her things away, she took stock of the woman holding the baby.

About thirty, she guessed, and very timid. Probably quite attractive when she took the trouble, but that clearly hadn't been the case today. The woman wore no makeup at all, not even lipstick. She had long brown hair tied back at her neck in a limp ponytail, and freckles across the bridge of her nose. Her eyes were large and blue, deeply set and ringed with shadows so dark they seemed like bruises, and her mouth looked wide and vulnerable, almost childlike.

The infant in her arms appeared to be a few months old, though Jackie didn't know all that much about babies. Probably a boy, since he wore a blue fur-trimmed bunting suit with perky little fabric ears. His eyes, like his mother's, were wide, blue and on the verge of tears.

The other two children looked to be identical twins. Jackie guessed about three or four years old, and probably girls. Their brown hair was cut straight across their foreheads and down around their ears, framing wide hazel eyes. They stood one on each side of their mother's chair, presenting an air of unity.

All four pairs of eyes watched Jackie with an unwinking gaze under furrowed eyebrows as she seated herself at her desk and got out a pen and notebook.

"My name is Detective Kaminsky," she said, giving the woman a reassuring smile and receiving a timid grimace in response. "You can call me Jackie if you like."

The woman cleared her throat. "Thank you," she whispered.

One of the twins reached cautiously toward a small foam-rubber basketball on the adjoining desk belonging to Brian Wardlow, Jackie's partner. The mother whispered something and the child drew back hastily, jamming her thumb back into her mouth.

At that moment Wardlow himself arrived, shrugging out of his topcoat, and saw the little group near his desk. He exchanged a quick glance with Jackie, then hung up his coat, took the basketball and held it out to the child, gesturing at a hoop mounted above a big wastebasket along one wall.

"Hey, you guys wanna shoot some hoops while your mom talks to Jackie?" he suggested.

Both of the older children ventured over to him, looking cautious but interested. Their mother relaxed visibly and settled back, clutching the baby, who seemed to be falling asleep within his furry blue cocoon.

Jackie tossed her partner a grateful smile, then turned her attention back to the woman. "Your name, please, ma'am?"

"Carolyn Stevenson. But people..." The woman paused and licked her lips nervously. "Most everybody calls me Carly."

"Address, Carly?"

She gave an address in the Franklin Park district, which was a modest residential area lying between Jackie's neighborhood and the substation.

Jackie leaned back in her chair to study the woman.

Carly Stevenson seemed utterly crushed by fatigue and worry. Her arms were trembling as she held the baby.

"Looks like he's fallen asleep," Jackie said, watching the fan of eyelashes fluttering over the baby's plump cheek. "Maybe you could lay him down on my desk."

The woman still looked frightened, but too weary to object. "All right," she murmured. "If you're sure it's no problem...."

Jackie got up and spread her coat out on the desktop, then lifted the baby gingerly, aware of Wardlow's bright amused glance. She was surprised by the solid substance of the little boy, the way he felt in her arms.

And he smelled so good.

Carly Stevenson might not trouble much with herself, but she took good care of her kids.

Carefully, Jackie placed the sleeping baby on her folded coat and tucked the shawl up around his chin, feeling ridiculously moved when she saw how he pursed his lips and pressed a fat hand against his cheek, then sighed and went back to sleep.

His mother shifted in her chair, looking limp with relief. She smiled shyly in gratitude when a blond woman in a blue uniform came by with a cup of coffee for her, along with a plateful of decorated cookies.

"Thanks, Brenda," Jackie said to the young patrol officer.

"Can I get you a cup, Jackie?"

"Oh, thanks, I'd love it. Just black, please."

Jackie returned to her notebook, sensing it might be best to ask a few more easy questions before she launched into the reason for Carly Stevenson's early-morning visit.

At the other desk, Wardlow and the two little girls seemed to have tired of basketball. The children were now sitting in his lap, one on each knee. They clutched pencils and scribbled on yellow legal pads, their heads close together.

Jackie made a private resolution to take her partner out to lunch as soon as she got the chance.

"Are they twins?" she asked the woman.

Carla nodded jerkily. "Rachel and Emily. They'll be four in March. We have another little girl named Caitlin but she's in school right now, second grade."

"And the baby?"

"That's Patrick," the woman said, looking at her child's plump sleeping face. "He'll be five months next week," she added with a tired smile.

Jackie jotted down the children's names and ages, then looked up.

"What brings you here this morning, Carly? Is there some kind of problem?"

"My husband…" The woman paused. A tear slipped from her right eye and trickled down her cheek, followed by a few more. She sniffled and rummaged for a tissue in the big plastic diaper bag on the floor beside her.

He beat up on you, Jackie thought, waiting impassively. He hurt you and scared the kids, and you're thinking you should lodge a complaint. But you won't, Carly. You'll change your mind because you don't know where to go and you're scared of him, and besides, he's really, really sorry. So you'll go home and he'll do it again, until he kills you or one of your kids.

No matter how often she witnessed this, Jackie always felt a sickening fury at the situation in which so many women—often mothers with small children—found themselves.

But Carly Stevenson's next words surprised her.

"He's gone. I don't know where he is. And I'm so worried..." Her voice caught and she clutched the tissue tightly.

"Your husband's name?"

"John Stevenson."

Jackie wrote the name in the notebook, hoping an air of calm would help settle the woman down. "Age and place of employment?"

"He'll be thirty-two in February. He works for... he's a bookkeeper at White Wolf Enterprises. I don't have a job right now because day care's so expensive that it doesn't make sense for me to work."

Without the baby to hold, Carly seemed unsure what to do with her hands. She shredded the tissue she'd extracted from the bag, then pulled a strand of long hair forward to curl it around her finger, flicked it off her shoulder and began to fiddle with the drawstring on her ski jacket.

"How long has your husband been gone?"

"Since last night. He went out to get some formula for the baby because I'd forgotten to pick it up in the afternoon. It was early, around five o'clock. And he...didn't come home."

Jackie caught a quick glance from Wardlow, who was listening while the children sat on his knee. She turned back to the woman.

"Have you checked with the local hospitals?"

"I've called everywhere," Carly said, her voice rising. "Friends, hospitals, both this substation and the police station downtown...I'm just crazy with worry."

"He's never done something like this before?"

The woman shook her head. "Never. John's not...he's not like that."

"Have you had any arguments recently? Problems in the marriage?"

"Nothing more than what's normal for any couple raising four kids." She looked up and met Jackie's eyes steadily. "John and I love each other, Detective. And he's crazy about the kids. There's no reason in the world for him to go away and leave us."

"What was he driving?"

"Our van."

"Make, model and year?"

"It's a dark green Ford Windstar, 1995, I think. Just a minute..." She rummaged through her pockets, took out a sheet of paper and read off the license-plate number.

Jackie made a note of the details. "So what are you driving now?"

"We have an old Volvo station wagon. Usually John takes it to work and leaves me the van in the daytime. I don't even have the car seats with me. They're all in the van."

Jackie felt a growing uneasiness.

"Carly," she said gently, "I'm afraid we can't do anything about this right now. The standard procedure for a missing adult is to wait three days before launching an investigation."

"I know. They told me over the phone. That's why I had to bundle up all the kids and come down here. I just...didn't know what else to do."

Jackie caught another thoughtful glance from her partner, and took a deep breath. "If there's been no accident report and he's not at any of the hospitals," she said, "I really don't think you need to worry about him being hurt."

"But where is he?" the woman asked, an edge of desperation creeping into her voice again.

"People do this all the time, Carly. Even people who've always been reliable in the past. They get a little crazy from the pressures of work and family life and take off. After a day or so they come home again, or at least call to let people know where they are. Do you have family or friends nearby to help you in the meantime?"

The woman lifted her chin and gave Jackie a look of cold challenge that was a little disconcerting. Despite her timidity and emotional trauma, Carly Stevenson was obviously a person with some steel at the core.

"Our families are both in Wyoming," she said. "My parents are dead and John's mother isn't well. I don't want to bother them with something like this unless..." She swallowed hard, then continued. "We have friends, of course, and a neighbor who helps me out with the kids when I need a sitter. That's not the problem."

Jackie was quiet, waiting.

Carly began to shred the tissue again, tearing it into little strips and lining them up on her denim-clad knee. One of the twins scrambled down from Wardlow's lap and came over to lean against her mother's chair, looking up at Jackie with unnerving hazel eyes.

"Something's happened to him," Carly said in a low voice. "If you knew John, you'd realize that. John's the most stable, reliable person in the world, and the best husband and father. He'd never, ever do anything like this on purpose. Never in a million years.''

Jackie closed the notebook. ''Okay,'' she said. ''I'll see what I can do. In the meantime, call me right away if he turns up, all right?'' She handed the woman one of her cards.

Carly got up reluctantly and wrapped her baby in the shawl while Wardlow and Jackie fitted little plaid coats on the two girls.

''You'll call?'' Carly asked Jackie, who escorted her to the door of the squad room. ''As soon as you hear something, you'll let me know?''

''I'll do what I can,'' Jackie said. ''Meanwhile, try not to worry. I'm sure you'll hear from him soon.''

She watched the little group trail out through the reception area, then went back in and sat at her desk.

Wardlow leaned back in his chair, hands behind his head, suit jacket falling open to reveal the gun in his shoulder holster. ''So what do you think, Kaminsky?'' he asked.

''I think it's a really sad story. She's all alone with four little kids, and the rotten bastard even took their car seats.''

''You don't think he's bleeding in an alley somewhere, or lying in a pile of twisted wreckage?''

''Somebody would have found him by now. He's been missing more than twelve hours and he was only going to the grocery store for baby formula. Supposedly,'' Jackie added grimly, taking a gulp of coffee.

''But,'' Wardlow said with a teasing grin, ''you promised her you'd do something.''

Brian Wardlow was the same age as Jackie but had less seniority as a detective. Still, he'd matured considerably since his recent divorce and all the suffering that went along with it. He had curly red hair, a good-looking freckled face and a lean, athletic body, and was one of Jackie's favorite people in spite of their periodic disagreements.

"I didn't promise anything," Jackie said. "I only told her I'd try."

"The poor woman." Wardlow looked down at his telephone, wrapping the cord idly around his fingers. "They're cute little kids. Well-behaved, too."

"At this stage it's not a police matter, Brian. You know it isn't." She sat down and began to leaf through the files stacked in her wire basket.

Wardlow nodded and leaned over to take one of the decorated cookies, munching it thoughtfully. "Chris and I went to see Desiree last night," he said.

Jackie smiled, thinking about the strange girl who was Christine Lewis's half sister, and who had been one of the chief suspects in Brian and Jackie's first homicide case. "How's she doing?"

"Pretty well. She likes the junior college she's going to. Feels she's not as conspicuous there as she used to be at high school."

"No kidding," Jackie said dryly.

Desiree Moreau had long jet-black hair and a nose ring, wore transparent dresses and army boots and practiced some kind of weird pagan religion. At college, she'd probably fit right in.

Wardlow studied the plate of cookies and selected a Christmas tree covered with lurid green icing. "She and Laney are getting along just fine. They've taken a couple of other boarders into the house and they're a big happy family group. A bunch of barefoot hippies and country-music fans, all living together under one roof."

Laney Symons, another of the suspects in that homicide case, was a part-time singer at a downtown club. She and Desiree had discovered they were kindred spirits, and now roomed together.

"Poor Maribel would turn over in her grave if she knew what was going on in that house." Jackie chuckled, then sobered when she remembered the grisly murder they'd investigated. "But," she added, "it's probably a whole lot better for your relationship than having Desiree living with Chris."

"God, you can say that again," Wardlow stated fervently. "She and Chris get along better these days, but I still wouldn't want them sharing a house."

"How's Gordie doing with the diet?"

Wardlow brightened at the mention of Christine's young son. "Great. He and I go running every night, and he's lost twenty pounds. He's a good kid, Jackie."

She smiled again, then glanced around the noisy room. "What's going on this morning, Brian? I haven't had a chance to talk to anybody since I got here."

Wardlow's grin faded. "Ugly thing," he said. "You know Jason Burkett?"

"That's the guy who's running for Congress next spring. According to the newspaper, our city's most handsome and charismatic politician."

Wardlow examined his thumbnail, nodding. "Burkett's kid died this morning. Little eight-year-old girl, killed by a hit-and-run driver."

Jackie turned to stare at him. "When?"

"She wasn't killed outright. Apparently she was building a snowman at the edge of their property just before bedtime last night. A car barreled off the street, plowed into the yard and hit her, then took off without stopping.''

"A car?'' Jackie asked. "Model? Color?''

"Uniforms have been out canvasing the neighborhood all night but nobody's come up with a more accurate description of the vehicle.''

"And you say she died this morning?''

"She was on life support for most of the night. They only disconnected it about three hours ago.''

"God, that's awful.'' Jackie hesitated, frowning. "Who's got the case?''

"Steve Baumgartner from Traffic Division.''

Jackie tapped her fingers rapidly on the desktop.

Wardlow looked at her with sudden interest. "What are you thinking, Kaminsky?''

"Brian,'' she began slowly, "remember when we investigated a break-and-enter last year at White Wolf Enterprises?''

He nodded in satisfaction. "Stolen money and a lot of vandalism. The Identification guys lifted a good print off one of the countertops and we nailed the little buggers who did it. Right?''

"That's right. But do you remember who owns White Wolf Enterprises?''

His eyes widened. "Hey, it's Jason Burkett, right? White Wolf's a holding company for most of his business interests.''

"It's also where Carly Stevenson's husband works as a bookkeeper.''

Wardlow whistled softly, staring at her. "And Stevenson went out last night around five o'clock and didn't come home.''

She opened the notebook and began to type a new case file into her computer.

"Shouldn't you hand this over to Baumgartner?" Wardlow asked.

"I want to talk to Sarge about it. Maybe we should start a full-fledged investigation of John Stevenson as a missing person, even though he's only been gone twelve hours."

"Baumgartner's going to have to know about him."

"Of course," Jackie said. "I'll call downtown and tell him right away."

"Okay." Wardlow got to his feet. "Let's go talk to Sarge. Bring your notebook." He started across the room with Jackie at his heels, then paused, returned to her desk and picked up the plate of cookies, carrying them with him to Lew Michelson's office.

3

"**G**et that crap out of my office," Michelson said when he saw the cookies.

Wardlow grinned and set the plate on the sergeant's desk, near the sleeve of his dark blue uniform. "Come on, Sarge," he urged. "Live a little. It's Christmas."

Jackie settled in a vinyl chair and smiled at her immediate superior. Lew Michelson was in his late forties, with a broad face and thinning gingery hair. He'd recently lost a fair amount of weight and still looked uneasy in his new, streamlined body.

"Sarge, just ignore Brian," she said. "He's one of those annoying skinny people who's always pressing food on everybody else. I don't know how Gordie ever sticks to his diet."

"Hey, Brian, how's the kid doing?" Michelson asked with the warm interest of any dieter in another's progress.

"Twenty pounds," Wardlow announced. "He looks great. It's a good thing the kids wear baggy clothes nowadays or we'd have to buy him a whole new wardrobe."

Michelson smiled with genuine pleasure and pushed the plate of cookies toward the edge of his desk.

"What's up?" he asked Jackie. "Who was the woman with all the little kids?"

Jackie told him while he listened in silence, doodling on a notebook.

"Seventy-two hours," he said when she was finished. "That's the standard waiting period for adult missing persons, Jackie."

"I know it is. But I thought because of the tie-in with Jason Burkett, maybe we could…"

Michelson shook his head. "It's pretty thin. Besides, we've got a tentative ID on the hit-and-run vehicle and it wasn't a van."

"For sure?" Wardlow asked.

Michelson reached toward the plate of cookies, then pulled his hand back and returned to his doodling.

"The door-to-door finally turned up a guy who saw the accident while he was leaving for his night shift at the water-treatment plant. He didn't realize the kid was hit, just saw a car in his rearview mirror as it swerved into Burkett's yard, then back out onto the street again. It was dark and snowing heavily, but he thought it was some kind of small sports model."

"Any confirmation of that?" Jackie asked.

The sergeant nodded. "A boy out shoveling walks saw a little sports car driving away really fast at the same time, weaving and fishtailing as it turned the corner. He couldn't give a model or color."

"But it definitely wasn't a Ford van."

"Definitely not." Michelson sighed, broke a pink Santa in half and began to nibble its feet.

Jackie looked down at her notebook, conscious of the sergeant watching her.

"You've got a feeling, don't you, Jackie?" he said at last.

She nodded. "I've got a feeling. I'd really like to go with this now instead of waiting three days."

"Okay," he said, surprising her a little. "Put out a call on the guy's van and get in touch with Steve Baumgartner to let him know what you're doing. But if you can't come up with any more connection to the hit-and-run today, you'll have to leave the Stevenson thing until we can start a formal missing-person investigation on the weekend. Okay?"

"Okay." Jackie watched fondly as the sergeant picked up the other half of the Santa.

"Wardlow," he said when they got up to leave, "*please* take this stuff with you."

Jackie's partner followed her into the squad room carrying the plate of cookies, which he deposited on the desk of one of the other detectives.

"What are you doing this morning?" she asked him.

"Interviews up in Loma Vista about the Sullivan baby," he said with a grimace.

Jackie nodded in sympathy.

Little Matthew Sullivan, aged four months and three days, had been found dead in his crib by his shocked parents the previous morning. Investigating a sudden infant death was one of the most unpleasant kinds of police work.

"It has to be done, Brian," she said gently.

"I know." He shrugged into his topcoat. "But it's damn hard."

She patted his arm and sat at her desk, reaching for the telephone. "If you get back in time and I'm still here, I'll buy you lunch, okay?"

"Sorry, not today. Chris is driving in from Reardan to bring a horse to the vet, and I'm meeting her for lunch. Are you putting out the call on the Windstar?"

"Right away," she said.

"It's been more than twelve hours, you know. The guy could be in California by now."

"I know."

Jackie waved as Wardlow left the squad room. She dialed the Traffic Division and waited to be connected, then passed on the details of John Stevenson's green van and left a request for Steve Baumgartner to get back to her.

Twenty minutes later a patrol officer, Dave Pringle, called to report that they'd found the van in a parking lot at the Northtown Mall, just a few blocks from the Stevenson home.

"Anything unusual about the vehicle?" Jackie asked.

"Not that I can see. It's all locked up and sitting there covered with snow."

"So it's been in the parking lot all night?"

"Must have been. There's a lot of snow on it."

"Are the car seats still inside?" Jackie asked. "Kids' car seats?"

"Three of them," the officer said after a moment. "All lined up in the back."

"Okay, thanks." She stared down at her notebook, thinking.

"Do you want it towed, Jackie?"

"You said it's locked?"

"Tight as a drum."

"Okay. Leave it there for now and I'll swing by as soon as I can to have a look at it, then let the owner know it's been located. Thanks, Dave."

"No problem."

He signed off and Jackie made an entry on her computer, then took another call.

It was Steve Baumgartner, sounding harried and impatient. "Hey, Jackie," he said. "Have you got something for me?"

Jackie told him about John Stevenson. A brief silence followed while he digested the information.

"Sounds interesting," he said at last, "but I don't know if we can make a connection. The vehicle that hit the kid was a small red car, probably some kind of sports model."

"Have you got physical evidence?"

"A bit. The car grazed a metal fence behind the little girl and left a red paint smear along with some fragments of a broken headlight in the snow. We're having them analyzed in the lab. Within a day or so they should be able to give us a make and model."

"Great. Sergeant Michelson thinks we should follow up on the John Stevenson thing," she said. "Mostly to see if we can dig up some kind of connection for you. But I don't want to step on anybody's toes. Is it all right with you if I go ahead on this?"

"Hell, yes. We're going crazy down here."

In the background she could hear ringing telephones and a steady buzz of voices. "What's going on, Steve?" she asked.

"Mostly the press. They're all over this thing. It's like an armed camp around the building. We'll have to give them something pretty damn soon or I don't know what's going to happen."

"Okay, I'll get back to you right away if I find anything."

* * *

The storm was over and a fitful sun glimmered between wisps of clouds that drifted across the blue arch of prairie sky. Jackie drove east on Wellesley, heading for Division Street and the Northtown Mall.

She found the late-model green van near the entrance to the Sears store and parked as close to it as she could, then got out to investigate.

The van was still covered with snow as Dave Pringle had reported. Jackie peered in the window at the row of children's car seats in the back. There was no sign of a struggle, nothing lying on the floor or across the seats. The van was neat, locked and empty. Any footprints nearby would have been long since obscured by falling snow.

She studied the vehicle for a while, then got back into her unmarked car and headed north to a light industrial area on the outskirts of the city.

White Wolf Enterprises sat well back from the road in the middle of a row of office buildings. It was a small, modern-looking fieldstone structure surrounded by drifts of fresh snow that obscured the landscaping.

Jackie parked and made her way up the walk to the front door. A hand-printed sign was fastened to the glass on the inside, announcing that the business was closed due to a family tragedy. But when Jackie peered in through the door, she could see a woman working at a computer.

The interior looked modern and comfortable, with thick blue plush carpeting, darker blue furniture and oak trim. A Christmas tree glittered in one corner. The tree was attractively decorated, but under the circumstances it seemed out of place.

Jackie knocked on the glass. The woman glanced up sharply, her face difficult to see in the shadows.

After a moment she came to the door and looked through the slats of the venetian blind. Jackie held up her badge and pointed to the door handle.

With obvious reluctance, the woman opened the door and stood aside for Jackie to enter. "The police have already been here this morning," she said.

"I know they have. I'd just like to ask a few more questions, if I could."

The woman turned and walked back toward her desk, gesturing at a chair nearby. She appeared to be about sixty, plump and matronly, with gray, tightly curled hair and eyeglasses hanging around her neck on a silver chain. Despite the flowery rayon dress and flat shoes, she moved with the stately dignity of a ship in full sail.

"I see that the business is closed today." Jackie settled herself in the chair and got out her notebook. Up close, she could tell that the woman had obviously been crying. "But you're still here working."

"I didn't know what else to do. I couldn't just...sit at home and do nothing."

"I understand. It's really a tragic, awful thing," Jackie said gently.

They were both silent for a moment while the older woman took a fresh handful of tissues from a box on her desk.

"Could you tell me your name and position in the company?" Jackie asked.

"Gladys Wahl. I'm the office manager here." The woman looked up at Jackie, blinking rapidly, her lips trembling. "I've been with the Burkett family in various capacities for almost thirty years now."

"We investigated a break-in out here last year,"

Jackie said, "but I can't remember the exact organization of the company."

Gladys Wahl looked down at her keyboard. A tear trickled down her cheek and she wiped it away with the back of her hand.

"White Wolf is an umbrella corporation for Mr. Burkett's six business interests. The cabinet company maintains a showroom here," she added, pointing at a carpeted area beyond an alcove where Jackie could see samples of wooden doors and cabinet hardware.

"So the cabinet salespeople would work out here as well?" Jackie asked.

"Just one person at the moment. It's our smallest company. And the cellular-communication division is here temporarily while they're trying to find a new sales location downtown. Mr. Burkett also maintains an office in the building, but he's so busy that he's not here very often."

Jackie looked at a closed oak door with a brass nameplate attached. "Then White Wolf is essentially Mr. Burkett's head office?"

"Yes, that's right. I work out here full-time, handling Mr. Burkett's appointments and personal schedule. There are also a few other people employed by the family who use the space for various purposes, and a full-time bookkeeper who maintains records relating to all six businesses."

"And you've been employed by the family for almost thirty years?"

Gladys nodded. "My husband was killed in Vietnam and I had three children to support. I started as a saleswoman in James Burkett's hardware store downtown."

"That would have been Jason Burkett's father, I assume?"

"Yes, the family has always been so good to me. This…" Another tear slipped down her cheek. "It's just a terrible thing."

"You knew the little girl?" Jackie asked.

"Since she was born. Her name was Angela, and it really suited her. She's…she was a little angel. Their only child, too. I can't imagine how they're…"

She gulped and turned away, riffling aimlessly through a pile of letters while Jackie watched.

"Jason doted on that child," Gladys continued in a thick, choked voice. "She was the light of his life. He and his first wife never had children, and he was almost forty when Angela was born."

Jackie nodded in sympathy. "Have you spoken with him today?"

"He called this morning from the hospital and told me to close the business for the day. The poor, poor man, he sounded so…" Gladys blew her nose loudly into the wad of tissues.

"You said there's a full-time bookkeeper who keeps records for all the businesses?" Jackie asked, hoping to get the conversation back on a less emotional footing.

"Well, the separate businesses each have their own bookkeepers, of course." Gladys sniffled and took a fresh handful of tissues. "This is Mr. Burkett's personal corporation. The paperwork from all six businesses comes up here to be organized and entered, then goes back downtown to the accountant."

"And the organizing and entering…that's John Stevenson's job?"

The woman looked up, giving Jackie a startled

glance from reddened eyes. "Yes. The head book-keeper collects all the paperwork, and keeps it filed and organized. It's a big job. He has a full-time assistant."

Jackie looked down at the notebook, choosing her words carefully. "Does John Stevenson get along well with everybody in the office?"

"He was always polite to people. I don't think I ever heard him say a cross word to anybody."

This time it was Jackie's turn to be startled. "You're referring to him in the past tense," she said. "Why is that?"

Gladys dabbed at her eyes. "John quit his job two weeks ago," she said. "I haven't seen him since."

Jackie's mouth dropped open in surprise. "He quit two *weeks* ago?"

Gladys nodded. "It was very irresponsible. I couldn't believe it of John. He came in one morning with barely a word to any of us, cleared his desk out and said he wouldn't be back. Poor Chantal has been going out of her mind ever since. She has no idea how to keep the books on her own."

"Chantal…Mr. Stevenson's assistant?"

"That's right. Chantal Biggins."

"Will she be here tomorrow?" Jackie asked.

"Yes, the office will be open again tomorrow," Gladys said. "The…the funeral is Friday afternoon, so we'll probably close at noon that day."

"I see. Can you tell me where Mr. Stevenson's office was?"

"In there." Gladys indicated another closed door. "But there's nothing left in the desk. John took every single thing he owned. We've been trying to hire another bookkeeper but it's not easy on such short notice.''

Jackie got to her feet. ''Thank you, Mrs. Wahl.'' She paused with the notebook in her hand. ''What was your personal opinion of John Stevenson?''

''I always liked him. He was a quiet, hardworking, responsible person, and he absolutely adored his wife and children. I can't imagine why he quit like that. I've been wanting to call and talk with him, but it's...sort of embarrassing.'' Her cheeks turned pink. ''I mean, there must have been something to make him do it, but I can't imagine what.''

''Maybe he had some sort of argument with Mr. Burkett?'' Jackie asked casually. ''Did you know if there were hard feelings of any kind between them?''

''Goodness, no. Mr. Burkett was very fond of John. He was stunned when we told him the man had up and quit out of the blue. I think Jason was planning to call and talk with him. In fact, that's another reason I haven't tried to get in touch with John,'' she said, looking a little defensive. ''I thought it best to leave the whole thing to Mr. Burkett, rather than all of us calling and interfering.''

''I can understand that.'' Jackie put the notebook in her shoulder bag and headed for the door. ''Thank you for your cooperation, Mrs. Wahl. Maybe I'll come back out tomorrow and have a talk with some of the other employees, if that's all right?''

Gladys nodded, opening a file. She put her glasses in place and the overhead light glinted on the heavy metal frames.

Jackie let herself out of the building and plodded through the snow to her car where a man stood leaning against the front fender, hands thrust deep in the pockets of the baggy tweed sports jacket he wore over a gray turtleneck.

He was about forty years old, good looking, with a hawkish nose in a thin dark face, curly graying hair and a look of shabby elegance. His eyes glittered with intelligence and an air of mocking humor that set her teeth on edge.

"Sorry," she said when he displayed his press card and settled more comfortably against the car. "I can't help you."

"Karl Widmer." He grinned, clearly not troubled by the curtness of her response. "The *Spokane Sentinel*. And you would be...?"

"I'd be in a hurry," she said. "Look, could we do this some other time? I've got nothing to tell you."

He grinned and hoisted himself onto her car, where he sat swinging his worn leather hiking boots. "It's not nice to be rude to the press," he said. "What's your name, and when did the police department get so gorgeous? I just got transferred to the crime beat," he added. "Now I'm not sorry."

Jackie walked around the car and opened the driver's door, tossing her shoulder bag inside. She stood erect to speak to him across the hood. "I really don't have time for this."

"Your name?" he asked calmly, flipping open a ragged notebook.

Jackie sighed.

The *Spokane Sentinel* was a small independent newspaper, currently jostling for a place amongst the established heavyweights of the city press. It made its mark by hard-nosed journalism, relentless investigation and the kind of gossipy "soft" news that often bordered on tabloid fare.

But the *Sentinel* was also generally supportive of the police department, and these days they needed all the good press they could get.

"I'm Detective Kaminsky from the northwest sub-station."

He glanced up at her sharply. "And you're working on the Burkett hit-and-run case? I thought it belonged to the downtown Traffic Division."

"We're not working on the hit-and-run. I'm investigating a related matter."

His eyes brightened with interest. "What's that, Detective?"

"I can't tell you. It's not even an official investigation at this point, just a few inquiries about something. Look, Mr...."

"Widmer. Call me Karl." He leaned over to hand her a business card and gave her a winning smile, but his eyes were hard and shrewd.

"Okay, Karl." Jackie took the card and slipped it into her pocket. "What I'm doing involves one of the Burkett group's employees but has no relevance to the little girl's hit-and-run death. If a time comes up when it appears you and I can trade useful information, I'll be sure to give you a call. Okay?"

"Do you have a card, Detective Kaminsky?"

She handed him one and he studied it thoughtfully. "Jackie," he said. "Nice name. It suits you."

She shook her head and reached for the door again. Widmer slid off the car, hurried to the driver's side and inserted his body next to the open car door as Jackie settled behind the wheel.

"Have the police been able to recover any kind of physical evidence from the accident scene?" he asked.

"You'll have to talk to Sergeant Baumgartner about that. He's in charge of the case."

"I know." Widmer bent low to peer in the door at her. Jackie smelled tobacco smoke and damp tweed. "Is there any truth to the rumor the Burketts were on the verge of a messy divorce?"

She felt a rising tide of annoyance. "I've never even met the Burkett family, and I can't see what relevance that rumor has to anything. What does their marital status have to do with the death of their only child?"

He grinned. "Ah, moral outrage. I like that in a cop. Especially a beautiful one."

"Get out of my way, all right?" Jackie tugged on the handle.

He stood up, holding the door with a thin brown hand. "Don't forget, Detective Kaminsky, that you and I might be able to help each other."

"I can't imagine how, but I'll bear it in mind. Now, if you'll excuse me…" She tugged on the door again, leaving him no choice but to release it or have his fingers crushed.

As she drove off, she glanced in the rearview mirror. Karl Widmer stood watching, the notebook in his hands. When she turned the corner, he waved casually and strolled off toward his battered Volkswagen. Jackie felt another sharp wave of impatience.

But her mind soon returned to the puzzle of John Stevenson's behavior.

How was she going to break the news to Carly Stevenson that her husband's van seemed to have been deliberately abandoned in the parking lot of a local mall?

More to the point, how did she impart the fact that this upstanding man had been lying to his wife every day of the past two weeks when he got up and pretended to leave for a job he no longer had?

4

About an hour remained until lunchtime, and since there was nothing more she could do on the Stevenson case, Jackie glanced at her to-do list. She drove back to the mall to interview several merchants who'd been stung by a rash of bad checks that had begun surfacing at Northtown during the previous week.

By noon she was starving, tempted to stop in at the mall's food court and grab a hamburger. But she knew she'd regret it later, so she checked her watch, hesitated for a moment, then went to her car and headed for her own apartment about two miles north of the mall.

Maybe a dish of cottage cheese, she thought as she drove, trying to remember what was in the fridge. A little fruit salad and toast, something light...

But when she pulled into the parking lot, all thoughts of food vanished from her mind.

A big four-wheel-drive truck sat in one of the visitor spaces. The truck was smeared with mud and bits of hay, its fenders and undercarriage packed with dirty snow. Jackie looked at it for a moment, feeling a rush of happiness, then got out and ran upstairs, her heart beating noisily.

But when she let herself into her apartment, the

place was utterly silent. No radio or television playing, no cheerful clatter in the kitchen.

No sign of Paul.

She went cautiously into the living room and found him sprawled full length on the couch, sound asleep.

Jackie took off her coat and laid it on a chair, then removed her blazer and took off the belt containing her gun and handcuff pouch. She tucked them all away on top of the coat and tiptoed across the room to approach the sleeping man on the sofa.

Paul Arnussen lay on his back, partially covered by one of the old knitted afghans she kept on the couch. He was big, lean and well-muscled, with smooth blond hair, blunt cheekbones and a finely sculpted mouth. Jackie studied him in silence, feeling an unaccustomed tenderness as she drank in the sight of his face and body.

She hardly ever had a chance to look at him like this without his knowledge. Usually his dark eyes were open and watchful, so penetrating that Jackie often had the uncomfortable feeling he was reading her thoughts.

In fact, this man was a reluctant psychic. On more than one occasion she'd been astounded by his ability to pick up emotions from others. But his paranormal gift, which embarrassed and distressed him, was both random and very specialized. Paul could sometimes tell when another person, even at a distance from him, was in great trauma or pain.

But he assured her that he couldn't read minds, and if he were able to foretell the future he'd never have risked so much money on the cattle market.

That last part, Jackie tended to doubt. The man was born to be a rancher. He'd worked all his adult life to acquire land of his own after his father gambled away the family ranch while Paul was still a teenage boy.

She reached down to touch him, stroking the soft golden hair with a gentle touch so she wouldn't wake him up. He looked so exhausted that her heart was wrung with sympathy and guilt.

I should be out there with him, she told herself, still gazing at his sleeping face. *I should be making sure he gets enough sleep and has somebody to talk to. He's alone so much...*

Paul was finally making his dream come true. The previous spring he'd bought a tumbledown ranch near the town of Reardan, about twenty miles west of the city, and was laboring to build the place up and make it profitable. He worked in lonely isolation except for the times when Jackie had a few days off and went out to the ranch to join him, and he did the work of four men.

Paul was tearing down and restoring the barns and outbuildings, renovating the old ranch house, trenching in an auxiliary water supply, feeding and tending a growing herd of cattle throughout the winter.

His hands were callused and scarred with cuts. Jackie saw a heavy bandage on his left thumb and bent to examine it more closely, wondering what he'd done this time.

A nick with a power saw, an injury from handling livestock, a gash from a barbed-wire fence...he was always hurting himself. What if one day he was hurt badly and there was nobody around to help him?

Gently she pulled the afghan away, lay down with him and settled her body on top of his, nestling into the strength of him.

He stirred and muttered, then closed his arms around her and relaxed against the pillows.

"Mmm," he muttered, still half-asleep, his mouth moving against her face.

"Don't wake up," she whispered.

His hands began to caress her body, drowsily at first, then with more purpose.

"You're not sleeping," she told him.

"Sure I am," he whispered huskily. "I'm having an erotic dream."

He pulled her shirt out and slipped his hand underneath, caressing her back with long, gentle strokes. She lay against him, pressing her body into his, suddenly on fire with need.

She could feel the rough cotton and tape of the bandage as his hands moved across her skin. He reached up to unfasten her bra and brushed it aside to fondle her breasts, kissing her with hungry urgency.

"Oh, Paul." She ran her tongue over the column of his neck, the hard line of his jaw.

He slid a hand under the waistband of her slacks, stroked her hips and reached between their bodies to fumble with her zipper and his own, then began to remove their trousers and underclothes. She arched herself upward to help him and settled back on top of him, conscious of his thrusting hardness against her body.

"This is a nice dream," he whispered, gripping her buttocks and pulling her closer. "It's a really nice dream."

She smiled at his closed eyes and the taut, passionate look on his face.

"Well, don't wake up. It's going to get even

nicer," she murmured against his ear, moving her body against his until he groaned with arousal.

She reached down to caress him gently, then held him and guided him inside. He sighed and moved slowly as their bodies merged with the practiced ease of lovers well accustomed to each other. Jackie lifted herself on her elbows and began to rotate her hips gently, loving the feeling of him. She rocked back and forth, using him for her own pleasure, lost in emotion.

Finally her body melted in widening ripples of sensation and she collapsed against him, moaning with fulfillment. He held her while she began to move again, slowly and purposefully, until she brought him to a shuddering climax.

At last they lay together, utterly spent, their lips touching.

"See, I told you," she whispered. "Wasn't that a nice dream?"

He smiled, his eyes still closed, and gripped her in his arms.

"Marry me, Jackie," he said.

She glanced at him, startled. His eyes opened and gazed into hers.

"Marry me," he said again. "Let's do it this weekend. I can't keep living without you."

She looked down ruefully at their bodies, still joined. "Come on. You're hardly living without me," she said.

"You know what I mean. I want you out there at the ranch with me every day. I want you to be my wife. I love you, Jackie."

She smoothed his hair. "I know you do. And I love you."

Paul reached to the floor to grasp the afghan, drawing it up over their bodies. He hugged Jackie and held her close while she told him about her visit to the Calder house and Adrienne's suggestion that they have their wedding in Barbara and Alden Mellon's mansion over on the South Hill.

"What do you think of that idea?" he asked.

"I don't know. What do you think?" She kissed his ear, then disengaged from him reluctantly, climbed down from the couch to gather her clothes and hurried into the bathroom.

Paul came down the hall, zipping his jeans, and stood leaning in the doorway, watching as she got dressed and combed her hair.

"I'm pretty sure I don't want to be married in their house," he said. "I'd like something a little more low-key and personal. Wouldn't you?"

She frowned at his reflection in the mirror. "I don't know," she said again. "I keep thinking that if we have a formal ceremony, we'll have to invite my family and send the plane tickets to L.A. for them to come here, and I never know what shape my grandmother's going to be in."

"I know."

"And then," she added restlessly, "there are so many people from work. If I invite any of them, like Brian and Lew, I should probably invite everybody..."

"Jackie," he said, reaching out to touch her arm.

"What?"

"Let's talk about what you're really afraid of. It has nothing to do with what kind of wedding we're going to have, does it?"

"Paul, I'm on my lunch hour," she said with

forced casualness. "I don't have time for soul-searching, okay?"

He hesitated. "Okay," he said at last.

She moved past him toward the kitchen. "I'm starved and I don't have much time to eat, either," she said over her shoulder. "What brings you to town anyhow?"

"I just needed a little affection," he told her as he strolled over to look inside the fridge. "Want some fruit salad?"

"I'd love it." She opened the cupboard and took out a loaf of bread. "Some cottage cheese, too, if there's any left."

"Good idea," he said approvingly, setting a plastic carton on the table. "Actually, I needed a load of block salt for the cows. *And* some affection," he added, crossing the room to drop a kiss on her cheek.

Jackie turned to wrap her arms around his neck and pull his mouth down to hers, relieved that he'd apparently chosen to drop the topic of weddings for the moment.

After lunch they walked down to the parking lot together, where Jackie said goodbye to him and watched sadly as he got into his truck and drove off.

Just three more days, she told herself as she climbed into her own car, and they'd be together again. She was going out to the ranch on Friday night to spend the whole weekend.

A mood of melancholy settled over her—just as it had last night at Adrienne's. But Jackie didn't want to examine those feelings. She started her own car and headed back past the mall, then west a few blocks to the address in Franklin Park that Carly Stevenson had given her. She parked outside, looking thought-fully at the house.

It was a modest bilevel about fifteen or twenty years old, conspicuous only by its tidiness and well-maintained look. Everything about the house was in apple-pie order, from the freshly painted window trim to the shrubs around the foundation, all neatly tied and staked for winter.

The garage door was open, showing banks of metal shelves containing an assortment of tools and garden-ing equipment. No junk stacked in corners, no toys or paint cans lying on the floor, nothing out of place. A blue Volvo station wagon, old but in good shape, stood in one of the parking bays, and the other was empty.

Jackie looked at the vacant parking spot for a mo-ment in silence, dreading her upcoming conversation with Carly Stevenson. At last, reluctantly, she got out of her car and went up the walk to ring the doorbell.

The door was answered by either Rachel or Emily, who hung from the knob and gave Jackie one of those long, unnerving stares. In the distance, Jackie could hear the sounds of other children, yelling and laugh-ing boisterously.

"My mommy's busy," the child said.

"Who is it?" Carly's voice called from another room as Jackie smiled awkwardly at the little girl and moved past her into the house. "Emily, did you..."

She appeared in the far doorway, holding a naked baby and a handful of cloth diapers. When she saw Jackie, her eyes registered surprise, then fear.

"Detective," she whispered. "Have you...is there some news about John?"

"Nothing specific," Jackie said hastily. "Just a few things we should talk about. If I could…"

"Of course." Carly hurried across the room, shifted the baby to her other arm and reached for Jackie's coat.

"Don't worry, I can put it here." Jackie took off the topcoat and hung it over an armchair, then rummaged in her bag for her notebook. "I'll only keep you for a few minutes."

Another woman appeared in the doorway, which apparently led to a kitchen. She was young and attractive in a lush, careless kind of way. Her long hair was an improbable shade of blond, and she wore a lot of makeup. She was barefoot, her toenails painted with chipped orange polish. Her curves bulged in a pair of black tights and she wore a mauve T-shirt dusted with glittery flowers.

"This is Lavonne Dermott," Carly said. "She lives next door. Lavonne, this is the police detective I told you about."

"Hi," the young woman said, giving Jackie a sudden, penetrating glance. She smiled coldly, showing teeth that needed some work. "How's things?"

"Fine," Jackie said.

"Lavonne comes over a lot to help me with the kids," Carly said, still holding her baby, the diapers clutched nervously in her hand. "She has two of her own, about the same age as the twins."

The women seemed like unlikely friends. Even here in the security of her own home, Carly Stevenson had a buttoned-down, austere look, while the neighbor was blowsy, almost sluttish. It appeared, Jackie thought, to be one of those odd relationships women tend to develop based on little more than physical proximity and small children in common.

The other twin had arrived along with two yellow-haired children, apparently boys, in dirty T-shirts and small blue jeans with tears in the knees. The children stood clustered around Lavonne, watching Jackie with the unwavering gaze that was becoming familiar.

"Come on, kids," the blond woman said. She reached for the baby and took him into her plump embrace. "Let's all go into the bedroom and put some clothes on this boy. Then we'll watch 'Sesame Street' while Mummy talks to the lady. All right?"

She swayed from the room, followed by the group of children. When they were alone in the living room, Carly gestured nervously at one of the armchairs, then moved a small pile of Barbie dolls and clothes so she could sit on the couch.

Jackie held the notebook and looked around. The furnishings were modest but comfortable, and the place was surprisingly tidy for a home with four small children. Plants filled the big front window, arranged on a well-made wooden stand.

Pride of place was given to a large gold-framed photograph above the couch, showing a slender and radiant Carly wearing a long white wedding gown. In the picture she gazed adoringly at a sturdy young man with a square, pleasant face, who looked uncomfortable in his pale blue tuxedo and bow tie.

"Is that a good photograph of your husband?" Jackie asked, studying the sandy-haired groom.

Carly glanced over her shoulder at the wedding photo, her face softening. "Yes, I'd say it is. Although we both look awfully young, don't we?" she added wistfully. "It was almost ten years ago. John and I were high school sweethearts."

A large toy box sat near the fireplace. It was skillfully crafted of polished wood, with the names Rachel and Emily inlaid on the lid.

"John made it for the twins last year," Carly said when she saw Jackie looking at the box. "He's a real homebody. He loves making things and puttering with tools downstairs in his workshop."

"So does my boyfriend," Jackie said. Involuntarily she glanced up at the wedding photo again and cleared her throat.

"Could I get you anything?" Carly asked timidly. "Some coffee, maybe?"

"No thanks, I just had lunch." Jackie opened the notebook and paged through it to avoid looking at the woman. "We've located your van," she said.

"Where is it? Did John..."

Jackie shook her head. "There was no sign of your husband, Carly. But the van's parked over at Northtown Mall, near the Sears entrance. Do you have an extra set of keys for it?"

Carly nodded, looking confused.

"If your neighbor can stay with the kids a few minutes, I'll drive you over there now to pick it up, all right?"

"But...I don't understand. How could the van be there if John's not..."

"Carly, has your husband shown any signs of stress lately? Has he talked to you about problems at work, for instance?"

The woman frowned in concentration, then shook her head. "No, not at all. He did say on the weekend that they're really busy right now with Christmas coming up and everything, but afterward he might be able to take a couple of weeks off and we could go to Wyoming to visit his family.''

''I see.'' Jackie watched her thoughtfully.

''He even said maybe we could…'' Carly hesitated, brushing aimlessly at her hair. ''He said we could leave the kids with his sister for a few days and have a little time to ourselves. Maybe take a run down into Colorado and do some skiing. John and I both love to ski,'' she added. ''But for the past few years with the kids and all, we haven't had much chance.''

Jackie took a deep breath. ''I should tell you that I went over to White Wolf this morning and talked with Gladys Wahl.''

Carly's face twisted with emotion. ''I just heard on the radio about the Burketts' little girl,'' she whispered. ''I've been so crazy with worry about John that I didn't even know it happened until a little while ago.''

''It's a sad thing,'' Jackie said.

''I was going to phone them.'' Carly looked around miserably, toying with her limp ponytail. ''But I don't suppose it's right to bother them today. Anyhow, I thought I'd wait until John came home so we could…''

Her voice trailed off.

Jackie looked at her, watching her reaction. ''Carly,'' she said, ''Gladys Wahl told me your husband quit his job at White Wolf two weeks ago.''

The woman's face turned so pale that the freckles stood out in sharp relief. She stared at Jackie, her eyes wide with shock.

''What?'' she asked. ''What did you say?''

"He quit his job two weeks ago," Jackie repeated. "They haven't seen him since."

"But that's just..." Carly shook her head in disbelief. "No, no," she muttered. "No, that's not true. He's been going to work every morning. He gets up and has breakfast just like always, plays with the kids and helps me with Patrick's bath. Then he takes his lunch and his briefcase and leaves for work. Every single day."

"It's been two weeks since they've seen him," Jackie said. "Wherever he's been going in the morning, it hasn't been to work."

"But...that's just crazy. Where would he go? And why would he quit his job? John loves working at White Wolf. He's been there more than six years, since Caitlin was a baby."

"According to Gladys, he didn't say why he was quitting. He just cleaned out his desk one morning and left without giving any notice. They haven't been able to replace him yet. Apparently it's been quite a problem for them."

Tears gathered in Carly's eyes and began to trickle down her cheeks. She tugged a handful of tissues from the pocket of her cardigan and rubbed distractedly at her face.

"I just...I don't know what to say," she whispered. "It's like a nightmare. This is all so awful."

Lavonne Dermott appeared in the doorway, still carrying the baby who was now dressed in a blue terry-cloth sleeper.

"I'm putting him down for his nap," she said. "And the kids are watching TV." She looked sharply at Carly's tear-streaked face, then at Jackie. "Is something the matter here?"

Carly got up and stumbled across the room. Lavonne took her in an embrace and held her along with the baby, glaring at Jackie.

"She says…" Carly's voice was choked. "She says John left the van in the parking lot at the mall. And he…he quit his job two weeks ago! He hasn't even been going to *work*." Her voice rose to a wail of despair on the final words.

Lavonne patted Carly as if the distressed woman were one of the children and murmured soothing words. Jackie began to wonder if perhaps she'd been overly harsh in her appraisal of the neighbor.

She got to her feet, picked up her coat and looked at the plump blond woman. "Mrs. Dermott, if you could stay with the kids for a few minutes, I'd like to take Carly over to Northtown to pick up their van. She's going to need her kids' car seats. Is that all right with you?"

"Of course. You go on, honey," the woman said to Carly. "Go get your van. I'll watch the babies till you get back."

"But where is he?" Carly asked piteously. "Where's John? What's going on?"

"Whatever's going on," Lavonne said, "it'll be okay. There's got to be some explanation for all this."

Carly sniffled and brushed at her tears with the sleeve of her cardigan. "You really think so?" she asked. "You think he's all right?"

"Of course he's all right," Lavonne said, exchanging another inscrutable glance with Jackie. "This is some kind of mix-up, that's all. Now off you go," she added. "Don't keep the lady waiting. I'm sure she's a busy person."

Carly turned obediently and went to the closet to

get her duffle coat. She followed Jackie out the door and down the walk to the police car.

When Jackie glanced over at her, she saw the face of a shattered woman.

5

Carly hesitated next to the locked van, looking around at Jackie who stood behind her.

"Are you sure it's all right for me to just…take it?" she asked timidly. "I mean, you don't want to check it for fingerprints, or anything?"

Jackie shook her head. "We don't have the right to proceed along those lines. To hold or examine a vehicle, we need to have some kind of probable cause, and as far as we know, there's been no crime committed here."

Carly dug in her pocket for the keys. She unlocked the door, opened it and looked inside at the neat, unrevealing contents of the van, the little row of car seats in the rear. Then she squared her shoulders and turned back to Jackie.

"I know what you're thinking," she said. "You think John's just another discontented husband and that he probably left us and ran off with somebody. Don't you?"

Jackie hesitated, wondering what to say.

"Well, I can see how you'd think so." Carly frowned at the snowy parking lot in the afternoon sun. "But if you knew John, you'd realize how impossible that is. It's all so…"

Her voice caught. She turned away for a moment,

then went on. "Something's happened to him, and I don't know what to do. I feel so helpless. It's like I'm caught in one of those awful nightmares where you can't move or think properly."

Jackie looked at the woman's pale, taut face, touched by her loyalty.

"You don't doubt him at all, Carly?" she asked. "Not even for a second?"

"No, I don't."

"Even though you know he quit his job and lied to you about it for all that time?"

Carly blinked rapidly to hold back tears. Her chin trembled and jerked like a child's. "No, because there had to be some kind of reason. Something terrible must have happened to him at work, something Gladys doesn't know about. Poor John, he must have suffered so much, and been afraid to tell me…"

Carly scrambled behind the wheel of the van. Jackie watched her, amazed at the woman's refusal to accept the obvious.

Because it's unbearable, she thought with a wave of sympathy. *I guess we all try to avoid dealing with the things we can't endure.*

She watched as Carly shifted the vehicle into gear and drove out of the parking lot, back toward her neat little houseful of children.

Finally, still brooding over the Stevensons and their situation, Jackie got into her own car and headed southwest across the city, toward the upscale residential area along the Spokane River where Jason Burkett's family lived.

The white mansion, though gracious and costly, probably wouldn't have stood out among its neighbors except for the mass of press and police vehicles parked outside and the yellow tape still fluttering across the snow-covered expanse of the yard. The house had a tall Grecian facade with slender pillars and ornate upper moldings, set well back from the road behind a profusion of shrubbery and mature trees. A three-car garage stood off to one side of the house, at the end of a long curved driveway now barricaded by the plastic tape.

Jackie parked and got out, ignoring the noisy crowd of journalists as she crossed the tape and waded through the snow. A group of police technicians worked near the fence under a pine bough that jutted from the adjoining yard. She greeted them and stopped for a moment to watch.

They had a small camp stove set up near the fence, with a pot of brownish yellow liquid bubbling cheerfully on one of the burners.

"Really cute, guys," she said. "It looks like you're having a picnic."

"Some picnic." Sergeant Welsh glanced up from a snow-covered bank where she knelt studying the ground. "You don't want to snack on this stuff, Jackie."

Claire Welsh was a slim blond woman in her forties, one of the senior Ident technicians. She wore white coveralls over her working clothes, and a pair of hiking boots.

Jackie leaned closer to sniff the bubbling liquid. "Phew!" she said, wrinkling her nose. "That's really awful. What is it, Claire?"

"Sulfur." Sergeant Welsh moved over to help one of the junior technicians, who was mounding snow carefully along the edges of a tire track near the fence.

"We heat it until it liquefies, then pour it onto the tread. The sulfur hardens so quickly that it takes an impression before the snow melts."

"But you've already got photographs of this, haven't you?"

"Of course we have. All kinds of them, in boring, painstaking detail."

Claire gestured to another of her assistants, who tipped the boiling liquid onto the ground. Jackie watched, fascinated, as the brilliant yellow flowed over the snow, congealing instantly.

Claire reached out with her gloved hands, lifted the mass carefully and turned it over, brushing snow from its edges. All the technicians bent closer to study the impression.

"It looks like a good one, boys," Claire said. "Really good."

"Just like a fingerprint." Jackie gazed in astonishment at the neat treads reproduced on the sulfur cast.

"It's not exactly like a fingerprint," Claire said. "What we're primarily looking for are accidental characteristics." She touched a portion of the neat herringbone track. "See, right here there's a piece of the tread missing. We know it's the right front tire, because the car swerved at this point to avoid crashing into the fence and hit the little girl just a few feet farther on. So once we find the car, we can do test impressions and match that bit of missing tread with a pretty high degree of reliability."

"And it'll stand up in court?"

Claire nodded. "Usually it's solid enough that we don't get to court. But," she added, "this impression's worthless until we have the actual tire for comparison. You guys find us the tire, and we'll do the matching."

Jackie straightened and looked around. "With all that snow last night, I didn't think you'd get any tracks at all."

"We didn't get much." Claire stood up next to her, brushing at the knees of her coveralls. "Just this one, where the fence and that overhanging branch helped to block the snow. My guys were out here last night a few minutes after the ambulance left, and managed to get some things covered for me."

Jackie watched another technician who was pumping a little bellows at the mounded snow, sending puffs of white into the air.

"We're still trying to find another tread under there," Claire said, "and see if we can determine a track width. It helps to narrow down the size and make of the car. But it's just about impossible to locate anything now. Even if we did, it would be hard to do a proper measurement."

Jackie looked down at her feet, where the tire tread had been melted and obliterated by the liquid sulfur. She glanced around at the rest of the yard.

A blue plastic pail stood next to the fence nearby, containing a withered carrot, some black buttons and an old cloth hat.

"She was building a snowman," Claire said, following Jackie's eyes. "I suppose it got mashed to pieces when the car hit her."

Jackie nodded, still looking at the pail.

"Hey, how come you're working on this?" Claire asked, beginning to pack her equipment. "I thought Traffic was in charge."

"I'm doing something kind of related. It's a complicated story."

"Oh, yeah." Claire gave her a wry smile. "They always are."

Jackie walked gingerly across the snow to a white plastic sheet pegged down by stakes. She glanced back at Claire, who nodded.

"Go ahead. We're pretty much finished here."

Jackie raised the sheet and looked at a small impression in the snow. The hollow was soaked with a pinkish stain and dusted by snow that had fallen after the child's body was removed, before the technicians were called to protect the site.

She tried to picture a little girl out here in the safety of her own yard, building a snowman in darkness starred with Christmas lights.

And the kind of person who could destroy that child and drive off into the night without stopping....

Claire came up beside her, carrying an aluminum case and a couple of cameras. They both gazed down soberly at the bloodstain in the snow.

"Let's get this one, Jackie," Claire said with sudden passion. "The goddamn bastard."

Jackie looked at her colleague in surprise. The Ident technician was usually so calm and efficient, and hardly ever expressed this sort of emotion about the cases she worked on.

"We'll get him, Claire," she said. "Count on it."

Jackie watched a moment longer as the technicians loaded equipment into their vans. Finally she turned and headed up the walk to Jason Burkett's house.

The door was answered by a thin, wiry little woman of indeterminate age, wearing jeans, a Sonics sweatshirt and a checked apron.

The woman peered at Jackie's badge, then sighed heavily. "I don't suppose you could put off talking to them?" she asked. "Because they've had an awful day, you know. I'm not sure how much more they can stand."

"Maybe you could give me your name first." Jackie stepped into the foyer and took off her boots, leaving them on a tray near the door. "And your position in the household, if you don't mind."

"Sadie Frank. I'm the housekeeper." The woman's eyes were red-rimmed, and she kept wringing her hands nervously in the apron. "This is the most awful thing," she whispered. "Just the most awful thing."

"Yes," Jackie said. "It really is." She paused to give the woman a chance to compose herself. "Do you think I could speak for a moment to Mr. Burkett? I don't need to bother his wife, but I'd really like to have a word with him."

"I'll go see. Could you wait here for a second?" The woman indicated an oak deacon's bench along one wall. Jackie sat down, shrugged out of her topcoat and took a notebook from her shoulder bag. She leaned back and looked around at the Burkett home.

As was often the case when she investigated crimes among the wealthy and powerful, Jackie found herself battling a deep chill of uneasiness bordering on panic. No matter how professional she tried to appear, it was still hard to overcome a lifetime of conditioning.

A treacherous inner voice kept whispering to her that Jackie Kaminsky didn't belong in a place like this. She had nothing in common with the kind of people who lived here, didn't even speak the same language.

And despite the authority of her badge and position, these people could look right through her, the voice whispered. They could see all the way to the sullen, dirty, impoverished little girl she'd once been, the child who was angry with everybody who had so much when she had nothing.

Years ago, Jackie had come to recognize this voice as her grandmother's. Ever since she could remember, the old woman had been telling her, by word, action and implication, that she wasn't good enough and she'd never find a place in the world.

For most of her early life Jackie had believed the message without really thinking about it, though she'd also been dedicated to a grim battle against her own fate. Only lately had she begun to wonder why Irene Kaminsky had felt the need to be so harsh. From an adult perspective it seemed like the behavior of a frightened person, though in her childhood Jackie had believed Gram wasn't afraid of anything but running out of liquor.

Maybe the old lady had been frightened of something she saw in Jackie's own personality. Perhaps she was terrified the girl's restless striving would one day bring her into the kind of world she now caught glimpses of, and the reality of it would be too much for her to endure....

Jackie shook her head to clear the memories, and took stock of the house.

Like many of the very expensive homes she encountered, the place had a beautiful austerity that she found instinctively satisfying. There were no frills here, no swirls or patterns or bright colors. The floor was gleaming parquet hardwood covered with faded tapestry rugs. The walls were smooth plaster, the furniture upholstered in pale shades. Flower arrangements sat on low wooden tables, massed and beautiful, and every piece of artwork that Jackie could see looked as if it cost a small fortune.

They had so much beauty in their lives, these people. It seemed almost prodigal.

Again Jackie remembered the child she'd been at eight years old, cutting pictures from magazines and keeping them behind the broken baseboard in an upstairs closet so her cousins wouldn't get them. Images of waterfalls and green fields starred with wildflowers, little bits of distant loveliness that helped her to endure life on those gritty streets.

A child the very same age, Jackie remembered, had lived in this house, and probably taken all the luxury and beauty for granted.

But that child was dead now, and the person who'd killed her was walking free, going about his business...

She felt hot and tired, with the beginnings of a dull headache. For a moment she sprawled wearily on the wooden bench and closed her eyes, then looked up with a start when Sadie Frank reappeared.

"They'll see you together," the housekeeper said. "They're in the morning room."

Jackie got up, trying to smile, and clutched her notebook. "Thanks a lot, Sadie."

"Come this way, Detective," the housekeeper said.

Jackie followed the woman through a wide hallway to the back of the house, which was lighted by rows of clerestory windows high above. As they walked, she stepped gingerly on the rich Persian carpets. They felt thick and silky under her stocking feet, their colors glowing like pale jewels.

They reached a room at the back of the house,

where the far wall opened into a greenhouse filled
with plants. Many of them were in bloom, filling the
air with a damp fragrance. The room was furnished
with couches, chairs and love seats made of raw
wicker, cushioned in earth-tone linens.

If I had a place like this, Jackie thought, *I'd never
want to leave. I'd just stay here all day.*

Aloud, she said, "I'm Detective Kaminsky. What
a beautiful room this is."

One of the people watching her was a small woman
with chin-length hair of such a pale blond that it was
almost silver. She wore pink nylon jogging pants and
a white T-shirt, and was curled on one of the wicker
couches with her feet tucked under her, clutching a
fringed cushion in her lap. Obviously Norine Burkett.

A man—Jason Burkett—sprawled in an armchair
across from the blond woman, wearing jeans and a
gray sweatshirt, his legs extended wearily. He held a
drink in his hand that appeared to be mostly melting
ice.

"Sadie?" he said, holding the glass aloft and giving the housekeeper an imploring glance.

The little woman hesitated in the doorway next to
Jackie. "Same thing?" she asked.

He nodded.

Sadie looked over at Norine. "Anything for you,
ma'am?"

Norine Burkett shook her head and stared out the
window at the snow-covered yard that formed an in-
congruous backdrop for the lush greenery inside the
room.

Jackie sat in another of the wicker armchairs and
looked at the couple. Her first reaction was that she'd

never, in all her years of police work, been in the presence of such powerfully controlled grief.

Jason Burkett had a haggard, haunted look, and stared fixedly at Jackie from sunken eyes, though she suspected he wasn't even seeing her. The congressional candidate was a big, well-built man with a head of thick brown hair, and was almost boyishly handsome though he was probably close to fifty.

She glanced at her notebook for confirmation. Gladys Wahl had said Jason was forty when his daughter was born, and Angela had been eight years old.

"I'm so terribly sorry about your little girl," she said at last. "I can only imagine how you must feel."

Jason shook his head from side to side, like a big animal in pain.

"She was outside," he muttered, his voice thick and slurred. "She was building a snowman and she didn't want to come in until it was finished. I said she could stay for a few more minutes. When she didn't come in, I went to the door and called for her, then went outside. I found her in the—"

He stopped abruptly and took a sip from his glass, then rattled the ice chips and squinted at them in confusion.

"So you didn't see anything unusual outside the house?" Jackie asked.

"Didn't see anything," he muttered. "Not a goddamn thing. Just my little angel lying in that..." He choked, his mouth widening into a grimace of agony.

"Jason," his wife said, speaking for the first time.

Her voice was low and clear, like the flick of a whip, and had a visible effect on her husband. He sat up straighter, put the glass on a low table nearby and composed his face.

Jackie glanced at Norine Burkett. She was very dainty and fine-boned, with skin so pale it was almost translucent. Her eyes were huge and flower blue, ringed with shadows. She looked at least fifteen years younger than her husband.

Jackie remembered Gladys Wahl's remark that this was her employer's second marriage.

And somebody...who was it?...had suggested earlier in the day that the Burketts were having marital difficulties.

She hesitated, wondering what line of questioning to follow. The hit-and-run wasn't her case. All the physical details of the accident would certainly have been covered by investigators from the Traffic Division.

"Actually," she said, clearing her throat and feeling uncomfortable, "I'm here to ask you about a...related matter."

The man looked up at her without interest, his eyes dazed and expressionless. But his wife stiffened and sat more erect on the couch.

Neither of them spoke.

"I wanted to know a little about your bookkeeper, John Stevenson."

"Stevenson?" Jason asked blankly. "What about him?"

"He seems to have disappeared," Jackie said. "According to his wife, he went out last night to get some baby formula and never came home."

Norine Burkett said nothing, but her thin hands tightened on the cushion in her lap, gripping so hard that the knuckles whitened. Jackie watched the woman with sudden interest, then turned back to her husband.

"Could you tell me anything about John Stevenson, Mr. Burkett? What kind of man he was, and if his work was satisfactory?"

Jason held his glass aloft and stared at the watery liquid. "He was a damn good bookkeeper. I never had any complaints with him."

"And you have no idea why he quit his job?"

It seemed to take a major effort for the man to concentrate enough to carry on a conversation. Jackie wondered if he was also sedated, and showing the combined effects of liquor and drugs.

Norine Burkett sat stiffly on the couch and watched him. Occasionally she turned to glance at Jackie with unfathomable blue eyes.

The room seemed charged with emotion and deep, strange undercurrents. It was intensely uncomfortable. Somewhere in the distance a phone rang and was quickly stilled. Jackie had to fight an urge to shift nervously in her chair.

"Mr. Burkett?" she prompted.

"What?"

"Do you have any idea why John Stevenson resigned so suddenly?"

"No," the man said with a miserable glance at his wife. "We were all taken completely by surprise. One day he just cleared out his desk and left, and never said a word about why he was going. Not like John at all."

"And you say he's disappeared?" Norine asked, the first time Jackie had heard her speak more than a monosyllable. Her voice was quiet and sweet, almost childlike, but the expression in her eyes remained cautious and watchful.

"He vanished last night. His wife came into the station this morning and reported him as a missing person, but we can't launch an official investigation until he's been gone for three days. At this point I'm just making a few inquiries."

"Is Carly all right?" Jason asked. "Does she need any help?"

"I think she's managing, but she's pretty upset. She asked me to express her sympathy," Jackie added, "about your little girl, but she didn't want to call today in the midst of what you're going through."

"People keep calling," Jason said vaguely. "They're just trying to be kind, I suppose."

"I'm sure they are." Jackie got to her feet and reached in her pocket. "Mr. Burkett," she said, handing over one of her cards, "if you remember anything odd about John Stevenson's behavior, anything he might have said to give a hint as to why he quit his job, I'd be most appreciative if you'd give me a call."

"Of course." He took her card and set it on the table next to his empty glass. Jackie wondered if he even saw it.

The last thing she was conscious of as she left the room was the man's grief, so dark and heavy it was almost palpable.

6

Carly Stevenson moved restlessly in bed, trying to get comfortable. She leaned up on one elbow to look at the bedside clock. It was just after 1:00 a.m. Less than ten minutes had passed since the last time she'd checked.

Sighing, she turned her pillow over, burying her face in its welcome coolness, then reached for John's pillow and wrapped her arms around it.

She couldn't stand sleeping alone. They'd hardly spent a night apart in all the years of their marriage, except for the times she was in hospital having babies. Even then John had always stayed as late as he could, lingering at her bedside, reluctant to leave her and go home.

She smiled wistfully in the darkness.

Sometimes he'd even climbed into her hospital bed so he could hold her, because it comforted both of them so much. One night after Caitlin was born, the nurse had caught them together like that but she hadn't said anything, just smiled and slipped out again....

This was the second night since his disappearance.

Carly grasped the pillow and burrowed closer to it, thinking about men. Could a woman really have so little knowledge of men in general that she could be completely wrong about her husband?

That's what everybody seemed to think. Lavonne said none of them could be trusted, they were all bastards. She'd certainly had experiences with a lot of men.

And the tall police detective, with her striking good looks and her air of calm authority...it was easy to see that she thought Carly was foolish for her blind faith in her husband.

There was no doubt Detective Kaminsky, too, saw a lot of what happened in the world, and knew what men were capable of.

Carly had never really, truly known any man but John. She'd been raised by a single mother after her father was killed in Vietnam when she was three years old. And she'd been a virgin when she and John first started going out together in high school. He'd been all her girlhood dreams come true, a sturdy handsome boy who thought she was wonderful.

They started sleeping together when Carly was in her senior year and John was taking business classes at a college in Cheyenne. He'd been so gentle with her, so awed and worshipful, that her first experience with sex hadn't been as terrifying as it seemed to be for a lot of girls. In fact, it was a night so achingly sweet, she still treasured the memory.

Carly had never in all her life slept with anybody but John. She didn't really know what other men were like physically. But she understood John all the way to his core. After so many years, there was probably nothing about her husband she didn't know.

Except, Carly thought miserably, where he was right now....

She turned over, still clutching the pillow, and stared at the window. It was snowing again, big soft flakes that hissed and spattered on the glass.

Carly slipped from her bed and walked across the room to look out, leaning her hot forehead against the window. Several of the neighbors had left their Christmas lights on all night. The colors glimmered through the snowfall, misty and beautiful, evoking long-ago feelings of childhood and wonder.

A sob rose in her throat and she struggled to hold back the tears. She'd been crying ever since John had failed to come home. But she really had to pull herself together because the kids needed her to stay calm. They needed her to be strong.

Caitlin, in particular, crept around the house looking worried and trying to keep the twins quiet, casting frightened glances at her mother when she thought Carly wasn't watching.

She stared again at the glow of lights, wondering what kind of Christmas her children were going to have this year.

"Oh, John," she whispered. "Where are you? What's going on?"

Something caught her attention, a sound carried on the dark stillness. She gripped the edge of the ruffled curtain and listened tensely.

It came again, a breath of noise from the other end of the house, near the back door. A small, stealthy noise, a series of muffled thuds and scrapes.

Carly glanced around nervously, then slipped from the room and paused in the hallway to check on her children.

Rachel and Emily shared a small room next to the master bedroom, filled with toys and stuffed animals.

They were both sleeping soundly in their bunks, only their thatches of messy brown hair visible above mounded blankets in the faint glow of the night-light.

She moved quietly across the hall to the room where Caitlin had a small bed and Patrick slept in his crib. Carly slipped into the room and glanced at her eldest daughter who was sprawled awkwardly, her leggy body mostly uncovered. Caitlin was getting to be a tall girl, losing the sweet pudginess of early childhood.

My little athlete, John called her, proud of her prowess at the school track meets, when Cait's shirt was usually covered with ribbons.

John always took a day off work and volunteered to help at the track meets. They took a picnic basket and spent the day together as a family, enjoying the sunshine and the crowds of laughing children.

Carly drew the covers over Caitlin's body, touched her forehead with a lingering hand and went to the crib to look at the baby.

Patrick wore a terry-cloth sleeper and crouched on his stomach like a little blue snail, his diapered rump high in the air. One hand was curled near his fat cheek, the other outflung on the crib mattress, fingers spread wide.

John had been so thrilled to have a boy at last. While Carly was pregnant, he'd never even allowed himself to think about it.

"Girls are just great," he'd assured her a hundred times. "I love all my girls. I wouldn't trade them for anything."

But in the delivery room when Patrick was born the doctor had held the baby aloft to display his tiny genitals. Through a fog of weariness Carly had seen her husband burst into tears, actually sobbing with emotion.

Remembering, she felt her eyes stinging again and brushed at them with the back of her hand. She pulled the cotton blanket up to cover Patrick warmly, then slipped out the door and paused in the hallway.

The noise came again. It had a cautious, deliberate sound, not something random like a tree branch rubbing against a window.

"See?" John would say after she'd wakened him and made him go outside to check some troubling noise. "See, punkin? It's just a little piece of the shutter, broken loose and flapping in the wind. That's all it is."

And then, laughing, he'd hold her and kiss her to show that he didn't mind, that he loved her even when she forced him from his bed in the middle of the night and sent him out on a wild-goose chase....

She moved down the hall to the kitchen and edged toward the back entry. The room was bathed in a ghostly half light. John kept night-lights in every room for safety, in case one of the girls got up and went looking for a drink of water or something.

The floor tiles were cold against her bare feet. Carly curled her toes away from the chill and stared at the door. Suddenly her eyes widened in horror.

The doorknob was moving.

She covered her mouth with both hands and stared, then looked around wildly at the phone, sitting on the counter. She moved toward it, her heart thundering with panic, planning to dial the emergency number. But near the counter she paused and looked at the door again.

What if it was John outside that door? What if he'd

lost his key and needed to get into the house but didn't want anybody to know?

She moved closer to the door, trying to calm herself and catch her breath.

"Who's there?" she called softly. "Is somebody out there?"

The doorknob stilled abruptly. The silence was so profound that she could hear the thudding of her heart and her own ragged breath.

"John?" she said. "Is that you?"

Footsteps pounded down the steps, off the back deck. Carly opened the door and went outside, crossing the deck in time to see a dark shape vanish around the back of the garage and into the alley.

Her bare feet stung and burned with cold. She hurried back inside and looked at the telephone again, then slipped into her coat and boots, took a flashlight from a shelf near the door and went outside, examining the blanket of fresh snow. A single set of men's footprints led up the steps to the deck, then back down and off into the yard where the dark shape had vanished.

Carly backtracked, following the row of prints that were already dusted and filling with snow. They came to an end under the window of the room at the back of the house where Caitlin slept with Patrick.

She shone the flashlight on the snow, all at once feeling sick with dread. Now there seemed to be two sets of prints, both large enough to belong to men wearing heavy boots. And it appeared they'd spent a lot of time under the children's window, milling around and moving back and forth.

She looked up at the window. Their house was a bilevel built on property that sloped away at the rear, so the basement was mostly aboveground. The bed-room window stood at least ten feet above the grade.

Who had been out here? And why were they concentrating their attention on the window of the room where her baby slept?

Carly stared tensely into the shadows of the back-yard.

"John?" she called, her voice small and thin in the darkness. "Are you out here?"

There was no answer. The snow fell steadily, settling on her hair and eyelashes, and the Christmas lights glistened through a pale shroud of white.

Finally she went back inside and spent a long time checking the house, securing locks, making sure all the windows were fastened.

Her stomach was clenched with fear. Still, Carly didn't call the police.

She knew she wasn't going to tell Detective Kaminsky about her midnight visitors.

Jackie had to go to the mall on Wednesday morning for a couple of final interviews regarding the forged checks. On the way back, she swung a few miles out of her way to chat with Chantal Biggins, the young woman who'd been John Stevenson's bookkeeping assistant at White Wolf Enterprises.

Poor Chantal was plump and pasty-faced, suffering from a bad case of acne that had persisted into adult-hood, and obviously so burdened with unfamiliar work that she seemed on the verge of tears.

Like everybody else, Chantal thought John Stevenson was an exemplary person, a terrific supervisor, a completely reliable and accurate bookkeeper, a warm and caring family man. And she had no idea why he'd quit his job, leaving her in this terrible dilemma, or where he could be now.

Jackie left the building close to lunchtime and headed downtown, toward the main police station. As she drove, she frowned and tapped her fingers on the wheel.

John Stevenson sounded too good to be true. And in Jackie's experience, that was usually a bad sign. In real life most people had at least a trace of a gritty underside, a few problems or flaws. When none showed up at all, she took it as a sign that something was being concealed.

At this stage, she wouldn't be surprised to discover Carly Stevenson's husband had some kind of ugly secret life, a whole part of his existence that was hidden from both spouse and co-workers.

Although, she had to admit, it was hard to speculate when the man found time to indulge in anything off-kilter. If her sources were reliable, until he'd gone off the rails, Stevenson seemed to spend all his time either at work or with his family. How much trouble could a man get into when he was working overtime without pay and attending track meets and T-ball practices with eight-year-old kids?

Still thoughtful, she parked outside the downtown station, went inside and made her way to the Traffic Division, where she found Steve Baumgartner just leaving on his lunch break. He was harried and curt.

"Goddamn media," he told Jackie, shrugging into his overcoat and heading for the door. "They're hounding the life out of us. Did you see that circus out front?"

"No, I parked in the lot and came through the back."

"They're just relentless. They want the driver of that hit-and-run vehicle, and they want him *now*."

She nodded in sympathy. "I wonder if I could read the file, Steve? I want to see what the Burketts said in their statements."

"Sure." He paused to unlock a tall file cabinet along one wall and pulled a manila folder. "Here, you can use my desk. Put it in the top drawer when you're finished, okay? I'll be gone for an hour or so."

Jackie smiled her thanks, settled at Baumgartner's desk and opened the file, reading the reports from the patrol officers who'd responded to the initial call, the detectives who'd visited the house the next day and the Burketts who had given individual statements.

None of the police reports held anything she didn't already know. The press, avid for details of the accident, had already obtained and run most of this material, along with a heart-wrenching picture of the little girl and her parents that had been taken for their annual Christmas card.

Jackie looked at the child's face. Angela Burkett had been truly lovely, with a mischievous, engaging smile and a pair of sparkling blue eyes under a boyish haircut. She'd inherited her mother's golden delicacy, but in the child that austerity had been lightened by the same easygoing humor that endeared Jason Burkett to local voters.

A beautiful child, Jackie thought, setting the picture down and touching it thoughtfully.

The Burketts had given their statements individually at eight o'clock on Tuesday morning, two hours after their daughter's life-support system had been disconnected. They were interviewed separately. Jason Burkett had still been at the hospital, but his wife was home, in the kitchen with the housekeeper.

It seemed odd to Jackie that they wouldn't be together at such a time, but she knew how these things tended to unfold. Events got so crazy and confused in the middle of a crisis. Decisions were made to go places and do things, and afterward people looked back and recalled nothing but a disordered blur. They often had no memory of where they'd been at any given time, or even how they got from one place to another.

Jason's statement had been taped and transcribed because he didn't feel able to write. It recounted how he'd been at home alone for the evening while his wife was at the gym. He was reading the paper and watching television. Larry King was interviewing a group of senators embroiled in the tobacco debate and he'd been looking forward to watching the program. He let Angela go outside and play, telling her she had to get ready for bed by eight o'clock.

He went to check on her regularly during commercials and gave her ten minutes' notice when she had to come in. She begged for a few more minutes so he allowed her to stay a little longer.

"She was close to the house and the yard is brightly lighted," he said. "I didn't see how any harm could come to her."

A few minutes after the program ended, he went to the door and called, but she didn't answer. He called again, thinking she was hiding from him. She often liked to tease him by making him search for her. Finally he put on his boots and jacket and went outside, where he found his daughter's body crumpled in the snow, bleeding profusely from the mouth, nose and ears. He ran into the house and told the housekeeper to call an ambulance, then went back out and covered the little girl with a blanket, afraid to move her before the paramedics arrived.

Angela had been unconscious when he found her, and never spoke again.

"After the ambulance came," his statement read, "it's all pretty much of a blur."

Jackie remembered the dazed, grief-stricken man in his beautiful home, and wasn't surprised. No doubt that blur had been merciful.

Norine Burkett's statement was written in longhand on a standard police form. The handwriting started out neat and precise but grew progressively more sloppy, the letters large and wavering. This wasn't unusual for handwritten statements, especially those given by people under stress. She wrote:

I was out for a couple of hours, having coffee with some friends. We were discussing the final details for a charity ball we're giving to fund Christmas hampers for disadvantaged children. When I got home at nine o'clock the house was in an uproar, with police vehicles all over the place. Sadie told me what happened and I went straight to the hospital. Angela was in the ICU. They were preparing her for surgery and the doctor said it would take a miracle. We waited all night, hoping for that miracle, but it didn't happen.

Jackie frowned, then set the statement aside and paged through the detective reports again.

After giving their statements willingly, it appeared

the Burketts had begun to stonewall. After Tuesday morning they refused to answer questions separately, and there was no explanation for their differing versions of where Norine had been on Monday night. Jason's statement said that his wife had been at the gym.

Jackie studied the reports from the two eyewitnesses, both of whom saw a sports car speeding and fishtailing along the road about the time the girl was hit.

As things stood, Jackie knew she had no right to insert herself into the hit-and-run investigation. It wasn't her case, and protocol was strict in these instances. But if John Stevenson could be clearly established as a missing person, perhaps the victim of foul play, then all the rules changed. She could talk to the Burketts again because they were relevant to her case, particularly Jason as the man's former employer. Norine, too, since she'd known him and his family.

But the Burketts were a prominent family with a lot at stake, and they were already apparently closing ranks. With every hour that passed, Jackie would be less likely to get anything from them.

She felt a rising urgency.

If only she could find something that would convince Michelson to go with the missing-person angle right away instead of waiting until Friday...

Jackie got to her feet, put the file away in Baumgartner's desk, grabbed her jacket and headed for the door.

But when she reached her car the journalist was sitting on the hood again, obviously waiting for her, his curly hair glistening in the bright morning light.

Jackie searched her memory to recall his name.

Karl Widmer...

"Well, here's the detective goddess," he was saying with a lazy grin. "Guess what? You've been selected from among thousands of applicants to go for lunch with me today. Aren't you excited?"

"I'm overwhelmed." Jackie unlocked the car and tossed her shoulder bag and notebook inside. "Simply overwhelmed."

"Don't be so quick to walk away from me," he said. "I might have something you can use."

"Related to what?"

"Jason Burkett's little girl."

Jackie hesitated for a moment, then shrugged. "Okay, I guess I have to eat. You drive, and I'll follow in my car."

7

They sat in a vinyl booth at a fifties-style café, near a window that looked out on a downtown street. A little wire basket at the end of the table held a napkin dispenser, a ketchup bottle, two laminated menus and a pair of salt and pepper shakers. Above the table hung a jukebox terminal with a series of selections listed in plastic slots.

Jackie turned the jukebox pages, feeling unaccountably ill at ease. She found a recording from Carole King's "Tapestry" album and punched in her quarter to select it.

"I can't believe my luck." Karl Widmer reached for one of the menus. "I never thought you'd actually have lunch with me."

"You said you had information for me," Jackie muttered. "Otherwise I'd never have agreed."

"You cops are always so intimidated by the press," the journalist said with a teasing smile. "Why all this adversarial crap, Jackie? Can't we just be friends?"

He leaned back expansively, annoying her with his air of sardonic insouciance. Despite the friendliness, his shrewd eyes seemed to be watching her closely, waiting for some kind of misstep.

"Why should we be friends?" she asked.

"Because we have a lot in common. We grew up in the same place, we're committed to the same noble fight for truth and justice, we both like Carole King—"

"We grew up in the same place?" she interrupted.

"You come from L.A., right?"

"How did you know that?"

"Oh, come on, Jackie. I'm a reporter. I can find out whatever I want to know about anybody. With someone in the public eye like you, it's no problem at all."

"Look," she said impatiently, "cut the crap, okay? I'm not impressed by flattery. Just tell me what it is you want to know, and I'll decide whether I want to give it to you."

Their waitress arrived, wearing a ruffled gingham apron and a little pink cap with a matching frill. She was a tall, no-nonsense kind of girl with muscular arms and level dark eyebrows.

"I'd like a toasted BLT," Karl Widmer told the waitress, "with side salad instead of fries, wheat bread and no mayo. And a coffee."

"I'll have the same," Jackie said.

The waitress scribbled busily on a yellow pad. "Exactly the same?"

"No coffee for me. I'll have a glass of milk."

Widmer studied Jackie with warm interest. "Well, well," he said. "Similar background, and now an identical taste in food. Isn't this interesting?"

"Look, I forget what it feels like to have somebody hit on me," Jackie said, accepting the glass of milk the waitress brought her. It was icy cold and tasted delicious. "But since that's what seems to be happening here, I should tell you I'm in a relationship."

"Serious?" he asked.

"I'm getting married."

She caught a flicker of disappointment on his thin, clever face, quickly masked. "So when's the wedding?"

Jackie moved uneasily on the vinyl seat. "We haven't actually set a date yet. Sometime in the spring, I guess."

"In the spring," he said, his face expressionless again. "That sounds nice."

Jackie gave him a suspicious glance, then murmured her thanks to the waitress who delivered their salads.

Widmer spooned a bit of dressing onto his salad from the little paper cup. "What does he do, this boyfriend of yours?"

"He has a ranch out by Reardan. He just bought it last spring."

Widmer saluted her with his fork and gave her a mocking grin. "So the uptown girl is going to move out to the sticks and live with coyotes and polecats. Ain't love grand?"

"I'm hardly an uptown girl," Jackie said.

"Which part of L.A. did you grow up in?"

"South Long Beach," she said curtly.

His eyebrows shot up. "Pretty tough area."

She munched on her lettuce and thought about Irene Kaminsky's apartment. "No kidding."

"So where exactly did you live?" he asked.

"Just south of Anaheim Street. My grandmother has a suite in an old apartment building. She raised me along with a whole crew of cousins. Most of our parents were in jail, or just not all that interested.

Not," she added, "that my grandmother was very interested either."

"Was the neighborhood down there as bad when you were growing up as it is now?"

Jackie shook her head. "Not quite. It didn't have the filth and rampant crime. Last time I was there," she added with a shudder, "it looked like downtown Beirut. Trash and squalor filling the yards, old mattresses rotting in the alleys and gang tags all over the place."

He listened quietly, eating his salad.

"When I was a kid," Jackie went on, "the 'hood was actually too tame for me. I used to go over to Compton for my social life."

"You're joking."

She shook her head, wondering why she felt compelled to tell him all this. "I was pretty restless as a teenager. Got into some bad trouble."

"Gangs?" he asked.

She didn't answer.

"Of course," he said in response to his own question. "Over in Watts-Compton, what else would it be?"

Widmer glanced at her thoughtfully. His eyes were gray, flecked with brown, deep-set and penetrating under heavy dark eyebrows.

"I took a journalism course twenty years ago at Cal State," he said. "We used to dare each other to walk through those streets at night, as a sort of rite of manhood. I'd see young kids hanging on the street corners out there and wonder how they managed to survive."

"What a coincidence. Twenty years ago, I was one of those kids."

The waitress delivered their sandwiches. Jackie glanced up, smiling her thanks, and was rewarded by a brief answering grin.

"I'd be willing to guess," she said to Widmer, "we didn't have exactly similar childhoods, even though we both grew up in L.A."

"Worlds apart," he agreed cheerfully. "I lived in Fullerton. My father worked for Disney as a technician. He retired two years ago but they're still letting him work as a consultant so he feels useful. They're pretty good to their employees."

"High school sports," Jackie suggested. "Debating team. Piano lessons."

"Violin." He grinned at her again. "My grandparents paid for the lessons. You sound scornful, Detective."

She felt a little abashed. "Sorry, I don't mean to. I really think it's a crock, this whole reverse-snobbery thing you find out on the streets, like if somebody isn't as poor and disadvantaged as you were, they're not worthy of your time."

"Detective Kaminsky, I'm liking you better all the time. How did you get from there to here?"

Jackie shrugged, suddenly uncomfortable. "It's not important. I got into some bad trouble when I was sixteen and realized I'd better straighten out if I wanted to stay alive."

"So you became a cop?"

"What else could I do? There was no money for college or anything like that. Being a woman and also representing a couple of ethnic minorities, I got a double boost at the start from the LAPD hiring policy. And I figured—"

She stopped abruptly and looked down at her sandwich, feeling her appetite begin to wane.

"You figured it was a way to help people," he suggested. "Maybe keep other kids from going down the same road."

"That makes me sound so sanctimonious."

"You know, Jackie, you really are a hell of a woman," he said quietly.

Her cheeks reddened with embarrassment. She glanced up at him to see if he was joking, but he seemed completely sincere.

"Look," she said abruptly, "can we talk about something else? I can't believe I've told you as much as I have. You obviously know how to get your subject to talk. I guess that's the sign of a good journalist. But you said you had information for me."

"First, I want to know what you're working on that's related to the Burkett kid's death."

She hesitated, watching him thoughtfully. "And if I give it to you, what do I get in return?"

"A fair trade," he said promptly. "An interesting tidbit of information that seems thus far to have eluded all the mental giants in our local constabulary."

Jackie pushed her plate away and got up, reaching for her shoulder bag. She tossed a ten-dollar bill onto the table. "That should cover my share plus the tip."

He reached out and grasped her arm. His fingers felt like thin bands of steel. "Sit down, for God's sake. Don't be so touchy."

She stood in the aisle, glaring at him. "I don't appreciate it when a guy who spends his life shuffling paper when he's not digging up dirt on people thinks he can bad-mouth the police force."

Widmer chuckled, looking genuinely amused. "Yeah, sure," he scoffed. "Like the police don't spend ninety-five percent of their time shuffling paper. Look," he added, "I was *kidding*. Sit down, Kaminsky. You're making a spectacle of yourself."

Jackie glanced around at the other patrons who were watching them with interest. She sank onto the vinyl bench, leaned forward and lowered her voice.

"Do you know how much shit we have to take from the media, Widmer? Do you know what it's like to have you and your eager-beaver friends constantly dogging our footsteps, messing with crime scenes, playing at being cops, interviewing witnesses and contaminating the evidence before we can get to it?"

"Then maybe you should all learn to move a little faster," he said calmly, sipping his coffee.

Her fury mounted. "But that's not the worst of it," she went on. "The worst part is having to read the kind of garbage you print. Anytime you and your buddies want to grab a headline, you run something detrimental to the police and the public seizes on it. Cop-bashing sells papers. Do you know how hard it is for us to do a decent job in the kind of climate you create?"

"Our paper is usually supportive of the police force," he said mildly, leaning back and resting an arm along the seat back. "You guys have to screw up royally before we publish something even mildly critical."

She fell silent, still glaring at him. What he said was true. Of all the local papers, the *Sentinel* was probably fairest to the police. Unfortunately, in Jackie's opinion, that wasn't saying a whole lot.

"So, is your little tantrum over?" He watched her

with maddening calm. "Because if it is, I'm still interested in an exchange of information."

She settled back against the seat, looking at her half-eaten sandwich.

"Finish your lunch," he said. "I've been watching the schedule you keep. You need to maintain your strength, kiddo."

"I'm not hungry." She drained the last of the milk, thinking about his offer.

In all likelihood, Michelson was going to sanction a missing-person bulletin on John Stevenson by tomorrow morning. It would be twelve hours short of the required seventy-two, but under the circumstances, and in the light of her own coaxing, Jackie was pretty sure her sergeant would be willing to bend the rules a bit.

So any information she gave to Widmer was only going to be a little in advance. If John Stevenson, or somebody who'd harmed him, was out there watching, it couldn't hurt to let them know his absence had been noted by others besides his wife and family.

"This is just from me to you," she said warningly. "I don't want to find a whole crowd of vultures following me around."

"Believe me, Jackie," he said fervently, "you're going to remain my closely guarded secret. In fact, I want to avoid being seen with you in public in case some of my colleagues tumble to you."

"Okay." Jackie leaned back in the booth and twisted her hands together nervously. "I'm investigating a missing person," she said at last. "John Stevenson, the bookkeeper for White Wolf Enterprises. He went missing on Monday night. Tomorrow morning we'll probably be launching a full-scale search for him.''

Widmer's eyes brightened with interest. He took a notebook from his pocket and flipped to a fresh page. Jackie watched, fascinated by his rapid shorthand as she gave him details about John Stevenson, his position in Jason Burkett's holding company and his disappearance on the same night as Angela's death.

"So what do you think?" he asked.

"I have no idea what to think. From everything I've learned about the man, it seems to be a coincidence. And we haven't ruled out that he might have been the victim of foul play. Tomorrow we'll be asking formally for public assistance in locating him or learning what's happened to him."

Widmer nodded, rubbing a forefinger along his jaw. "Interesting. Very, very interesting."

"So," Jackie said reluctantly, "what do you have for me?"

He chuckled. "You really don't like making deals with the press, do you, Detective?"

"It's not exactly my favorite thing."

"Then I won't keep teasing you." He sobered, sitting erect to put his notebook away. "Have you been out to the Burkett residence?"

"I was there yesterday. Why?"

"Did you see that big three-car garage?"

"Of course."

"Well, as far as I know, nobody's made any attempt to find out what the Burketts drive."

Her interest sharpened. "And you have?"

"Yes, I have. Jason drives a midnight blue Lincoln. They have a new sport utility vehicle. And the gracious Lady Norine..." He settled back in the booth and watched Jackie intently. "She has a snazzy little BMW sports model. It's bright red."

Jackie stared at the man, openmouthed. "You're not saying…"

"I'm not saying anything. I'm just telling you an interesting fact that's probably been overlooked, since I assume the police are being as gentle with the bereaved couple as everybody else is."

She nodded and got to her feet, reaching for her coat. "I have to leave."

"Jackie," he said quietly.

She paused and gazed down at him.

"I know it's none of my business," he said, looking awkward for the first time in their interview, "but you know, I really don't think you're cut out to be a farmer's wife."

"You're right," Jackie told him. "It's none of your business."

She gathered her bag and left the restaurant without looking back.

8

By now the atmosphere of holiday silliness around the police substation was intensifying. Gag gifts littered desktops, and food was everywhere...cookies, half-eaten boxes of chocolates, trays of dried fruit artistically arranged with tiny plastic forks and cheese wrapped in colored cellophane.

In the squad room someone had set up an artificial tree on top of a file cabinet and decorated it with tiny pinpoints of light and dainty spun-glass decorations. A group of junior traffic patrols had further enhanced the tree by hanging condom packs from most of the branches. The little plastic squares glistened under the fluorescent lights and twirled slowly in gusts of moving air from the vent overhead.

Jackie found them surprisingly pretty.

"Hey, Kaminsky, you got a Christmas tree at home?" Wardlow asked. He sat at his desk, typing files onto a computer.

Jackie shook her head. "No, I'm not really into trees and Santas and all that stuff."

"We put one up at Chris's place on the weekend. Gordie wanted a real-live tree so I had to drive all over town in a damn blizzard with half a forest attached to my ski rack. Now I feel as if I'm coming down with the bug that seems to be going round."

"Quit complaining. Everybody knows how much you're loving all this," Jackie said calmly, hanging up her coat and pulling her boots off. "You're a real domestic kind of guy."

"Kaminsky, do you think I should get married again?" he asked. Something in his tone alerted her, and she glanced up quickly.

"Is that a serious question?"

He nodded, looking at his keyboard. "I was wondering about maybe buying her a ring for Christmas. What do you think?"

She concentrated on setting out her notebook along with an armful of files. "I don't know, Brian. It's a big step. You've only known Chris for about eight months, right?"

"So when does a person feel sure enough to make the commitment?" he asked.

Jackie laughed without humor. "God, don't look at me. I could be married for forty years and probably still not be sure. The whole commitment thing really scares the hell out of me."

"But I think she's the one, Jackie. I can't imagine being without her. I can't even remember how I got along before I had her in my life."

"Then," Jackie said briskly, "I suppose you should go for it. Buy the ring." She gathered a couple of files. "Is Sarge around?"

"He just came back from lunch. Had a budget meeting downtown this morning."

"Oh, hell. Did he look in a really bad mood?"

Wardlow chuckled. "You know Sarge. And trying to stay on his diet over Christmas isn't making his disposition any sweeter. At least he didn't kick any puppies or junior officers on the way in."

Jackie sighed and checked the sergeant's office window, then set her files down again, picked up the telephone and dialed.

"Hey, Rennie," she said when her friend answered. "I need some help."

"Jackie! Oh, God, I'm so *glad* you called!" Adrienne said in a breathless rush. "Look, I have to talk to you. I want to see you right away. Something wonderful has happened."

"Whoa," Jackie said darkly as she sank into her desk chair. "Who are you and what have you done with Adrienne Calder, the jaded society lady?"

Adrienne laughed. "Sorry," she said. "I'm just a little overwhelmed, that's all. Dying to tell you all about it."

"So tell me."

"Not over the phone, Jackie. No way. When can you get here?"

Jackie pondered. "How about if I drop in tonight for a few minutes right after dinner?"

"Can't you come for dinner? Come on," Adrienne coaxed. "I'll make that seafood lasagna you love so much."

Jackie hesitated wistfully, then shook her head. "I just can't make it, Rennie. I still have a million things to do today, and time keeps slipping away on me. I'll try to stop in around eight o'clock tonight for some eggnog, okay?"

"You turkey."

"Is that on the menu," Jackie asked, "or are you calling me names again?"

Adrienne giggled, then hiccuped. Jackie wondered in alarm if her friend had been drinking. She'd sometimes been known, especially in the past, to get into the daiquiris a little too early in the afternoon.

"Seriously, Rennie," Jackie said, "I need some information."

"Sure, Ossifer," Adrienne said solemnly. "At your service. Fire away. Always happy to be of assistance to the police."

"It's about Norine Burkett."

"Oh, God," Adrienne said, instantly serious. "Those poor people. We sent flowers, of course, but I haven't spoken with her or Jason yet. How are they bearing up, Jackie?"

"Pretty much the way you'd expect."

"They both adored that child, absolutely doted on her, and she was such a little sweetie. Not at all spoiled. Just a darling."

Jackie hesitated, feeling awkward. She'd suspected that Adrienne might know the Burketts, but she hadn't realized how hard it was going to be to ask questions under those circumstances.

"So what can I help you with?" Adrienne asked.

"Well, mostly I just wanted to know a little more about this charity ball Norine was working on. It's something about using the proceeds to give Christmas hampers to poor kids?"

"Oh, Norine's off that committee," Adrienne said. "And I certainly don't blame her."

"Do you know this for certain?"

"I was there when it happened, sweetie. Buffy Grange told Norine she had no more taste in music than a mushroom, right in front of everybody. It was a breathless moment, one of those rich emotional crises that society ladies positively *live* for," Adrienne said cheerfully. "Norine got up and swept from the room, and sent the committee a stiff little note saying she would be pleased to assist in a monetary sense but felt that her time could be best spent elsewhere. The ladies have been chewing it over and taking sides ever since," she added with relish. "So much fun, Jackie. You simply can't imagine."

"Oh, yeah," Jackie said. "It sounds real entertaining, all right. So," she added carefully, "how long ago did this happen?"

"Early in November. And Norine's stuck to her guns. We haven't seen a glimpse of her at any of the meetings since then."

"And the meetings are…"

"Monday nights. We've been quite faithful, considering what a bunch of lazy dilettantes we all are."

"But Monday night," Jackie said, "I was at your house. Wasn't I?"

"That's true," Adrienne said, sounding contrite. "I wasn't feeling well in the afternoon so I canceled. And with the bad weather that night, apparently only Buffy, Carrie and Alison showed up at the meeting, so they didn't get much done."

"I see." Jackie paused, thinking. "Rennie, do you know much about Norine Burkett?"

"Why?"

"I mean," Jackie said, improvising rapidly, "what kind of person she is. How's she likely to be bearing up under this kind of tragedy? People around here are really concerned about her."

Which, she thought grimly, wasn't such a complete lie.

"We're worried, too. Listen, Jackie, can we talk tonight? I've got a cake in the oven and I have to run."

"All right," Jackie said. "Thanks, Rennie. See you later."

"I can hardly wait to tell you my news. Jackie, hurry up and get here, okay? This is so damn *wonderful!*" Adrienne hung up, still bubbling.

Jackie replaced the receiver and looked at her telephone thoughtfully. Adrienne's behavior was as bizarrely out of character as if Lew Michelson had suddenly broken into a tap-dance routine during a police briefing.

Shaking her head, she made a second call and got a very different response.

"Hello?" a timid voice said.

"Carly, this is Detective Kaminsky. Have you heard anything from your husband today?"

She heard a quick, nervous catch in the other woman's breath.

"No," Carly said. "Nothing at all. But I..."

"What?" Jackie prompted. "Has something happened?"

"I'm...scared," Carly whispered. "I'm worried about the kids."

Jackie's interest sharpened. She kept her voice calm and offhand, knowing it was the best way to get people talking.

"I know you're worried," she said casually. "After all, it must be really scary for them to have their daddy missing. But they'll be all right, Carly, if you just—"

"No, it's not that!" Carly interrupted, her voice rising a little. "I'm scared because of—" She stopped abruptly.

Jackie waited, holding her breath.

"Because of...of the money," Carly said at last.

Jackie suspected the woman had been on the verge of saying something different, but Carly sounded so fragile that she decided not to press.

"The money?" she said.

"I still needed baby formula for Patrick. That's what John was going to pick up when he...when he didn't..." She coughed a couple of times, obviously struggling to compose herself.

Jackie waited patiently, staring at the glistening plastic squares on the Christmas tree.

"So yesterday I went to pick some up, but when I looked in my purse at the checkout stand, both my credit cards were gone."

Jackie's eyes widened at this new development. She pondered rapidly. "Do you only have two credit cards, Carly?"

"That's right. A Sears card and a MasterCard. We use them for everything. So I had to write a check for the baby food, and this morning the bank called me and told me..."

Jackie felt a sinking feeling, followed by a hot flood of anger. But she kept her voice carefully neutral. "Was it a joint account, Carly?"

Carly swallowed and gulped, then went on. "Everything is in both our names. The house, the cars, the checking and savings accounts. He...on Monday, John went and..."

She was now sobbing in earnest.

"Now, now. Calm down," Jackie said soothingly, though her mind was racing.

More and more, John Stevenson looked like a deliberate walkaway. So what did that do to a missing-person investigation? She was pretty certain Michelson wouldn't agree to commit any of their scarce resources under those conditions.

"Carly, did he clean out your bank account?" Jackie asked.

"Both of them," Carly said. "He took everything from the checking account and left only seven hundred dollars in the savings account, but that's because it's tagged for automatic withdrawal on the second day of every month so he couldn't touch it."

"It goes to pay the mortgage?" Jackie said.

"Yes."

"Carly, how much money did he take altogether?"

"About…nine thousand dollars. Everything we've managed to save in the last few years."

"And how much do you have to live on?"

"The only money I have is…" Carly paused, then went on. "I have about fifty dollars and the money from the kids' piggy banks, and maybe a hundred dollars in each of their bank accounts, but that's mostly gifts from their grandmother that we're saving for college."

Jackie was reluctant to point out that college was looking very far away indeed for Carly Stevenson's children.

In light of present circumstances, this little family had more immediate concerns, like losing their house and finding themselves out on the winter streets with the rest of the city's homeless population.

The woman at the other end of the phone was weeping quietly now, timid little sniffles that went straight to Jackie's heart.

"I don't understand how he could do this to us," Carly said. "John's always been such a wonderful husband. So thoughtful and protective."

Yeah, sure, Jackie told herself bitterly. *Hold that thought.*

Aloud she said, "Look, Carly, I'm going to see what I can do for you. Right now I'll talk to my sergeant and see if we can get the missing-person investigation under way a little early, all right?"

"All right," Carly whispered. "Thank you. Is there...anything I can do?"

"Find me a good picture of your husband," Jackie said. "As recent as possible, okay? One that we can use in the newspapers and on television."

"Should I bring it down to the station?"

Jackie thought about her overcrowded day, and the amount of time she'd already given to the Stevenson case, which wasn't even officially on her duty roster.

But then she remembered Carly Stevenson packing up four kids, zipping them into snowsuits and boots and lining them up in their row of car seats.

"No," she said at last. "Your place is almost on my way home. I'll stop by later to pick it up when I'm finished here."

"Thanks, Jackie," Carly whispered. "I really appreciate it."

Jackie hung up and stared at the phone for a minute, then went to Michelson's office and knocked.

He sat at his desk munching from a Tupperware container full of carrot sticks, cherry tomatoes, sliced celery and raw mushrooms.

"Yummy," Jackie said dryly, looking at the box.

"My wife's idea of guerilla warfare," he said. "She's trying to combat all the fat, sugary crap lying around the place this time of year."

"Is it working?" Jackie settled into a chair.

He selected a tomato and popped it into his mouth,

then chewed thoughtfully on a carrot stick. "You acquire a taste for this stuff, Jackie. You really do. After a while your body starts to crave it."

"My body doesn't crave anything right now," she said restlessly. "I seem to have completely lost my appetite. And dealing with scumbags on a daily basis doesn't help to bring it back."

"When do you see Paul again?" he asked, rummaging among the celery.

"Look," Jackie said warningly, "don't make me mad, okay?"

"Now, why would that make you mad?"

"Because you seem to keep implying," she said, only half in jest, "that I'm not a stable, functioning person unless I can get together with my boyfriend and have sex on a regular basis. And you know how insulting I think that is."

Michelson leaned back in his chair, chewing on a celery stick. He waved the half-eaten stalk at her while he swallowed.

"God forbid I should insult you, Detective. In fact," he added, reaching for a mushroom, "it often seems to me you were easier to get along with when you didn't have a boyfriend at all."

"Really?" she asked, startled.

The sergeant fitted a lid on his plastic container. "Are you here to discuss your love life, or what?"

"I want to talk about the Stevenson case."

"Tomorrow night it'll be seventy-two hours. If he still hasn't turned up by then, we can go ahead on Friday morning."

"I want to go ahead tomorrow morning, Sarge. Twelve hours early, not twelve hours late."

"Why? Have we got some compelling new evidence?"

Jackie told him about her conversation with Carly and that John Stevenson had apparently cleaned out the family bank accounts before disappearing.

Michelson shook his balding head. "But it doesn't wash, Jackie. What you've got here is positive evidence the guy just took a walk. It looks like a domestic issue, not a police one."

"But there are so many weird things about the Burkett family and their little girl's death, and somehow they're all tied in to John Stevenson," Jackie pleaded. "I just know they are."

"Tell me all these weird things."

Jackie opened her notebook and summarized her visit to the Burketts, and the fact that they'd refused to answer more questions about the accident or the discrepancy in their statements regarding Norine's whereabouts on the night their daughter was killed. She added that Norine had apparently been lying to everybody about her activities on Monday night.

The only thing Jackie kept to herself, for the moment, was Karl Widmer's revelation about the red sports car belonging to Norine Burkett.

Michelson listened and shook his head. "This isn't our case, Jackie. You should turn whatever you've got over to Traffic and let Steve handle it."

"Steve's already up to his ass in alligators. The press is riding him so hard he can barely make a move without tripping over them. But so far," Jackie argued, "only one of the reporters is showing any interest in me, and I really think the John Stevenson thing is related to the little girl's death. I've got a feeling, Sarge, that if we find this man, we'll solve the hit-and-run."

"Despite the Traffic angle, this missing person is still our case," Michelson said, toying with a pen. "Theoretically, at least."

"It came right to my desk, first thing Tuesday morning." Jackie leaned forward. "I don't need to pursue the Burketts, except where the cases overlap because Jason Burkett was Stevenson's employer. But I have every right to launch a hard-and-heavy search for John Stevenson and see what we can turn up."

She watched him, waiting tensely.

"Okay," he said at last. "Tomorrow morning. But if we find him on a beach in Acapulco, sucking back margaritas with his girlfriend, it's going to be your rear on the line."

"If we find him on a beach any goddamn place," Jackie said, "I'll personally haul *his* rear back home to face charges of abandonment and nonsupport."

Michelson shook his head in awe. "Women are so scary when they get mad."

"Does it bother you, Sarge?" she asked with a sweet smile.

"Hell, no. I like that kind of passion. Carrot stick, Jackie?"

She accepted the offer and left his office, munching thoughtfully.

Carly stood in the fenced backyard looking anxiously at the twins. They were dressed in their red nylon snowsuits, a gift from Grandma Stevenson last Christmas and now a little too short in the leg. But Carly had pulled sturdy woolen socks up to their knees and fastened their boots tightly to keep the snow out.

"Stay in the yard," she told them. "Don't you *dare* open the gate and go outside the yard."

Her voice was a little shrill, even to her own ears. The children stood close together and stared up at her from identical hazel eyes under their white knitted hats.

Carly stretched her mouth into a smile that she hoped was reassuring. "Captain will look after you," she said, glancing into Lavonne's untidy yard next door.

Captain was a rottweiler-shepherd cross with heavy forequarters and a menacing blunt jaw that looked as if it could take off a man's arm. He'd been the property of Lavonne's former boyfriend, recently departed, who had apparently left the dog in lieu of a cash settlement.

Carly was afraid of the big animal, but had to acknowledge he was a good protector for the children. He barked at anybody who came and went through the alley, including old ladies with shopping carts and kindergarten children taking the shortest way home. If trespassers weren't prepared, his booming, bell-like tones could send them jumping right out of their skin.

But, Carly recalled, the dog hadn't barked the night of the mysterious intruder, and, now that she thought about it, he'd seemed sick and groggy for most of the next day. He was fine now, so she pushed the memory aside.

"We don't need Captain," Emily said scornfully. "We got Beanie."

Beanie was the smaller of Lavonne's two dogs, a half-grown black Lab who was just a baby himself, all paws and ears and lolling tongue. He loved to come over and play with the children, rolling in the snow and racing hysterically around the yard.

Unlike Beanie, Captain was never allowed out of his own yard. The rottweiler spent his days pacing the length of the clothesline on a running chain, ever-vigilant, his yellow eyes darting everywhere and a low growl rumbling from his throat at the slightest provocation.

"Are Jamie and Kyle coming out to play?" Rachel asked.

Carly shook her head. "They're downtown with their mummy."

"Doing what?" Emily said.

"I don't know. honey. Maybe they're shopping for Christmas presents." Carly tugged Rachel's hat lower around her ears.

In fact, Lavonne was applying for social assistance, and Carly was very much afraid that soon she would be doing the same thing.

It was all such a nightmare.

"I have to go check on Patrick," she said. "You two play nice, don't hurt Beanie, and don't go out of the yard, okay?"

She tried to keep her voice light and pleasant this time, but their faces still looked wary as they watched her go back into the house.

Carly looked in on Patrick, who slept in his crib, smelling of milk and powder. She patted his diapered rump, then gently turned the baby over on his back and tucked the covers up around him. Carly stroked his fragile skull and watched the pulse under the soft bones, her own heart melting with love.

Finally she slipped out of the room and went down

the hall to the little spare room, furnished only with a desk, sewing machine and foldout couch. She and John both used the room as an office and storage compartment.

Carly drew a large box from under the couch, opened it and set out a series of small plastic trays, then began to sort her buttons.

This was something she always did when she was troubled or upset. Since the children liked playing with them, the boxes were usually in disorder. Sorting through the masses of buttons helped to calm her and organize her mind so she could think clearly.

And every button was a special memory.

Plastic pineapple buttons from the gaudy Hawaiian shirt John bought on their honeymoon. The little duck-shaped fasteners on Caitlin's baby sweater. Gold buttons with rhinestone centers from the dress Carly wore to her senior prom...

She let the masses of buttons fall through her fingers in a rustling waterfall, then picked through them and began to arrange them in matching groups, thinking about John.

It was inconceivable that her husband would go away and leave her without any way of taking care of herself and the children. Something terrible must have happened to him.

Carly swallowed a sob and wiped her eyes with the back of her hand, frowning at the buttons.

She couldn't deny, of course, that the withdrawals from their bank accounts had been made before he left the house on Monday night. The proof was right there in black and white.

But how could a woman possibly be so wrong about a man? After fifteen years of friendship and ten years of marriage, could she have formed an entirely false impression of John Stevenson?

She remembered his face, the quiet steadiness of his eyes, the way a dimple flashed in one cheek when he said certain words.

There was nothing Carly didn't know about John Stevenson. He was afraid of spiders, he loved pumpkin pie, he'd once dreamed of playing professional baseball. And he was so generous. When John was a boy, he'd suffered agonies because his father was tightfisted and wouldn't let him dress well or have the things the other boys had. John always vowed his own kids would never have to feel the same way.

He was a tender, considerate lover, though perhaps more interested in sex than Carly had been lately, what with three babies in less than four years. Still, he was always mindful of her, and so gentle.

She moaned and plunged her hands into the mass of buttons.

What was she going to do about money? They barely had enough for food. She certainly couldn't afford the January mortgage payment. And with all the bills John's parents had paid for Ethel's heart surgery, she doubted they could help her much. Besides, she hated to ask. She'd have to tell the whole story, and Ted Stevenson, who was as tightfisted as he'd ever been, would have his own opinions about the situation which he would voice loudly and endlessly, in front of the children or whoever was listening.

But if she couldn't find the money anywhere else...

Suddenly a blood-chilling clamor rose from the backyard, driving all other thoughts from Carly's mind.

She ran outside, her heart thudding madly, in time to witness a dreadful sight.

9

Rachel stood at the end of the yard near the back gate, screaming hysterically. Beanie, the half-grown puppy, was crumpled in a snowbank, twitching in convulsive jerks with blood flowing from his open mouth. In the other yard Captain paced along the low picket fence, growling and emitting an occasional booming howl to chime in with Rachel's shouts.

Not caring that she was in her stockinged feet, Carly ran to the child.

"Where's your sister?" she shouted, kneeling in the snow to grasp the little girl's shoulders. "Honey, *where's Emily?*"

Rachel sobbed and struggled to draw breath, her face smeared with tears and mucous.

Carly released her and ran to the gate.

A man was fleeing down the alley, by now just a dark shape near a leafless hedge next to the street. He vanished almost as soon as she saw him. Soon afterward she heard a car start up and race off.

"Oh, God," Carly whispered, her hand to her mouth. *"Emily!"* she screamed.

The alley was still and deserted, the silence broken only by Captain's furious barking. Carly stared into the gray distance, frozen with terror.

Suddenly a small red snowsuit appeared from behind the neighbor's trash stand and came stumbling toward her. Carly collapsed against the gate, weak with relief.

"Mummy!" Emily shouted.

Carly ran and lifted the child in her arms, touching Emily's head, her arms and legs, her flushed little face. One of her red boots was gone, and the knitted hat was missing.

"Sweetheart," Carly whispered, burying her face in the child's tousled hair. "My sweetheart."

Rachel, still shouting, ran to her side and tugged at her arm. "Beanie's hurt, Mummy. He kicked Beanie! Mummy, come and help."

"I want my boot," Emily muttered, twisting in her mother's arms. "My boot's gone."

"Not now, dear." Carly looked fearfully down the alley. "First we should—"

"There it is," Rachel shouted. "I can see Emily's boot!"

She ran toward the wooden trash stand. Carly looked at the little red boot lying in the snow and felt her stomach heave sharply with nausea.

"Oh, God," she muttered again, hoping she wasn't going to vomit and upset the children even more. She leaned against the fence to steady herself, still clutching Emily so tightly that the child squirmed in discomfort.

Rachel trotted back toward them, holding the boot, and tugged at Carly's sweater. "We hafta help Beanie!" she insisted.

Carly walked into their yard with Emily in her arms, holding Rachel's shoulder. The little dog was sitting up now, trembling and whimpering. Blood still dripped from his muzzle.

"We'll help Beanie in a minute," Carly said. "First we need to check on Patrick. Come with me, both of you."

She ran inside the house over the twins' noisy protests and found Patrick sleeping peacefully in his room. The baby had rolled onto his stomach again and lay with his cheek flattened against the crib mattress.

When Carly went back to the kitchen, Beanie had dragged himself to the porch where the twins squatted next to him, muttering in low worried tones.

Carly picked the little dog up, hugged him and examined his mouth.

"He's all right," she told the girls after a moment, pulling back the soft muzzle to show them. "He just bit his lip, see? The bleeding's almost stopped."

She kissed the dog's silky head and set him back on the floor, suddenly conscious of how badly her hands were shaking, and the icy coldness of her wet feet. The puppy tried to sit up, his front paws splayed on the linoleum. He shook his head and whined, looking dazed.

"The man kicked him," Rachel said, her eyes wide with remembered horror. "He kicked Beanie like a football."

"Beanie was barking and jumping up," Emily said. "He was trying to bite the man. I heard the man swear. Mummy, he said a really bad word."

Carly took a deep breath and closed her eyes briefly, sitting back on her heels. "Did the man come right into our yard?" she asked, trying to keep her voice casual.

Both children nodded. "We weren't outside the yard, Mom," Rachel said earnestly. "We were inside like we're supposed to be. We were playing dragons with Beanie.''

Dear God, Carly thought. *Help me, God...*

"What happened when the man came into the yard?'' she asked. "Did he say anything to you?''

Another earnest headshake, in unison.

"He just grabbed me,'' Emily said. "And he started running away.''

Carly put her arms around the child, who began to cry again.

"Beanie barked and jumped and the man kicked him,'' Rachel said.

She patted the little dog who whimpered and licked her hand, leaving a bloody smear on the nylon mitten.

"But in the alley, the man tripped and started to fall down, and he dropped me and kept on running,'' Emily said in a choked voice. "I bumped my head on the ground when he dropped me, Mummy. And,'' she added, touching her hair, "I lost my hat.''

"We'll find your hat, sweetheart.'' Carly kissed the child's tangled hair. "Did either of you see what the man looked like?''

Both children shook their heads again. "He was wearing a blue thing over his face with funny holes for the eyes and mouth,'' Rachel said. "He looked like a monster.''

"He was big,'' Emily said after a moment's thought. "Big as Daddy.''

Carly hesitated, then looked directly into the child's troubled hazel eyes.

"Emily, I want you to think very hard,'' she said. "*Was* it Daddy?''

Both little girls stared up at her in disbelief.

"But why would Daddy scare us like that?" Rachel asked.

"Maybe he was…just playing a game," Carly said lamely.

She hesitated, agonized. If John had somehow gone out of his mind and was posing a threat to the children, she needed to warn them. But she couldn't bear to make them frightened of their father.

Emily shook her head again, setting the mop of hair swinging. "Daddy would never, ever kick Beanie," she said firmly.

Carly got to her feet and drew the children close to her. "Come on," she said with forced cheerfulness. "We have to get busy, kids."

"What are we doing?" They pressed against her legs, still chastened by their experience.

"Well, we're going to get all cleaned up and give Beanie something good to eat," Carly said. "And then we're—"

"I want my hat," Emily interrupted.

"We'll find your hat," Carly promised. "But first we have to dress Patrick up in his cozy bunny suit because we're all going out for a walk."

"Where?" they asked.

Carly swallowed again and tried to smile at them. "We're going down to Cait's school," she said, "so we can walk her home. That'll be fun, won't it?"

She hurried to clean them up and wake the baby, who was cranky and fretful at having his sleep interrupted. And all the time her heart kept thudding noisily, erratically, making her feel shaky and sick.

Jackie worked for a couple of hours after her shift ended, trying to clear her desk and dispose of paperwork. By the time she finished, the station was empty, its square bulk looming dark and silent in the snowy chill of evening.

She put on her coat and boots, locked all the security doors behind her and headed for her own car, choosing a homeward route that would take her past Carly Stevenson's house.

When she knocked at the front door, Jackie heard a flurry of activity on the inside, along with muffled voices. Finally the door opened and Carly appeared, looking pale and frightened.

"Please," she said, standing back. "Come in, Detective."

Jackie shook her head. "There's no need for me to take any of your time," she said. "I just wanted to pick up the picture of your husband, if it's handy."

Carly glanced over her shoulder, then lowered her voice. "I'd like to talk to you for a minute. It's really important."

"Sure, no problem. I'm on my way home anyhow."

Jackie didn't add that she hadn't eaten since lunch. She wasn't all that hungry, anyway. After stamping the snow from her boots, she stepped into the house and unbuttoned her topcoat.

A little girl about eight years old sprawled on her stomach in front of the television set, clutching a pencil and making careful entries in a school notebook. She looked much like her mother, with big blue eyes, freckles and russet-colored hair pulled back into ponytails that stuck out from both sides of her head.

"This is Caitlin," Carly murmured. "Cait, this is Detective Kaminsky."

"My name's Jackie. How are you, Caitlin?"

Jackie extended a hand, which the child shook, scrambling up from the floor to examine the newcomer solemnly. For the first time, Jackie noticed the baby on a blanket next to the little girl. He lay on his back, holding a set of giant plastic keys in front of his eyes, cooing and gurgling.

"Hi, Patrick," Jackie murmured, kneeling on the rug to pat the baby's stomach. He was fat and cheerful, looking cozy in a yellow sleeper, and he kicked his legs with rhythmic energy when she touched him. She was surprised by a sudden urge to pick him up.

"Do you have a gun?" the older child asked, her eyes wide with awe.

Jackie was used to this question, which was often the first thing children asked her. She drew aside her blazer to show the leather holster at her waist and the flap that fastened across the handle of her pistol.

"Wow," Caitlin breathed, staring at the gun.

From somewhere at the rear of the house Jackie could hear the sound of shouts and noisy splashing, followed by a sudden ominous silence.

"Cait, could you run and check on them, please?" Carly asked. She gave Jackie a timid smile. "The twins are having their bath."

"It sounds like a lot of fun." Jackie smiled back and sat on the couch. Carly's face had a pinched, anxious look and she seemed thinner, as if she'd lost weight since their first meeting just a couple of days ago.

"Cait, listen," Carly called into the hallway. "Could you please get them dried and into their pajamas for me? And then read them a bedtime story while I talk to the detective?"

"Okay, Mom," the little girl called back.

Carly turned to Jackie and held out a brown envelope, her hands shaking badly. "Here's the pictures of…of John," she murmured. "We had some family photos taken last Christmas, so they're pretty recent…"

"Hey," Jackie said gently. She set the envelope down next to her shoulder bag. "What's the matter?"

Carly's eyes were bright with tears, her lips quivering. "I'm so scared," she whispered. "I don't know what to do."

"Why are you scared?"

Carly shook her head and looked down, picking nervously at the fringed edging on a throw cushion.

"Has something happened, Carly?"

There was no response.

"I think you'd better tell me," Jackie said quietly, "if the safety of your kids is involved in any way."

This was clearly the right approach. Carly took a deep shuddering breath, straightened her shoulders and looked up. "Somebody's been…at the house," she muttered.

"At this house? Your husband's come home?"

"I don't think it was John. But I'm not…" Carly moaned and hunched forward, burying her face in her hands.

Jackie crossed the room, sat on the chair, and gripped the woman's shoulders.

Carly rested against her as if grateful for the comfort. "Two nights ago there was somebody outside. It was late at night. He ran away when I went out."

While Jackie listened, Carly went on to tell about the midnight intruder, the ominous turning doorknob and the mass of footprints under the baby's window.

"You're sure it was more than one person?" Jackie asked.

Carly nodded. "There were different kinds of prints, lots of them. They must have been out there for quite a while."

Jackie felt a harsh stab of impatience, which she suppressed firmly. The last thing Carly Stevenson needed at this point was an official scolding.

"Why didn't you call right away and tell me about this, Carly?" she asked, keeping her voice gentle.

"Because I thought maybe he..."

"You thought maybe it was John, trying to contact you," Jackie said when the woman stopped talking. "You're afraid he might be in some kind of trouble, and you wanted to protect him. Right?"

Carly nodded miserably, turning her head away.

Jackie watched her closely. "What makes you think he might be in trouble?"

"I don't know," Carly said. "The way he...quit his job and didn't tell me, and then..." She gulped and swallowed. "And the little Burkett girl..."

Jackie went back to the couch and sat down, looking thoughtfully at the distraught woman. She wanted to get her notebook out but was afraid to interrupt the flow of their conversation, so she decided instead she'd record everything as soon as she got home, while it was still fresh in her memory.

"Do you think John had something to do with Angela Burkett's death?"

"I don't *know!*" Carly flung her head up and stared at Jackie briefly, her eyes glittering with tears. "It's all such a nightmare," she whispered, looking down again. "And then today..."

"Yes?" Jackie leaned forward tensely. "What happened today?"

Carly began to sob. Jackie watched while she cried, then composed herself and took a tissue from the pocket of her cardigan to mop at her face.

"It was in the afternoon. Patrick was having his nap," Carly said at last. "I dressed the twins and put them out in the yard. Beanie was with them."

"Who's Beanie?"

"One of Lavonne's dogs. He's just a puppy, actually."

"Where was Lavonne?" Jackie asked, reaching for her notebook.

No way she was going to remember all of this, and Carly was fully embarked on the story now, so she probably wouldn't be distracted by the notebook.

"Lavonne was downtown with her kids. Beanie came over to play with the girls, and Captain was out on his clothesline leash in Lavonne's yard, watching them."

"Captain?"

"That's Lavonne's big dog. He's one of those killer guard dogs."

Oh, swell.

That was a great animal to have around little kids, Jackie thought grimly.

She didn't say anything, just wrote steadily in her notebook while Carly told her about the intruder in the backyard who'd snatched Emily and tried to run away with her.

Jackie set the notebook aside and got to her feet, reaching for her coat. "Do you have a flashlight, Carly? I could go out to the car and get mine if you don't."

"That's okay," Carly said. "John keeps one right by the back door. Just a minute, I'll get my things." She gathered Patrick up, wrapped him in his blanket and handed him to Jackie, who held the baby while Carly pulled on her boots and coat and called to Caitlin.

The two women—Carly now holding Patrick in her arms—went outside where Jackie shone the beam of light around the tidy backyard. A pair of wooden sleds leaned against the garage and a swing set was covered with a plastic tarp, neatly tied around the legs to keep it from flapping in the wind.

"Where were the girls playing?" she asked.

"Out there in the deep snow. You can still see the blood where Beanie...where he was kicked."

Jackie waded into the trampled drifts of snow. For the second time that week, she knelt looking at a pink wash of blood across fresh snow.

Finally she stood up and ran the trail of light along the ground. "Can you pick out any of the man's footprints?"

Carly shook her head. "The kids have been running all over the place. I had to let them play outside later, after Caitlin came home, because they were so restless and I didn't want them to be afraid of their own yard. So I sat on the back step with Patrick bundled in his car seat, and I watched them."

Jackie looked at the myriad tracks in the snow. She walked out into the alley where the situation was no better. Children coming home from school had apparently trooped up the alley in small herds, obliterating everything in their path.

"Just the same," she said aloud, "I'll send a couple of patrols out here tomorrow morning to look around. Somebody might have noticed something.''

She came back to the deck where Carly huddled on the top step. Jackie looked around at the darkness again, shining her flashlight into the opposite yard where two doghouses stood side by side, one large and one much smaller.

In the beam of light, a pair of yellow eyes glittered from the depths of the larger doghouse and a low growl rumbled.

"That's Captain," Carly whispered. "Try not to get him roused, all right? He's really scary. He comes charging out of there and barks at strangers like some kind of monster.''

Jackie looked thoughtfully at the doghouse, the low picket fence and the clothesline with the empty running chain that hung from it.

"But he didn't bark when the man came into the yard, did he?'' She frowned, trying to remember Carly's story as she'd just written it in her notebook. "You heard the kids and the puppy, but at first you thought they were just playing. If the big dog had barked, you would have been concerned right away, wouldn't you?''

Carly's eyes widened. "You're right," she said. "I never thought of that. Captain didn't bark at all. That's really strange. And he didn't bark the other night, either, but he seemed sick the next day. Could somebody be poisoning him, do you think?''

"Either that," Jackie said, "or the intruder is somebody he knows.''

Carly stared at the doghouse, then shook her head. "Let's go in," she suggested, "and have a cup of coffee.''

Jackie's stomach, already far too empty, churned uneasily at the thought of coffee.

She worried that she was getting sick. Wardlow was developing a bad case of flu and had threatened to stay home on Friday if he didn't feel any better. Michelson, a notorious workhorse, had also begun to complain of not feeling his best, and Brenda Howe and Dave Pringle had both been off duty since Tuesday morning.

These winter flu epidemics seemed to be an occupational hazard of police work, where people worked long hours without proper food or rest, dealt with the public all the time and spent their workdays crowded into vehicles or hurrying in and out of overheated buildings.

"Sorry," she said aloud, "no coffee for me, thanks. I still need to go home and find something to eat in my apartment."

Inside the kitchen, Carly looked apologetic. "I'm really sorry. I shouldn't be taking up so much of your time. Can I make you a sandwich or something?"

"No thanks. I really have to get home." Jackie held the baby while Carly removed her coat and boots. Patrick gazed up at her solemnly from the folds of the blanket and reached out to grasp a fistful of her hair, tugging with surprising strength.

She grinned at him. He smiled back, his face dimpling and glowing. Jackie laughed, feeling absurdly pleased, and hugged him while Carly looked on with a shy smile.

Jackie sat at the table, still holding the baby. "Carly," she said, "do you have any idea who tried to snatch Emily today?"

Carly was at the fridge getting out a bottle of baby formula. She flinched, her head turned away.

"Do you?" Jackie asked.

Patrick blew a series of damp bubbles, obviously tickled by the noise they made. Jackie held him upright, smiling. She squeezed him and kissed his plump cheek, then felt guilty when she remembered she was probably coming down with the flu.

"I thought it...might be John," Carly murmured. "The kids said he was wearing a ski mask."

"Does your husband own a ski mask?"

Carly shook her head.

"Did he take any of his clothes, Carly?"

The woman's shoulders began to tremble. Jackie could see the way she pulled herself together with visible effort, then ran hot water into a saucepan and set it on the stove, putting the bottle into it.

"He took quite a few of his things. Older clothes that he thought I wouldn't miss, I guess. At first it looked like everything was still here, but when I checked the basement and the storage rooms, I could tell things were missing."

Oh, shit, Jackie thought wearily. *Wait'll Sarge hears about this.*

"So he wasn't involved in any kind of accident," Jackie said. "This was obviously something he planned in advance. Particularly in the light of the money that's missing from your bank accounts."

Carly nodded, brushing at her eyes. "But there has to be an explanation. I know he's in some kind of terrible trouble. John's not the kind of man to desert his family. He just isn't."

"Do you think he could have become emotionally

unbalanced by pressures at work?'' Jackie asked. ''You told me he's been working pretty hard lately.''

''John's always so stable,'' Carly said. ''I'm the one who gets upset and frets over things, and he always talks me around and makes me feel optimistic again. He's just like a rock.''

Carly took the formula out of the saucepan and tested it by shaking a few drops onto her wrist. She brought the milk across the room and handed it automatically to Jackie, then turned away in distracted fashion and began to rummage through boxes of baby cereal in the cupboard.

Startled, Jackie looked at the bottle, then at Patrick who flailed his fists and tried to sit up, puffing anxiously as he reached for the bottle. She fitted it in his mouth, gratified to see how he latched on to the nipple and settled back, sucking noisily.

One chubby hand rested against the side of the bottle. The other reached up to touch Jackie's cheek in a gentle, reflective manner. She held him closer, enjoying the moment.

''Carly,'' she said.

''Yes?''

''Do you think John could be a threat to your children?''

Carly barely hesitated. ''Not unless he's completely changed from the man I know.''

''And if he was a threat,'' Jackie asked curiously, ''how would you feel about him?''

''I'd still love him. I could never stop loving John, no matter what he did.''

''No matter what?'' Jackie repeated.

Carly nodded with slow emphasis, watching Patrick suck lustily at the bottle.

"How are you going to manage?" Jackie asked at last. "With Christmas coming, and so little money? Do you have family who can help you out?"

"There's John's parents and his sister but I couldn't ask them now. I just couldn't. I don't know what I'm going to do. The mortgage is looked after for one month and I have enough to buy a bit of food, but if any kind of emergency happens, we'll be in big trouble. And as far as Christmas goes..."

Jackie handed the baby over reluctantly, went into the other room and rummaged in her shoulder bag for a checkbook.

"Here's five hundred dollars," she said, writing quickly. "It's all I can afford right now, but it should help a bit with Christmas."

Carly stared at her, wide-eyed. Her cheeks drained of color, then turned red in mottled patches. "I can't...I couldn't possibly."

Jackie set the check down on the coffee table. "Call it a loan." She picked up the manila envelope containing the pictures of John Stevenson. "Tomorrow morning we'll get this missing-person investigation launched and find out where your husband is, and then your situation should improve a whole lot. Okay?"

"Okay," Carly said numbly. She lifted the check and stared at it. "Thank you, Jackie."

Jackie laced up her boots and paused in the doorway. "Carly," she said, trying to keep her voice casual.

"Yes?"

"Is there anyplace you could go to get the kids away from here for a few days until things get sorted out?"

Carly pondered, then shook her head. "Just La-vonne's, and that wouldn't make much difference, would it?"

"Not much," Jackie said. She paused, thinking about Harlan and Adrienne, whom she was supposed to be visiting in a few minutes. "Look, I have some friends who own a big house, and I know they'd be happy to—"

Carly shook her head. "No," she said. "Please, I don't want to go away. I want to stay here with my kids where all their things are."

"Okay," Jackie said. "I'll report what happened, but this is still a domestic issue at this point, so we can't give you any kind of protection. But call us right away if something scares you, all right?"

"All right."

"I mean it," Jackie said sternly. "Be sure to call. And keep a real close eye on the kids, all right? Maybe Caitlin could stay home from school tomor-row since it's Friday. Don't let them out of your sight for the next few days."

Carly nodded. The last thing Jackie saw as she left was the woman's thin face in the doorway, once again so pale that the freckles stood out sharply on the bridge of her nose.

It bothered her that Carly Stevenson would choose to stay in the house after what had happened that afternoon. Her decision didn't seem rational.

The only explanation was that she still believed the mysterious intruder was her husband, the father of her children, and that the kids weren't really in any dan-ger from him.

Jackie hoped fervently that Carly Stevenson was right.

10

By the time Jackie got home, she didn't feel hungry anymore. She stood in the kitchen, staring at the contents of the fridge and wondering if she should just make herself some popcorn.

Popcorn was a vegetable, wasn't it?

She frowned, trying to decide.

The phone rang, and she crossed the room to answer.

"Hi, sweetheart," Paul said.

"Hi, Paul. Is popcorn a vegetable?"

"No," he said promptly. "Popcorn is a snack food. And you'd better not be planning to have it for supper."

She made a face at the telephone receiver, then decided she didn't feel like arguing with him. "Okay," she said. "I'll cook some macaroni and vegetables. How are you?"

"I'm tired. I spent the whole day working on the tank heater. I still can't get it to work so I've been out chopping water holes in the ice with an ax."

"What's a tank heater?"

"It's a little gizmo that goes in the bottom of the trough and keeps the water from freezing. Very delicate to operate since it's always submerged. How was your day, Jackie?"

She thought about Karl Widmer and his hints about Norine Burkett, about the flu epidemic in the office and the mountain of extra work that was going to result from it, about John Stevenson's disappearance and the specter of a mysterious intruder trying to snatch one of Carly's children.

"Jackie?"

"It was crazy," she said, "the same as always. And I'm coming down with something, Paul. Everybody at the office is getting sick. You should see Brian, he looks like death warmed over."

"You're still coming out here on the weekend, though?" he said.

Jackie thought about the coming day, in which she hoped to launch a missing-person search for John Stevenson, provided Michelson remained agreeable. If things went as planned, tips would start coming in by Friday afternoon and would continue all through the weekend.

"Jackie?" he said.

"All right." She sighed. "Sure, I'm planning to come out to the ranch. But if something comes up, I might have to leave early and I don't want you to be mad at me."

"Is everything all right?" he asked. "Are you upset about something?"

Jackie thought about him in his isolated ranch house out on the star-dazzled blackness of the prairie, and had the sudden impression that he was a thousand miles away, impossibly beyond her reach. She felt so lonely and desolate that she had to fight back tears.

"No, Paul," she said. "I'm fine, just tired. I still have to make myself something to eat, then drop in at Rennie's for a while."

"You were just there, weren't you?"

"I went over on Monday to see their Christmas tree. But when I talked to her today, she had some big secret she wants to tell me, so I promised I'd stop by for a few minutes."

"Okay," he said. "Drive carefully if the streets are slippery."

She laughed. "Paul, I spend my whole day driving around in a police car."

"I love you," he said, his voice suddenly intense.

"I know, sweetheart. I love you, too." The sadness grew and spread, almost engulfing her.

"So you'll be out here tomorrow night?"

"I'll try. But it'll probably not be until Saturday morning, okay?"

"Jackie, you promised you'd—"

"Oh, hell," she said in pretended alarm. "The macaroni's boiling over! I have to go, honey. See you soon."

She hung up the phone and stood looking at it for a moment. Finally she wandered over to the pantry and took out the popcorn maker.

Adrienne greeted her at the front door, wearing black tights and a long tunic of gold lamé. Her sleek head glistened and her eyes were bright with repressed excitement.

"Wow," Jackie said, feeling dowdy and tired in her jeans and sweatshirt. "You look great. What's the occasion? Tell me this news of yours."

"Not right away." Adrienne looked almost shy. "I have to build up to it."

"Rennie, you'll make me crazy."

"Let's just chat about other stuff for a while, okay? Be patient for once."

Jackie looked at her friend. "You *are* okay, aren't you? You look wonderful."

Adrienne gave her a self-deprecating grin. "New haircut, that's all." She took Jackie's coat and examined her closely. "But I gotta say, you don't look so hot, kiddo."

"I don't?"

"You're pale, and you've got huge bags under your eyes."

"I've been working too hard. What else is new?"

Jackie wandered into the family room where a holly-decked cheese ball sat on the coffee table flanked by antipasto, crackers and wineglasses.

"Yummy," she said, suddenly ravenous.

"Help yourself. I made the cheese ball for you because I know how much you love it."

Jackie sat on the couch, tucking her legs under her. She attacked the food, dipping crackers into the savory cheese, spooning antipasto on them and munching them hungrily.

Adrienne sat in the opposite chair and watched in disapproval. "What did you have for dinner?"

"Popcorn." Jackie reached for another cracker. "Don't start with me, okay? Paul's already weighed in on the subject."

"You should get married, Jackie."

Jackie made an impatient gesture. "What would that solve? Would my diet somehow miraculously improve if I got married?"

"Your life would be more stable and orderly," Adrienne said.

"I doubt it." Jackie selected another cracker.

"This is so delicious." She chewed and swallowed, then glanced up. "I've got an inherently disorderly job, you know. It's supposed to be eight to four, five days a week, but it never works out that way. If I get married and live with Paul at the ranch, the only difference will be that I'll have to drive fifty miles every day."

Adrienne watched her closely. "I was right. You *are* getting cold feet."

"I didn't say that. I just want to point out that getting married isn't the solution to achieving stability in my life."

"So what is?"

Jackie shrugged. "Quitting my job, I guess."

"But is that likely to happen? Could you stand to quit and work with Paul at the ranch, not be on the police force anymore?"

"I don't think so. It's a hellish job but I seem to be addicted to it."

"That's what I thought." Adrienne got up and crossed the room to the wood-fronted bar fridge. "You want to know what I think?"

"No," Jackie said promptly.

"I think," Adrienne said, "that you're scared to make the commitment so you keep looking for excuses."

She glanced at Jackie, who concentrated on the antipasto.

"Want a drink?" Adrienne asked.

Jackie shook her head. Adrienne poured some eggnog into a crystal glass and came back to curl up in the chair.

"Where are Harlan and Alex?" Jackie said after a moment.

"Ice skating. They always go on Thursday nights."
Jackie smiled, then sobered. "Rennie..."

"Hmm?"

"What do you know about Norine Burkett? I mean, about what kind of person she is?"

Adrienne frowned, sipping her eggnog. "Not much. Isn't that strange? We've moved in the same social circle for ten years, worked on all kinds of committees together, attended the same parties ad nauseam, but I know almost nothing about the woman."

"She's Jason Burkett's second wife, isn't she?"

"Yeah." Adrienne grimaced. "The classic blond trophy wife. He dumped poor Sandra when she turned forty. Then he produced this little blond cutie, and we all had to get adjusted to her."

"Where did she come from?"

Adrienne leaned forward and helped herself to part of the decimated cheese ball. "Nobody knows. There was a lot of fevered speculation at first, as I recall. The older women in our crowd kept hinting that Norine had a past, but I think they were just being catty because she was so young and beautiful."

"What kind of past?"

"I don't know. Something shady, maybe even criminal. I didn't pay much attention." She gave Jackie a wry grin. "I was also a young wife at the time, and my own past didn't exactly bear close inspection."

"And you can't remember any of this gossip?"

"It's been years since I've heard anything at all. After Angela was born and Norine settled in to the social rhythm of the group, people just accepted her as Jason's wife."

"What happened to the first wife?"

"Sandra? She pretty much dropped out of sight. I heard she gouged Jason for a ton of money, went back to school and finished her psychology degree. I think she's a family counselor in Seattle."

"And you can't remember any of the rumors about Norine, or where she might have come from?"

"It was ten years ago, Jackie. I only remember there was talk, that's all."

"Do you know where he met her?"

Adrienne grinned. "Where do men meet these little blond cupcakes? As I recall, it was on a ski hill or a scuba-diving trip, something wholesome and out-doorsy. At least, that's the party line."

"The party line?"

"Jason Burkett's a politician first and foremost, and so is Norine. Their entire lives are orchestrated and dedicated to one goal—reaching Washington. I wouldn't be surprised if Norine aspires to even loftier heights." Adrienne drained the last of her eggnog and got up to pour another.

"Like what?" Jackie asked.

"Pennsylvania Avenue," Adrienne said briefly. "Want some eggnog? It's nonalcoholic."

"Thanks. You think she wants him to be *president?*"

"I think she wants to be First Lady. I have the feeling little Norine has a mass of seething ambition under that dainty pink-and-white exterior."

"What makes you think so?"

Adrienne handed Jackie a glass full of the rich liquid, then sat opposite her again. "I guess after a lifetime with my mother, I can smell political ambition.

I hate it so passionately that I have some kind of sixth sense for recognizing it.''

''So if there were some kind of scandal threatening them,'' Jackie said, ''how far would Norine go to cover it up?''

''She'd kill without a qualm,'' Adrienne said calmly. ''God,'' she added, ''what a way to talk about the woman when I'm going to her child's funeral tomorrow. But I still think it's the truth.''

''You society ladies are pretty terrifying,'' Jackie said dryly. ''I grew up in a place where people kill for passion, not ambition.''

Adrienne laughed. ''Same thing, sweetie. In my world, ambition is the most passionate thing of all.''

Jackie nodded, considering.

''What did you want to tell me, Rennie?'' she said at last.

Adrienne looked down at the glass in her hand. ''Damn, this is embarrassing,'' she muttered. When she looked up, her eyes were wet with tears.

''Hey,'' Jackie said. She leaned forward and took her friend's hands. ''Rennie, what's the matter?''

Adrienne shook her head. ''Nothing's the matter. It's just so... I can't help it. Sorry.''

She took a tissue from a box on the table and wiped her eyes, then blew her nose while Jackie watched in concern.

''I'm pregnant,'' Adrienne said at last.

Jackie's mouth dropped open. ''You're *what?*''

''Isn't it the most amazing thing you ever heard?'' Adrienne gave her a misty smile. ''After all these years of trying, finally giving up, and suddenly it happens out of the blue. Jackie, I'm so—''

Jackie got up and hugged her, laughing. ''Rennie,

I don't know what to say! How long have you known?''

"For a while. At first we never even suspected anything. I've always been so irregular, I never know what's going on with my body. It was one of the reasons I could never conceive. The doctor says I probably only ovulate a couple of times a year.''

"Hey, I'm exactly the same,'' Jackie said. "I never talked to other women and God knows my grandmother didn't tell me anything, so for years I thought everybody was like that.''

Adrienne laughed. "Well, the doctor discovered this a couple of months ago during a routine checkup. When she told me, I almost fainted.''

"A couple of months?'' Jackie stared at her. "You've known for a couple of *months?*''

Adrienne nodded, gazing at the Christmas tree. "Harlan and I were so scared,'' she murmured. "It seemed too good to be true. We wanted to wait until they could do a second ultrasound and make sure everything was okay. That just happened yesterday.''

"So how pregnant are you?''

"Four and a half months.'' Adrienne looked up shyly. "I felt the baby move earlier this week.''

"It moved?'' Jackie looked down at Adrienne's slim body.

"There's already quite a little bump, you know.'' Adrienne took Jackie's hand and held it on her abdomen. "See?''

"Hey, there is.'' Jackie laughed and hugged her again. "Isn't this amazing?'' she said. "Rennie, you're going to be such a great mother.''

"You think so? I'm thirty-seven years old, Jackie.

And," she added gloomily, "nothing in my life has taught me very much about mothering."

"Oh, come on. You've been a wonderful mother to Alex. You and Harlan saved her life."

"But Alex is almost fully grown, and a terrific kid to start with. This baby's going to be so *small*." Adrienne held up her cupped hands to indicate something tiny and fragile.

"You'll be great," Jackie said firmly. "Does Alex know?"

"We told her today, and she's so excited. She's already planning to take a baby-sitting course at school so she can learn all about caring for infants."

Jackie laughed, then shook her head. "How long have you and Harlan been married?"

"Almost seventeen years. Jackie, he's so…" Adrienne looked down at her hands.

"What?" Jackie said.

Adrienne glanced up, her eyes bright with tears, her face soft. Jackie could hardly believe this was the brittle, sardonic woman she'd first met two years ago.

"It's scary to be so happy," Adrienne murmured. "You feel really…vulnerable."

"I know." Jackie felt a sudden wave of sadness and repressed it firmly. "When's the baby due?"

"The end of April. My doctor's monitoring everything pretty closely since it'll be a first child for me at such an advanced age, but she says everything looks fine so far."

"Advanced age," Jackie scoffed. "You're in great shape, Rennie, and you swim and work out all the time. You're not going to have any problems."

"Maybe not, but Harlan and I are going to look like grandparents in the maternity ward with all those young kids having their first babies. He's fifty-two this year, you know.''

"You and Harlan," Jackie said firmly, "are going to be the best parents in the whole world. This is one lucky kid.'' She hesitated, feeling awkward. "Do you know if it's a boy or a girl?''

Adrienne shook her head. "The doctor knows, but we asked her not to tell us. It's more fun to be surprised. Harlan was there yesterday for the ultrasound,'' she added. "It was so amazing, Jackie. You can see the spinal column, all the little vertebrae like a string of pearls, and the head and hands and feet…''

Jackie looked again at her friend's stomach and touched it tentatively. "Incredible,'' she murmured, "to think there's a little person in there. It's a miracle, isn't it, Rennie?''

"It truly is.'' Adrienne dashed at her eyes again. "And if I don't quit blubbering, I'm going to make a complete idiot of myself. Come look at the little clothes.''

She led Jackie upstairs to the master bedroom and opened a dresser drawer filled with tiny cotton shorts and nighties.

"We didn't want to start planning a nursery or anything until after the ultrasound,'' Adrienne said, "but I couldn't resist buying some things.''

Jackie touched the little garments in wondering awe. She held up a minuscule shirt, touched its softness to her cheek and thought of Carly's baby, his pudgy hand resting against the side of his nursing bottle.

Finally she said her goodbyes and drove home through the multicolored stillness of the Christmas lights. All at once her spirits lifted, and she felt happier than she had in weeks.

11

"So he took his clothes and cleaned out the bank accounts?" Michelson sat behind his desk on Friday morning, studying Jackie's file.

"That's right. But—"

He glanced at her over the tops of his reading glasses. "And you honestly still think this sounds like a police matter?"

"There's a whole lot of other stuff going on here, Sarge." Jackie told him about the intruder at Carly Stevenson's house, and the attempted abduction of one of the twins the previous afternoon.

He waved his hand in dismissal. "I already know all that. Bill Klementz went out and talked to the neighbors this morning, but nobody saw a thing. You're sure this poor woman isn't just looking for a little attention? Maybe some help in tracking down a wandering husband?"

Jackie thought about Carly's pale face and trembling hands, and her houseful of little children. "I'm sure she's not. And I can't shake the feeling that it all ties in somehow to the Burkett hit-and-run. I really want to follow up on this guy, Sarge. We need to ask him some questions."

He raised a hand, ticking items off on his blunt fingers.

"Wardlow's out with the flu. Brenda's been gone since Tuesday. Dave Pringle's looking a little green today, and I don't feel so hot myself. We're low on staff and we don't have the resources at the best of times to get involved in domestic problems, Jackie."

"Please," she said.

The sergeant sighed. "Okay. But if anything comes up, I'm going to pull you off this right away. You're prepared for that?"

"Sure." She got to her feet, gathered her papers and gave him a grateful smile. "Thanks, Sarge."

"Jackie," he said.

"Yes?"

"How are *you* feeling?"

She paused in the doorway. "Fine, Sarge. I'm just fine."

He gave her a keen glance from under his bushy eyebrows, then opened a file. "Okay. Get out of here," he said with a brusqueness that didn't fool her for a moment.

Jackie hurried to complete the paperwork and put out a missing-person bulletin on John Stevenson, then drove downtown to talk to Steve Baumgartner, who looked more harried than ever.

The pre-Christmas flu epidemic was thinning the ranks at the main police station as well, and the spell of icy weather had further overburdened the Traffic Division, already struggling against relentless pressure from the media and the public to solve little Angela Burkett's hit-and-run death.

Jackie sat near Baumgartner's desk, sipping lemon tea, and watched him in sympathy. "Have you got anything at all?" she asked.

"Not very much." He tossed the file across the

desk. "The headlight fragments are an aftermarket brand, no help in identifying the vehicle. Eyewitnesses say it was some kind of small sports model, and the paint smear on the fence was red. Ident believes the tread they picked up was a summer tire."

"So it could even be a vehicle that's garaged most of the winter and not normally driven?"

He nodded gloomily. "Which, of course, makes our job even tougher. And you know that searching for a hit-and-run driver is always like trying to find a needle in a haystack because there's no motivation or connection to the victim."

Jackie gazed into her cup. "Did you get my message about Norine Burkett's car?" she asked.

He glanced at her sharply. "Yeah. I never got a chance to ask you what that was all about, Jackie. Surely you don't think the woman ran over her own kid?"

"I don't think anything. I just passed on the information."

"Well, we can't get a look at her car. It's locked inside that bloody big garage of theirs and they won't let us in there without a warrant."

"You've already tried to get into the garage?" she asked in surprise.

"We had to be really delicate about the request. For some reason this Burkett is antsy as hell. We told him we wanted to examine the treads on their car tires so we could eliminate them from all the other tracks outside the house and try to isolate the hit-and-run vehicle."

"And he didn't buy it?"

"He refuses to let us into his garage without a warrant. And we certainly have no probable cause to get one.''

''Don't you think it's strange,'' Jackie murmured, ''that he'd turn down a straightforward request like that?''

''Not really. I think he's a nice guy who's getting bad advice from his lawyers.''

''But why not let you into the garage?''

''Like I said, he's got a crew of lawyers advising him, and they're telling him to refuse everything. The man won't even talk with us. But apparently he's planning to offer a huge reward for information leading to the arrest and conviction of the hit-and-run driver.''

''Oh, great,'' Jackie said.

''I know. That's going to make this even tougher. Every amateur detective in the city's going to be running around getting in our way.''

Jackie set her teacup down on the desk and ran a finger slowly around the handle. ''So I guess you've already put out a bulletin to all the autobody shops, to watch for a red sports car with damage to a front headlight?''

Baumgartner laughed without humor. ''Come on, Jackie,'' he said. ''You've been watching too much television. Either that or you haven't worked traffic for a long time.''

She looked up at him in surprise. ''You mean it doesn't work that way?''

''Not worth a damn. There are so many chop shops and back-alley body workers, we could never begin to cover all of them. And who's going to take their car into a licensed body shop when they've just killed a little kid with it and they know everybody's looking for the vehicle? They'd have to be crazy.''

"So what do you think about the John Stevenson angle? Have you turned up any connections?"

"We're hoping you'll do that for us." He opened the file and leaned back. "I've got ten people working this, Jackie. You know what they're doing right now?"

"I can guess, but tell me anyway."

"They're using computers to check out every red sports car registered in the state and locate the owners. Can you imagine how time-consuming that is?" Without giving her a chance to respond, he continued. "Let me tell you, it's not fun. So where do you want to start?"

"I'm looking for John Stevenson. I really want to talk with that man. We've distributed his photograph to the media, put a description on the tip line, notified other departments, all the usual stuff. Now we're waiting for feedback."

"And right now?"

Jackie looked at her watch, then pushed the chair back and got up. "Right now I want to stop by Angela Burkett's funeral. I'm hoping to get another look at her parents."

Cars lined the streets for blocks in all directions. Jackie found a parking spot, got out and started briskly up the street toward the Episcopal church on Grand Boulevard, noticing the crush of media people ranged against a row of limousines and a long black hearse parked out front.

She kept her head down, hoping none of this boisterous crowd would recognize her and begin shouting questions. Jackie pushed her way through the cameras and microphones toward the massive doors, annoyed to feel herself being jostled and shoved.

Suddenly she felt a hand on her elbow and a wiry body next to hers, moving with her into the throng. She smelled tobacco and tweed, and recognized Karl Widmer.

"Hi, Detective," he murmured. "Just stay close to me, all right?"

Jackie tried to pull her arm away. "Leave me alone."

But he held her with surprising strength. "Hey, Jackie, don't be so touchy. I'm going to get you a good seat inside the church."

They mounted the steps and moved past an usher at the door, who offered Widmer a couple of printed leaflets with an illustration of a sleeping lamb surrounded by flowers. Still holding her arm, he led her into the hushed sanctuary, already crowded with people.

Organ music swelled and throbbed, and a cloying scent of flowers drifted on the warm currents of air. Without hesitation, Widmer guided her around the end of the pews and up toward the front of the lofty cathedral, pausing a few rows behind a curtained alcove.

"In there," he murmured, indicating a length of polished wooden bench.

Jackie glanced at him dubiously, then slid onto the bench. He followed and sat next to her, leaning close to whisper in her ear.

"The Burkett family's in there." He gestured toward the alcove. "I thought you'd probably want to be as close to them as possible."

She stared at the thin draperies and the blurry outlines of people sitting beyond them.

"Thanks," she said, turning away from him to look around.

The beautiful cathedral was filled with well-dressed people. Many of them dabbed at wet eyes and studied the printed leaflets.

Widmer handed her one of them. It contained a summary of the service, a photograph of Angela Burkett and some words about her short, happy life, and a few selected verses from poems by William Wordsworth.

A simple child,
That lightly draws her breath,
And feels her life in every limb,
What should she know of death?

Deeply moved, Jackie stopped reading after the first verse, lowered the pamphlet and looked around again. She noticed Adrienne across the sanctuary, sitting quietly next to Harlan and clutching his hand. Adrienne didn't see Jackie. She was gazing at the front of the church where a small white coffin, its cover half opened, lay buried under flowers.

The music swelled, then ebbed, and the service began. The minister spoke with simple eloquence about the innocence and purity of childhood, the comfort of faith and the sweetness of the little girl whose life had been snatched away so abruptly.

Jackie closed her eyes as she listened, almost sickened by the warm stillness of the room and the overwhelming scent of flowers.

Scenes flashed in front of her mind, images of her

own childhood filled with violence and hunger, with fear and loneliness and rage. She saw the filthy streets and alleys, shrubs withering in the smoky sunlight, front yards that were dirt instead of lawn, garbage piling up outside the doors and bedsheets hanging crookedly across the windows.

Beside her, Karl Widmer touched her arm briefly and moved closer to her on the bench, his hard face gentle with sympathy.

Jackie glanced at him, startled, and realized that she was crying. She edged away to rummage in the pocket of her coat for a tissue, wiped her eyes and concentrated on the service.

When the eulogy was over, the family filed from behind their screen to walk past the casket. Jason Burkett led the way, looking almost destroyed by grief. He stumbled along like a man in a trance, his face flushed and bloated with tears. Jackie was close enough to notice a blue, pinched look around his mouth and nostrils. He seemed dangerously near collapse.

His wife caught up with him and walked at his side, wearing a simple black coatdress that accentuated her pale loveliness. Norine's head was high, her face as composed and still as a cameo carved from fine marble. She gripped her husband's arm so tightly that her knuckles were white against his jacket sleeve.

But she wasn't clinging to Jason for support, Jackie realized. In fact, Norine Burkett was holding her husband upright. Without her, he would probably have fallen.

"She's a pretty cool little customer, isn't she?" Widmer whispered.

Jackie nodded and watched, fascinated, as the

child's parents moved past the casket, flanked by people who were obviously close relatives. They all looked prosperous and well-dressed, and most of them were crying openly.

Only Norine Burkett remained dry-eyed. Jackie leaned forward to watch as the woman looked at her daughter's face against the satin pillows. Norine gazed for a long time at the child's still profile while her husband shuddered next to her and moaned aloud, then turned away, shaking his head like a wounded animal.

Finally Norine reached out with a gesture that looked consciously graceful, almost studied, and lifted a single pink rose from a huge bouquet at the foot of the casket. She placed it on the little girl's folded hands, touched her daughter's cheek and turned away, gripping Jason's arm and leading him back to the privacy of the alcove.

Jackie exchanged a thoughtful glance with her companion, then got up and walked to the front of the church with him, following the rest of the congregation as they filed past the casket. At the front of the church, the rich fragrance of the flowers was almost overpowering. Jackie swayed briefly, and Widner reached out to steady her.

In the course of her career she'd seen a lot of victims of violent death, but none as lovely as Angela Burkett. The little girl was dressed in a white ruffled dress with a pink sash. Her close-cropped blond hair lay sleekly around her head. Long eyelashes fanned out across pale cheeks, and her mouth seemed relaxed, half-smiling, as if she were enjoying a pleasant dream.

Gravely, Jackie studied the sweet face on the ruffled pillow and found herself making a silent vow.

We'll find out, she told the earthly remains of Angela Burkett. *We're going to catch the person who did this to you. I promise we will.*

Karl Widmer, too, stood silently next to her and gazed at the child's face, his aquiline profile stern and unrevealing. After a moment he took Jackie's elbow and guided her down the aisle to the rear of the church.

They went through the wide doors into pale winter sunlight. Jackie stood at the top of the steps, taking huge gulps of fresh cold air.

"I thought I was going to pass out from the smell of all those flowers," she said, then looked down in distaste at the milling hordes of photographers and journalists. "God," she muttered bitterly. "You people really are vultures, aren't you?"

Apparently unruffled by her comment, Widmer grasped her arm and hustled her down the steps, then off through the waiting lines of cars, ducking past the noisy mob of reporters.

"You risked a lot coming here," he muttered as they ran. "If any of them recognized you, they'd have hounded you all the way back to the station trying to find out why you were here."

"I didn't realize they'd turn out in force for the damn funeral," Jackie said as they passed thinning crowds of people and emerged onto an empty side street. "I guess I should have known better."

They slowed their pace and walked past snow-covered yards toward her car.

"There's a tremendous amount of interest in this case," Widmer said, pausing next to the unmarked police vehicle. ''People want to know who did it and what the police are doing to catch him.''

Jackie hesitated, then got in and leaned over to flip the lock on the passenger door. Widmer climbed inside and sat next to her, stretching his long legs. There was a brief, awkward silence.

''Thanks,'' she said at last.

''What for?''

''For getting me inside the church and close to the family.''

He laughed with genuine amusement. ''It doesn't exactly come naturally to you, does it, Detective?''

''What?'' she asked.

''Saying thank-you.''

She considered, feeling vaguely defensive. ''Mostly I've made my own way in the world,'' she said. ''I guess I never had much practise expressing gratitude because I never had much cause.''

''That sounds pretty self-pitying,'' he said casually. ''I don't read you as that kind of person.''

She felt her cheeks warm with embarrassment. ''You're right, it does. Sorry, I guess my only excuse is I'm not feeling well these days, and that funeral service didn't help.''

He patted her shoulder, then stared out the window at the distant spires of the church. ''You're a trained observer of people,'' he said at last. ''What do you honestly think of Lady Norine?''

Jackie frowned. ''I'm not sure what to think. In my experience, people who look the most composed in a crisis are often feeling things just as deeply as everyone else. They stay calm while people are panicking, then fall apart later.''

He gave her a skeptical glance. "You really think that woman's going to fall apart?"

Jackie opened her mouth to reply, then stopped herself, realizing she was becoming dangerously comfortable with the man.

"I never know how safe it is to talk with you," she said. "Am I on the record here?"

He looked genuinely hurt. "I thought we were friends, Jackie."

"We're not friends. In fact, we barely know each other. How can I be sure you won't quote me if it serves your purposes?"

"I promise I won't quote you," he said. "And I'd be crazy to break that promise, considering how valuable your information could be to me in the future. Whenever our conversation is on the record, I'll let you know in advance, okay?"

"That sounds fair, I guess."

"So tell me what you think of Mrs. Burkett."

"I don't know what to think," Jackie said. "I'd need to talk to her again before I could form any kind of impression. From what I've been able to gather, that won't be easy. Neither she nor her husband are talking to the police any longer."

"Or to the press," he added, then cocked an eyebrow at her. "You look to be in pretty good shape," he said, gazing down with frank admiration at her body in slacks and blazer. "Tell me, do you work out?"

"What the hell does that have to do with anything?"

He threw his head back and laughed. "Well, it doesn't mean I'm lusting after your fair young body, although I must say the prospect wouldn't be totally unappealing.''

She glared at him with cold suspicion, unsure what to say.

"Norine Burkett seems to be something of a fitness nut," he said. "She goes to an aerobics class at the Lakewood gym on Monday, Wednesday and Friday afternoons. She missed today because of the funeral, but her instructor expects her to be back on Monday.''

"Did she go on Wednesday?" Jackie asked in disbelief.

"A full workout," he said grimly. "The day after her kid died, two days before the funeral. Didn't talk to anybody, shrugged off all offers of condolence, just sweated through her routine, had a shower and left the building.''

"Maybe she finds it relieves stress," Jackie said after a brief silence. "Working out usually helps to do that for me.''

"Maybe," he said with a noncommittal shrug.

"Did she go on Monday? The day of the accident?''

"She was there. I asked about that specifically. The instructor said Norine never misses a class. Two o'clock in the afternoon, in the upstairs aerobics room.''

"Two o'clock," Jackie repeated thoughtfully. "But she said...''

"What?" he asked.

"Nothing.''

"Hey." He touched her arm, looking hurt. "I'm bending over backward to help you, Jackie. This is supposed to be a reciprocal thing.''

She paused, feeling awkward.

Despite their public sparring, a lot of detectives maintained regular working relationships with certain members of the press, and the mutual exchange of information helped her colleagues bypass some tedious slogging. But Jackie had never been comfortable with the whole process.

"I'll tell you what I can, as soon as I feel okay with it," she promised. "I'm just learning how this works. It's all new to me."

He set his jaw with brief impatience, then nodded. "All right, but don't keep me waiting too long, Jackie. I have the potential to be very valuable to you in all kinds of ways."

She shot him a quick glance. "About this gym Norine Burkett goes to," she said at last.

"Lakewood, on Sixth Avenue. The class is at two o'clock, drop-in aerobics. You can buy a ticket for five dollars, but I have to warn you, it's a pretty strenuous workout."

Jackie smiled grimly. "No problem, as long as I have enough breath left over to have a chat with her in the locker room afterward."

"I'm laying my money on you, Detective," he said, giving her a sardonic salute.

"We put out a missing-person bulletin on John Stevenson this morning," she told him after a brief silence. "We're counting on getting a ton of tips. Apparently Jason Burkett is planning to offer a big reward for information about Angela's death but he hasn't got around to publishing it yet, thank God. Our tip line offers a reward, but we sure can't compete with Burkett's kind of money."

"Well, we've got all our feelers out, too," Widmer

said. "If anything comes in that looks even remotely interesting, I'll let you know right away."

"Thanks."

"So where can I reach you on the weekend?" he said casually.

"You can't. I'll be at my boyfriend's ranch most of the weekend and there's no phone. Just leave a message for me at the main switchboard and I'll get to it as soon as I can."

He looked at her for a moment, then nodded, got out of the car and strode off down the street, hands jammed deep in his pockets, shoulders hunched in the shabby tweed jacket.

12

On Saturday morning Jackie drove out to the ranch, her head so filled with random thoughts that she hardly noticed the scenery.

She'd stopped at the station before she left to find that tips were already pouring in concerning the whereabouts of John Stevenson. In response to the photographs and the public appeal, people had called to say he'd been seen everywhere from the greyhound track at Coeur d'Alene to a gay bar in San Francisco.

As usual, most of these tips were useless, but all of them were being logged onto the computer where they waited to be studied and cross-referenced to determine if any of them showed a pattern.

Following up on tips had once been a painstaking, labor-intensive job that police forces dreaded. But with the kind of software now available, hundreds of hours could be condensed to a single day's work for a skilled analyst.

She frowned and gripped the wheel, feeling a reluctance to leave the city just when things were starting to happen.

Paul still didn't have a telephone at the ranch and probably wouldn't be able to get the poles planted and the lines run in until spring. The place was isolated and located in a valley, so it was beyond cellular range. Jackie's portable police radio usually functioned when she was at the ranch, but at that distance was subject to the vagaries of weather and atmosphere and not completely reliable.

Besides, the portable was officially supposed to be used for emergency transmissions only, not off-duty officers checking up on cases.

Jackie tapped her fingers impatiently on the wheel, watching a hawk that circled and dipped its wings across the snow-covered prairie.

She should be happy, heading out here to spend a couple of days in a peaceful, rural setting away from the demands and complexities of her daily life, sheltered in a cozy house with the man she loved.

But more and more, Jackie found herself chafing at the isolation and quietness of the ranch.

She pulled off the highway and headed down the graveled road toward Paul's land. The prairie spread all around her, blanketed in snow, shimmering like a sun-washed ocean in the bright daylight. The world seemed muffled in white, silent and still, as if time had ground to a halt and nothing would move again until the warm breath of spring came sweeping over the land.

Driven by a cold wind, wraiths of snow slithered across the road like white snakes. Jackie shivered and peered ahead through the misty brightness to the cluster of buildings, still mostly unpainted. When she thought of Paul, she felt a lift of her spirits, along with a hot surge of sexual excitement.

She parked in a shed at the side of the house, got her duffel bag and a couple of sacks of groceries from the trunk and ran up the path to the back door, where she paused to stamp the snow from her boots, then unlace them.

"Hello?" she called, opening the door. "Paul, are you home?"

There was no answer. She went into the kitchen, looking around with pleasure as she unpacked the groceries.

He'd done a mountain of work since buying the place last spring. Even though much of his time had to be spent restoring outbuildings, repairing fences and looking after his herd of cows, Paul found time to work on the house as well.

The kitchen boasted a new set of glass-fronted oak cabinets, lovingly built and fitted, polished to a rich sheen. He'd also laid hardwood floors with careful precision and refurbished most of the old wooden moldings and wainscoting.

But there were still rooms in the big old house where the plastered walls were riddled with holes and windows hung crookedly in their frames. None of the upstairs had yet been touched. Jackie sometimes felt weak when she thought about the amount of work that needed to be done, but Paul remained serenely confident.

"I like hard work," he'd told her during her last visit. "Nothing makes me happier than having a big project to work on, and a pile of new lumber to use. Well, almost nothing," he'd added, sweeping her into his arms and kissing her with lusty passion.

She smiled, remembering, and crossed the sunny kitchen to pick up a piece of paper from the table.

"Hi, sweetheart," she read in his blunt, firm handwriting. "Outside doing chores, make yourself comfortable. I'll be in as soon as I can."

She set the paper back on the table and stroked it tenderly, then carried her bag down the hall to the bedroom.

This room, too, had been fully restored, outfitted with sprigged wallpaper and handmade oak furniture. The brass bed was covered with a gorgeous wedding-ring quilt that Adrienne had bought at a craft sale and given to Paul as a housewarming gift.

Jackie looked at the bed fitted with clean sheets, the quilt folded back invitingly, and felt her heart pound with anticipation.

She might have all kinds of questions and fears about the commitment of marriage, but there was no doubting how much she craved the man's body. She'd never known the kind of lustful yearning Paul Arnussen aroused in her.

Jackie left the bedroom, went back to the kitchen and put the kettle on, then rummaged through the cupboards until she found a packet of instant soup. She made herself some vegetable soup and toast and sat at the table eating reflectively, staring out the window at the expanse of snow rolling all the way to the horizon.

Paul loved the space and distance out here, but then, he'd grown up with this kind of landscape on his Montana ranch. Jackie, though, often found the vastness disturbing, as if she were trapped at the small end of a telescope, somehow out of proportion with the rest of the world.

She wasn't used to feeling so tiny and insignificant in the overall scheme of things. In the world she'd grown up in, nature definitely took a back seat, except during something cataclysmic like an earthquake.

The door opened and Paul stood in the entry, smiling. He wore a denim parka lined with sheepskin, a woolen cap and gloves, and heavy boots laced almost to his knees. He whipped the cap off, ruffling his pale blond hair, and held out his arms.

Jackie ran to him and burrowed against his chest, feeling the coldness of his jacket, smelling the mingled outdoor scents of hay and animals.

Paul bent his head to find her mouth. His kiss was deep and long, and his mouth clung to hers as he gripped her in a powerful embrace.

"I love you," she whispered.

He kissed her again, then drew away to look at her, his eyes sparkling.

Paul's face—like hers—was a mixture of racial heritages, but his was predominately Scandinavian and Native American, with blond hair that contrasted dramatically with blunt cheekbones and dark eyes.

Jackie could never get enough of looking at him. Just the slope of his tanned cheek was enough to turn her knees to jelly.

"You really love me?" he said, looking down at her with teasing intensity.

"Passionately."

"Enough to give me a bit of help with something?"

"What?" she asked, instantly wary.

"Just a little job out in the barn. Put your coat and boots on."

She dressed in her outer clothes and followed him outside. "I tend to hate jobs that need to be done in the barn," she said.

He laughed, seizing her mittened hand. "Oh, come on," he scoffed. "A big tough detective, and she's worried about a little heifer?"

"What's wrong with this heifer?"

"She's been indiscreet," he said. "And now she's paying for it, poor girl."

He held the barn door open and followed her inside, switching on the overhead light. The building was newly restored, snug and tidy, with green hay bales and sacks of feed piled along one wall, and riding gear stored in a corner.

Paul led Jackie to one of the box stalls where a little Hereford cow lay on a mound of loose hay, heaving and panting.

Jackie looked over the top of the stall at the animal's rough coat dusted with bits of hay, her lolling tongue and panicky liquid eyes.

"What's the matter with her? Is she sick? Oh, my God," she added when the cow shifted on her bed of hay, revealing a pair of tiny yellow hooves protruding from her vaginal opening.

"She's just been having a little problem," Paul said calmly, taking a coiled rope from a hook on the wall and moving into the stall. "And you and I are going to help her."

While Jackie watched in horrified fascination, he looped the rope around the little hooves and pulled to tighten the noose.

"I could put the calf-puller on her, but I don't think we'll need it," he said.

She looked nervously at the rope when he handed it over. "Paul, I don't have the slightest idea what I'm supposed to do."

"Just hold on to that while I get ready." He took off his jacket, then his shirt, stripping all the way down to his bare torso. Jackie studied the lean, half-naked body, then remembered the rope in her hand and turned away.

Paul hung his clothes on a hook and moved inside the stall. He knelt beside the little heifer, murmuring softly as her eyes rolled back at him in panic. She emitted a deep guttural bellow and shuddered, scrabbling her legs weakly on the hay.

He put his arm inside her and reached up along the body of the calf, frowning in concentration. Jackie watched, wide-eyed with shock.

"Ow!" he shouted as a contraction squeezed down hard against his arm.

He closed his eyes in pain, then opened them and smiled ruefully up at Jackie.

"That hurts like hell. Next time we'd better be ready for her," he said. "When I tell you, grab the rope and pull as hard as you can."

Jackie nodded tensely, hoping she wasn't going to be sick. Just the sight of his arm in that bloody opening was enough to make her stomach churn.

"Pull!" he shouted. "Hard!"

She leaned back and tugged on the rope with all her strength.

"Okay, ease off for a minute." He continued to manipulate the calf's body. A pair of legs appeared, then a damp tail.

"It's backward," Jackie said. "Isn't it?"

"That's what caused the whole problem. Pull again, as hard as you can."

She threw her whole weight against the rope. Paul's muscles strained and the heifer bellowed in agony. They continued to work, going through the procedure again and again until Jackie thought she would collapse.

She was ready to tell him she couldn't go on and plead for respite, when the body of the calf suddenly fell clear and dropped onto the hay, lying at Paul's feet in a slick bloody mass.

The little cow turned wearily and nosed at her calf, then struggled to her feet and began to lick the baby's damp body. Paul got up, stretching his arms, and knelt again to examine the calf.

"A nice little bull," he told Jackie in triumph. "And no ill effects that I can see."

The calf was already floundering to his feet. He stumbled around the stall on long wobbly legs while Jackie watched in amazement.

Paul left the box stall, plunged his arms into a bucket of water and scrubbed them with a cake of yellow soap from the windowsill, then dried himself on a piece of clean sacking.

"Why is she having a calf now?" Jackie asked, watching as the newborn animal faltered toward his mother and butted against her front legs, looking vainly for milk. "Isn't this supposed to happen in the spring?"

"Ideally," Paul said. "But a few of the heifers are ready to calve. The fences were in bad shape last spring before I bought the place. One of the bulls must have crawled out and done some lady-killing."

"How long does it take?"

"Lady-killing?" He cocked an eyebrow and gave her a meaningful grin. "That depends on the lady."

"No, you idiot, I mean gestation."

He pulled on his shirt and fastened the buttons, then unzipped his jeans to tuck the shirttail inside while she watched with covert interest.

"It takes nine months," he said. "Just like it does with people."

Jackie looked at the cow and calf. The little mother stood patiently, reaching back to nudge her calf in the right direction. At last he found the udder and began to nurse greedily.

"Guess what?" Jackie said abruptly. "Adrienne's pregnant."

Paul stopped with one arm in a jacket sleeve and stared at her.

"Adrienne?"

Jackie nodded. "You should see her, Paul. She's so happy, the woman hardly knows what to do with herself. They tried for years, you know, and finally gave up. The baby's due in April."

He zipped his jacket thoughtfully. "When did you find out?"

"A couple of nights ago. Remember when I told you on the phone I was going over to see her? Well, that was her big news."

He smiled. "That's really great. Tell her and Harlan I'm happy for them, all right?"

"Why don't you come home and tell them yourself? You're hardly ever in the city anymore."

"I know." He washed his hands again and dried them carefully, then pulled his gloves on. "But I hate to leave the ranch in case I get snowed out while these heifers are calving."

She folded her arms on the top of the stall and rested her chin on them, still staring at the calf. By now he was dried and beginning to look almost fluffy, with a bright copper coat and white face. His tail switched erratically as he nursed.

"Would you want kids?" she asked. "I don't think we've talked about that."

He glanced at her and went to toss the pail of bloody water onto the snow. A gray barn cat emerged from the piled hay and crossed the floor to rub against Jackie's legs, purring loudly.

"Sure, I want kids." Paul stood next to Jackie and looked at the calf. "Don't you?"

She bent to stroke the cat, suddenly nervous. "I guess I haven't thought about it much," she said. "It never seemed likely that a baby would ever be part of my life."

"Why not?" Paul put an arm around her and cuddled her, bending to kiss her hair.

"I don't know," Jackie said, brooding over the newborn calf. "I guess because I had such an awful childhood, and no father or mother to speak of. I never learned anything about parenting. I wouldn't have the slightest idea how to go about it."

"I didn't have much parenting either," Paul said. "But I think we could do a pretty good job. I'm looking forward to having kids."

She felt a sudden deep chill of alarm that she couldn't explain.

"One thing, though," he went on, still holding her close. "You wouldn't be able to keep your job if you got pregnant."

"Why not?" She looked up at him in surprise. "Lots of people do. We have officers away on maternity leave all the time."

His jaw set with the grim look that meant he had no intention of discussing the issue. "Lots of people may do it," he said. "But that doesn't make it right."

"That seems just a bit old-fashioned," she said,

trying to sound casual. "To say nothing of the arrogance."

"It's not arrogant at all. I'm just saying that when a woman has a baby, she shouldn't be out doing a job where people can shoot at her."

Jackie opened her mouth to protest, then stopped abruptly. He was touching her, reaching under her coat to finger the place on her abdomen where she'd been shot the previous summer. The scars from the exit wound, though long since healed, were a constant and painful reminder to Paul of the dangers of her job.

"Well," she said, turning away, "let's not waste any of our weekend fighting about something that may never happen, all right?"

"Suits me. Did you bring us something good to eat?"

"I brought lots of goodies. Come and see."

They went out into the blue and white stillness of the morning and walked toward the house arm in arm, talking and laughing.

But something was weighing on Jackie's mind, clouding her happiness and making her feel uneasy, and she knew that sooner or later they were going to have to talk about it.

The crisis came sooner than she expected, creeping into the midst of their relationship later the same day without drama or fanfare, changing everything.

It was just before midnight. They lay together in Paul's brass bed in a warm tangle of arms and legs, weary and content.

Jackie rolled her head on the pillow and looked at his profile, delicately etched with silver. She reached up to run a forefinger along the line of his nose and lips, then burrowed her hand into the mat of gleaming hair on his chest.

"Delicious," she murmured against his shoulder. "You're such a delicious man."

He smiled and caressed her naked hip, then ran his hand slowly over her buttock and down to her thigh. "You're pretty tasty yourself," he said, his voice husky.

She sighed and stretched out in the bed, moving closer to him and pressing against him. Jackie always liked the feeling of touching him with all the length of her body, her face and breasts and hips and legs.

He grasped her and lifted her effortlessly onto his chest. She lay sprawled comfortably on top of him, her face buried in his neck. Beneath her, the big, hard-muscled body was as solid as a ledge of rock, but silken-smooth and warm.

He continued to stroke her, running his hands down her back, touching the narrowness of her waist and the flare of hips and thighs. The long slow caresses were both soothing and arousing, making her intensely conscious of her own femaleness.

"Paul," she whispered, reaching down between their bodies to touch and fondle him.

"Mmm?"

She smiled, feeling him begin to stiffen and swell in her hands. "What a man," she teased. "You're ready to do it again."

"Not quite. But if you keep doing that, neither of us will get any sleep tonight."

"I'll stop," she promised, running her fingers along the shaft. "Right away."

"Oh yeah," he scoffed. "Sure you will." He

laughed and hugged her, then lifted her gently onto her side again and leaned over to cup her breast, flicking the nipple with his tongue.

Jackie moaned and grasped him more tightly. "I love being with you," she said. "I wish we could sleep together every night."

He held her breast gently and looked down at her. "So do I. Why can't we?"

"Because we…" She paused, still gripped by passion, and opened her eyes.

"Why?" he asked again.

"I forget the question." She sat up and knelt beside him, bending over to kiss his flat stomach, sliding her mouth downward.

But he grasped her and drew her gently back into his arms. "Not now," he said. "I want to talk about this."

"Oh, Paul," she protested. "This isn't a time for talking."

"Yes, I think it is."

Something in his voice alerted her. She tensed, glancing at him nervously. Paul held her close and she nestled against him so she wouldn't have to look at his face.

"I want to marry you, Jackie," he said.

"I know," she murmured into the warm skin of his neck. "We've agreed we're going to get married just as soon as we can."

"But when will that be? Why can't we get married tomorrow, since both of us want to?"

"Come on," she said. "It's not that simple. We have a lot of things we need to work out first."

"What kind of things?"

She felt a rising impatience. "Practical things," she

said. "Like my job, and how I'm going to commute when the weather's bad, and being out of telephone range when I need to be contacted—"

"So how," he interrupted her, "are these problems going to get resolved? Should we move the ranch about ten miles closer to the city, or what?"

"You'll have a telephone by spring," she said, seizing on the idea with relief. "Maybe we can get married then."

"Sorry," he said calmly. "I'm not waiting until spring."

She drew away and looked at him in disbelief. "Just like that?"

"Exactly like that. You know why?"

"Why, Paul?" she asked stiffly. Fear clutched at her and she struggled to keep her voice steady.

"Because when spring comes and the telephone's installed, there'll be some other excuse. None of this has anything to do with the phone or the isolation of the ranch or any other damn thing. You know what it's all about, and so do I."

She felt chilled suddenly and slipped from the bed to put on her plaid nightshirt. Reluctant to lie down with him again, she sat on the padded oak rocking chair and drew her knees up, resting her chin on them.

"We both know what's going on here," he repeated, watching her from the bed.

"No, Paul," she said wearily. "I have no idea what's going on here. Why don't you tell me, since you seem to know everything?"

He climbed from the bed, pulled on his shorts and T-shirt and sat on the edge of the mattress, still looking at her intently. She met his eyes for a moment, then turned away.

"You don't want to get married," he said. "You're quite happy to come out here and sleep with me, but you're afraid of making a lifetime commitment. You'd rather keep on just the way we are, forever, with each of us maintaining a separate world and getting together on weekends."

"I'm not afraid of anything." She gazed out the window. "It's just not practical right now, that's all."

"Not practical," he echoed grimly. "I see. And you're more concerned about being practical than defining our relationship and what we're going to do with the rest of our lives. Is that the idea?"

She turned back to him, stung by the sarcasm. "Look, there's no need to talk to me that way," she said. "I don't know what's wrong with being sensible about this. I have no intention of quitting my job, any more than you're going to sell this ranch and move back to the city. And that means we have problems we need to work out."

"They could all be worked out in ten minutes if you wanted to make an effort."

"You think I'm not making an effort?"

"That's what I think." He met her eyes steadily. "I think you're afraid."

"Bullshit." She buried her face against her knees, feeling a rising misery.

"Jackie, come on." He got up and moved toward her, kneeling by the rocking chair. "Let's not fight, sweetheart. I love you. Let's just get married and deal with the problems as they come up."

She kept her face hidden and shook her head, not trusting herself to speak.

"Okay," he said after a moment, getting back into bed. "Come over here, you're starting to shiver. I want to tell you something, and then we'll drop the whole topic.''

Jackie hesitated, then realized that it was, in fact, becoming very cold in the room. She got up reluctantly and climbed into the bed, holding herself stiffly away from him.

"I want to make you a deal." He rolled his head on the pillow to look at her steadily.

"What kind of a deal?" she said after a brief, charged silence.

"I'll give you until Christmas," he said. "That's a little less than three weeks."

"What for?"

"To make a decision about marrying me," he said. "In the meantime, we won't talk about it anymore. You can go home, think it through and reach a decision. At Christmas, tell me what you've decided."

"And?" she asked.

"And if you want to get married, we'll do it right away and deal with the issues later."

"What if I don't want to get married?"

"Then it's over between us. I don't want to go on like this for the rest of my life. It's too painful and disorganized."

She was so outraged that she sat upright and grasped his shoulder.

"An ultimatum?" she shouted. "You're giving me a goddamn *ultimatum?*"

"Yes, Jackie, I am. We've known each other almost two years. I'm closer to forty than thirty, and soon you will be, too. If we want to build a life and family together, we need to get started."

"I can't believe you're ready to end the relationship over this," she said, her voice shaking. "You'll throw it all away if you can't get everything your own way.''

"How are you being any different?''

"I'm not the one forcing issues,'' she said angrily.

"I know. You're too busy dodging and ducking issues to force anything.''

"Oh, Paul,'' she said wearily. "For God's sake.''

He reached up and pulled her down into his arms. She came unwillingly, her body stiff with reluctance.

"Let's go to sleep,'' he muttered. "No point in talking about it anymore right now.''

"But you really mean it?'' she said. "This whole ultimatum thing?''

"I really mean it. You're going to have to make some decisions, Jackie.''

13

The next morning Paul didn't mention their midnight argument, and neither did Jackie. They had breakfast, went outside together to finish the chores, then came in for lunch and spent the afternoon hanging wallpaper in the dining room, a task that both of them usually enjoyed.

They even managed to talk and laugh almost normally, but Paul's ultimatum drifted beneath the surface of their conversation like a shark circling in murky waters. When Jackie announced soon after supper that she was going to leave for the city, he didn't try to change her mind.

Instead, he went over to the old mullioned window and peered into the gathering darkness.

"Not such a bad idea," he said. "Looks like there could be a storm blowing up."

Silently, she went down the hall to the bedroom and packed her duffel bag, then came back to find her jacket and stood near the kitchen door, watching him. He leaned against the archway to the dining room, a roll of wallpaper in his hand.

"Will you be all right here on your own?" Jackie asked. "With that, I mean," she added hastily, gesturing at the wallpaper.

Paul smiled without humor. "I can always manage

on my own, Jackie. I'm like you, remember? I've had a lifetime of doing things by myself.''

She looked down at her boots, then bent hastily to put them on, well aware that the conversation wasn't just about wallpaper. Tears rose in her throat and she held them back fiercely, determined not to cry in front of him.

"I'd come over there and give you a hug," she said in a deliberately casual voice, ''but I've already got my boots on.''

He crossed the hardwood floor of the kitchen and took her in his arms, holding her tightly. She sighed and gave herself up to the warmth of his embrace, feeling both pleasure and sorrow.

Because these were, possibly, going to be their last moments together....

Jackie reached the freeway and merged with the traffic heading into the city, still thinking about Paul's ultimatum.

Did he really mean his threat, that if she refused his marriage proposal their relationship was over?

Just the thought of that was enough to suck the breath from Jackie's body and leave her feeling hollow and sick with fear.

Never to see that face again, to touch his cheek and stroke his chest, feel his arms around her. Never to sit at the table laughing over some shared joke, or walk with him in the fading daylight as they went around the ranch yard doing chores.

Never to lie with him at night in the rumpled moonlit bed, feeling him moving and thrusting inside her, filling her world with joy and tenderness...

"Oh, *shit*," she muttered aloud, scrubbing at her eyes again.

She looked around for something to distract her and thought of the nearby police substation which would be closed and silent on this early Sunday evening. She could check out the computers, see if she could figure out what was happening with the John Stevenson tip line.

But as soon as Jackie got the idea, she was forced to dismiss it. She hadn't brought along the security key to deactivate the station's entry alarm. It was at home in her nightstand along with her handgun and the rest of her work keys.

She could always go home, grab the keys and head over there. The thought of her empty apartment certainly wasn't all that appealing right now.

Jackie tapped her fingers restlessly on the wheel, then turned left off Division and headed for the Franklin Park area, pulling to a stop in front of Carly Stevenson's house.

Everything looked in order. The garage door was closed, Christmas lights glittered along the roof in orderly rows and the walks were freshly shoveled.

Had John Stevenson come back? Perhaps the man had finally come to his senses and dragged his sorry ass back home. That would certainly be a huge saving in time and emotional strain for everybody concerned.

She checked her face in the mirror, making sure no trace of the embarrassing tears remained, then walked up to the front door and rang the bell, feeling a little cheered. It was about time things started to work out right for somebody.

And she was anxious to ask John Stevenson what

he knew about his former employer, and the death of little Angela Burkett.

But as soon as the door opened, Jackie's optimism faded. Eight-year-old Caitlin stood in the doorway, looking up at her with a frightened expression.

"Caitlin?" a shrill voice called. "Who is it? Honey, get out of that doorway! How many times do I have to tell you…"

Carly appeared, grasping the child's shoulders and thrusting her daughter back out of sight. When she recognized Jackie, she sagged with relief against the door frame.

"Oh, thank God," she whispered. "I thought it might be…" Her voice trailed off.

"Who?" Jackie asked, stepping inside onto the jute doormat. "Who did you think it might be?"

"I don't know." Carly looked thinner than ever, and her hands were unsteady. Her chin trembled in little spasmodic jerks.

The woman was falling apart. Carly Stevenson looked as if she couldn't make it through another day.

While Jackie looked at her, wondering what to say, the twins came racing into the room, both naked. One of them had a green plastic water gun and she was squirting jets of water at her sister, laughing hysterically while the other screamed.

Carly covered her ears with her hands, leaned against the back of the couch with her eyes closed.

Lavonne Dermott, the next-door neighbour, wandered languidly into the room, grasped the little naked girls by the arms and gave them a couple of firm shakes that made them howl in alarm. Then she dragged them from the room while they cast glances of rebellious appeal in the direction of their mother, who ignored them.

The older child edged closer to Carly and touched her arm timidly.

"Mom, I'm going to check on Patrick," she whispered. "He's in his playpen. I think those boys are bothering him."

As Caitlin spoke, Jackie could hear the baby's frustrated howls amid some raucous laughter from other children, whom she presumed to be Lavonne's two little boys.

Carly nodded at her daughter, clearly making an effort to smile. "Thank you, dear. Make sure they're not hurting him, all right?"

When they were alone, Jackie put an arm around Carly and murmured soothingly, then led her to the couch and sat next to her.

"I was away for most of the weekend," she said. "What's been going on?"

"Just some…" Carly gulped and swallowed. "I've had some phone calls."

"From your husband?"

Carly looked up, her eyes shocked and pained behind reddened lids. "Not John! This call was awful. They said they were going to…kill the baby and…and hurt the girls…." She choked and began to moan softly, rocking back and forth on the couch.

"Did you save the calls?" Jackie asked. "Were any of them on the machine?"

Carly shook her head from side to side like a child. "There were only two calls, in the middle of the night. The first one woke me up. The second time I answered but nobody was on the line. If they were, they didn't say anything."

"When?"

"Last night."

"What was the voice like?" Jackie asked. "Male or female?"

"I couldn't tell. It was sort of a loud, rough whisper."

"And what did it say?" Jackie kept her arm around the woman, holding her firmly, conscious of the thin body trembling like a bird in her arms.

"It said I should pack up and leave, that my baby would be hacked to pieces and my little girls would be..." Carly gulped and swallowed, then continued. "They'd be...raped. This voice said there were people who loved to rape little girls, but it was too bad because the children usually died. That's what he said," she added, her voice trembling, rising close to hysteria as she attempted to imitate the caller. "'It's too bad, the way they almost always die. They're so...small, you see. Inside, I mean.'"

"Son of a bitch," Jackie muttered with feeling. "You're saying 'he' said this," she added. "You're sure it was a man?"

"I guess so." Carly twisted her hands together and looked down at them. "It didn't seem like anything a woman would say."

"And it must have been somebody who knew about your kids and that your husband is gone. Did he seem to believe you were alone?"

"I think he did. He called me Carly, and said I had to get away." She looked up, her face mottled with red patches. "I tried to call you, even though it was the middle of the night. But you weren't home."

"I'm sorry." Jackie hugged her again. "So did you call the downtown station like I told you to?"

Carly shook her head. "I didn't want to bother somebody I...didn't know. So I called Lavonne and she packed her kids up and came right over. She's going to stay here a few days so I won't be alone."

As if in response to her name, Carly's neighbor appeared in the hallway entrance holding one of the twins, now wearing a pink sleeping suit and looking round-eyed and chastened.

"They want a bedtime story from their mommy," Lavonne said with a hoarse bark of laughter. "My stories are no good, they say."

"Come here, Rachel." Carly got up and took the child from her neighbor's arms. The little girl straddled her mother's body and clung to her, face buried against her neck. Carly patted her daughter's back and murmured something in her ear.

As soon as she held the child in her arms, she straightened and looked more competent. Jackie realized the responsibility of her kids was probably the only thing holding Carly together.

"I'll go and tuck them in," she said to Lavonne. "Caitlin's watching the other kids, okay?"

Lavonne shrugged. "Sure, fine with me." She sat on the arm of the couch and watched over her shoulder as Carly left the room, then gave Jackie a conspiratorial grin and took a pack of cigarettes and a lighter from the pocket of her sweatpants.

"Carly doesn't like me to smoke in here," she said, leaning forward and lowering her voice, "but a person can hardly be expected to sit outside in a snowbank every time they need a smoke, can they?"

Jackie watched without expression as the other woman cupped the flame expertly and took a deep drag on her cigarette. "I suppose it's not all that good for the kids," she said.

"I guess not." Lavonne tipped her head back and exhaled a long plume of smoke.

Her blond hair was tousled, her clothes sloppy and not entirely clean. But she wore a lot of makeup, all of it skillfully applied. On closer inspection Jackie could see that the heavy foundation covered some pits and acne scars in the woman's cheeks.

"So you're staying here with Carly for a while," she said, wondering what the two women found to talk about when they were alone.

"Not much choice, is there? The poor kid's totally freaked out."

"Do you have any idea where John Stevenson might be?" she asked.

Lavonne concentrated on a scab on her bare foot, biting her lip as she tried to lift it with a long painted fingernail. "I think he's dead," she muttered.

Jackie looked up, startled, but the woman's head was bent and her hair tumbled forward to hide her face. Dark roots showed for almost an inch in the bright gold mass.

"Dead?" Jackie asked. "Why would you say that?"

Lavonne pried the scab loose and reached into her pocket for a tissue.

"Because he'd never stay away otherwise. You have no idea what the man's like."

"Maybe you could tell me what he's like," Jackie suggested.

Lavonne gave her a quick glance from narrowed eyes, then took another drag on her cigarette. Jackie suspected it wasn't the first time Carly's neighbor had experienced discussions with the police.

"Johnny-boy's a total straight arrow." Lavonne gestured at her bleeding foot with grim humor. "All the way down to his toes."

"You don't believe he's got a secret life of some kind?"

"John Stevenson?" Lavonne hooted coarsely with laughter. "He doesn't even have a secret life inside his head. I bet he's one of those men who think it's a sin to have lustful thoughts."

"So in all the time you lived next door to him, you've never had any indication that he's anything but an upright, law-abiding family man?"

Lavonne nodded. "Oh, yeah, that's what he is, all right. Uptight, buttoned-down, honest and sincere as hell. The most boring man I ever met. If I was lying outside in my bikini and he was mowing the lawn, he'd scurry round to the other side of the yard so he wouldn't have to look at me."

"And he loves Carly?"

"He's crazy about her. You can tell when they're together. His face goes all soft, and his shoulders get big and broad, you know? She doesn't look like the sort a man would feel that way about," Lavonne added carelessly, "but I guess it takes all kinds."

Jackie wished she'd thought to have a private interview with Lavonne Dermott earlier in her investigation. The woman was turning out to be a lot more forthcoming than she'd expected.

"So you don't think there'd be any circumstances that would make him voluntarily desert his family."

"Shit, no!" Lavonne shook her head firmly. "This little house, Carly and the kids, they're the whole world to John Stevenson. He's one of those men like you see in the movies, who'd die protecting his own,'' she added, looking briefly wistful.

Jackie glanced at the hallway and leaned forward, lowering her voice. "So if he's dead or injured somewhere and can't make his way home," she said carefully, "who do you think is threatening Carly?"

Lavonne shrugged, looking bored. "Who knows? Maybe it's somebody who thinks Carly's got money. Or,'' she added, frowning at her toes again, "maybe she's imagining the whole thing."

"You think she'd be capable of—"

"Mom!" a child howled. One of Lavonne's sons rushed into the room. His nose was running and he rubbed it with his forearm.

Lavonne looked at him and, grimacing in distaste, reached for another tissue and wiped his face while he squirmed in her grasp.

"Now what's the matter?" she asked, shaking him. "What's this all about?"

"Caitlin hit me," the little boy howled. "She hit me hard, Mom!"

"Well, you prob'ly deserved it, you little bugger," Lavonne said calmly. "Were you teasing that poor baby again?"

The child turned and stared sullenly at Jackie who got to her feet and reached for her jacket, telling Lavonne to let Carly know she was leaving.

"No problem," Lavonne said. "Look, try and find him, okay? I'd just as soon be able to take my kids and go back home. I get tired of all this goddamn fighting."

"I'm sure Carly gets tired of it, too," Jackie said neutrally.

"I'm sure she does," Lavonne mimicked.

But when she looked up, her blue-shadowed eyes were shrewd and level. The boy continued to stare at Jackie too, still sniffling in his mother's grasp.

"Just find the uptight bastard," Lavonne said, "before somebody really gets hurt. Okay?"

"We're doing our best," Jackie said.

She left the house and drove home, where she found a message from Karl Widmer on the answering machine.

"I've got something interesting for you, Detective," he said. "At least I will have by tomorrow afternoon. Meet me at our downtown café at four o'clock, okay?"

Jackie was annoyed by the man's assumption she'd make time for him in the middle of her day. She dug out Widmer's card and dialed his home number but there was no answer.

She stood listening to his taped greeting, then hung up and wandered into the living room to pick up her flute.

She sat cross-legged on the ottoman near the sliding glass doors, staring at the falling snow as she began to pick out the first notes of a piece by Vivaldi and tried not to think about anything but the music.

14

The instructor shouted something that was inaudible over the pounding beat of the music. Jackie watched, puffing, trying to follow the intricate steps of the aerobics routine. But as soon as she mastered a series of moves, they changed. Around her, the rest of the class maintained an uneven rhythm as they stepped and kicked.

Okay, she thought, staring grimly at the leader's flying feet. If everyone else can do this, I can do it.

"Side to side and heel and toe, and front and back and front... Now double up!" the woman shouted, her black high-tops flashing.

Jackie swore and floundered, feeling sweat dripping into her eyes. She worked out regularly in the basement gym at the substation, but mostly alone with weights and treadmill. This hard-driving aerobics routine was something else.

The instructor was a trim brunette, probably in her late thirties, wearing black bicycle shorts under a zebra-striped leotard. Her tanned legs bulged with muscle, and she seemed cool and comfortable though most of the class was gasping for breath.

But not Norine Burkett. Jackie glanced across the room at the slim blond woman next to the ballet bar by a mirrored wall.

Norine wore yellow spandex tights, a plain yellow bodysuit and a pale green headband. She looked like a slender daffodil in the wind, swaying and bobbing effortlessly though her face was drawn with concentration as she watched the instructor. She danced through the aerobics steps, taut and straight-backed, keeping perfect time with the leader and the music.

Jackie had last seen the woman at her daughter's funeral two days ago, but Norine's expression hadn't changed since then. She still looked composed and distant, as if she was focused on some private goal not visible to the rest of the world.

"Push!" the instructor shouted over the music. "Double time! Come on, people, look alive!"

Jackie sighed and struggled to keep up, wondering if she'd have enough breath left to talk with Norine Burkett after the class. If not, this whole project was going to be a huge waste of time and effort.

But as it turned out, she had all kinds of recovery time before their conversation. Norine headed for the locker room as soon as the music ended and disappeared into a shower stall.

Jackie hurried to grab her shampoo and position herself in the next stall. She lathered rapidly, listening to the rush of water in the adjoining cubicle. After a few moments she came out with a towel wrapped around her body and tucked in firmly above her breasts, rubbing at her hair with a smaller towel.

Keeping an eye on the door of Norine's shower stall, Jackie dried herself and hurried into her slacks and shirt, figuring that if she was dressed and the other woman was wearing only a towel, she'd have the psychological advantage.

Her gun and holster were outside, locked in the

trunk of the car because gym lockers weren't secure enough to suit her. As always in a public setting, she felt more undressed without the gun than without her clothes.

She took a blow-dryer from her duffel bag, plugged it in and began to dry her hair, keeping an eye on the shower.

Norine Burkett didn't emerge even when most of the others were showered and gone. The locker room began to fill up with members of the next class, changing into their sweats and leotards.

What the hell's she doing in there? Jackie thought impatiently. *Tweezing her leg hairs?*

Finally Norine Burkett stepped from the stall, wearing a towel wrapped tightly around her slim body and another wound turban-style on her head.

Her eyes met Jackie's with a flicker of anger and dislike, quickly masked.

She recognized me, Jackie thought in surprise. *She knew I was out here and that's why she took so long, hoping I'd go away.*

"Hi," Jackie said aloud, sitting on the bench to tug at her socks. "Hey, that woman gives a pretty brutal workout, doesn't she?"

The other woman unwrapped the towel from her head and rubbed at her hair. The wet strands clung to her delicate little skull. Even without makeup, Norine was beautiful. Her face was translucent and fine-featured, the eyes enormous and wide-set under eyebrows so pale they were almost invisible.

She took the towel from her body and tossed it aside, standing casually naked in front of the locker. Her body was slender and boyish, without an ounce of extra fat. After that initial flash of recognition, she seemed totally unaware of Jackie's presence.

She put on a sports bra and a pair of white cotton panties, then pulled a mauve T-shirt over her head. It fell just below the bottom of her panties, covering most of the dainty little body.

A fresh burst of music sounded intermittently through the door of the locker room as people headed out for the next class. Soon the two of them were alone except for a pair of teenagers giggling near the long mirrors as they exchanged makeup.

Jackie watched covertly while Norine tugged on a pair of mauve tights and began to dry her hair. She debated how to approach the woman and decided it was best to be direct.

"I don't know if you remember me," she said, shrugging into her navy blazer and adjusting the shoulder pads. "I was at your house early last week. My name's Jackie Kaminsky."

"I remember you," Norine said.

Her eyes flashed contemptuously over Jackie's pleated flannel slacks and blazer, making Jackie feel hot and uncomfortable, hopelessly frumpy.

But she couldn't let the woman's cool superiority get to her, or she'd have wasted this whole afternoon. Not to mention the sweaty agony of the aerobics workout.

"A friend of mine recommended this class," she said, raising her voice over the hum of Norine's hair dryer. "In fact, I think you probably know her. The name's Adrienne Calder?"

That got the woman's attention. She switched off the dryer and looked at Jackie, clearly startled. "Adri-

enne's your friend?'' she asked with a skeptical lift
of her delicate eyebrows.

"We've been friends for a couple of years," Jackie
said casually while Norine began to dry her hair
again. "I told Adrienne I was looking for a good
class," she lied, "but I'd prefer to find one I can go
to in the evenings. I wonder if you could tell me what
the Monday-night class is like."

"What Monday-night class?" Norine switched off
the dryer again and stared at her reflection in the mirror. Her hair fluffed around her small head, so well
cut that it fell into soft perfect layers like the petals
of a windblown chrysanthemum.

"I had the impression..." Jackie pretended confusion. She drew her belt through the loops in her
slacks, reaching back automatically to adjust the holster before she remembered her gun wasn't there.
"Didn't somebody say you went to the gym on Monday nights?"

Norine stood erect, gazing at Jackie's reflection in
the mirror. She bent to gather her belongings, shoved
them into her nylon sports bag and turned away with
quick, angry gestures.

"Mrs. Burkett?" Jackie moved around unobtru-
sively to block her path.

Norine hurried past her, heading for the door, and
allowed her duffel bag to bump hard against Jackie's
knees as she went. Jackie followed the woman toward
the entry, conscious of a scent of gardenias, faintly
sweet on the damp air of the locker room.

Norine Burkett paused with her hand on the doorknob and looked over her shoulder. Her blue eyes
were stormy with anger. She glanced at the two

laughing girls by the mirror, then leaned close to Jackie.

"Go fuck yourself, Detective," she murmured, and slammed into the reception area.

Karl Widmer was in the same booth where they'd met before, smoking a slender brown cigar. When Jackie arrived, he stubbed out the cigar and grinned, waving a hand at the opposite seat with exaggerated gallantry.

"You're looking even more wonderful than usual, Detective. Positively radiant."

She smiled without humor and slid into the booth. "I just had a refreshing aerobics workout."

"Ah." He nodded, still looking amused. "And did you get a chance to speak with Lady Norine?"

"Not much." The waitress arrived and Jackie ordered a cup of tea with lemon, then glanced at Widmer. "She told me to go fuck myself."

"The poor little bereaved mother. Obviously beside herself with grief."

"Obviously."

"And was she driving her shiny red sports car?" he asked.

"No, I followed her to the parking lot and saw her get into a shiny black Land Rover. Probably cost close to two years of my salary."

Widmer chuckled aloud. "You sound so bitter. It's your slum background showing, Jackie. Mustn't be envious of the upper classes, you know. It destroys all that police objectivity that's so important."

Jackie felt a surge of annoyance that made her stomach clench. But she realized he was baiting her and forced herself to ignore his comment.

She smiled at the waitress who'd arrived with the tea. Jackie peered into the small metal pot, inhaling the lemon fragrance.

"So how was your weekend in the country?" Widmer changed the subject. "I'll bet the boyfriend was glad to see you."

Jackie looked up at the man's watchful eyes. She thought of Paul and felt a stab of pain but repressed it quickly.

Years of training had taught her how to keep her personal life separate from the job.

She'd worry about Paul and his ultimatum later. Right now she had to concentrate on what she was doing.

"My boyfriend's always glad to see me," she said, sipping her tea.

"Lucky bastard." Widmer leaned back in the booth and rested one arm along the vinyl seat back, staring out the window with a brooding expression.

"Your message said you had something for me," Jackie told him.

"I sure do." He reached into an inner pocket and took out a dirty white envelope, placing it on the Arborite tabletop.

Jackie looked down at the envelope, then into his face. "So what's in there?"

He grinned and put a hand on the envelope. "All in good time, Jackie. First it's your turn."

"What for?"

"We're business partners, you and I. Before I show you what's in this envelope, I want a little information from you."

Jackie hesitated. Again she had an uneasy feeling. Widmer watched her and chuckled with genuine amusement. "God, you really are a straight arrow, aren't you? Never cut a deal in your life. Anybody would think you're taking a bribe or committing some other dastardly deed, not doing everyday police work."

"I've always preferred to work alone," she said, feeling stiff and awkward.

"I'm sure you have, but in this case I think you'll want to see what I've got here."

Jackie glanced at the envelope. "Okay," she said with a sigh. "What do you want to know?"

"Two things." He touched the thumb and forefinger of his left hand. "First, what do you honestly think of Norine Burkett?"

Jackie sipped her tea, studying the gleaming metal controls of the jukebox. "I think the lady's hiding something," she said at last. "I suppose she's afraid I'm going to find it out, but I doubt that her secret is any of my business. Most likely she's got a boyfriend or something."

"You don't think she had anything to do with her little girl's death?"

Jackie shook her head. "I've always thought that was a pretty far-fetched scenario."

"Then why are she and her husband stonewalling and refusing to cooperate with the police investigation?"

"I don't know," Jackie said. "They're just being careful, I assume. Politicians are notoriously wary of any kind of publicity they aren't able to orchestrate and control."

"So what are you planning to do about Norine Burkett?"

"My instinct would be to leave her alone from now

on, because I have no valid reason to pursue the woman any further.''

''Fair enough,'' Widmer said, then hesitated, looking down at the envelope. ''What about this Stevenson guy who disappeared?''

Warning bells sounded in her mind. ''What about him?'' she asked.

''What's the story? Who is he and why did he go missing last Monday night?''

Jackie told him what she knew about John Stevenson, keeping it brief, stressing his reputation as an upstanding employee and a reliable family man.

Widmer listened intently.

''Very interesting,'' he said at last. ''Do you happen to know why he quit his job two weeks before he decided to vanish?''

''How did you know he quit his job?''

Widmer shook his head in disappointment. ''Jackie, Jackie,'' he murmured. ''You think you're the only one who can go over to that office and ask Gladys Wahl a few questions?''

''For God's sake, Widmer. I hate to think about you following me around and getting involved in my investigation.''

But her companion appeared unruffled. ''When you see what I've got in here,'' he said, tapping the white envelope on the table, ''you'll be grateful to me for getting involved. I'll bet,'' he added, his teeth flashing, ''you'll even want to give me a big hug and I'll have to fight you off.''

''Look,'' she said wearily, ''I'm tired and sick, and I don't feel like playing games with you. So cut the crap, all right?''

He sobered at once and reached for a notebook in

his pocket. "One more thing," he said, "and I'll let you open the envelope."

She drained her tea and refilled the cup from the little pot. "Go ahead. I'm listening."

"I want to know just a bit more about John Stevenson," he said.

"Like what?"

Widmer shrugged. "Human-interest stuff. Something about the family. Anything you can give me."

Jackie fingered the handle of her teacup. "Is this off the record?"

"For now. Look, I told you, if I ever decide to use anything you tell me, I'll let you know and get your approval first."

She looked at the envelope, then back at his face. "What's in there?"

"It's worth making a deal, Jackie."

"Where did it come from?"

"A friend of a friend," Widmer said. "A reliable source."

Jackie sighed. "Stevenson's wife has been threatened," she said at last. "She says somebody tried to snatch one of her kids and made threatening calls to her in the middle of the night."

Widmer leaned forward, his eyes bright with interest. "No shit," he muttered. "What do you think's going on? Is this woman for real?"

"I have no idea, but she seems genuinely terrified." Jackie looked into the brown depths of the cup, frowning. "You know, she loves the man, absolutely adores him, even after all this. I don't understand it."

"What do you mean?"

"She can't seem to think anything negative about him, even though he's taken off without a word and left her alone, broke and crazy with worry. She keeps making excuses for him, saying he must be hurt or in some kind of trouble.''

Widmer leaned back, watching her thoughtfully. "You've never been in that place, Jackie?" he asked. "You don't know what it's like to feel unconditional love for somebody?"

"Unconditional?" She shook her head. "No way, Karl. I think where two adults are involved, love is always conditional.''

"Not always."

Widmer gazed out the window with a faraway look, and for the first time Jackie found herself wondering about the man's past and his personal situation.

"Carly Stevenson's a timid little person," she said after an awkward silence. "Quiet and shy but with some steel at the core. And she's a great mother. I feel so sorry for her," Jackie said, wondering why she was telling him so much. "This guy even cleaned out the bank accounts and left her without enough to buy groceries. She's out of her mind with worry.''

He leaned back in the booth, watching her with amusement. "Tell me the rest, Jackie," he said.

"What?"

"You gave her some money, didn't you? You actually handed over some of your hard-earned cash to help this little family.''

She sipped the tea and fiddled with a slice of lemon to hide her discomfort.

"Have I mentioned," Widmer said, "that I think you're just a hell of a woman?''

"Look," she began stiffly.

He smiled and opened the envelope, sliding out a handful of photographs. "These came to me from a guy who happens to know a friend of mine," he said. "This guy wants to collect some money from the police tip line but isn't anxious to reveal his identity. So I'm handing them over for him."

"What are they?" Jackie looked suspiciously at the pictures.

"They're pirated photographs. This guy works in a local photo lab. When he saw what was on this roll, he printed an extra run and kept it for himself."

"That's theft," Jackie said. "He could lose his job and face charges for doing it."

Widmer nodded agreement. "But he's not going to face charges. Is he, Jackie? He's going to remain anonymous and get some reward money for helping the police, and nobody's going to pursue him any further."

"Why would he want to copy somebody's film?" she asked.

"You'll see." Widmer handed her a few of the photographs. They showed a young man standing in the doorway of a room. The man was John Stevenson, wearing a pair of jeans and a down-filled jacket, his shoulders dusted with fresh snow.

Jackie turned the pictures over and glanced at the dates on the back. They'd been processed on the nineteenth of November, about two weeks before John Stevenson abandoned his vehicle in the mall parking lot and vanished into thin air.

She looked at the photos again, studying the man's face. He looked boyishly handsome, with the same square-jawed, wholesome appearance he had in all the pictures she'd seen. The kind of man who loved dogs, took his kids fishing on weekends and was considerate and faithful to his wife.

"The salt of the earth," she muttered. "A great all-American guy."

"He sure seems that way." Widmer handed over a couple more pictures.

A woman appeared in the frame, approaching Stevenson, visible only from the rear. She was slim and blond, wearing a belted silk dressing gown, her hair carelessly upswept.

"What the hell?" Jackie muttered.

In the next photographs the woman had shed the dressing gown. She was nude, her body trim and shapely with a tiny waist and firm buttocks.

"Do you have any that show her face?" Jackie asked intently.

Widmer handed over the last of the photographs without comment. By now Stevenson's back was to the camera and the woman stood smiling up at him, frontally nude. Her breasts were heavy and well-shaped with large brown nipples, and her pubic hair had been shaved into a dainty triangle. The woman's face was lovely, full-lipped and sultry, but also strangely girlish and innocent-looking in spite of her nakedness.

She faced the camera and reached up to touch the man's face. In the last of the photographs she was in his arms, kissing him, most of her body obscured by his shoulders and torso in the bulky winter parka.

Widmer watched Jackie while she studied the pictures. "I think," he said at last, "that if you find that pretty blond girl, Detective, you'll also find your runaway husband."

Jackie nodded thoughtfully. "Does your source have any idea who she is?"

"She has a vaguely familiar look, but I can't place

it.'' The reporter shook his head, frowning. ''Anyhow, I'll bet that's why our boy printed and kept the pictures.'' He took out the photograph showing the blonde's nude body. ''Your friend Stevenson,'' he said with a wolfish grin, ''has excellent taste in women.''

15

The following morning Jackie sat in Sergeant Michelson's office and looked out through the opened door at the squad room. The little Christmas tree shimmered as gusts of air from an overhead vent disturbed it. The bright cellophane condom packs had been removed in anticipation of a visit from Captain Alvarez, one of the high-ranking officials from the downtown police station, and replaced with golden angels holding trumpets.

"I really liked the condoms," Michelson said, arriving with a mug of coffee and an armful of file folders. "Didn't you?"

Jackie nodded absently. "They were pretty, all those different colors. The captain would probably have appreciated them."

The sergeant settled behind his desk and opened a file. "Is Brian here yet?"

"He's out there with Alice, picking up his messages. The first day back is always such a bitch," she added, "trying to catch up with everything."

"How's he feeling?"

"Still pretty shaky, apparently. I haven't talked with him much."

He glanced at her over the top of his reading glasses. "How about you?"

"I'm not going to think about it. If I don't admit I'm sick, maybe I can keep from getting the damn flu until after Christmas, at least."

"Mind over matter?" he asked.

"Something like that."

The sergeant grinned. "You're a tough woman, Jackie. But I don't think you're that tough." He sipped his coffee and glanced at her again. "How's Paul?"

"He's fine," she said more curtly than she'd intended.

Michelson raised his eyebrows and studied her. "Are you having problems?" he said after a few moments of silence.

She leafed aimlessly through a file in her lap. "A few."

"Want to talk about it? I'm only asking," he said, "because I know Paul's had some objections to your job in the past. If that's still an issue, maybe there's something we can do to help."

"Like what?"

"I don't know. We could look at some more flexible scheduling, maybe a shift change or something."

"My job's only one of the issues." Jackie felt a resurgence of the anxiety that had been plaguing her ever since the weekend, accompanied by a dull headache and rising nausea. "God," she muttered, rubbing a hand across her damp forehead. "I think the flu may be winning."

The sergeant looked on in concern while she fiddled aimlessly with a typed evidence-release form in one of her files, bending and creasing the upper corners into neat alignment.

"Paul gave me an ultimatum on Sunday," she said.

"What kind of ultimatum?"

"Either I agree to get married or the relationship's over. He wants an answer by Christmas."

"I see. And what did you say to that?"

"Nothing, really. We haven't talked since. I told him I'd think about it." Jackie took a deep breath. "And I am. I'm thinking all the time. It's making me feel worse than the flu bug."

"Why don't you just marry him?" the sergeant asked. "I've been telling you for months that you should."

"I know you have." She moved restlessly in the chair. "Everybody's been telling me that. But there are a whole lot of things that need to be considered, Sarge. It's really complicated."

"What makes it so complicated?"

"Our jobs, mainly. Paul's got his ranch and he's not about to give it up anytime soon. But I don't want to quit working either."

"Why should you have to? I thought he agreed not to stand in your way after…"

The sergeant's broad face creased with discomfort and he looked down at his desk.

Lew Michelson still couldn't bear to talk about Jackie's gunshot wound the previous spring, or the events leading up to it, and had never mentioned the incident after the internal investigation was concluded.

"Well, for instance," she said, "Paul tells me he wouldn't want me working if we had kids. Just like that, no discussion or compromise. If there's ever a baby, then the job is over."

"So are you all that anxious to have babies?" Michelson asked. "I can't recall that you've ever talked about it much."

"I'm hardly the maternal type," she said with a wan smile. "Paul's the one who wants kids, not me. But that's not the point."

"What's the point, then?"

"The point is that he agreed long ago he wasn't going to object to my job as long as I wanted to stay," Jackie said. "Now he's changing his tune, and I don't appreciate it."

"But he cares about you so much. You two could work this out if you'd just talk about it. That's how a marriage works, Jackie. My wife and I talk things to death until we reach a compromise."

"Paul doesn't often give up on things once he's established a position. He's a very controlling kind of person."

"Oh, I see. And you're not?" Michelson said, raising an eyebrow.

"Sure, you're right." She closed the file folder. "I've been making my own decisions for a long time. It's not easy to give up that kind of independence."

"But if you want to be in a partnership," he said, "you have to give up some of your freedom. It goes with the territory."

"I guess so. It's just that..." Jackie wanted to end the conversation. She glanced at her watch and turned to peer out into the squad room. "What the hell's keeping Brian? He was supposed to be here by now."

"Jackie," the sergeant said.

"What?"

"You're not going to give up this guy, are you? I know how much you love him. Seems to me two grown-ups should be able to work out a few problems without throwing everything away.''

She felt another wave of nausea, and her head began to throb painfully. ''Two adults should be able to give each other enough freedom to breathe,'' she said. ''If not, I don't see how—''

Wardlow strolled into the room, carrying an armful of files. ''Good morning,'' he said, dropping into a chair next to Jackie.

She smiled at him, grateful for the interruption.

''So how are you feeling, Brian?'' she asked. ''You're still white as a sheet, and you look like you've lost about ten pounds.''

''Only five,'' Wardlow said. ''But that flu's a real bugger. I was sick as a dog.''

''Five pounds,'' the sergeant said wistfully. ''I wish I could lose five pounds just before Christmas. I must have had a different bug. Maybe I should get one of you to breathe on me.''

''One of us?'' Wardlow glanced at Jackie. ''You're sick, too?''

''I'm fighting it off,'' Jackie said, ''by drinking tons of lemon tea and wrapping a sock around my throat every night when I go to bed.''

Wardlow grinned. ''A sock?''

''That was always Gram's remedy for colds or flu. Wrap an old sock around your neck at bedtime to keep your throat warm. Other kids got hot soup and medicine. We got dirty socks.''

''Your grandmother's such a warm and lovely person,'' Wardlow said with a chuckle.

Jackie grimaced at him, then turned her attention to Michelson who launched into a standard briefing on their roster of cases to bring Wardlow up to date.

Michelson concluded with the Stevenson case and glanced at Jackie. "Anything new from the tip line?"

She looked down at the soiled white envelope in her file folder. "Nothing that cross-checks at all. Just a whole pile of dead ends. The man's apparently been seen all over the state, but so far no two people have spotted him in the same place."

"What about the Burkett hit-and-run?" Wardlow asked. "Have you talked to Baumgartner lately?"

Jackie told them about the status of the investigation, including the evidence from the crime scene, the eyewitness reports and the Burkett family's refusal to cooperate with the police.

"Jason Burkett must be crazy," Michelson said flatly. "Doesn't he realize he's fueling the gossip and speculation by not answering questions. People will think they're hiding something."

"Do you think they have something to hide?" Wardlow asked Jackie.

"Not related to this hit-and-run," she said. "I think there might be some other secrets they don't want revealed, so they've decided to stonewall on everything. They have a high-profile public relations consultant and a whole army of lawyers advising them to play their cards close to the chest."

Michelson shook his head. "Well, I still think it's a foolish decision. This is going to do him a lot of political damage."

"Not if we can find the hit-and-run driver," Jackie said. "As soon as that happens, there'll be all kinds of sympathy for the Burketts. And if Traffic's checking every red sports car in the state, they're bound to turn something up before long. Baumgartner's got a ton of guys working on this."

"Hit-and-runs are never a sure thing," Michelson said. "I'm glad it's Traffic and not us who has to deal with this one."

He closed his file and glanced up at the two detectives. "Well, I guess that's it. Anything else?"

"One more thing." Jackie lifted the envelope. "This came to me from a private source."

"A private source?" Michelson asked.

Jackie's face warmed with discomfort. "I've been playing footsie with a local journalist," she said. "It's sort of a new experience for me."

"Which journalist?" the sergeant asked.

"Karl Widmer, from the *Sentinel*."

Michelson looked interested. "The guy's got a reputation as a pretty straight shooter. He's sure not easy to deal with, though. I guess that tragedy made him a bitter man."

"Tragedy?" Jackie asked.

"His wife was killed. It happened years ago, before you came to the city," Michelson told Jackie. "Molly Widmer was out for a jog along the river trail when a gang of teenage boys jumped her. They raped and beat her, apparently just for kicks. All five were caught and convicted, but Juvenile couldn't do much more than slap their wrists."

"Was his wife killed outright?" she asked.

Wardlow shook his head. "I was on patrol that day, and we responded to the call along with a lot of other cars. She was lying in a ravine, naked and beaten so badly that she wasn't recognizable. She never regained consciousness, hung on in a coma for about three weeks before she died. Apparently the poor guy hardly left her bedside during all that time."

"My God," Jackie muttered.

They were silent for a moment. Finally Jackie shook her shoulders and pulled herself together.

"Anyhow," she said, "Widmer's been making these little deals with me. I feed him a bit of information and he tells me stuff." She glanced at the sergeant. "I've never done this before."

"Everybody does it," Michelson said calmly. "Has he given you anything useful?"

"Just something that proves you were right all the time." She tossed the envelope onto his desk. "John Stevenson's a cheating bastard who left his wife for reasons of his own."

Michelson opened the envelope and studied the photos, then handed them to Wardlow. Jackie waited for the sergeant to announce the missing-person case closed, but he surprised her.

"I don't like this," he muttered, twisting a pen in his hands.

"Why not, Sarge?" she asked.

"Hey, I like it." Wardlow stared avidly at the nude woman in the photos. "In fact, I like it a whole lot."

"Where did these pictures come from?" Michelson asked. "How did Widmer get them?"

"He claims they belong to a friend of a friend," Jackie said. "Somebody who works in a photo lab and ran an extra set of the pictures because he liked the look of the girl. But when he saw the bulletin on John Stevenson, he thought he could earn a little cash from the tip line by turning them in anonymously."

"So who took the photographs?" Michelson said. "Why did Stevenson and his girlfriend have their little rendezvous recorded on camera? And who's been threatening this poor woman and her kids?"

In spite of her nagging sickness, Jackie's spirits

lifted. "You think we should stay on it for a while longer, Sarge?"

"I'd really like to find your Mr. Stevenson and have a chat with him."

"We have nothing to charge him with when we find him," Jackie said. "Cheating on your wife isn't a crime."

"So? We can just say we need his assistance in another investigation. Let's get him and see what's going on."

"Come on, Brian," Jackie said to her partner, reaching for the photographs. "Hand them over."

Wardlow gave her the pictures reluctantly, taking a last look at the nude woman with the shaved triangle of pubic hair. He cleared his throat and leaned back in the chair, looking sheepish.

"What is it, Brian?" the sergeant asked.

"I know her," Wardlow said.

The other two stared at him. He ran a hand through his curly red hair. "I don't exactly *know* her," he said, "but I'm pretty sure I know who she is and where she works."

"You know where she works?" Jackie said.

"It's not easy to forget somebody who looks like that." Wardlow gestured at the photographs, then looked at the sergeant. "She's a hostess at the Prairie Club."

Michelson nodded thoughtfully while Jackie searched her memory. "The Prairie Club?" she said. "I've never heard of it."

"It's sort of a..." Wardlow exchanged another glance with the sergeant.

"It's a private club downtown," Michelson said. "For men only."

"Men only?" Jackie stared at them. "I didn't think that kind of stuff was even legal anymore."

"This isn't a commercial establishment. At least not openly," Wardlow said. "The Prairie does business on sort of an invitational basis. They have members who pay an annual fee. The only way an outsider can get in is to be invited by a member."

"And you've both been there?" she asked.

"I haven't," Michelson said. "I'm a happily married man. But I've heard about it."

Wardlow grinned at her. "I was invited a few months ago. My sister's husband went there one night along with his boss and some visiting executives."

Jackie looked at the photograph of the sultry blonde with the childlike face. "What kind of club is it? A strip joint?"

Wardlow shook his head. "Not even close. It's sort of a..." He hesitated. "I guess you'd call it a pleasure palace for men."

"A brothel?" she asked.

Wardlow and the sergeant exchanged another glance, and Jackie's patience began to fray. "For God's sake, could you two knock off all this secret-handshake stuff and just tell me where the place is? I don't really give a damn what you do for fun, Brian. I just want to find this woman and talk to her."

Wardlow cocked an eyebrow at her. "My, my," he said with infuriating mildness, "aren't we cranky this morning?"

"Look, Brian—"

"From what I've heard," Michelson said, interrupting her, "the Prairie is just what Brian told you. It's a place for men to relax and have fun. Very high-end and exclusive. There's a lounge, a reading room, a couple of rooms for playing cards and billiards, a first-rate kitchen and some nice young ladies to keep you company if you're lonely."

"And let me tell you, these are very high-class ladies." Wardlow gestured at the photographs. "Like that one."

"So has the vice squad ever looked at this place?" Jackie asked.

"Years ago when I was on Vice, we used to check it out from time to time," Michelson said. "But the Prairie's a well-run operation and it was always clean when our boys paid a visit."

Jackie looked sharply at the sergeant's face, which remained bland and noncommittal. "You mean, the proprietors got tipped off in advance whenever you were coming?" she asked.

"They might have been," Michelson said. "Who knows? I've heard that a few of our top brass have been there now and then. The place has been keeping a low profile for years."

She sighed and looked at the photographs. "You're sure this girl works there, Brian?"

"Pretty sure. She was sitting at another table with some big computer-software honchos who were in town for the weekend. She was wearing more clothes at the time," he added cheerfully, "but I still recognize her."

"But how do you know she's a hostess?" Jackie asked. "Maybe she was just with one of the computer guys."

"Kaminsky," her partner said with exaggerated patience, "women don't *go* to this place. They aren't allowed in the door unless they work there."

"Oh, for God's sake," Jackie muttered. "You guys kill me. You really do. Come on, Brian," she added, getting up and heading for the door. "I want you to take me there."

16

The Prairie Club appeared to occupy the upper two floors of a big downtown hotel. But there were no signs to indicate its existence, no evidence of any kind that a private club operated in the building.

Jackie rode up silently in the express elevator with her partner, looking at the brass-trimmed compartment and the rich wood paneling on the walls.

"You really seem to know your way around here," she said.

"I was only here once, but I've known about the place for years. Everybody does."

"If they're male," she said bitterly.

Her partner chuckled but didn't respond.

On the tenth floor the two detectives walked down a hallway more plushly carpeted than any of the lower floors. The decor was forest green and dark brown, luxurious but heavily masculine. Jackie caught a whiff of stale cigar smoke masked by some kind of spicy air freshener.

Wardlow knocked at a broad oak door with a brass plate marked Office, and a female voice inside told them to enter.

They stepped into a room carpeted in the same rich green. A thin woman with graying hair sat behind a massive desk littered with papers. She was immaculately groomed, wearing bifocals and a pale blue linen suit over a black turtleneck. She looked coldly at the two visitors.

"Have you come to the wrong floor?" she asked. "I'm not expecting anybody this morning."

When Wardlow showed his badge, the woman's severe features registered a flicker of annoyance. She glanced at Jackie, who also displayed her credentials in their leather folder.

"I'm Detective Kaminsky, and this is my partner, Detective Wardlow. We'd like to ask you a couple of questions."

The woman sighed. "My name is Madeleine Feldman."

She indicated a couple of leather chairs trimmed with brass studs. Jackie and Wardlow sat down.

The woman folded her hands and watched them calmly. Wardlow took one of the photographs from the envelope Jackie handed him, and gave it to the woman behind the desk. It showed the blond girl still demurely belted into her dressing gown, smiling up at John Stevenson, whose back was to the camera.

"We're interested in talking to this woman, Ms. Feldman," he said. "I believe she's employed here."

Madeleine Feldman peered at the photograph through stylish bifocals. Her expression didn't change. "What do you want with her?"

"We're hoping she can give us some information, that's all. It should only take a couple of minutes."

She gave him a long measuring glance, ignoring Jackie as if she weren't in the room. Finally she nodded abruptly. "That's Darla Drake. She's a hostess in the club."

"Is she here now?" Wardlow asked.

"The club opens at eleven o'clock to accommodate those of our members who wish to come here for lunch. The hostesses don't usually arrive until late afternoon at the earliest."

"Will Miss Drake be working this evening?" Jackie asked.

The woman tossed her a look of dislike, opened a leather-bound folder and consulted a schedule. "Darla's had the weekend off," she said, addressing herself to Wardlow again. "She hasn't been at work since Friday, but she's due to arrive here tonight at 9:00 p.m."

"How about this man, Ms. Feldman?" Wardlow handed over another of the photographs, showing John Stevenson in the doorway wearing his bulky parka. "Does he look familiar at all?"

The woman lifted the photograph and studied it for a moment through her bifocals. "I've never seen him before," she said at last. "He's certainly never been to the club." Her voice was faintly contemptuous.

"Could you give us Darla Drake's home address?" Jackie asked, taking back the picture. "We'd really like to talk with her."

Madeleine Feldman met her eyes coldly. "Not without a warrant, Detective."

"A warrant?" Jackie asked in genuine surprise. "Look, there's nothing serious going on here, Ms. Feldman. We'd just like Darla's help with regard to a missing-person case we're investigating. We were hoping we wouldn't have to wait until this evening."

"We don't give out the home addresses for any of our hostesses," the woman said to Wardlow. She gave the photo back to him and he handed it silently to Jackie, who put the envelope away in her notebook. "Not even to the police."

She opened another file with a dismissive air. Jackie and Wardlow exchanged a glance, then got to their feet and headed for the door.

"Especially not to the police," Jackie muttered as they walked soundlessly back down the hallway toward the private elevator. "God, this damn place gives me the creeps."

"It's not as glamorous in the cold light of day," he agreed. "But the club really swings after dark. It's a lot of fun." He looked at her awkwardly. "Kaminsky, if you insist on going in there with me tonight, you're going to be pretty conspicuous."

"Don't worry," Jackie said. "I won't spoil the fun for all the boys. I can just wait in perky little Madeleine's office and let you bring the girl in to talk with us, okay?"

"Okay," he said, looking relieved.

"Do you mind having to work a shift in the evening?" she asked, pressing a button to summon the elevator. "You still don't look all that steady on your feet."

"I'll go home and grab a couple hours of rest after supper. Actually," Wardlow said, "I'm glad to pull an evening shift. That way I can justify taking off all of Friday afternoon."

"What's happening on Friday?" she asked.

"It's the staff kids' Christmas party, sponsored by the Police Wives Club and the civilian workers. They're having it downtown in the shooting range. It's a great party. They decorate the targets to look like Santas and drape tinsel all over the place, make the range look really festive. Captain Alvarez and the chief and his wife help serve the turkey dinner, and Lieutenant Hatch is always Santa Claus. He brings a present for every kid.''

"And you're taking Gordie this year?''

"The kid's still young enough to get a kick out of games and presents. Besides, he thinks it's going to be awesome to see the shooting range.''

Jackie smiled and stepped from the elevator into the lobby. Wardlow followed her. "You should come, Kaminsky. Book the afternoon off and come to the party.''

"I don't have any kids,'' she said. "Remember?''

"You can come along with Chris and me. Or maybe you could borrow a kid somewhere. How about those poor little Stevenson kids?'' he suggested. "They could probably use some fun in their lives right now.''

Jackie turned to him in surprise. "Could I do that? Bring kids that aren't related to me?''

"Sure. They encourage officers who don't have families of their own to invite kids who wouldn't get much of a Christmas otherwise.''

"Maybe I'll do that,'' she said thoughtfully. "It'll give me an excuse to check in with Carly and see how she's doing. Thanks, Brian.''

They passed through the lobby and out into the sunny winter morning, where their cars were parked at the curb. Both of them had full schedules for the rest of the day, and they'd traveled downtown separately so they could part after visiting the club.

Wardlow bent and opened his driver's door. "If I don't see you again today, I'll come by your place and pick you up about nine o'clock,'' he said. "Okay?''

"Sure," Jackie said. "Thanks."

She watched him get into the car and drive away, still thinking about Carly Stevenson and her children, and that disturbing handful of photographs in her notebook. At last she put her car in gear and headed north toward the substation.

Twelve hours later they were at the club again, but there was no sign of Madeleine Feldman. The office was now occupied by a middle-aged man in a three-piece suit and tie, with a flap of gray hair combed over a bald spot. The man introduced himself as Avery Feldman, manager of the Prairie Club.

"Oh, yes," he said when the two detectives displayed their badges. "My wife told me you'd be dropping by. But I'm afraid Darla's not here."

Jackie looked at him carefully. Feldman's broad face was faintly greasy and pitted with old acne scars, but he looked well-groomed and seemed competent and anxious to cooperate.

"Is Darla late for work, or what?" she asked.

The manager's eyelids flickered. He looked down at the desk, then back up at the two police officers. "Actually, I'm a little worried about her," he said. "She's always been a reliable kid, never misses a shift. But she's not answering her phone, either. I just keep getting the machine."

Wardlow glanced at Jackie and inclined his head slightly toward one of the leather side chairs. "Do you mind if I just go in and take a quick look around, Mr. Feldman?" he asked. "My partner will wait here."

Jackie sat down and smiled politely at the manager, who looked morose as he leafed through his leather-bound notebook. She showed him the photograph of John Stevenson but, like his wife, Feldman appeared not to recognize the man.

Wardlow returned in a few minutes. "No sign of her," he told Jackie. "But one of the other hostesses confirms that Darla never misses a shift."

They both looked at the manager, who shifted uneasily in his chair.

"I really think we'd better check it out, Mr. Feldman," Jackie said. "She might be hurt or in some kind of trouble."

"But we don't like to..." He continued to fidget, doodling aimlessly on a page in his notebook. Finally he wrote down an address, tore off the sheet and handed it to Wardlow, who took the paper and showed it to Jackie.

"Looks like it's one of those new condo complexes out in the Valley."

"Okay, let's go." She got to her feet. "Thank you, Mr. Feldman."

The manager waved a hand and returned to his folder, still looking uncomfortable.

Jackie and her partner headed east toward the area of the city known as the Valley. They drove through snow-covered streets to a well-maintained town-house complex near the golf course. Wardlow, who was driving, opened the window to press a button at the entrance, causing the metal security gates to swing open.

The condo units were all narrow two-story structures, beige with white trim, attached in long rows with single garages facing the street. Wardlow parked at the end unit occupied by Darla Drake.

A light shone dimly through the largest downstairs

window, probably from a room somewhere near the back of the dwelling. Another window was illuminated on the second floor, a small frosted square that looked as if it might be in a bathroom.

They made their way up a walk that apparently hadn't been shoveled for several days. Wardlow rang the bell, then knocked at the door while Jackie tried to peer through the sidelight.

Nobody answered. A curtain twitched in one of the condos across the street and a face peeked out, then vanished.

"Maybe she's gone on holiday," Wardlow said. "Looks like the garage hasn't been used for a few days, either."

Jackie studied the unmarked snow in the driveway, then waded over to test the garage door. It was locked. She played her flashlight on the little window, tensed suddenly and leaned forward to cup her hands behind the beam of light.

"Jesus," she whispered.

"What is it?" Wardlow crowded up beside her. She moved over silently to let him look inside.

A sporty little red Del Sol was parked in the garage. The right front fender, clearly visible in the beam of the flashlight, was crumpled, sprouting a couple of electrical wires from a broken headlight.

"What the hell?" Wardlow muttered.

Jackie stood next to him, frowning. "What should we do? I don't suppose," she said wistfully, "that this is enough to get a warrant and break into the condo?"

"No way," he said decisively. "I think we have to tell Baumgartner and let him take it from here. The Burkett hit-and-run isn't even our case."

She stared at the garage window, then at the locked front door of the town house. "I want to get inside that place."

"Dammit, quit being such a cowboy. You'll get us both in trouble, Kaminsky."

Jackie glared at her partner. "I'm not being a cowboy. We're here at a scene where we've found a vehicle that was probably used in a homicide and it ties in to a case we're working on. I'm not walking away until we've at least exhausted all the possibilities."

Wardlow sighed. "Okay, what do you want to do?"

"Well, first I'm going to walk around the main floor and see if I can look in any of the windows."

Suiting actions to words, Jackie plowed off through the snow with Wardlow at her heels, pausing at each window. But all of them were fitted with venetian blinds that were closed tight.

"It really looks like she went away for a while," Wardlow said. "The place is tight as a drum."

Jackie paused at the rear corner of the unit, playing her flashlight across the snow. "Wait," she said, raising a hand.

He stood behind her. "What is it?"

"I thought I heard something." She strained to listen. "It sounds like a cat. Did you hear that?"

Wardlow nodded. "Or it could be a baby crying somewhere."

"It came from in here." Jackie moved around the back of the condo and across a covered terrace. She stood near a bare trellis and looked tensely at her partner, then jerked her chin upward.

Wardlow raised his head and sniffed. "Oh, shit," he whispered.

The two police officers looked up at a small window on the second floor that stood partly open. A downdraft floated toward them on the calm night air, rank with the smell of decay.

"We need to find a key," Jackie said over her shoulder, hurrying back around to the front. "You check the neighbors across the street and I'll go down this side."

They parted without another word and began knocking on doors. The first neighbor Jackie encountered was a grizzled old man in carpet slippers who seemed annoyed at having his television program interrupted. He'd never spoken to the young woman who lived next door, and didn't even know her name.

"I think maybe she talks sometimes with the people down in number twenty-seven," he said, edging the door closed. "I seen her walking over there a while ago."

The door lock clicked in Jackie's face before she could express her thanks.

At unit twenty-seven, a blue tricycle sat in the shelter of the front porch next to a plastic ride-on duck. Jackie rang the bell and a young baby-sitter answered, clutching a bowl of popcorn. She smiled shyly, displaying a mouthful of metal braces.

Jackie showed her badge. The teenager studied it carefully, then nodded.

"My partner and I need to get into unit twelve," Jackie said. "We think the lady who lives there might have had an accident. Her name is Darla Drake. Would you happen to know if your employers have a key to her place?"

"I think maybe there's..." The girl hesitated, then

turned away. "I'll be right back," she called over her shoulder.

She reappeared almost at once with a tagged key. The name Darla was printed on a red label stuck to the tag.

The baby-sitter gave Jackie a worried glance. "Are you sure this is okay?" she asked. "To give out somebody's key, I mean?"

"Under normal circumstances, it's certainly not something you should do," Jackie told her. "But it's different when it's the police who are asking."

"Okay." The girl took a mouthful of popcorn from her bowl and stood in the doorway, munching thoughtfully. Jackie hurried down the path, waving to her partner across the street.

He came back to join her and they approached Darla Drake's condo reluctantly.

"God, I hate this," Wardlow muttered at her side.

"So do I," she said. "But this is why they pay us the big bucks, right?"

Jackie stopped at the car to call in their location, mentioning only that they had a key and were about to enter the residence. She kept the transmission deliberately noncommittal in case anybody was monitoring local calls, looking for excitement.

When she was finished, Wardlow took the key and unlocked the front door. They stepped inside the foyer and were instantly assailed by a gust of warm air and the stench of rotting flesh.

Both of them took gloves from their pockets and held them over nose and mouth, stepping gingerly into the darkened living room. Wardlow used his forearm to flick a light switch near the door. He and Jackie stood looking at a room that was more luxurious than the exterior of the condo would have indicated.

The living room was decorated in trendy shades of teal blue and dusty rose, with plush carpeting and flowered couches. The lamps were glossy china figures of shepherdesses holding crooks and urns. Pastel water lilies in gilt frames hung on the walls.

Wardlow nudged Jackie and she heard his sharp intake of breath.

A white Siamese cat appeared in the lighted kitchen doorway, where it sat glaring at them with pale blue eyes. The cat lifted a bloodstained paw and licked it.

"Poor thing, it's hurt?" Jackie whispered.

"It doesn't look hurt," Wardlow said.

"Oh, hell," she muttered, feeling a sharp wave of nausea. "Jesus, Brian, maybe it's stepped in blood."

He cast her a concerned glance. "You want to wait here, Kaminsky? I'll go have a look."

"I'm coming with you."

They unstrapped their holster flaps in unison and headed for the kitchen, where the smell was almost overwhelming. Both of them held the gloves over their faces and looked at the remains of Darla Drake, lying on the pink and white floor tiles in a pool of dark congealed blood.

She was still recognizable from her photograph, but only vaguely. Her dark blond hair was done up in foam rollers, and the once-pretty face was distended and blue. Darla's eyes were half-closed, the whites gleaming faintly from beneath long eyelashes.

Her body was also grotesquely swollen in death, stretching the seams of her white cotton nightshirt. A cheery image of a cartoon character adorned the front of the shirt, looking miserably out of place in the midst of such carnage. Her legs were neatly crossed at the ankles, the feet close together in worn slippers with holes along the edges of both soles.

Darla appeared to have been a big fan of popular cartoons. The slippers were printed with bright images of a well-known canary.

The girl's wrists were slashed and had bled profusely. The brown stain had seeped under the table, along the bottom of the cupboards, even as far as the doorsill where the cat's empty dish stood next to a pair of black winter boots. The room was heavily tracked with bloody paw prints.

Jackie's stomach heaved and a sour taste rose in her throat. She turned aside, looking desperately for a place to vomit that wouldn't contaminate the scene. Finally she ran back out through the front door and retched into the massed shrubbery under the living-room window.

Wardlow arrived with the cat at his heels and stood by the railing to peer down at her.

"Are you okay, Kaminsky?"

She wiped her mouth, feeling shaky and miserable. "I've never done that before at a scene," she muttered. "But I'm feeling sick to start with, and that goddamn cat..."

Wardlow took a roll of mints from his pocket. "Here, have a candy."

"Thanks." She accepted the mint and climbed the steps, covered her nose and mouth again and forced herself to enter the house. "Did you see any kind of weapon in there?" she asked.

"There's an Exacto knife under the table by her right hand."

"So it's a suicide?"

"Well, it makes sense, right?" Wardlow said. "She ran over the kid, panicked and fled the scene, then realized from all the media reports that the little girl was dead. Poor Darla couldn't hide, couldn't get her car fixed, couldn't even run away without arousing suspicion. So she finally took the only way out."

"But what about the connection with John Stevenson?" Jackie asked through the woolen fabric of her gloves. "He disappears exactly the same time as the little girl gets hit. Somebody's apparently been threatening his family. Now we have hard evidence tying him to the owner of the hit-and-run car and she turns up dead."

Wardlow nodded thoughtfully.

"To be safe, maybe we'd better treat it as a homicide to start." Jackie looked around for a telephone. "And I'd like to use a landline to call it in. We don't want this place flooded with ambulance chasers."

Wardlow crossed the room beside her. They stood looking down at the phone, an ornate style with a gold-trimmed receiver resting on a white porcelain column. The answering machine next to the telephone blinked with messages.

Jackie used one of her gloves to wrap the receiver and pulled the other one onto her hand before she gingerly punched in Michelson's home number.

The stench in her unprotected nostrils was almost unbearable. Jackie swayed on her feet and began to feel sick again as she passed on the address and pertinent information to her sergeant.

"Can you make the other calls for me, Sarge?" she asked. "I'm using a phone at the scene."

"Okay. I'll be there as soon as I can," Michelson said. "Brian's with you?"

"Yes, he's been holding my hand while I barf like a rookie."

"Good for him. Is it a definite suicide, Jackie?" the sergeant asked.

She hesitated, thinking.

"Jackie?" he asked.

"I don't know, Sarge. She's got her hair in rollers and she's wearing tatty old slippers, a cartoon nightshirt, the same kind of stuff I wear around the house."

"So?" Michelson asked while Wardlow watched from the doorway.

"I don't know," Jackie repeated, frowning. "I think, judging from those photographs, this was the kind of girl who'd want to look nice even if she was committing suicide."

"You mean she'd have staged it a little better?"

"Unless she was high on something and didn't even know what she was doing. But it does make me wonder."

There was a brief silence. "Okay," Michelson said at last. "You two know what to do. I'll see you in a few minutes, Jackie."

"So is this our case?" Wardlow asked when she hung up.

"Maybe not permanently, but it's ours right now," Jackie said grimly, getting out her notebook as she steeled herself to cross the room again and look at Darla Drake's swollen, mutilated body.

17

The discovery of Darla Drake's body gave rise to a number of sensitive jurisdictional issues within the police department, since Traffic Division had prior claim on the hit-and-run case, but the woman's death was outside their area.

After some late-night wrangling among senior administrative personnel, it was decided to allow Traffic personnel to investigate the events in Darla Drake's recent past leading up to the Monday-night hit-and-run accident. They would concentrate on Darla's job and would interview her fellow employees at the Prairie Club.

Jackie and Wardlow were assigned the investigation into the woman's actual death, which involved custody and analysis of the scene at the condo, as well as the questioning of neighbors within the complex. The two groups were scheduled to meet in a downtown squad room late on Wednesday afternoon for an initial exchange of information.

Just before leaving to attend the meeting, Jackie and her partner stopped in at Michelson's office to brief him on their investigation.

"None of the neighbors saw anything unusual," Wardlow said. "She was supposed to attend a meeting of the condo association on Saturday morning but she never showed. They all thought she'd worked late and was sleeping in, so nobody called her.''

"And we're assuming she died on Friday night?"

"The pathologist thought it was a reasonable estimate from a preliminary examination of the body. The autopsy's scheduled for tomorrow afternoon.''

Michelson frowned at the notes. "Did the woman regularly attend condo-association meetings?''

"Apparently," Wardlow said. "She was a good tenant. The couple who supervise the complex really liked her. They were pretty shaken.''

"How about the scene?" Michelson looked at Jackie over the tops of his reading glasses. "Did the techs find anything?"

"Not much. She was a tidy housekeeper," Jackie said. "The only mess in the place was made by the cat.''

"What happened to the cat, by the way?" Michelson asked, flipping through papers.

"I dropped it off at an animal shelter this morning,'' Wardlow said.

"No signs of a struggle or anything unusual at the condo?'' the sergeant asked.

Jackie shook her head. "But it looks as if she might have had company just before she died. There was a cut-glass whiskey decanter in the living room and a couple of shot glasses. Both glasses had been used and left out on the coffee table along with the decanter.''

"Ident has them now?"

"They dusted all the glassware at the scene before they took it away. Claire says the decanter will be tough to lift prints from because there are almost no smooth surfaces, but she had some hopes for the two glasses. That was all she'd tell me.''

''And what about all these phone messages?'' Michelson asked.

Wardlow glanced at his notes. ''The first message was Saturday morning from the chairman of the condo committee, telling her what they'd decided about changing rules for garbage pickup. Two calls from a co-worker at the Prairie Club named Jennifer, just calling to chat. The guys from Traffic are talking with Jennifer today. One call from her mother, checking to see if she was okay.''

''Has anybody talked to the girl's mother?'' the sergeant asked.

''I called her this morning,'' Jackie said. ''She's a widow in Florida, fifty-nine years old, two other daughters living in Texas. She fell apart completely. Said Darla was always such a good girl, and she couldn't believe she'd ever take her own life.''

''Had this woman talked to her daughter lately?'' Michelson asked.

Jackie shook her head. ''Not for a couple of weeks. Darla was planning to fly to Orlando for Christmas, and the mother was all excited about seeing her for the first time in more than three years.''

There was a brief, strained silence before Michelson returned to his file. ''What about the other calls?'' he asked.

''Two from Avery Feldman, asking why she wasn't at work. Those would have been made last night before ten o'clock when we spoke to him.'' Wardlow consulted his notes. ''And a final one from an unidentified male who asked her to call him at the usual number, said it was urgent. We're trying to trace the caller by matching it up on her caller-ID box, but it only lists numbers, not names.''

"We won't know the full story on any of this stuff," Jackie said, "until we get together with Baumgartner's guys and see what they found out. They're doing the interviews over at the Prairie Club."

"Well," Wardlow said, "it's only a matter of tying up some loose ends. The little Burkett girl was struck by a hit-and-run driver, and now the driver's killed herself. All nice and tidy. Nobody has to build a case or go to court and try for a conviction."

"Too nice and tidy," Michelson commented.

"And we all know," Jackie said, "life's never like that."

A half hour later, Jackie sat next to her partner in an office at the downtown station, accompanied by some senior personnel and the investigators from the Traffic Division. Probably because of the intense media interest in the hit-and-run case, more than the usual number of high-ranking officers were in attendance.

Captain Alvarez sat on Jackie's other side, neat and dapper in his dark blue uniform. The captain was in his late fifties, with graying temples and a chiseled profile, and was much loved by the rank-and-file officers.

"You're looking a little pale, Detective Kaminsky," he said to Jackie, his dark eyes warm with concern. "Not feeling well?"

She gestured at Wardlow. "It's Brian's fault. He got the flu and gave it to me."

Alvarez laughed. "I think he gave it to everybody

in the department. Are you folks coming to our Christmas party on Friday afternoon?''

"I'm bringing my girlfriend's little boy," Wardlow said.

"And I'm bringing the three older Stevenson kids," Jackie told the captain.

"Stevenson," he said thoughtfully. "That's your missing person, right? With a tie-in to this case, as I recall?"

"Apparently John Stevenson was a...close friend of the woman who killed herself."

"Interesting," the captain murmured. "That's very interesting."

He settled back in his chair and looked up at Steve Baumgartner who cleared his throat and prepared to address the group of police officers.

"We have a positive ID on the vehicle," he said. "Ident's already matched the tread on the right front tire to the cast they took at the accident scene last Tuesday. We're prepared to issue a statement to the press later today, telling them Darla Drake's sports car, a 1995 Honda Del Sol, was the vehicle involved in the hit-and-run on Angela Burkett."

A murmur of relief and approval rippled through the room. Baumgartner's team weren't the only members of the department who'd been hounded by the press over their failure to solve the child's death.

Jackie made a mental note to call Karl Widmer right after the meeting. Since the news was going to be released anyway, it wouldn't hurt to give the journalist a scoop, and it might keep some nuggets of useful information coming her way.

Maybe Widmer knew something about the Prairie

Club and its clients, though he hadn't recognized Darla Drake from the photographs...

Baumgartner continued to outline the results of his team's investigation and their interviews with Darla's co-workers, all of whom reported that she was a nice, pleasant person, friendly and helpful, but everyone thought she had seemed troubled and preoccupied lately.

He glanced at Jackie and Wardlow. "The last call on her answering machine came from the Prairie Club, by the way."

"Which one?" Wardlow asked, flipping through his notebook.

"The one from an unidentified male. He talked about something urgent and said for her to call the usual number. That call was made from a telephone in the hall outside the lounge at the Prairie Club. Nobody knows who made the call. A lot of club members use the same phone, and it's not visible from inside the lounge."

While Wardlow scribbled in the notebook, Jackie raised her hand. "These co-workers you talked to, didn't any of them associate Darla with the hit-and-run?" she asked. "Knowing that she drove a red sports car and hearing the vehicle described in the press, nobody made the connection?"

"She never drove her Del Sol in the winter. It was more or less a summertime toy, garaged from November till March," Baumgartner said. "Darla grew up in Florida and was afraid to drive on snow. In the winter she used the bus or cabs, or rode with friends."

"But she was in the Del Sol last Monday," Wardlow said. "And it was practically a blizzard that night. Does anybody know why she was driving?"

Baumgartner shook his head. "Like I said, her friends found her hard to get close to lately. Not like her usual self at all."

"For how long?" Jackie asked.

The Traffic sergeant frowned. "Look, maybe you two should go out there and talk to these people yourself," he said to Jackie and Wardlow. "We're satisfied we've found the hit-and-run vehicle, and that was the main concern for us."

Claire Welsh appeared in the doorway, knocked twice and came into the room, wearing a tweed blazer over flannel slacks and an open-necked white shirt. The assembled group looked at her with interest as she walked to the front next to Baumgartner and smiled at him.

"Anything new, Sergeant Welsh?" he asked. "I'll give you the floor."

The senior Ident technician faced the group. "This has been a lucky case for us," she said. "We got a positive match on the tire tread, some good prints from the car, and now we've also got hits on two sets of prints we lifted from those whiskey glasses at the condo." She glanced around the room. "Is Detective Kaminsky here?"

Jackie raised her hand again and Claire smiled at her. "We just got them back a few minutes ago, Jackie, and they're good ones."

Jackie tensed. "What's the word?"

"Positive ID's on prints from both glasses," Claire said, looking at her file. "One set matches prints taken this morning from the deceased at the morgue, left index finger and thumb."

"And the other set?" Jackie asked, her throat tightening.

"Several smudges and a positive match to John Allan Stevenson, right middle finger."

"John Stevenson," Jackie breathed.

"His prints are also in the Del Sol," Claire said. "Two good matches, from the steering wheel and signal-light lever."

The room buzzed with murmurs of excitement. Jackie and Wardlow exchanged a glance.

"Why were Stevenson's prints on file?" Wardlow asked the Ident technician. "The guy didn't have any kind of record."

"While John Stevenson was in college, he had a summer job at a national park in Wyoming. The position required low-level security clearance, so the FBI had his prints in their bank."

"That means he was at Darla Drake's house on Friday night," Jackie whispered to her partner. "Four days after he left home."

"Are you going to tell his wife?" Wardlow asked in an undertone.

"I don't know." Jackie looked up at Steve Baumgartner, who had thanked Sergeant Welsh and was now continuing his case summary. "I don't know what the hell I'm going to do about this."

On Wednesday evening, Jackie took a couple of aspirin to soothe her dull headache, then curled up on the couch under one of her knitted afghans, wearing ragged navy sweatpants, fuzzy socks and an old patrol shirt with the departmental patches removed.

An animated Christmas special flickered on the television set in the corner, something about a baby reindeer trying to find its mother who was lost in the Land of Ice and Snow.

She hugged a pillow, then rolled over to bury her face in its softness. Something kept bothering her about the whole John Stevenson–Darla Drake problem, a loose thread she couldn't seem to put her finger on.

Everybody else in the department was relieved. The child's killer had been found, and had conveniently tried, convicted and executed herself without any costly and time-consuming intervention from the judicial system.

"Everybody's a winner," Jackie muttered.

She stared absently at the television, where a snow fairy guided the frightened little reindeer through the dark woods.

Everybody won except two sets of parents grieving over their lost daughters, to say nothing of poor distraught Carly Stevenson with a houseful of little kids and no money....

Jackie began to feel hot and sweaty. She unfolded herself from the couch, went over to her desk and sat down, pulling a notepad toward her and rummaging in the drawer for a pen. After a few moments of thought, she began to jot down questions.

1.) Darla Drake's suicide—Suicide note? Where is it?

2.) John & Darla—how did they meet? At Prairie Club? [Unlikely] Where is he? Why no pos. sightings?

3.) Who phoned D. on Tues. night with urgent prob.?

4.) Who's threatening Carly/kids?

5.) Norine Burkett—why so hostile a few days after funeral?

6.) Why John quit job, not tell wife?
7.) CONNECTIONS…between John/Darla/Burkett girl… Why so many? Weird coincidence?

She studied the questions until her head began to throb again, then turned away and wandered back to the couch, picking up the cushion and hugging it in her lap.

Jackie felt tears stinging her eyes as she watched the poignant special. She picked up the remote to switch off the television and looked around for something else to do.

Her flute case was stored beneath the ottoman, but she wasn't in the mood for music today. Even the thought of it made her head ache.

Instead, she opened the ottoman and took out a cloth bag containing a pattern book, some metal needles and a few balls of beige yarn. This was a brand-new project, and more challenging, she often thought, than basic training at the police academy.

Jackie Kaminsky was learning to knit, and she wasn't very good at it.

She looked at the few rows of uneven stitches on one of the needles with little cable holders hanging crookedly from the whole mess.

At first she'd had ambitious intentions of knitting new afghans for the ranch house, so that when she and Paul got married and moved in together she wouldn't have to drag along those garish old afghans her grandmother had knitted, with all their unhappy memories.

Not that Jackie could ever bring herself to throw Gram's afghans away. But she was feeling more and more anxious to get them out of sight, wrapped in tissue and stored away in a wooden chest up in the attic at Paul's house.

Out of sight, far away and forgotten, like the rest of her past.

All this symbolism was becoming too overpowering, and in her sick and weary state, the problems loomed impossibly large. No matter how hard she tried, Jackie couldn't see herself being able to make pretty new afghans to replace the ugly ones from her past...

"A psychologist would have a field day with me and my goddamn knitting," Jackie muttered aloud, then felt nervous hearing her voice in the silent apartment.

I should have a pet, she told herself. *If you've got a pet, you can talk out loud when you're alone and you don't feel like an idiot.*

With sudden clarity, she recalled the dainty Siamese cat licking blood from its front paws. Her stomach heaved.

This time Jackie rushed to the bathroom and retched, losing most of the tuna casserole she'd eaten for supper. Afterward she felt a little better, though weak and shaky.

She splashed cold water on her face and gazed soberly at her pallid reflection in the mirror, then went back to the living room and settled to her knitting with dogged determination. But after a while, her eyes stung when she tried to read the little symbols on the pattern, and she dropped the messy rows of knitting into her lap.

Just two weeks remained until Christmas, when she and Paul were supposed to go to Adrienne's home for a festive dinner. Later Jackie would have to respond to his ultimatum. What was she going to tell him?

"I'll marry you even it means giving up control of my own life and letting you be in charge of everything. I love you too much to lose you."

Could she really say that?

Or, "I'm sorry, Paul, but I'm just not ready to do this. I love you and I always will, but I've looked after myself too long to hand my life over to someone else. So I guess this is goodbye."

Jackie pictured herself saying this, even smiling bravely, kissing his cheek and telling him to have a nice life before she turned and walked slowly away from him into the falling snow.

But she could also imagine the aftermath of such a scene, her own loneliness and pain, the sheer anguish of never seeing him again, not talking and laughing with him, being unaware of what he was doing and thinking.

Not sleeping with him, holding him, feeling his body close to hers...

Tears gathered in her eyes again and slipped down her cheeks, blurring her vision. She brushed at them angrily, picked up her knitting and promptly dropped the next stitch, leaving a gaping hole with no place to insert the cable holder.

"Oh, *shit,*" she muttered, staring at the crooked length of knitting.

Finally she sat up, pulled the phone toward her and dialed.

"Hi, Gram," she said when a quavering voice answered. "It's Jackie. How are you?"

"Well," her grandmother began, "I got a bad pain

in my left knee, shoots right up into my thigh something awful in the morning, and I can't—''

"Did you go to the doctor?"

"The *doctor?*" her grandmother said bitterly. "Who can afford a doctor?"

"Gram, I sent you some money last month." Jackie felt a familiar sense of despair. "Seven hundred dollars, remember? Joey put it in the bank for you. It was supposed to be a sort of emergency fund if you needed medical care or anything."

"That was real nice, Jackie," her grandmother said, the petulance switching to a cautious tone. "Real generous to send that money for your poor old gram. I sure appreciate it."

"But what happened to the money, Gram?"

There was a brief silence. Jackie's head began to ache more fiercely as her frustration mounted. It was all she could do to keep herself from gathering up the telephone and flinging it across the room.

"Gram?" she prompted with forced gentleness. "You're not drinking again, are you?"

"No!" Irene said indignantly. "I haven't had a single drink since Halloween, Jackie. Not even one of Joey's beers."

"That's good. I'm really glad to hear it." Jackie took a deep breath. "So where'd the money go?"

"We had a little problem down here," Irene muttered evasively.

"What kind of problem?"

"Well, this girl down the street claimed Carmelo got her pregnant. The little bitch," Irene said with venom. "Could've been any guy in the neighborhood. Why pick on Carmelo?"

Jackie thought of her youngest cousin with his dark

good looks, his gleaming white-toothed smile and arrogant swagger.

"If Carmelo wasn't responsible," she said wearily, "he shouldn't have to give money to the girl."

"He just wanted to get it over with, poor kid. So how you been, Jackie?" her grandmother asked with the falsely bright tone she used when she was anxious to change the subject.

"Actually I'm learning to knit," Jackie said. "And I'm having trouble with this pattern, Gram. I wondered if you could help me."

"Maybe I can." Irene sounded flattered. "But I haven't knitted in a long time, you know. My fingers hurt too much with the goddamn arthritis."

"Lucky you can still hold a bingo marker."

Her grandmother was silent. Instantly Jackie regretted her sarcasm and frowned at the pattern.

"Now, when it says cable F and cable B, that means front and back, doesn't it? But when I try to move this little extra needle—"

"Jackie," her grandmother interrupted. "You aren't trying to knit a cable pattern?"

"Yes, I am," Jackie said. "It's an afghan. It looked nice in the picture, and I thought—"

"Well, you can't do it," Irene said flatly. "It's too hard."

Jackie's stomach clenched, then heaved ominously again. "If this afghan is impossible to make, why would they print the pattern?"

"Oh, a good knitter could do it," her grandmother said carelessly. "But you're all thumbs, girl. You always were."

Jackie gripped the receiver, suddenly furious. To

hear this now, from the same woman who'd been saying such things to her ever since she was born....

You can't, you'll never be able to, they won't let you, you should just give up.

No nice boy is ever going to take you out, a girl like you. What makes you think you could work for the police? Play the flute? Learn to knit? You must be crazy. You can't marry a man and be a decent wife. How could you ever raise a baby, when your own mother couldn't even be bothered with you?

"Thanks for the advice, Gram," Jackie said coldly. "But I think I'll keep plugging away at this until I figure out the pattern. I'll talk to you again before Christmas, okay?"

She hung up quickly before her grandmother could say anything else, and sat staring out the window into the wintry darkness.

The doorbell rang. Jackie wandered across the room to peer through the peephole, then gasped and opened the door. Paul stood in the outer hall, gazing down at her with a quiet, intent look.

18

"Paul!" Jackie said in a voice she hoped was casual and pleased. "What a nice surprise. Come in."

She stood aside to let him enter the foyer, watching while he unlaced his boots, removed his jacket and put it in the closet.

For the first time in months, she didn't hug him on his arrival and he didn't comment on the fact. But the omission hung awkwardly between them.

"How are you?" he asked, his dark eyes devouring her. "You look upset."

She moved into the kitchen. "I'm fine. I was just talking to Gram. You know how she gets to me."

"What did she say this time?"

He opened the fridge and poured himself a glass of orange juice, then leaned against the counter drinking it and watching Jackie.

She stood by the sink, reaching out to set the faucet in perfect alignment. "Oh, just the usual. I'm still struggling with that rotten knitting. I called to ask her for some help, and she said knitting was too hard for me and I'd never be able to learn." Jackie gave him a bleak smile. "She said I'm all thumbs."

He set the glass down hard. "That damn old woman has been saying the same kind of thing to you for years." He scowled. "You've got a hard job and you do it well. You're looking after yourself with no help from anybody. Where does she get off, telling you you're not competent?''

Irrationally, Jackie found herself annoyed by his criticism of her grandmother. ''Gram's had a hard life,'' she said. ''It wasn't easy raising me and that whole crew of cousins.''

''She didn't raise you.'' Paul picked up his glass, drained it of juice and set it on the counter again. ''She just drank and ran around and let you raise yourselves as best you could. Why give her any credit?''

''Let's not talk about my grandmother, okay?'' Jackie looked up, meeting his eyes directly, surprised by her own anger.

He held her gaze for a moment, then turned aside. ''Suits me. I don't like talking about that woman anyhow. What have you been doing besides knitting?''

He walked past her to rinse his juice glass at the sink. Then he went into the living room, padding softly in his thick woolen socks.

Jackie followed and watched him settle on the couch. She longed to nestle with him and curl up in his arms. Instead, she put some music on the stereo, then retrieved her knitting and sat in an armchair facing him.

''I'm just doing the usual,'' she said. ''Mostly working, eating and sleeping. What brings you to town so late at night?''

God, she thought in despair. *We sound like a couple of casual acquaintances meeting on a street corner.*

Paul glanced at his watch. ''I've got a sick calf, had to come in to pick up some more antibiotic tablets. I can't stay long because he needs another treatment before midnight.''

She nodded, both disappointed and relieved that he wouldn't be spending the night.

"Will the calf be okay?" she asked, frowning at her knitting.

"I don't know. He's pretty listless, hasn't been eating well for days.''

She tried to smile. "Hey, that's exactly the way I'm feeling right now. Maybe you should leave a few of those tablets for me.''

"Are you still sick?''

"Not as bad," she said. "Brian says I'm probably through the worst of it by now. We've just been working on this…''

A sudden image of Darla Drake's body nagged at her mind but she pushed it away before the nausea could rise again.

"What?" he asked.

"Just a kind of ugly suicide. It's tied to that hit-and-run on the little Burkett girl.''

"Did you find the driver yet?" He leaned back on the couch and extended his legs wearily. "I haven't heard any news since breakfast.''

Jackie told him about the case, including the death of Darla, then stopped and fingered the uneven length of knitting.

"Jackie?" he prompted after a moment. "What are you thinking?''

"I just feel so sorry for his wife," she said. "Carly Stevenson, I mean. She loves the man, and she's so loyal to him even now. She still won't let anybody say a word against him. And yet he's been lying to her, he stole all her money and left her penniless, he's been running around with this other woman..."

She looked up, feeling her cheeks turn warm with emotion.

"Maybe he's even involved somehow in this woman's death," she went on. "I think he could actually be a threat to his own kids. And yet she still loves him. How can the woman be so *blind?*"

"Love and loyalty aren't necessarily rational," Paul said. "Maybe she knows things about her husband that nobody else does. It could be none of this situation is what it seems to be."

"Well, I'm an investigator, not a psychic like you. I have to deal with facts. And the facts show that John Stevenson is guilty as hell."

"Jackie," he said gently.

She ignored him, still looking down at her knitting. "I can't stand to think I might be like that someday," she said. "So besotted with a man that I could ignore all logic and let my emotions tell me he's a great guy even though the facts are—" She stopped abruptly, winding a loose strand of wool around the ball.

"Just because this guy's a cheat and a liar doesn't mean all men are the same," he said. "And it doesn't mean a loving marriage makes you blind to the truth."

"But how can anybody be sure?" She moved the wool restlessly in her hands. "I've never been in a committed relationship except with you. How do I know what it might do to me?"

"We've been together for more than a year," he said. "As far as I can see, the relationship has done you nothing but good."

"So what are you saying? You mean I was such

an awful person before I met you?'' she asked, and instantly regretted the question, especially when she saw the look of disappointment on his face.

''That's not the kind of thing you usually say,'' he commented. ''It sounds like a...''

''Like a woman,'' she said when he paused. ''Isn't that what you were going to say? I sound just like a woman. Don't I, Paul?'' Her voice rose.

''You're usually more rational,'' he said quietly. ''It's one of the things I've always liked about you, the way you're able to be so levelheaded and objective.''

''But what if I'm losing that ability?'' Her anger subsided, replaced by uneasy tension. ''What if being in love is making me turn bitchy and unreasonable, the kind of woman I never wanted to be?''

He watched her in silence for a moment. ''Tell me what you're really afraid of, Jackie.''

She looked down at her knitting, tugging restlessly on the needles. ''I'm not afraid of anything.''

''Of course you are. That's what this whole conversation is about, isn't it? We're talking about your fears. Are you really afraid you'll lose yourself in marriage and not be the person you want to be?''

She stabbed at the yarn and began knitting blindly, not even trying to follow the intricate pattern.

''Or have you been listening to your vicious old grandmother again, and letting her scare you into thinking you can't be a wife and mother because you're somehow not good enough?''

She was shaken by a flood of outrage that burned through her like white heat, then left her feeling empty and sick. ''I don't want to be a wife and mother,'' she said. ''I want to be a person. You can't shove me into one of those boxes.''

''I'm not talking about putting you into any kind of box,'' he said. ''I love you and I want you to be my wife. I hope someday you'll be the mother of my children. Is that such a terrible, devious plan to have?''

''It's terrible if I'm your wife and the mother of your children so I don't get to work at my job anymore. It's devious if all you really care about is getting your own way.''

Jackie was seized by a growing recklessness. On some level she knew the things she was saying were both false and hurtful, but she felt a terrible, uncontrollable need to say them anyhow.

''You're being selfish,'' she went on in a shaking, furious voice, not looking at him. ''You're dictating all the terms. We have to get married on your timetable, not mine, and afterward you're going to make me into the woman you want because what I am isn't good enough for you. And all the time—''

''That's enough,'' he said sharply. ''For God's sake, stop talking before you say something we're both going to regret.''

He got up and moved toward the door, then paused to look back at her.

''I'm leaving now, Jackie. But before I go, I want to tell you one thing.''

She couldn't look at him. Instead she stared at the ball of wool in her hands, choked with misery.

''I don't think this is about a loss of independence or a struggle for control within our relationship,'' he said. ''Those are important issues, but we can deal with them if we love each other enough.''

He opened the closet and shrugged into his jacket, then put on his boots.

"This is all about your fears," he went on as Jackie approached the door, clutching the knitting in her hands. "It's about those insecurities that were planted in you by your grandmother, thirty years before I met you. You're afraid of being close to anybody. You can't give your heart for fear of losing it. You can't trust or love anybody."

"That's not true," she whispered. "It's not true at all."

"And," he went on grimly, "I can't go on competing with your grandmother and your fears. I love you, but there's nothing more I can do to convince you that if we have a life together, you won't lose your identity."

The note of finality in his voice was terrifying to her. She dropped the knitting onto the floor and took a few steps toward him.

"Look," she pleaded, "why can't we just forget about the whole marriage thing? Couldn't we keep seeing each other the same way and not make any big changes or commitments right now? I'll admit I'm not ready, Paul. But I love you," she added, distressed by the way her voice trembled. "I really love you."

He stood watching her, his handsome face expressionless. "I think you do," he said at last. "But only with the part of you that lets you reach beyond your fears. It's not enough for me, Jackie. I want your whole heart. If you can't give it, I'm not interested."

"What are you saying?" She stood in the doorway and gripped the molding.

"I guess I'm saying goodbye. Call me if you ever change your mind. I'll be waiting."

"Paul!"

He opened the door and stepped into the hallway, then turned to look at her, his face so full of love and sorrow that she felt her heart breaking.

"Goodbye, Jackie," he said.

Then he was gone, walking down the hall with the lithe, hip-swinging stride that she loved.

Come back, she screamed silently. *Paul, come back, I'll do what you want! I'll do anything to keep from losing you like this...*

But the voice was locked inside along with her tears. She watched, dry-eyed and still, as he vanished into the stairwell, leaving the hallway empty in the melancholy quiet of the winter evening.

The next day she was still numb with pain and disbelief, unable to grasp what had really happened.

How could all those months of love and laughter end in a few cold sentences?

And why? After a night of lying awake, tossing and turning and staring with gritty eyes at her bedside clock, Jackie was no closer to understanding.

She went through her morning routine mechanically, then headed over to the hospital, where she sat in a waiting room near the morgue, still thinking about Paul.

The things they disagreed about had always been there, but until now they'd put them aside and managed to go on loving each other, even to grow closer with every day and week that passed. Now the differences had risen like a shoal of rocks in shallow water tearing the bottom from a ship, dealing a mortal blow.

No, she thought in despair. *I can't bear it to be over. I'll die if I can't see him again.*

"God, you look awful, Kaminsky," her partner said cheerfully, coming through the door of the hospital autopsy room with Claire Welsh. "You've got bags under your eyes as big as suitcases."

The slim blond sergeant looked at her in concern. "You do seem awfully pale, Jackie. Are you feeling all right?"

"I didn't sleep well," Jackie said, avoiding Wardlow's keen glance. She looked around restlessly. "Where's everybody else? We're late already."

Dr. Klein, the chief pathologist, appeared through another door as if in response to her question.

"Come in, everyone. Raelynn will be along soon with the body," he said. "Hello, Detectives. And Sergeant Welsh," he said, beaming up at Claire who topped him by at least three or four inches.

"Hello, Dr. Klein," the sergeant said with the warm respect of a professional for a trusted colleague. "I'm taking the pictures today. My department has a special interest in this case."

"A very intriguing case," he agreed, pulling on his rubber gloves and glancing at the police officers. "You might choose to take some precautions," he said quietly to Claire, who was unpacking cameras and flash equipment from her aluminum case. "Decomposition is fairly advanced."

Claire nodded and took a handful of paper masks from her equipment bag, handing a couple to Jackie and her partner. The masks were made of several layers of white tissue with a flexible metal nosepiece and an elastic strap to hold them in place.

"Here," Claire said, handing Jackie a small blue jar. "Use some of this, too."

"What is it?" Jackie asked.

"Vicks VapoRub," Claire smiled briefly. "Just rub a bit inside the mask. It helps a lot."

Jackie took the bottle gratefully and did as she was instructed, then handed the ointment to Wardlow and fitted her mask in place.

"Here's Raelynn," the pathologist announced, smiling at his assistant who arrived wheeling a metal gurney containing the bagged corpse.

Raelynn was a dark-skinned girl with beautiful eyes and a sweet, shy smile. She wore a white zippered jumpsuit and white rubber boots.

The assistant murmured a greeting to the police officers and positioned the body in the center of the room.

Jackie and Wardlow prepared to take notes while Claire moved closer with her camera in one hand and a flash unit in the other.

"Darla Elizabeth Drake," the pathologist began in a calm monotone after the seals had been examined and the body bag removed. "Caucasian female, aged twenty-seven years."

Jackie looked at the corpse on the gurney while Raelynn unbuttoned the nightshirt caked with dried blood. The girl made a couple of deft cuts in the fabric to remove the shirt, then deposited it in an evidence box along with the patterned slippers.

Darla's body lay on the metal table, naked except for the pink foam rollers in her hair. Jackie moved closer to look at the young woman, grateful for her paper mask with its smear of medicated ointment that filtered most of the odor.

The swollen, bluish hulk on the table bore little resemblance to that lovely seductive girl in the photographs Jackie had been given by Karl Widmer. As always in the autopsy room, she was stunned by the gross indignities death committed on the human body.

"The hair rollers as well," Dr. Klein murmured to his assistant. "We'll want to examine the brain tissue. Sergeant Welsh, are you ready?"

Claire moved up to photograph the young woman's hair and face from several angles. "Okay," she said. "I've got it, Raelynn."

The pathologist nodded to his assistant who took out the pink hair rollers, then reached for a small flexible hose hooked to a water supply at the side of the room. The two of them worked together with such practiced efficiency that they seldom needed to exchange words, just looks and gestures. Neither Dr. Klein nor Raelynn wore a mask, and both seemed unaffected by the odor of the corpse.

Raelynn cast an inquiring glance at the police sergeant with the camera who was now taking pictures of the torso and limbs, particularly the arms and wrists. Claire moved along the table to get a better shot of the left arm, holding her flash aloft.

"All right," she said. "Got it."

The assistant began to hose blood from the body, plying the nozzle skillfully, concentrating on the slashed wrists.

Jackie moved restlessly. Wardlow shot her a quick glance, his eyes concerned above the white cotton mask. She frowned at him and turned back to her notes.

"I suspect you people are primarily interested in these cuts to the wrists, but we'll begin with the internal organs," the pathologist announced. "Raelynn, we'll want to take a blood sample, a urine specimen from the bladder and all of the stomach contents."

She nodded silently and went to fetch a series of specimen jars from the counter.

Dr. Klein made the initial cut on Darla Drake's swollen abdomen and a gush of trapped air escaped, so fetid that it penetrated the cotton of the mask and made Jackie feel light-headed.

She watched in grim silence as the doctor exposed and removed the major organs. Soft tissue like the liver was already turning mushy and formless.

"Drugs and alcohol are quite volatile within the human system," Dr. Klein told the police officers. "We'll test for their presence, of course, but negative results five days after death are not necessarily conclusive."

Jackie made notes in her book, feeling intensely grateful when the internal examination was finished and the organs, body fluid and tissue samples were stored in jars for transfer to the lab. Dr. Klein sewed up the body cavity with neat blanket stitches, then removed a portion of the skull to extract the brain.

Finally he moved to the slashed wrists and the police officers watched with renewed interest.

"Can you tell anything definitive about her injuries?" Claire asked, bending closer with her camera.

"Well, now, we'll just have to see about that," the pathologist murmured, peering intently at the damaged wrists.

"Hmm," he murmured, examining the deep gash in the left wrist, then bustling around the table to peer at the other arm. "You'll want close-up photographs of both these wounds, Sergeant Welsh."

Claire followed him obediently while Jackie and Wardlow looked on in tense silence.

"There appear to be no tentative cuts," the doctor told Raelynn over his shoulder. She nodded impassively and made a note.

"Tentative cuts?" Jackie asked through her mask. "What does that mean?"

"Except in cases of mental imbalance, there is a very deep human aversion to cutting one's own flesh," the pathologist told her. "In this type of suicide, we almost always see one or more experimental, superficial wounds that are inflicted before the fatal incision is made. There are none in this case."

Jackie and Wardlow exchanged a glance.

"But the incisions themselves are most revealing," the pathologist said. "They go right to the bone. If you look closely, you'll see that these major tendons on both wrists, known as the radial and ulnar flexors, have all been severed."

"Both wrists?" Claire asked, staring down at the body.

He nodded, his eyes twinkling, and looked at Jackie and her partner. "Of course you recognize the significance of this?"

Jackie nodded slowly, digesting this new information. If Darla had cut through the tendons in one wrist, she would never be able to hold the knife in that hand in order to cut her other wrist.

Dr. Klein confirmed Jackie's thoughts. "Suppose I've set out to cut my wrists," he said, pretending to slice with the scalpel. "Because I'm right-handed, my instinct is to slash my left wrist first. Then I transfer the knife to my left hand.''

He suited actions to words, and Jackie took over.

''But if your first cut has severed both tendons on your left arm, how can you grip the knife to cut your right wrist?''

''Correct, Detective Kaminsky.'' The doctor beamed at her. ''I could conceivably slash my wrist with the radial flexor severed, but not the ulnar flexor. That would be impossible.''

''So that means...'' Wardlow took a deep breath and moved closer to stare at the young woman's mutilated, discolored body.

''It means,'' Dr. Klein said cheerfully, ''that I was correct in my initial suspicions.'' He waved his hand at the corpse on the table. ''No doubt about it. This was not a suicide at all, but a very deliberate homicide.''

19

"So let's take a look at what we've got."

It was late Friday morning as Michelson leaned back in his chair and took a couple of celery sticks from the container on his desk.

"This Drake woman," he began, "is having an affair with John Stevenson who works for Jason Burkett. She goes out joyriding on Monday night, jumps the curb and hits the little Burkett kid, killing her. Stevenson disappears the same night, two weeks after he quits his job and forgets to tell his wife he's now unemployed."

He paused, chewing thoughtfully, and Wardlow picked up the narrative.

"Darla Drake frets for a few days about what she's done. On Friday night, John Stevenson drops by to chat with her. They have a drink together and he slits both her wrists, then disappears again."

"But why?" Jackie said abruptly, frowning at her notebook. "Why would he kill Darla Drake if he's already left his wife and kids for her? Wouldn't it be more likely they'd both just take off and leave the city, since she needed to get away and Stevenson was on the run already?"

Michelson munched thoughtfully on his celery. "So what are you thinking, Jackie?"

"Actually, I'm still wondering about Norine Burkett." Jackie looked up. "Why is the woman so resentful of us? Why keep being hostile and uncooperative with the police when they're investigating your child's death, unless you have something to hide?"

"But we know it wasn't the mother's car that killed the little girl," Wardlow argued. "It was Darla Drake's car, no doubt about it, and she had no connection with the Burkett family. Just with John Stevenson, whose prints were in the car, by the way..."

"John Stevenson certainly has a connection with the Burkett family," Jackie muttered. "And it seems like a pretty tidy coincidence. Who knows how in hell all these people are connected when we can't talk to any of them?" She stood up, shaking her head in frustration.

Michelson leaned over his desk. "Jackie, are you okay?"

"No, I'm not. There's a murderer—a child killer—on the loose. How do you think I feel?"

Michelson and Wardlow exchanged glances, then Wardlow asked, "How's Paul?"

"Paul and I aren't seeing each other for a while," she said curtly. "And in case either of you were going to make a comment," she added, giving both men a warning glare, "it's nobody's business but ours."

"But Jackie," Wardlow began, looking almost boyish in his distress.

"I said I don't want to talk about it, Brian," she told her partner wearily. "Leave it alone, okay?" She sat down again.

Wardlow started to speak again, then turned away awkwardly when a knock sounded at the door.

Officer Brenda Howe popped her blond head inside, smiling. "Hi, Jackie. I did what you said this morning and spent a few hours following Norine Burkett around. It was pretty interesting."

The two detectives and the sergeant all watched as Brenda came in and took an empty chair.

"Thanks, Brenda. So what did you find out?" Jackie asked.

"She was driving the Land Rover. She took about six big plastic sacks full of clothes and a ton of toys to the Salvation Army depot."

"Getting rid of poor Angela's stuff already?" Wardlow asked.

"I guess so," Brenda said. "She seemed very matter-of-fact about it. No emotion at all. Just like she was putting out the trash."

"Norine's a pretty cool customer," Jackie agreed. "What else did she do?"

"She stopped at Esmerelda downtown and did some shopping. Bought quite a lot of stuff, in fact."

"What's Esmerelda?" Wardlow asked.

"A clothing boutique," Jackie told him. "So expensive there's practically a cover charge to get in. I was there with Adrienne once and saw a little black handbag that cost three thousand dollars."

Michelson's eyes widened. "Three grand for a *purse?* That's obscene."

"It really is," Brenda said moodily. "When I think of all the little kids right here in this city who don't get enough to eat every day, while people like Norine Burkett—"

The young police officer stopped, looking embarrassed, and checked her notebook again. "Then our girl had coffee with a friend downtown and went back home.''

"Did you happen to recognize the friend?" Jackie asked.

Brenda nodded. "It was Karl Widmer. You know, that good-looking newspaper guy from the *Sentinel?*"

Jackie looked up, startled. "Did they really seem like friends?" she asked after a moment's thought. "Or was it just an interview for the paper?"

Brenda pondered, then shook her head. "No, it didn't look like an interview. They met at the Cavanaugh next to River Park and sat in a corner of the dining room behind a bunch of ferns and stuff. They seemed to be arguing. After twenty-five minutes she got up and left by herself, looking really ticked off."

"She always looks that way," Jackie said, but her mind was racing. She thought about Karl Widmer's initial approach to her, his insinuation that Norine Burkett might have been the driver of the red sports car that killed her own daughter, and those damning pictures he'd supplied of John Stevenson.

In fact, the journalist had been squarely at the center of everything that was happening in this hit-and-run case, although she'd never fully realized his involvement until now.

"Thanks, Brenda," she said, getting up and gathering her files. "I'll have a chat with our friend Widmer a bit later in the day. Right now, I have to take some kids to visit Santa Claus."

Jackie pulled up to the snowy curb and parked at Carly Stevenson's house behind a dark blue luxury car. The expensive automobile rang a distant bell in her mind, but she couldn't place it. She'd check her notebook later.

Maybe it was John Stevenson's parents, finally arriving to give Carly some help. They might even take her away from the city for a while. Jackie felt her spirits lift.

She hadn't realized how concerned she was getting about this little abandoned family until she pictured the huge relief of having all of them safely gone from Spokane while the murderer of Darla Drake was tracked down and captured.

She waded up the path through the snow, rang the bell and was greeted by an extraordinary sight when the door opened.

Rachel and Emily appeared in the opening, their normally solemn demeanor replaced by dancing, sparkling excitement. They wore matching tartan skirts and red velvet vests over white blouses with lace-trimmed collars, and each had a plastic Santa face pinned to her vest.

"His nose lights up," Emily told Jackie, beaming in delight.

"You pull the cord," Rachel added, suiting action to words. She tugged at a dangling string and the Santa's nose on her chest glowed bright red, making him look like a drunken gnome.

"Wow. Do it again," Jackie said, feigning fascination.

Rachel obeyed with a throaty giggle, and her sister imitated her. Caitlin arrived in the foyer, looking more subdued than the twins, though her blue eyes glowed with anticipation. She wore green tights and a white tunic patterned with a snowman.

"Hey, really cool threads," Jackie murmured,

smiling at the older child. "You all look like you're going to a party somewhere."

"We are." Emily gazed up at Jackie earnestly, gripping the hem of her gabardine topcoat. "We're going with you. Aren't we?" She began to look a little anxious, and her round cheeks flushed with emotion.

Jackie's heart melted when she thought of the fear and uncertainty these poor children had suffered in the past few weeks.

"Of course you're going with me," she said, ruffling Emily's hair. "You're going down to the shooting range under the police station for a big party with a whole lot of other kids. And..." She lowered her voice to a significant whisper. "I'm pretty sure Santa's bringing you a special present."

Emily sighed blissfully and jammed her thumb in her mouth. The three children dragged Jackie into the living room where she stopped abruptly.

Jason Burkett sat in an armchair by the little stone fireplace, sipping from one of the special teacups that Carly kept in a big glass-fronted china cabinet. The visitor looked up at Jackie with an easy, boyish smile, set his cup down and got to his feet to shake her hand.

"Hello, Detective. Carly tells me you're taking the older kids to a police Christmas party this afternoon. That's very nice of you."

She smiled back at him, trying hard to take the measure of the man. This was the first time Jackie had seen Jason Burkett without his wife, and he seemed strangely incomplete, as if Norine's presence was needed to bring him to life. The man's smile was courteous, even warm, but his eyes seemed empty and sad.

Of course, Jackie told herself with quick sympathy, being around a houseful of energetic children must be a painful experience for a man who'd lost his only child.

At any rate, he was a lot more pleasant than his cold, hostile wife.

He moved to the door, accepted his topcoat from Carly and smiled at her, taking her hands in both his own. "If there's anything we can do, Carly," he said with warm sincerity, "Norine and I are always glad to help. Just give us a call at any time."

"That's very kind," Carly whispered. "Thank you, Mr. Burkett."

He nodded courteously to Jackie and left the house. She stood by the front window and watched his erect, broad-shouldered figure as he plowed through the snow to his car.

Carly came and stood beside her. "What a nice man," she murmured. "He gave me a lot of money, Jackie. Enough to pay back what you loaned me and get us through the next few weeks. He said we didn't have to repay him until…until John comes home and this all gets sorted out."

"That really was nice of him," Jackie said cautiously, glancing at Carly's thin cheek, pale beneath the dusting of freckles.

The three little girls scattered to find their coats, and Jackie continued her covert examination of Carly Stevenson. The woman was looking more scared than ever.

Carly had been pushed almost beyond her limits of endurance, Jackie realized. The woman couldn't take much more.

"You do know, Carly," she began carefully, "that

when John...when we find him, he still might not be coming home for a while."

"He'll be home." Carly turned away to pluck a few dead leaves from among the plants in the window. Her hands were shaking.

"Listen, Carly," Jackie said with forced gentleness. "I told you about the autopsy. The woman was definitely murdered. We have pictures of her with your husband, and his fingerprints were found at the scene and in her car. So you have to—"

"I don't have to do anything!" Carly whirled to face Jackie, her face taut with passion. "I don't care what you say! John never hurt anybody in his whole life. Whatever's going on, it has nothing to do with him." She leaned closer, whispering harshly. "Nothing to do with him! *Do you hear me?*"

The little girls appeared in the doorway, trailing coats and mittens, looking curiously at the two of them.

Jackie and Carly both hurried to get the children buttoned and muffled in their outerwear, and the tense moment passed.

"You can take the van, okay?" Carly said, following them outside. "It's easier than transferring the car seats to your vehicle. And I'll still have the Volvo if I need to go anywhere."

Her voice was shaky but normal, and the burst of emotion seemed to have passed.

Jackie paused by the driver side of the van while Carly buckled the children in place. "I wish you could dress Patrick up and come along with us," she said. "Carly, a Christmas party would do you good."

Carly gave her a wavering smile. "The best party

for me would be a nice long nap. I'm hoping Patrick's going to sleep most of the afternoon, and so am I.''

Jackie wondered suddenly if Carly's terrifying nocturnal phone calls were still interrupting her sleep. But this certainly wasn't the time to bring the subject up.

"If you don't mind," Carly said from the sidewalk, "Caitlin needs to be taken to a friend's house after the party for a birthday dinner and sleepover tonight. Her friend lives on the west side, off Summit Boulevard," she added apologetically, handing over a sheet of paper with a neatly printed address. "I know it's out of your way, Jackie, but I don't see how I can…"

Jackie waved a hand in dismissal. "No problem. We should still be home by about four or five, okay?"

She got behind the wheel and buckled her seat belt. "Say goodbye to your mom," she told the children. They all waved and Jackie put the van in gear, heading carefully down the icy street.

As she drove, she glanced sidelong at Caitlin, strapped into the passenger seat next to her, and listened to the chatter of the twins in their car seats.

Jackie Kaminsky, she mused, taking three little kids to a Christmas party.

Life was strange. In fact, most of the time it was just too damn strange to figure out.

20

Jackie had never attended the annual Christmas party for city police officers and their families. In fact, she'd always been a little impatient with such festivities.

She sat with Wardlow and Christine, balancing a plate of turkey and stuffing on her knees and watching the children play games and squeal with excitement, and wondered why she'd avoided the event when it was so much fun.

Paul was right. She'd spent her whole life molding and shaping herself into a person who didn't need anybody. In fact, she'd practically made a private cult out of her loneliness and self-sufficiency. Now her behavior was so firmly ingrained that she had no idea how to change it. She was afraid to try, even though the future looked increasingly lonely and...

"Watch Emily," Brian's girlfriend, Chris, murmured, leaning close to Jackie so her voice could be heard above the chorus of young voices singing "Rudolph the Red-Nosed Reindeer."

Emily Stevenson stood in the front row by the Christmas tree with a group of smaller children, bellowing the song at the top of her lungs as she tugged self-consciously on the string of her plastic Santa. Her collar was askew, her skirt hiked up over cotton tights, her face flushed with happiness.

Chris gripped Wardlow's hand and gave Jackie a misty smile. "They're so cute, Jackie," she said. "It was nice of you to bring them."

Jackie took a mouthful of mashed potatoes slathered with gravy. "Well, you know me, Chris," she said when she could speak again. "I'm a real sweetheart. And a well-known fan of small children."

Chris gave her a quick glance, looking surprisingly shrewd.

"You're being sarcastic," she said. "But it's true, what you're saying. You *are* a nice person, Jackie. And you're really good with kids."

Jackie looked down at her plate, surprised and more than a little unsettled.

Something in the other woman's expression made her afraid that Chris was going to ask about Paul. Brian would certainly have told her about their problems already, since he and Christine shared everything.

After a brief, awkward silence, Jackie murmured something about food and got to her feet, heading back to the long table where the chief of police and his wife, both wearing Santa Claus hats, dispensed turkey and stuffing amid much hilarity.

It was surprising how festive the underground shooting range looked. Usually the place was as grim and cheerless as a military bunker. But now tinsel and holly covered the concrete walls, the human-shaped targets were dressed up as Santas and the gun lockers were concealed behind hand-painted murals depicting snow-covered landscapes, sleighs and reindeer.

"Having a good time, Jackie?" Captain Alvarez

asked. He paused next to her with his son, a solemn, dark-eyed little boy about the age of the twins, wearing a tartan suit jacket and a red bow tie.

"My, my," Jackie said, kneeling to smile at the child. "Don't you look spiffy?"

"Santa's coming here today," the child whispered, hushed with anticipation.

Overcome by a sudden rush of tenderness, Jackie leaned forward to hug him and kiss his plump cheek, then looked up at the smiling captain, feeling embarrassed and ill at ease.

She got to her feet and wandered around the room holding her plate of food, visiting with friends and colleagues. Lieutenant Hatch arrived from the back of the shooting range amid a noisy jangle of bells, plump and jovial in his red velvet outfit. He sat by the Christmas tree and distributed presents to each of the children.

Jackie watched their excitement, marveling at the selfless generosity and hard work that so many people put into organizing such an event, just to make little kids happy.

Caitlin unwrapped a wood-carving set, while Rachel and Emily got bright packets containing modeling clay and little plastic animal shapes.

By the time they left, all three children settled into their seats in the van and sighed in contentment, replete with food and excitement. The sky was already darkening and snow had begun to fall, swirling across the police parking lot on a cold north wind.

Jackie took the slip of paper from her pocket and checked the address for Caitlin's birthday party, then headed west on Broadway toward the steep road that bordered the river.

Beside her, Caitlin's dainty profile was etched with silver from the passing streetlights. She gripped the wood-carving set in her lap and examined it with grave interest.

"This is neat," she said to Jackie.

"It looks really neat," Jackie said, concentrating on the road ahead.

The sanding vehicles hadn't been out yet, and the pavement was slick. Snow had already begun to pile up along the curb.

"I would have loved something like that when I was a kid," she told the child. "What are you going to make first?"

"I'm making a Christmas present for my daddy," Caitlin said in her high clear voice. "I'm going to make one of those pictures like they show in the instructions, and then put all our names on it so Daddy can hang it in his office."

Jackie was conscious of the child watching her. "I'm sure he'll like that," she said.

"Yes, he will. He'll *love* it," Caitlin said with sudden fierceness, her hands tightening on the edge of the box.

"What's your friend's name?" Jackie asked after a brief silence. "At this place where you're having the birthday party, I mean."

"Brittany. Her mom and dad are both schoolteachers. She has five pet turtles."

"Five!" Jackie said. "My goodness, that's a whole herd of turtles, isn't it?" The snow was heavier now, and oncoming headlights bloomed out of the swirling mass.

She pulled off Summit onto a side street and found the two-story house where Caitlin's little friend lived with her schoolteacher parents and her family of turtles. Lights beamed from the lower windows, looking cozy and inviting.

Jackie helped the child carry her backpack and party gifts to the door, exchanged a few words with Brittany's mother and then plowed back through the snow to the van where both twins were nodding off in their car seats, weary after the day of party fun.

She started back down the road bordering the high ridge, concentrating on her driving. The height of the van gave her better visibility than she was accustomed to with her police car, but it didn't help much when the snow obscured most of the road and drove hard against the windshield.

While she drove, she thought about the Stevenson children: the twins in the back seat, Caitlin at her friend's house and baby Patrick at home with his mother. They were such a nice family, and the plight of the children tore at her heart.

Where in hell was their father?

All efforts to find him had come up empty. The standard police procedures for tracking missing persons were proving utterly futile in this case.

John Stevenson no longer had any work associates, and the people at his former place of employment hadn't seen him for weeks. He had no family in the state, and, ostensibly, no social life outside of his wife and children and the things they did together. Neither of his parents, or his siblings in Wyoming had spoken to him for at least a month. He was well supplied with cash, so the police had no credit-card trail to follow. The man had an ordinary appearance, with no obvious distinguishing characteristics. There was no vehicle they could track, and no other leads to follow.

Every promising tip they checked on turned out to be a false alarm.

They had nothing but that strange set of photographs, showing him with a naked and affectionate Darla Drake. And a whiskey glass covered with his fingerprints, placing him at the scene of a grisly murder…

A car's headlights loomed out of the storm with ghostly suddenness, dazzling in Jackie's rearview mirror. The vehicle hung on her tail, its brightness affecting Jackie's vision.

She frowned and increased her speed slightly, annoyed by the other driver's lack of consideration.

"Come on, dim those lights, you goddamn idiot," she muttered, wincing as she glanced in the mirror.

The vehicle increased its speed to keep pace with her, still tailgating. She swore softly and pulled onto the snow-covered shoulder to let the other car pass.

But by the time she parked, checked the twins and waited, the headlights were nowhere in sight. Jackie frowned into the whirling snow, puzzled.

The driver must have turned down a side road, though there weren't many avenues running off Summit at this point. She was high along the river where a steep dropoff beyond the driving lane was protected in places by guardrails and low concrete barriers.

Those barriers should be extended, Jackie thought idly, glancing to her right. In dark, slippery conditions like this, the steep roadbank looked pretty terrifying.

She slipped the car into gear and moved into the road again. After a minute or two, a pair of headlights loomed out of the snow behind her, coming up so quickly into her blind spot that her hands tensed on the wheel.

The car pulled close and ducked out sharply into the lane next to her, then fell back. Instinctively Jackie cranked the wheel to the right to avoid collision, and felt the van sliding toward the precipice.

She stepped down hard on the brake pedal and steered to her left, trying to stabilize the vehicle on the slippery road. The antilock braking system shuddered and held, pulling her gradually out of the skid.

As the van stabilized, the vehicle behind Jackie darted forward again and crowded her back toward the edge of the road.

"You *bastard!*" she whispered, gripping the wheel frantically, forcing herself not to panic and pump the brakes.

The van slipped so close to the edge of the road that she felt the tires grinding on the rough shoulder, felt the vehicle begin to tip and slide. In another two seconds they'd be over the edge and falling.

The brakes pulsed and grabbed beneath her, and sweat ran down her face as she pulled the wheel sharply to the left, beginning a long sideways skid.

The other vehicle spurted forward and vanished into the blackness. Through the whirling snow and mists of terror, Jackie recognized the outline of a dark, late-model sport-utility van.

She had no control of her own vehicle by now. It careened on the ice, turned sideways and plowed down the road into the opposite lane. If they met another vehicle coming up, everybody was going to die.

Or if the van started to skid in the opposite direction again and slipped over the edge…

She kept her foot pressed grimly on the brake and their dizzy slide began to lose speed. The vehicle swapped ends a third time as it reached the bottom of the hill, grated against a concrete barrier on the far side of the road and finally came to a halt heading uphill in the opposite direction.

The engine stalled and Jackie dropped her forehead to the wheel.

After a moment she turned and looked into the back seat. Rachel was sound asleep in her car seat. Emily sat watching, round-eyed and silent in the darkness, her thumb jammed into her mouth.

"No problem," Jackie told the child, trying to smile. "We hit a bit of ice and went for a little slide, but we're okay now."

Emily watched her gravely and didn't reply. Finally Jackie started the vehicle, made a turn in the falling snow and headed back into the bright lights of the city.

As she drove she thought about the van whose lights had come up behind her so quickly. The attempt to force her off the road had been deliberate and calculated. And the van that had driven alongside her had been dark and boxy, like a Land Rover—like the one Norine drove.

She thought about the two little girls in their car seats and gripped the wheel tightly, shuddering.

"Did you tell anybody we were going to that Christmas party?" Jackie asked Carly when she delivered the sleepy children back to their home. "Try to remember, Carly. Who knew we were going to be there?"

Carly looked up, distracted by Rachel who was displaying her box of modeling clay and talking loudly. "Why?" she asked. "Is something the matter?"

Jackie considered, wondering how much to say.

She hated to frighten the woman even more. But the attempt to force her off the road had been so deliberate, and she'd been driving Carly's van.

With a couple of kids in the back seat...

"Try to remember, Carly," she said. "Who knew about the party?"

"Well..." Carly frowned, kneeling to remove Emily's hat and smooth her cap of brown hair. "I told Lavonne yesterday, and Gladys Wahl when she called this morning to ask how we were doing. And of course Mr. Burkett was here when you came to pick up the girls."

"That's true," Jackie said thoughtfully. "He was here the whole time, wasn't he?"

Carly nodded and bent to pick up the children's coats, hats and mittens, holding them in her arms while she concentrated.

"And Mr. Burkett called his wife while he was here because he had to check with her about a package he was expecting, and he told her, too. They've always been fond of the girls."

Jackie nodded, considering. By now her panic had subsided. She was even beginning to wonder if she might have jumped to the conclusion that the other vehicle had deliberately tried to push her off the road. It *could* have been somebody driving too carelessly for the conditions, having trouble staying in control on the snow and ice.

If she'd been in one of the police cars, she'd have been annoyed, but certainly not terrified by the incident.

What upset her was that she'd been in Carly's van. It seemed incredible that anybody would deliberately threaten the lives of little children, but if Carly was telling the truth, it wouldn't be the first time these children had been targeted.

With sudden decision, Jackie opened her shoulder bag, took out her cell phone and dialed Adrienne's number.

"Hi," she said when her friend answered. "It's me. I need a favor, Rennie."

"For you, sweetie, I'd do anything," Adrienne said cheerfully. "God knows, you don't often ask me for favors."

"I have a little family here, a mother and four kids. The oldest is eight, and the youngest is a baby about five months old. I need a safe place for them to stay the next few days."

Carly turned to watch, clearly startled, her eyes wide with panic.

"Bring them over," Adrienne said without hesitation. "I need some practice looking after babies."

Jackie twisted the cord around her fingers, reluctant now that Adrienne had agreed so promptly.

"They've been the target of some pretty ugly stuff," she said at last. "I could be putting you in danger, Rennie. I'm not sure if..."

"Give me a break," Adrienne interrupted. "This place has a security system like a fortress. And the neighborhood committee hired a security guard a few months ago. He patrols all night."

Jackie didn't answer immediately. She wondered whether any of the local shelters had room for a mother and four children. They were always more crowded at Christmas—

"Harlan says to bring them right over," Adrienne said after a muffled conversation. "And do it right now!"

"Thanks, Rennie," Jackie smiled gratefully into the phone. "You're both terrific!"

"Of course we are," Adrienne said placidly. "When are you coming?"

"Right away." Jackie ignored Carly who was waving her hands in protest. "We'll be there as soon as we can get the kids dressed and pack some clothes for them. The oldest girl is at a friend's house but I'm going to go over and pick her up after I drop the rest of them off at your place. We'll probably be there in about an hour, okay?"

"Okay. I'd better go hunt up some bedding. See you soon."

Adrienne hung up. Jackie turned to face Carly, who watched her in silence.

"Somebody tried to force us off the road tonight after we dropped Caitlin at her friend's house," Jackie said quietly. "I'm pretty sure it was deliberate, Carly. I don't think you and the kids are safe."

Carly's freckled face drained of color. "Somebody tried to…"

"We could all have been killed. And I was driving your vehicle."

"But couldn't it…" Carly faltered across the room and sank onto the couch, covering her face with her hands. After a moment she looked up, her lips trembling. "It might have been just an accident," she whispered.

"Sure, I guess it could have been," Jackie said. "But coupled with all the other stuff that's happened, I don't think we can take the chance. I'd like to have all of you somewhere safe until we…"

Until we can find your goddamn husband, she wanted to say.

But there was no need. To her surprise Carly nodded agreement and got up without further argument, moving unsteadily toward the door.

"I'll pack some things," she said. "And you'll..." She looked at Jackie with naked appeal. "You said you'd get Caitlin and bring her to me?"

"I'll get her," Jackie promised. "As soon as you and the other kids are settled at Adrienne's house, I'll go back over and pick her up."

Carly hesitated in the doorway as if about to say something more. Then she nodded jerkily and vanished into the hall.

Once again Caitlin sat in the passenger seat, holding her new wood-carving set in her lap. But this time they were riding in Jackie's unmarked police sedan, heading south across the city. The little girl stared straight ahead, looking grim.

"I'm sorry to ruin your birthday party," Jackie ventured, glancing over at her. "But your mother wants you to be with her."

"That's okay. It was a dumb party, anyway," Caitlin said. "They were just talking about boys all the time."

"Eight-year-olds?" Jackie asked. "Isn't that a little young to be thinking about boys?"

"They're all crazy," her companion said scornfully. "They like to do their hair and pretend they're dating." She tossed Jackie a withering glance. "Most of them are on *diets*."

"Well, you're right," Jackie said. "That's just crazy." She smiled at the child. "How about you, Cait? What's your idea of fun?"

"I like to play baseball and collect bugs."

Jackie nodded. "That's pretty much the same kind of little girl I was."

"I have seventy-nine different bugs on a chart at home," Caitlin said eagerly, her reserve vanishing. "Daddy helped me catch them, then look them up and find out the names of every one of them. I won first prize at the science fair."

Jackie was spared the need to reply because they arrived and parked at Adrienne's home in the south end of the city. Caitlin peered out at the architectural angles and banks of sloped windows, the lavish display of Christmas lights on the snow-covered shrubbery.

"Are these people really rich?" she asked.

"They're comfortable," Jackie said. "And they're very nice. You kids will love having a little holiday here."

Caitlin made no move to get out of the car. She looked over at Jackie, her eyes gleaming in the darkness, then turned away. "Mom cries at night," she said. "All the time."

Jackie gripped the wheel, flicking nervously with her thumb at a bit of torn rubber. "This is hard on your mother," she said.

"Mom's really scared," the girl went on, surprising Jackie. "She acts like somebody's going to hurt us if we go out of her sight."

"I think she just needs a little rest," Jackie said cautiously. "It's not easy for your mom when...when your dad's away like this."

Caitlin seemed on the verge of replying, then looked at the police radio. "Does that thing work?" she asked.

Jackie demonstrated the function of the radio, wondering with a rueful smile if she'd just been skillfully deflected from the previous topic of conversation.

Finally she got out and helped Caitlin to carry her backpack and other supplies into the house.

The Calder family and their new house guests were all downstairs in the big comfortable family room near the decorated Christmas tree. Alex sat cross-legged on the floor next to the fireplace, accompanied by the twins. The three of them were playing noisily with the new packages of modeling clay, making a whole menagerie of chunky, whimsical animals.

Harlan lounged in a leather recliner with Patrick in his arms, feeding the baby a bottle. Both of them seemed blissfully content. Adrienne and Carly were curled up on the couch eating popcorn and talking in low tones. They appeared to be discussing the care of babies and small children. Carly looked relaxed, and prettier than Jackie had ever seen her.

Adrienne got up and crossed the room to take Caitlin's jacket, then bent gracefully to hug the little girl. Jackie felt her heart warm with affection for her friend.

"I'm so glad to meet you, Caitlin," Adrienne said gravely. "This party just wasn't complete without you."

Caitlin smiled, showing a couple of missing teeth, and crossed the room to climb onto the couch next to her mother, displaying the wood-carving set and talking about the birthday party. Carly cuddled her eldest child, smoothed her ponytails and dropped a kiss on the top of her head.

Adrienne squeezed Jackie's arm. "Come upstairs for a minute," she whispered.

Jackie hesitated. "Rennie, I need to get back to the

substation. I've been away all afternoon, and there's probably a ton of stuff to catch up on."

But Adrienne was already dragging her up the stairs. "This will only take a minute." She paused by the carved oak armoire in the upper foyer, rummaging in one of the drawers. "I know I put it in here somewhere."

Jackie watched curiously. "What are you looking for?"

"Here it is." Adrienne took out a piece of paper on which she'd jotted something.

Jackie accepted it and looked at the address written in Adrienne's bold, sloping hand. It appeared to be a downtown location, perhaps a store or office building. She gave her friend an inquiring glance.

"You've been asking me all these questions about Norine Burkett," Adrienne said, lowering her voice and drawing Jackie into the kitchen when they heard a burst of childish laughter from below.

Jackie felt a quickening of interest. "Yes," she said. "I know I have."

"Well, I told you, she's always been pretty much a mystery to her friends, too. But Buffy Grange told me her cleaner told her something about Norine that none of us ever knew."

"Which is?"

"Buffy's cleaner also does office buildings downtown in the evenings with her husband. Apparently they're working hard to earn the down payment on a house. She says they clean an office-supply place weekday evenings, and three times a week—Mondays, Wednesdays and Fridays—she sees Norine Burkett go into that address." Adrienne indicated the paper in Jackie's hand. "Always exactly at seven o'clock."

Jackie stared at her friend. "What kind of place is it?"

"It's a big professional building down on Lincoln, called Washington Center."

"I think I know the building. Five or six floors of doctors, lawyers and stockbrokers?"

"That's right."

Jackie leaned against the table, looking from the address to Adrienne's finely drawn features. "So what do you think, Rennie?" she asked. "Is the woman seeing a shrink? Has she got a boyfriend?"

Adrienne shrugged. "With Norine Burkett, who knows? Whatever she's doing, I can tell you it's a big secret. She never said a word about having a prior appointment when she signed on for our Monday-night committee. But I realize in hindsight that she took the first opportunity to get off that committee."

"I didn't think somebody like Norine could do anything in this town and not be noticed."

Adrienne grinned. "She certainly slipped through all our radar screens. I had no idea about this until Buffy told me. Buffy's cleaner says the woman always arrives dressed in jeans and a long coat, and runs into the building like she's being chased. The cleaner only knew it was Norine because she's had so many chances to watch for her."

Jackie looked at the address again, then checked her watch. "It's Friday night," she said. "I could get over there by eight o'clock. Do we know how long Norine stays in the building?"

Adrienne shook her head. "The cleaners have always finished and moved on to another building before she comes out.''

"Okay. I'm on my way."

"I wish I didn't have all this company," Adrienne complained. "I'd love to go along on stakeout with you."

Jackie gave her a brief hug. "You can't go on stakeout. You're a pregnant lady."

Adrienne chuckled and followed Jackie downstairs, where she said her farewells to the cozy group in the family room, then headed back out into the falling snow.

21

When Jackie arrived downtown in front of the Washington Center Professional Building, it was ten minutes after eight o'clock and most of the streets were deserted. A few cars huddled forlornly along the curbs with snow piling up around them and drifting across their hoods and fenders.

Jackie cruised up and down the block a few times, then ventured into some of the adjoining streets. She finally found the black Land Rover parked under a canopy next to a pizza restaurant a few blocks away, clearly intended to be unobtrusive.

Adrienne was right. Whatever Norine Burkett did in that downtown building three nights a week, she didn't want her actions observed by anybody.

When Jackie drove back toward the Washington Center and drifted along the one-way street, she suddenly noticed a familiar vehicle parked near the corner, almost obscured by the falling snow.

It was Karl Widmer's battered old Volkswagen. The journalist sprawled behind the wheel, his head resting against the closed window beside him.

Jackie parked well down the street, hesitated for a moment, then got out and locked her vehicle, pulled her coat collar up around her ears and settled the leather bag more firmly on her shoulder. She walked up the sidewalk and knocked sharply on Widmer's front passenger window.

The driver glanced up, startled. He hesitated, then leaned over and flipped the door open.

Jackie climbed into the smoky interior and settled next to him, glancing at his craggy face in the haloed glow of the streetlight.

"Did you bring coffee and doughnuts?" he asked.

"Was I supposed to?"

Widmer grinned, his teeth flashing white in the shadows. "I thought that's what cops always do on stakeout. They bring each other coffee and doughnuts."

"You're not a cop," Jackie said curtly. "In fact, what are you doing here, Widmer?"

"Same thing as you." He stretched his arm out along the seat back to grip her shoulder. "You're just a few steps behind me, that's all. As usual, I might add, Detective."

She shook his hand off in annoyance.

The silence deepened. Widmer examined his left hand and picked at a bit of loose skin by his thumbnail, smiling placidly.

"Oh, for God's sake," Jackie said at last, making him chuckle.

She resisted the urge to punch him. Instead, she took out her notebook and flipped it open.

"How did you find out about this place, Widmer?"

He cocked an eyebrow when he saw the notebook, but answered her question obediently.

"I've been following Lady Norine for days. I realized she was coming here to the building, but couldn't find out which office she visited. The doorman won't ever let me in to roam around and listen at doors.''

"So this morning you decided to ask her outright instead of just stalking her?"

For the first time he looked unsettled. "How did you know that?"

"You're not the only one who can follow people. I know that you met with Norine Burkett this morning at the Cavanaugh and had a twenty-five-minute discussion."

Widmer raised both eyebrows this time and gave her a look of grudging admiration. "Very good, Jackie. So if you wanted to know what that conversation was about, why didn't you just call and ask me?"

"Because I'm still not sure what the hell you're up to."

"I'm a journalist doing an investigation. I think there's a whole lot of mystery surrounding Jason and Norine Burkett, including the death of their kid and the disappearance of this bookkeeper. And I think Norine is the key to everything, but nobody can get a word out of either of the Burketts."

"Did you learn anything when you talked to her?"

"Did you?" he asked.

"Widmer, don't you remember? She told me to go fuck myself."

He threw back his head and laughed heartily. "Well, she told me pretty much the same thing, but with some added threats."

"Threats?"

Widmer shrugged. "You know, just the usual stuff. If I didn't leave her alone, she had enough power to make sure my newspaper sank without a trace and I'd never work in this town again. That kind of thing. Very boring and predictable.''

"Nice girl, our little Norine," Jackie murmured. "Why did she ever agree to meet with you in the first place?"

"I told her I had something incriminating that she might want to take a look at before I released it to the public."

"Did you?" Jackie asked.

He shrugged. "Nothing definite enough to show her at this point. And it didn't take her long to realize I was bluffing. But the woman's scared of something, I can tell you that."

Jackie shifted awkwardly in the passenger seat, feeling light-headed and a little sick. "God, I hate cigarette smoke," she said abruptly. "This car stinks, Widmer."

"Sorry," he said without contrition. "My only bad habit."

A tall, broad-shouldered man stepped out of a convenience store a few doors down the street, carrying a sack of groceries, and strode toward them through the wash of snowy light. He wore jeans and a windbreaker, and his smooth blond head was bare.

Jackie bent forward to stare at the man, her heart pounding. She felt a visceral surge of excitement, and a fierce hunger that made her throat tighten and her mouth go dry.

She was about to open the window frantically and call to him when he drew abreast of the car and she saw it wasn't Paul.

Not even close.

This was a stranger, a man with a wispy blond mustache, pitted skin and a blank, preoccupied look.

Jackie fell back against the seat and closed her eyes, gripping her hands tightly in her lap.

When she looked up, Widmer was watching her in thoughtful concern. "Is something the matter, Jackie?" he asked.

She shook her head, feeling foolish and miserable. "That blond man just…he reminded me of somebody, that's all."

"Who? Let me guess. The lucky farmer you're going to marry?"

"We're not getting married," she said, trying to sound emotionless. "As a matter of fact, we're not even together anymore."

He continued to watch her with that look of maddening sympathy.

"I think you—"

"I don't care what you think." Jackie tugged restlessly on the door handle. "Why are we sitting in this smelly car, anyway? What good will it do us when she comes out? We can hardly follow her and force her to tell us what she was doing in there."

Over Widmer's protests she opened the car door and climbed onto the sidewalk, breathing deeply of the chilly air.

He got out, locked the car and came around to join her. They stood side by side looking up at the building, where lights glimmered from banks of windows on upper floors.

Widmer waved a hand at the glass-fronted lobby. "After hours you have to be buzzed upstairs by somebody in one of the professional offices," he said. "I've tried to pretend I have an appointment, but it doesn't work."

"Is there a security guard?"

"Oh yes. He's a straight-arrow college kid, looks like Howdy Doody, takes his job very seriously. You couldn't get past that kid with a handheld nuclear weapon."

"Or a press card?" Jackie asked, briefly amused.

"Especially not a press card."

She smiled, beginning to recover from the shock of seeing the man who'd reminded her of Paul. But somewhere at her core there was an aching sorrow that she would soon have to confront.

Pushing open the lobby doors with Widmer close behind her, Jackie approached the glass security booth where a young man sat behind a desk, poring over a mathematics textbook.

Widmer was right in his appraisal, Jackie thought. The boy had freckles, large ears and ingenuous blue eyes. He looked clean-cut, serious about his work and totally emotionless.

"Hi," Jackie said through the grill, displaying her badge in its leather folder. "Detective Kaminsky, Spokane P.D."

The boy examined her credentials gravely, as if questioning their authenticity, then nodded. "What can I do for you, Detective?"

"A lady came in here a while ago," Jackie said, pretending to consult her notebook. "Small and attractive, blond lady probably wearing jeans and a long topcoat. I need to know what office she's visiting."

The boy pulled a logbook toward him and riffled through its pages, then peered up at Jackie again. "I'm only supposed to interrupt people in the case of emergencies."

"This is an emergency," she said, conscious of

Widmer standing tensely behind her. "It's related to her family. I can't tell you any more than that."

The boy nodded reluctantly. "That would be one of the rooms in the professional suite on the second floor to the left of the elevator. I'm not sure which number, but there aren't too many people up there tonight. You should be able to find her."

"Thank you very much," Jackie said, smiling politely at the young security guard.

She turned away with Widmer at her heels and waited for the guard to buzz them through the glass doors to the inner lobby.

The journalist held her elbow as they entered, and murmured admiringly in her ear. "Very impressive, Detective."

His breath was warm on her cheek and smelled of mint and tobacco. She pulled away.

"It's my job," she said.

They rode the elevator in silence to the second floor, then paused next to a service alcove containing ice and soft-drink machines while they took stock of the situation.

"So, what time does she usually come out?" Jackie asked.

"Never before nine."

She glanced at her watch. "Damn, that means we've got almost half an hour to cool our heels."

"Are you planning to confront her, Jackie?" Widmer asked. "Jesus," he added softly, staring at her in astonishment.

She was making automatic adjustments to her equipment, unfastening the flap on her holster and checking the gun handle, touching the handcuff pouch at her waist.

Jackie glanced up at him, then shook her head. "Just a habit," she said. "I like to make sure everything's in order."

"But you're not going into any of these rooms, are you?"

"Why would I? There's never any need to force a confrontation when ordinary investigative procedures will work just as well. We'll find out which room she comes out of and then go and check it after the fact without being conspicuous."

"I see. But what if—"

A door opened down the hall, and somebody came hurrying toward them. Jackie caught a flash of blond hair, a long black woolen coat and sneakers.

She knelt hastily by the ice machine, bent so low that only her back was visible, and pretended to be pounding in frustration at the delivery chute.

Widmer took the hint at once and crouched close beside her, also pounding at the machine.

Norine Burkett passed them without a second glance and disappeared into the elevator, leaving a scent of gardenias hanging on the air.

The detective and the journalist stood erect after she was gone.

"High five, Kaminsky," he said gravely.

Jackie hesitated, then slapped his upraised hand. "Room 267." She peered down the hall at an oak door set with tasteful brass numbers. "At least I think so."

"I agree," Widmer said. "Now what do we do, Detective?"

She punched his arm lightly. "Hey, for such an arrogant dude, you've become awfully docile and obedient all of a sudden."

Widmer gave her a wolfish grin. "There's nothing more fun than watching a powerful woman in action. It's a real turn-on."

Jackie started down the hall to room 267. For a moment she hesitated outside, wondering what line to take, and decided the best approach was to improvise, suiting her story to the person who answered the door.

At last she took a deep breath, touched the handle of her gun again and knocked. But she could hardly have imagined the person behind the door.

It was a woman perhaps in her seventies, but small, thin and erect, wearing a designer suit with a long tweed skirt and a soft blouse with lace at the collar. Her hair was dyed black and pulled back from a face that still exhibited wonderful bone structure. Gold hoops bobbed in her ears.

She gazed up at Jackie, her shrewd gray eyes set in a nest of wrinkles.

"Yes?" she said with some kind of soft European accent. "May I help you?"

Jackie and her companion stared at the woman in silence, then exchanged a nervous glance.

"Come, come." The elderly woman drew them inside and closed the door. "Don't be shy. There is nothing at all to be embarrassed about. My name is Madame Tassin."

"I'm Jackie. And this...this is Karl."

"Welcome to both of you, Jackie and Karl."

They were in an office decorated like a living room, with all kinds of expensive knickknacks, embroidered cushions, Turkish carpets and brassware. A business-like wooden desk in one corner, flanked by a tall steel file cabinet, seemed out of place in these surroundings.

Madame Tassin was obviously some kind of psychic, Jackie decided. The room had that look, and so did Madame Tassin.

"So, you are married?" the woman asked, gesturing for them to be seated on the couch while she brought them cups of fragrant dark coffee from a silver samovar on a low table nearby.

Jackie and Widmer exchanged another quick glance. "Not yet," Jackie said, improvising cautiously. "But we'll be...probably getting married soon."

Widmer moved beside her on the couch and she gave him a warning touch with her leg.

"And you need my help?" The woman studied Jackie for a long moment, then turned to Widmer. "Please, Karl, tell me something about yourself."

"What?" he asked.

Despite the bizarre situation, Jackie found herself secretly enjoying his discomfort. The journalist, usually so suave and sardonic, seemed to be on shaky ground here.

"Anything." Their elegant little host perched herself on an antique upholstered chair and spread her skirt so it fell gracefully around her. She folded her hands in her lap and waited impassively.

"Well..." Widmer exchanged a nervous glance with Jackie, who looked back at him without expression. "I grew up in Fullerton, California, graduated from university in Los Angeles and then decided I wanted to travel a bit, so I—"

"And what are you doing now?" Madame Tassin interrupted.

"I own a share in a business," Widmer said, beginning to recover his equilibrium. "I'm working in the print media."

"And you plan to rise in your business, do you not? You are ambitious."

"Sure I am," the journalist said, and Jackie realized he was speaking the truth. "I want to go as far as I can. In fact, I—"

"Yes, just as I thought." The woman waved her hand, cutting him off, and turned back to Jackie.

"So, Jackie," she said, smiling, "you are the one who needs my help, no?"

"Me?" Jackie said, startled, then nodded. "Yes," she murmured, looking down at her hands. "I guess so."

"Your new husband will be moving in circles of power," the woman said, watching her gravely. "Karl is handsome and well-educated, and he has important goals in life. You will be meeting many people who intimidate you, and you must learn to mingle and talk easily with all of them for the sake of your husband's career. No?"

No! Jackie wanted to shout.

She was finally getting a glimpse of what Madame Tassin did for a living, and it intrigued her. Especially when she thought about the woman's previous client. Norine Burkett.

22

The room was so still that Jackie could hear the ticking of an antique clock above the gas fireplace. She looked away from Madame Tassin, afraid those penetrating eyes could read the thoughts at the very center of her mind.

"Yes," she muttered at last, gazing down at her hands. "I guess I need your help."

"And your background is...California, I believe? One of the poorer areas of Los Angeles, perhaps?"

Jackie looked up again, startled. "How do you know that?"

Madame Tassin smiled. "I am very good at accents. And I can also tell a great deal by your bearing and manner. This is my job, Jackie," she added calmly. "I suspect that you had an impoverished upbringing, and that you know little about the arts and graces of life."

Jackie was surprised at her own outrage when she heard this cool appraisal, and at her urgent desire to get up and stalk from the room.

But that wasn't going to accomplish anything.

Instead she stared at her ringless hands again, gripped tightly together in her lap. "And you can help me?" she asked.

"Of course I can. It will take us some time, but

after a number of sessions you will be able to speak with confidence to anyone you might encounter through your husband's work. You will entertain gracefully, make elegant small talk and know more than the rudiments of art and culture. And," Madame Tassin added with a wintry smile, "you will lose that dreadful accent."

"Her accent sounds fine to me," Widmer said, speaking up for the first time.

Madame Tassin turned her calm gaze on him. "Your loyalty is quite admirable, Karl," she said. "But however attractive you may personally feel that she is, this woman will be a detriment to your career unless she learns some of the basic social graces. I have seen it happen many times."

Jackie put a hand on his sleeve, gripping his arm through the jacket. "How many sessions would I need?" she asked. "And how often would I have to come here?"

"That depends how much you wish to learn," the woman said. "I have clients who work with me as often as two or three times a week over a period of years."

"How much does it cost?" Widmer asked bluntly.

Madame Tassin looked pained and disapproving, as if talk of money was a social gaffe. "I can assure you," she said stiffly, "that I will give you more than adequate return on your investment."

"How much, Madame Tassin?" he said again. "What will you charge to turn my little street urchin into a great and gracious lady?"

There was a sharp edge to his words, but he softened them by putting his arm around Jackie to give her a warm cuddle.

"My usual fee is two hundred and fifty dollars an hour," Madame Tassin said. "But of course, if we should develop a long-term working relationship, those financial terms can be adjusted."

Jackie and her companion exchanged a brief, stunned glance.

"We'll have to talk about it," Widmer told the woman at last. "We're really interested, but you have to realize that's a pretty steep price, *madame,* no matter how good you are."

"As you wish. But you will go nowhere without help," she said, waving a hand toward Jackie as if she were an inferior object on display in a store. "Her accent and bearing are quite impossible. She needs a great deal of work."

Widmer got to his feet, pulling Jackie up with him. "That's funny," he said to the woman, gripping Jackie's arm so tightly that it hurt. "Because, you know, I think she's perfect just the way she is."

Jackie walked with him to the door. "Thank you for your time, *madame,*" she said with an apologetic smile. "We'll definitely be in touch."

"I will wait to hear from you." Madame Tassin moved toward them gracefully, handed Widmer a business card and followed them into the corridor.

She stood watching as they walked down the hall, then disappeared back inside her elegant office. They heard the soft click of the door just before they entered the elevator.

"My God," Widmer muttered. "Can you believe that, Jackie?"

She pushed the elevator button, saying nothing. In the lobby she hurried out past the young security guard into the falling snow, grateful for the fresh winter air.

They walked down the street together, still not speaking, and got into Widmer's car. While he switched the heater on to take the chill from the interior, Jackie stared through the glittering swirls of frost on the side window.

"Even if they've made some kind of financial arrangement," she said at last, "Norine Burkett has to be paying the woman a thousand dollars a week for her little sessions in culture and deportment. That's fifty grand a year."

"All so she can shed her past and become a great lady." He shook his head in disbelief. "Where do you suppose she comes from?"

"Who knows?" Jackie smiled bitterly. "Maybe she grew up right there in the 'hood. We might all have been neighbors."

"Wouldn't that be rich?" Widmer took a pack of cigarettes from his pocket and studied them longingly, then put them away again.

"Hell, I don't know where Norine Burkett comes from," Jackie said, "but I have a pretty good idea where she's going. I have a friend who knows her, and says Norine wants to get all the way to the White House."

"Well, she must want it pretty damn badly."

"Badly enough to cover up any little scandals in the family, that's for sure. No wonder they won't talk to the police about anything."

"So you think there's a scandal?" Widmer asked, giving her a keen glance.

Jackie sighed and rested her cheek against the window, enjoying the chill on her hot face.

"I don't know what to think. All I know is that they won't let us into their garage, and they refuse to talk to anybody about their little girl's death, that's all. If they'd been open and forthcoming with the police like normal parents, nobody would be giving any of this a second thought."

"Except that we have all these weird ties from the Burketts to their missing bookkeeper, and from him to this murdered woman, and from *her* back to the hit-and-run on their kid."

"I know." She stared at a blinking Santa in a store window across the street.

He cleared his throat awkwardly. "Jackie," he said.

"Yes?"

"Remember when I told you I didn't think you were cut out to be a farmer's wife?"

"Sure, I remember." Jackie scraped at the frost on the window, clearing a space so she could see the Christmas decoration more clearly.

"Well," Widmer said, stretching his legs in the cramped interior of the little car, "I've just changed my mind."

"You have?" She glared at him. "Because Madame Tassin thinks I'm not good enough to be a sophisticated career man's wife?"

"No. Because I saw the way you looked at that blond guy walking down the street a little while ago. You're really crazy about this man of yours, aren't you?"

Jackie exhaled deeply and continued to scrape at the window.

"Love like that only comes along once in a lifetime, Jackie," he said huskily. "It's a rare thing. You shouldn't throw it away when you've got it in your hands."

He was staring straight ahead, his hawklike profile sharply outlined in the darkness. Jackie remembered Michelson's story about the journalist's wife, and his devotion to her after her attack.

"I just..." She faltered, realizing with horror that if she said any more, she was going to burst into tears.

Abruptly, she gathered up her shoulder bag and notebook and opened the passenger door.

"I have to go home." Jackie climbed out onto the snow-covered sidewalk and held the door open to lean into the car. "Thanks for your help. Call me if you...if you hear anything else, okay?"

"Sure thing." He leaned forward to peer up at her. "Jackie?"

"Yes?" She paused, still gripping the door handle.

"I meant what I said to that woman. I think you're great just the way you are. A woman in a million."

On Saturday morning Jackie went to the office because she didn't want to be alone all day. Even her apartment, normally a cozy haven, seemed empty and cold.

The detective ranks and their superiors didn't normally work on weekends unless something out of the ordinary was happening. A few patrols were on duty, most of them already out in their vehicles cruising around the snow-covered city.

The squad room was deserted, a situation that Jackie usually enjoyed. She made a pot of coffee and sat down at her desk, staring at the file on her computer screen, but her mind kept wandering to other things.

Jackie wondered if Madame Tassin would drop some kind of hint about her late-night visitors to Norine Burkett, who was certainly no dummy. Jackie and Widmer had even used their own names, so if the woman mentioned them, Norine would know they were aware of her regular lessons in culture and deportment.

Obviously it was a part of her life that the politician's wife chose to keep hidden. So Jackie's knowledge of it could possibly be used as a pressure point, a way to make Norine talk to the police about her child's death, about John Stevenson's recent movements and the baffling series of links between him and his employer's family.

But using pressure on the woman definitely hadn't accomplished anything so far. Both Norine Burkett and her husband steadfastly refused to talk to the police about anything, and had issued a public statement saying that after the discovery of Darla Drake's body, they now considered their daughter's accidental death to be a closed issue.

Case closed.

Jackie grimaced at the sharp taste of the coffee and set her cup down, wondering if Wardlow had any tea stashed in his desk. But it seemed like too much effort to go and look.

Instead she sighed, frowning at the computer again, thinking about the baffling John Stevenson case. She wasn't happy with the way things were going.

She and Wardlow remained in charge of the Darla Drake homicide. Wardlow had been designated to coordinate the manhunt and work with the team of officers monitoring the tip files.

But even though it was their case, Jackie felt

strangely distant and uninvolved. She just couldn't get a handle on any of these people, not even Stevenson's wife, or the case history itself. Ever since Carly Stevenson had turned up in the detective squad room with her kids, Jackie had been floundering through quicksand, getting sucked deeper and deeper into personalities and irrelevancies.

There was none of the feeling that usually accompanied an investigation: the crisp methodical assembling of clues and facts, the slow development of a big picture and a working theory, and finally the visceral thrill of chase and capture.

That was how good police work felt. This was all just a confusing mess.

She got up restlessly, went into the little kitchen to throw her lukewarm coffee down the sink, and began to rummage through the cabinets.

A box of crackers, marked "Brenda" in felt pen, stood on one of the shelves. Jackie took the box down and helped herself absently, knowing she'd probably wind up eating all of them and have to replace the crackers before Monday.

She munched and swallowed without being conscious of the taste, still brooding.

A deliberate walkaway was the hardest kind of case to solve. The fact that their vanished man had apparently murdered Darla Drake a week after his disappearance didn't help at all, it only made the homicide equally difficult to work on. John Stevenson had now become a loose cannon, a kind of rogue animal operating outside all the normal means of interaction.

Crimes like this were usually solved either by eyewitnesses, or by numbers, those identifying strings of digits that trailed all people from birth until death.

But this man no longer had a home or work address, a license plate or a telephone number. Nobody had seen him come and go at Darla Drake's apartment, although he'd certainly left his fingerprints behind. Apparently there wasn't a living soul who knew where he was now, and strangers were unlikely to spot him because his appearance was so ordinary.

It was like chasing a goddamn shadow, Jackie thought bitterly.

Maybe someday in the future, if John Stevenson used a personal identification number somewhere to get a job or rent an apartment, it would ring a bell in some FBI computer and they'd be able to go and get him. But if the man had already managed to obtain some fake ID, he was gone forever.

Unless he erupted in another surge of violence and killed somebody else....

She took a fresh handful of crackers, munching gloomily.

People vanished all the time, thousands of them. The public would be stunned to know how many people just walked away from their jobs and families and were never seen again. Officially, after a certain time, they were labeled "Missing: Presumed Dead," and in seven years the life-insurance companies paid out on their policies.

But Jackie and other police officers knew the vast majority of these walkaways weren't dead at all. They were living somewhere, lost behind new identities, with a whole social structure built up around them as a barricade against the past.

In a case like John Stevenson's, they could only hope the criminal might be drawn back into his old orbit because of his children.

But they couldn't count on that in this case, Jackie thought, replacing the half-empty carton of crackers and shutting the cupboard door.

If anything, John Stevenson seemed more bent on harming his children than sneaking in to visit them and bring teddy bears.

She remembered the dark van so like Norine's that had tried to force her off the road. Feeling increasingly frustrated, she poured herself a glass of water and carried it back into the squad room, sat down at her desk and dialed Adrienne's number.

"Calder residence, good morning," Harlan said.

"Hi, Harlan, it's Jackie. I thought I'd better check and see how everybody's doing."

"Listen to this, Jackie." She heard him shift the phone away from his mouth, murmuring something. There was a brief silence, then a series of soft noises.

"Did you hear that?" he asked, coming back on the line.

"Sort of. What is it?"

"It's Patrick. I just changed him and gave him his bottle, and he's so contented now, he's making this funny little noise. It's kind of like singing, but with bubbles."

The dignified corporate lawyer sounded boyish and delighted. Jackie smiled, twisting the phone cord around her fingers. In the distance she could hear shouts of childish laughter and the sound of Alex's voice issuing some kind of instructions.

"So I gather things are going well over there," she said.

"Things are great. Don't worry about this group, Jackie. They can stay as long as they want."

"That's so good of you, Harlan," she said with warm sincerity. "All of you."

"We're practicing," he said. "Adrienne and I always wanted a houseful of kids, you know. We've been lonely for years. Now, thanks to you, we've got five in the house and another on the way."

"Hey, I'm only responsible for the five in the house. I had nothing to do with the one on the way."

Harlan chuckled, making her smile.

"Well," she said, "let me know if you need anything, okay?"

"Jackie..."

"Yes?"

"I never got a chance to talk to you privately about this whole situation. Are these little kids really in danger?"

She hesitated. "I made certain nobody followed me over there to your house, so I doubt that anybody even knows where they are."

"Who would have followed you? What's going on, Jackie?"

"I don't want to talk about it just yet. We should have it all resolved in a couple of days, Harlan. If not, I'll have to make some other arrangements for them. How's Carly?"

"She's looking a lot better this morning. Adrienne thinks the poor woman probably had her first good sleep in a long time last night."

Jackie thought about Carly's pale tense face and terrified manner. "I should have done something like this two weeks ago," she said.

"You can't look after everybody, Jackie. In your job, you deal with so much misery all the time, you'd get stretched way too thin if you kept getting personally involved.''

He was right, of course. Any police officer who didn't become somewhat hardened to the endless tide of misery he or she encountered on the job usually suffered from burnout and left the force within the first few years.

"Jackie?" Harlan said. "I think it's time to put this little fellow down for a nap. He's looking pretty sleepy.''

"Okay, thanks for everything. Tell Rennie I'm so grateful, and I'll be checking back with you later in the day.''

"Don't worry about us, everything's fine at this end.''

Jackie thanked him again, then hung up and stared at the fake Christmas tree with its dainty ornaments and strands of tinsel lifting in the warm air current. The tree looked forlorn, infinitely sad.

She thought about Paul out at the ranch, and the last thing he'd said to her.

"Goodbye, Jackie. Call me if you change your mind.''

Jackie shook her head, then buried her face on folded arms.

She wasn't going to be able to meet his demands and set a wedding date. The very idea terrified her, and fear made her angry and stubborn.

But neither was Paul going to back down and let Jackie take her time. He believed this pressure was in her best interest, and if she resisted, it was because she didn't truly love him.

They were at an impasse, and she knew it was going to break them apart.

She'd lost him.

But, with sad irony, Jackie was just beginning to realize how much she missed him, how deeply and completely she loved the man.

Widmer was right. Seeing that look-alike on the street last night had shaken her badly. Now she ached for his touch, but her longing wasn't just physical. With growing desperation, Jackie also missed their easy friendship, the long talks and laughter, the evening walks hand-in-hand on the prairie while they shared their dreams and memories...

Her cheeks burned with misery and her eyes stung, but she knew she wouldn't cry anymore. Tears were a luxury she could no longer allow herself.

You should have known you'd lose him, her grandmother whispered harshly. *You're not cut out to be somebody's wife, Jackie Kaminsky. You're too hard and selfish. And you don't know a single damn thing about looking after a man. You're so...*

"Shut up," she whispered into the warm cotton of her shirtsleeves. "Shut up, shut up!"

She lifted her head, rubbing at her eyes, and turned in response to a sound outside the building.

Somebody was hammering on the front door, beyond the receptionist's alcove. Ginny wasn't at her post on weekends, and the patrol officers came and went through the service door at the back.

Jackie ignored the pounding. There was a control box near the door containing a fixed line telephone where passersby could call in police emergencies and have their queries answered at the radio room in the downtown station. It wasn't her job to deal with public complaints, especially not when she was at the squad room after hours and wearing blue jeans.

The noise persisted for a while, then stopped.

Jackie returned her attention to the computer and the massive public tip file on John Stevenson. She picked up a pen and made some notes, concentrating especially on the instances where more than one person claimed to have seen Stevenson in the same place.

Wardlow and his team had been doggedly checking out every such situation, but none of them had yielded anything helpful.

Again a noise from outside the building penetrated her consciousness. Jackie got up and walked through the squad room to the entry foyer.

A man stood at the front door, his face visible through a square of steel-reinforced glass. He was pounding on the heavy door with violent determination.

Jackie unlocked the receptionist's cubicle, went over to Ginny's desk and spent a moment figuring out how to operate the intercom.

"What do you want?" she said.

The man jumped and glanced around wildly as her words boomed from a speaker above his head.

"I want to see Detective Jackie Kaminsky," he said, his voice crackling through the intercom. "It's really important."

Jackie peered at him again through the wire grid inside the glass. He was about thirty, wearing jeans and a heavy nylon windbreaker.

Actually, she thought, the man looked a little like John Stevenson. His hair was dark brown and he was a shorter, bulkier man, but he had that air of wholesomeness, the look of a solid suburban husband and father who spent his free time repairing tricycles in the garage.

Automatically she reached to unfasten the flap on her holster, then disarmed the alarm system, opened the front door and let him into the vestibule.

"I'm Jackie Kaminsky. You wanted to talk to me?" she asked.

"My name's Ken Dillard." The young man moved about awkwardly on the jute floor mat, stamping snow from his hiking boots.

"So what do you want, Ken?"

She watched him closely, noting the tension in his hands, now clenched into fists, and his nervous, evasive manner.

"I just went to see that guy down at the *Sentinel*," he said. "Karl Widmer. He said you were probably going to be at work this morning and I should come and talk to you. Nobody told me this place wasn't open on the weekend."

"Talk to me about what?" Jackie asked.

"I didn't tell Widmer anything about what I know. I only wanted to...I think the police should..."

Jackie looked the man over again, glanced through the door to the empty squad room behind her, then jerked her head in that direction.

"Come with me, Ken," she said. "We'll talk at my desk."

When he was settled opposite her, Jackie opened her notebook and reached for a pen.

"Now, what do you want to tell me?" she asked.

"I think..." He glanced up at her furtively and licked his lips. "I think I know where John Stevenson is."

23

Jackie gripped the pen tightly in her fingers and tried to look matter-of-fact, telling herself this might well be another of the useless tips they received every day.

But there had to be some reason Widmer had thought the man should be sent over to the substation on a Saturday morning.

"Let's start at the beginning," she said. "Tell me a bit about yourself."

"Like what?"

"Age, family, place of employment, that sort of thing."

Dillard relaxed a little, obviously relieved to be on more familiar territory.

"I'm thirty-two. I work as a welder at Midtown Farming Implements. I'm married with two kids and live not far from here, over by Corbin Park."

He gave his address and telephone number. Jackie made notes of all the information, then glanced up at her visitor.

Ken Dillard had a square, pleasant face, slightly marred by a scar on the left cheek that ran almost to the corner of his mouth. Probably the result of some childhood injury, she decided, because it looked as if it had healed a long time ago.

"So tell me what you know about John Stevenson," she said.

"John and I...we've been friends for years." He looked down at his hands. "We play on the same baseball team."

"What kind of team?"

"Just a bunch of guys who get together for fun. We're in a slow-pitch league in the Valley. We play about twenty games a season plus a couple of tournaments, usually bring our wives and kids along."

"And you and Stevenson have been on this team for a long time?"

Dillard cleared his throat and moved uneasily in the chair. "About six years, I guess. We sort of hit it off right away, and got to be really good friends. Most of the guys only see each other during the ball season, but John and I hang out quite a bit, and get together with our families sometimes for movies and cookouts, that kind of stuff."

She jotted notes in her book, then scanned through the computer program that contained the case file.

Carly had listed Ken Dillard's name among John's friends. Officer Pringle spoke with the man at his place of employment soon after they launched the investigation, but at that time Dillard said he didn't know anything about John Stevenson's disappearance, and hadn't seen his friend for several weeks.

"Nice guy, well-liked at work. Seemed a little tense, but maybe just doesn't like cops," Pringle had noted. "It's possible Dillard might be hiding something, but at this point we have no valid reason to press him for more information...."

Jackie felt a rising excitement but tried not to show it. Whatever information the man had, he was so nervous by now, she didn't want to spook him by appearing too eager.

"How old are your kids?" she asked.

"My boy's a little older than Caitlin, and my girl is the same age as the twins."

"I see. And your wife...she's also friends with Carly?"

"They get along okay. My wife's a more outgoing type, I guess you might say. Vivian teaches school and has her own friends, and she's always found Carly sort of shy and hard to get close to. But they like each other well enough."

"So when your families get together and do things socially, it's mostly because of the friendship between you and John?"

"I suppose it is. But the kids all have a lot of fun together, too."

"I see." Jackie looked up and met his eyes directly. "What makes you believe you know where he is, Ken?"

The young man flushed, making the thin white scar look even more prominent. "I didn't say I actually knew," he muttered. "I'm just...guessing. But I think I have a pretty good idea."

"So why haven't you come forward and told anybody about this before?"

His flush deepened. "I promised John I wouldn't tell anybody. But since there's been all this stuff in the news about the little Burkett girl being killed, and then...this other woman..."

He glanced up in naked appeal, then looked past her shoulder at the Christmas tree.

Jackie waited.

"I didn't know what to do," he said. "I really hate

to break a promise to a friend. And I still can't believe a guy like John is involved in any of this stuff. But if—'' He broke off abruptly.

"If he is, you don't want to shield him," Jackie said. "Because aiding and abetting a murderer is a pretty serious crime."

"I know," Dillard whispered, looking down at his hands again. He picked at a callus on one of his palms while Jackie watched. "I have a cabin up the river," he said at last. "A couple of months ago, after we closed up for the season, John asked me for the key."

"Where's this cabin?"

"North of the city on the Native reservation. My father got a ninety-year lease back in the fifties, and built a little fishing cabin. I inherited the lease nine years ago when my father died."

"And you only use this cabin in the summer?"

Dillard nodded. "Mostly. It's an isolated place, and fairly primitive. No indoor toilets, just a pump for drinking water and a little generator for electricity. It's not practical to use it during the winter. Except for a couple of snowmobile outings, we usually close the place up in October."

"So John Stevenson knows about this cabin?"

"Of course he does. We spend a lot of time there. John and I go fishing by ourselves for the weekend a couple of times a year, and we take the kids out there every summer for a family barbecue."

"And you gave him the key back in October?"

"Just before Halloween," Dillard said. "John told me he might...need to use the cabin sometime during the winter."

"Could you tell me the details of that conversation? Try hard to remember, Ken. Tell me everything both of you said.''

Dillard sprawled in the chair, passing a hand over his eyes.

"It was the weekend before Halloween. A really beautiful day. We took both families out to the cabin for a cleanup day and picnic. At the end of the day, the women and kids went home in one of the vehicles. John and I stayed to board up the windows and blow out the waterline, then followed them an hour or so later.''

He was silent, staring at the tree.

"And while you were there...?" Jackie prompted.

"John told me he was in trouble. He made me swear I wouldn't say a word about it to anybody.''

The man's expression was bleak. Jackie realized he felt this to be a betrayal of his friend, and the confession was causing him a great deal of pain.

"Did John say what kind of trouble he was in?''

Dillard shook his head. "He just said he might have to take off for a while and he didn't want Carly to know where he was.''

"But aren't he and Carly supposed to be such a close, loving couple? That's what everybody keeps telling me.''

"I know. And it's true. He wasn't making any sense. But when I asked about Carly, he grabbed my arm and shook me like a crazy man, and said he didn't want his wife to know anything about it. He made me swear on my kids' lives that I wouldn't tell Carly a thing about the cabin.''

"Sounds like he was pretty upset, all right,'' Jackie said carefully. "He must have been in some really big trouble.''

"He was frantic," Dillard said. "Totally freaked-out. I've never seen John act like that."

"What did you think was going on?" Jackie asked. "If you'd been friends for that long, you must have had some opinion."

He shrugged. "I guess I assumed they were having some troubles and John wanted to get away for a few days on his own. He's the kind of guy who couldn't stand any problems in his marriage, because family life is so important to him."

"Did you have any reason for suspecting they might be having marital difficulties?"

"None to speak of, but nobody's got a perfect marriage. Hell, even Vivian and I—" He broke off, looking uncomfortable.

"So you promised John you wouldn't tell anybody about the cabin," Jackie said, trying to get him talking again.

"Yes," he said grimly. "I promised. And I gave him the key. I said if anything happened, no matter what it was, I'd keep quiet."

"So what made you decide to talk now?" Jackie asked.

"I keep thinking about those two people being killed. First the little girl, then that woman in her condo. I haven't been able to sleep this past week. It's so hard to…" He ran a hand over his face, covering his eyes briefly again.

"Do you think your friend killed them?"

"I don't know what to think." Dillard glanced up, looking haggard. "I've sure never figured John Stevenson for a killer. What I'm really afraid of…"

"I think I know what you're afraid of," Jackie said quietly when he stopped. "You're worried that he's killed himself out there, and he's lying dead in your cabin. Aren't you?''

The young man nodded, tears glinting in his eyes. "Yeah," he muttered. "I guess that's what I'm mostly afraid of."

Jackie, too, was beginning to think this was a fairly strong possibility. She got to her feet and dropped a hand briefly on his shoulder. "Thanks for coming forward, Ken. I know it was hard for you."

"He's my friend. I didn't know what to do. And I...I couldn't stand to go out there myself. Just in case he's..." He trailed off.

"I don't suppose you have another key to the cabin?" she asked.

"No, but it's not hard to get in. I just have a shank padlock on the door, you could easily shoot it off. If he's inside, there's a slide bolt. We don't keep anything in the cabin that's valuable enough to worry about protecting."

"Can you give me exact instructions on how to get there?"

"It's best if I draw it on paper."

The man accepted a sheet from Jackie's notebook and drew a careful map showing the curve of the river through the Native reservation, the line of rural highway and a series of landmarks.

"You turn left at these three granaries, then keep heading south until you come to a big brick house with a private airplane hangar," he told her as he drew. "Turn right again and you'll find yourself on a gravel road running beside an old irrigation canal. Drive till you see a ranch gate with a set of buffalo horns..."

Jackie watched him carefully, memorizing the instructions.

"You're right," she commented when he was finished. "That looks to be a pretty isolated place. Can I get in there with a front-wheel-drive vehicle?"

"You should be able to. Most of the road gets plowed out every couple of days except for the last few hundred yards down the valley to the cabin. In the wintertime I usually leave my vehicle and walk in from the top."

"Okay. Thanks, Ken. We'll be in touch. I'll call you this evening for sure, after I've checked it out."

He stood up, looking alarmed. "You're not going down there by yourself, are you?"

Jackie gave him a thoughtful glance. "You just told me John Stevenson could never be a threat to anybody. You said he's the nicest guy in the world."

"I know I did, but with all this shit that's been happening...excuse me," he said automatically.

"You did the right thing, Ken," she told him. "Go home and enjoy your kids. Watch a football game. The police will look after this from now on."

"And you won't...hurt him?"

"Nobody will get hurt if we can help it."

Jackie escorted her visitor to the door, thinking about little Angela Burkett and Darla Drake, both of whom had already been hurt beyond repair.

And poor frightened Carly, with those sinister threats to her houseful of children...

She let Dillard out the front door and watched him trudge across the parking lot, shoulders slumped, hands thrust deep into his jacket pockets.

Then she went back inside and called Wardlow's number. There was no answer at his apartment so she tried his girlfriend's. Christine's twelve-year-old son answered the phone.

"Hi, Jackie," the boy said.

"Hi, kiddo. How are you? Having a good weekend?"

"Great," Gordie said. "Mom and Brian are out, but they let me have a couple of friends over this afternoon. We're making microwave popcorn." She could hear the muffled popping near the phone receiver, like a salvo of distant gunfire accompanied by boyish shouts.

"Sounds like fun," she said. "What are your mom and Brian doing?"

"Christmas shopping." Gordie lowered his voice. "Brian says I'm getting something awesome this year, but he won't tell me what it is."

"I think maybe I know what it is." Jackie smiled. "And Brian's right, it's totally awesome."

"Tell me!"

"And spoil the surprise? No way."

"You're no fun," Gordie complained. Jackie could hear him munching popcorn.

"So I'm told," she said dryly.

"If Brian calls here, what should I tell him? Is it something important?"

Jackie hesitated. "Tell him I'll probably check back with him around suppertime, okay?"

"Okay." Gordie hung up amid loud popping sounds.

Next she dialed the sergeant's home number and was told by a bored-sounding adolescent daughter that Michelson and his wife were attending a Christmas piano recital being given by a younger child.

This time Jackie didn't leave a message at all.

There was no need to bother anybody on a busy Saturday afternoon, she decided. For one thing, she had no idea at this point whether John Stevenson was actually holed up in Ken Dillard's cabin.

She drummed her fingers on the desktop, thinking. Maybe she could log on for some overtime, though Michelson would take a dim view of that, and drive a police car out to the cabin. That would allow her to maintain radio contact.

But she had no jurisdiction beyond the city, and she was reluctant to jump through all the bureaucratic hoops necessary to liaise with the adjoining county on an official police basis, especially for a nebulous case like this. It was a whole lot of trouble, just to be able to take a car out of the city.

The best course of action, Jackie decided, would be for her to drive out along the river in her own car and have a look at the place without making any attempt to go in.

If she saw any signs of life, like footprints in the snow or smoke coming from the chimney, she could come back and contact Michelson. The squad would have an emergency meeting and work out an operation to storm the cabin and take Stevenson into custody without anybody getting hurt, and without ruffling any jurisdictional feathers either. At this point, she was only going for a drive in the country, nothing more. No criminal would be confronted, no police action engaged. If Stevenson appeared to be in residence, she'd come back and get Michelson to liaise with the neighboring counties for a joint sweep. And if it turned out to be an unused cabin, she wouldn't wind up with egg all over her face in three jurisdictions.

Feeling better now that she had a plan, Jackie rummaged in her shoulder bag for her keys, let herself out of the substation and hurried across the parking lot to her car.

In spite of Ken Dillard's description, she was a little surprised to realize just how isolated his cabin was. After the three granaries, the irrigation canal and the buffalo horns, and almost an hour of driving, she found herself in open country a lot more rugged than the prairie around Paul's ranch.

Steep brush-filled coulees bisected the land and ran down toward the river valley. Massive boulders lay everywhere, evidence of long-ago volcanic activity. The road was fairly passable as Dillard had predicted, though she encountered places where drifts had blown across and formed hard, sculpted barriers.

Her little car floundered and got high-centered a few times, even with good winter tires, but wallowed through the drifts to open road again. Jackie gripped the wheel and frowned, thinking how much she'd hate to get stuck out here and have to call for help.

At last she reached the point where a narrow road left the graveled highway and curved down toward the river, running along a ridge that dropped away sharply in front of her. Jackie turned onto the road, which was little more than a rutted track.

She parked before she reached the brow of the ridge, not wanting her car to be visible from below.

According to Dillard's instructions, the cabin lay just below that ridge, nestled in a grove of trees at the water's edge. It backed onto the cliff behind it and had a wide veranda overlooking the water.

She walked through the snow to the edge of the

cliff and peered over, but could see nothing except a cluster of leafless trees, a few evergreens and the corner of a weathered roof. The road down to the cabin was solidly drifted in and hadn't been traveled since the last snowstorm.

"Well, dammit," Jackie muttered, hunching her shoulders against the chill of the wind. "I can't tell a thing from here."

She went back to her car, put on a pair of fur-lined gloves and tucked her jeans into her boots. Then she dragged a set of binoculars from under the passenger seat, the same ones that she and Paul sometimes used to watch the golden eagles that soared above his fields.

Jackie locked the car and set out to make her way into the brush-filled coulee behind the cabin. She climbed down slowly, grateful for the heavy crust, hardened by winds the previous night, that allowed her to stay on top of the snow without breaking through.

If this had been a fresh snowfall, she'd probably be floundering up to her waist.

Buck brush tore at her jeans and jacket sleeves, and a couple of magpies fluttered away in alarm from the naked branches of a cottonwood as she passed beneath them. Except for their raucous cries, the winter air was utterly silent. Clouds had begun to mass overhead, obscuring the deep blue of the sky, and a few snowflakes hissed against her face. The wind picked up again, threatening a storm.

She reached the edge of the coulee just above the cabin, and settled behind a screen of branches to look down. The cabin was fifty yards away, a rustic log building about thirty feet square with a shelter at the back covering piles of cut logs. Another open-sided lean-to at one side housed a shiny black snowmobile. There was no sign of any other vehicle.

Nothing else was visible of the cabin except for a small window at the back. Even when she trained her binoculars on it, the black square was impenetrable.

A couple of wooden slabs leaned against the cabin beneath the window. Jackie frowned at them, remembering Dillard telling her they'd come out in the fall to board up the windows.

Suddenly a shadow passed before the window. Jackie leaned forward, trying frantically to adjust the binoculars for a better look, and felt the snow suddenly give way underfoot, carrying her along in a small avalanche.

Swearing in alarm, she skidded out of the brush and into full view of the cabin, holding the binoculars aloft to keep from dropping them. A man's face appeared briefly in the window of the cabin and stared out at her, then vanished.

Jackie scrambled hastily back into her shelter of leafless branches, furious with herself for her lapse of concentration.

Whoever was inside the cabin had spotted her by now, and knew she'd come there deliberately to spy on him.

Furthermore, he had a snowmobile outside, parked and ready to go. He could head out along the frozen river under the cover of this snowfall and be long gone before she would have any chance to summon help.

There was no choice. Now that she'd been spotted, she had to go in.

24

Jackie huddled briefly in her screen of brush, watching the cabin while she planned her strategy. Then she ducked low and edged along the ravine until she was opposite the corner of the building and could see the whole outline of the snowmobile. She noted with satisfaction that the vehicle's rough shelter also covered the window on that side.

She hung her binoculars on a projecting branch, took out her gun and released the safety catch, then studied the mantle of snow between herself and the cabin, trying to spot any potential weak spots in the crusted expanse.

She couldn't afford to stumble and flounder again...

At last she took a deep breath, burst from the sheltering trees and approached the cabin in a running crouch, holding her gun in front of her. The snow crunched underfoot and dipped alarmingly in a couple of places but didn't give way. She reached the rough log wall of the building and moved into the shadows next to the snowmobile, breathing raggedly.

Now she was invisible from within the cabin and also had the snowmobile in her sights so nobody could rush her and get away. She moved along next to the vehicle, looking for a key.

Damn, she thought, staring at the empty ignition. *So much for that idea.*

Briefly she considered disabling the machine, then abandoned the idea. She was already out of her jurisdiction here, and it was possible that the man in the cabin was an innocent civilian. Michelson would be deeply unimpressed if Jackie was tagged for wanton destruction of private property.

Edging past the snowmobile, she slipped to the front corner of the cabin, and peered around it onto the veranda, empty except for a stack of firewood and an ax. A single front window overlooked the valley where a path had been cleared down to the riverside. A few ragged holes were chopped into the river ice.

Somebody's been doing some ice fishing, she thought. And fairly recently, too.

The cabin door was tightly closed, with no evidence of the padlock Dillard had described. That meant it was probably locked from within.

A slide bolt, he'd told her.

She ducked back against the wall of the cabin, thinking.

Finally she leaned out again and shouted toward the front window.

"Police!" she said. "Open the door and come out with your hands up!"

The cabin remained silent, eerily withdrawn in the gathering storm. Snow drifted across the river and powdered the branches of the evergreens.

"Look, Stevenson," Jackie shouted, "we know you're in there. The place is surrounded. We have sharpshooters in the trees along the river. If you don't come out, we're going to lob some tear-gas canisters through the windows. You have no way of escape."

Her voice echoed faintly down the river valley, mocking her.

"Come out for Carly's sake, John," she called. "I just spoke to her this morning. She's frantic about you. Think of your wife and kids, John. Don't let anything more happen."

She peered around the corner. After what seemed an eternity, the front door opened a crack. Heart pounding noisily, she edged forward with her gun leveled.

"Who are you?" a voice demanded, sounding hoarse and frightened.

"I'm Jackie Kaminsky, a detective with the Spokane Police Department. I just want to talk to you, John. We have to figure out what's best for Carly and your kids."

There was a silence so intense that she fancied she could hear each snowflake hitting the ground next to her boots.

"Okay, you can come in," he said at last. "But nobody else, just you. Come inside here and close the door behind you."

He believed her, Jackie thought. The poor fool really thought there was an army hidden in the trees. By inviting her inside, he probably had the impression he was taking a hostage.

She wrestled with herself, picturing Michelson's cold fury if he knew she was actually thinking of entering that cabin alone and without backup to confront the man holed up inside.

But his voice through the crack of the door, though frightened, had sounded reasonably coherent.

Besides, what choice did she have? If she turned aside now, he'd recognize that she'd been bluffing about the other police officers. And as soon as she left the valley, he could still get away on that damn snowmobile, even on foot if he had to.

Taking another deep breath, she leaned out to address the closed door. "Open up and then stand well back, John. I'm coming in. Don't make any sudden moves, all right? Nobody wants to have any problems here. I only want to talk to you."

Silence from within the cabin.

"John?" she called again. "For Carly's sake, and your kids, please let me know you're not planning to do anything foolish. A whole lot of people with guns are watching this cabin right now."

The door creaked open a few inches, then widened. "Okay," he said in a muffled voice. "Come in."

She mounted the veranda, sprinted past the window and kicked the door all the way open, holding her gun in front of her with both hands. Inside the cabin she paused and looked around, blinking rapidly while her eyes adjusted to the dimmer light.

John Stevenson was backed against the stone fireplace, looking pale and terrified. When he saw the gun she held, his hands flew up automatically above his head.

Jackie's eyes darted around, taking in details. The cabin was composed of a large room with two smaller spaces, obviously sleeping quarters, opening off the main area. The furniture was handmade and rustic, consisting mostly of a slab table flanked by rough chairs and benches. A black woodstove filled one corner and an oil lamp flickered in the center of the table where a pile of books was stacked next to some writing paper.

She noticed a .22-caliber rifle hanging above the mantel of the fireplace. Stevenson had apparently made no effort to get it down.

Jackie kept her gun leveled on the man next to the hearth. "Are the bedrooms empty?" she asked, moving cautiously into the room.

He gulped and swallowed. "Yes. There's...nobody here but me."

She moved over to glance quickly into each room in turn. Clothes hung from pegs and the beds were built on platforms attached to the plank floor, with no place for anybody to hide.

At least, Jackie thought with relief, she only had one person to deal with. And he didn't seem to have much fight in him.

In fact, John Stevenson looked like a beaten man. He was thinner than she'd expected from the pictures Carly had given her, and his hair grew over his collar in unkempt strands. His face still had the square, boyish look she remembered from the photos, even more pronounced in person. But his hands were shaking badly and he seemed on the verge of tears.

"Now, don't get upset, John," Jackie said soothingly, knowing a badly spooked fugitive was the most dangerous kind. "Nothing's going to happen. Could you turn around slowly, please, and put both hands on the mantel?"

He obeyed with jerky, awkward movements. She moved toward him, keeping her gun trained on him, and reached out to pat him down lightly.

"Okay," she said. "Turn around and face me."

He wore jeans, hiking boots and several layers of

clothing. Under a plaid flannel jacket and a denim shirt, she saw the neckline of a white T-shirt that was badly in need of laundering.

But it probably wasn't easy to get clothes washed out here...

She locked the cuffs on his wrists, then gestured with her gun toward one of the chairs.

He stumbled to obey, then buried his face in his manacled hands.

Jackie pulled up another chair and sat facing him, keeping the gun leveled on him, though she was rapidly coming to believe it wasn't necessary. Especially since he still believed she had an army hidden out there in the trees.

"So what's been going on here, John?" she asked quietly.

He shook his head, still keeping his face covered. Greasy strands of blond hair fell down across his hands.

The man had been an accountant until his sudden disappearance, but he had a working man's hands now. They were covered with scabs and fresh cuts, just like Paul's but not nearly as clean.

"Have you been out here the whole time, John?" she asked. "Ever since Angela Burkett was killed?"

"Angela?" He jerked his head up and stared at her. "What did you say?"

Jackie watched him closely. "Angela Burkett was killed the same night you disappeared. You're telling me you don't know anything about it?"

"Killed? Jason Burkett's little girl?" He seemed dazed, and kept shaking his head. "I don't know what... How was she killed?"

"She was struck in a hit-and-run accident. Don't you have a radio or anything out here?"

Again he shook his head. "I brought one that I found in the basement at home, but the batteries were dead when I got here and I'd forgotten to bring extras."

The whole story seemed highly implausible. But if John Stevenson was lying, the man was one hell of an actor.

"Angela Burkett," he muttered, looking down at his cuffed hands. "She's...almost the same age as Cait." He looked up, blue eyes full of pain. "How are my kids? Are they okay?"

"As well as can be expected, I guess." Jackie continued to watch him, trying to get the feel of the man. "It's been a tough time for them, and for Carly. Having your husband and father drop off the face of the earth with no explanation at all...it can't be easy."

"I know," he whispered.

"And then all these threats to the kids," Jackie said deliberately. "That's been hell for Carly."

"Threats to the kids?" He jerked in the chair and started to get up. "Like what?"

"All kinds of things." Again Jackie watched him closely. "Attempted kidnapping, people trying to get into the house, an effort to force the van off the road while the twins were in it...not nice at all, John. I hope you can imagine how Carly's feeling."

"Oh, *God*." He slumped back into the chair, his shoulders quivering. Jackie was afraid he might be crying.

"They're all right," she said. "Nobody's been hurt, and I have them hidden away in a safe place right now."

"Thank you. Thank you so much, Detective."

Again she met those frank blue eyes, now glittering with unshed tears.

She sat for a moment, wondering what to ask him.

Questions about Darla Drake were better kept for the police-station interviews, after he'd been read his Miranda rights and there was a tape recorder in operation.

The door stood open behind her, and the air was getting frosty inside the cabin. Jackie got up, still holding her gun on John Stevenson, and backed up to close the door, fastening the slide bolt to keep it from swinging open again.

Then she returned to the chair, selecting her words carefully. "You don't have to talk to me, John. Anything you say to me can be used against you in court. Do you understand that?"

"Are you arresting me?" he asked, his voice dull.

"Not yet. I was hoping we could just have an informal little chat, but I still want to let you know the things you say could be self-incriminating."

"Nice of you to be concerned," he said bitterly, "but it's going to be pretty tough to incriminate myself any more than I already have."

"So you don't mind answering a few questions?"

"Hell, why not? You found me, didn't you? Now I'll have to go back and face the music. As long as you promise to keep Carly and the kids safe, I don't mind telling you everything I know."

Jackie was becoming increasingly puzzled by his words and manner. "Look, John," she said at last, "let's start at the beginning, okay?"

"Start wherever you want."

"Why did you leave Carly and the kids and disappear like that? She's been out of her mind with worry.''

He glanced up, clearly startled, then smiled. His face was pleasant and handsome when the miserable expression vanished even briefly.

''But that's not the beginning. That's the end of the story.''

''Okay.'' She leaned back, still holding the gun lightly in her right hand. ''Suppose you tell me from the beginning, John.''

He stared out the window at the frozen river.

''I've been working for Jason Burkett at White Wolf for more than six years,'' he began. ''I was the accountant for the holding company, looking after funds that flowed in through all the other businesses.''

Jackie knew all this, but she let him describe his job to her again because he was talking comfortably.

''I always got along pretty well with Jason, though he can be an arrogant bastard at times. Not the aw-shucks local boy that people see when he's out campaigning, you know?''

He cast Jackie an inquiring glance.

''That doesn't surprise me,'' she said quietly.

''A couple of years ago I started having some money troubles,'' Stevenson went on. ''Personal ones, I mean.'' He looked down again at his clenched hands.

''What kind of money troubles?''

''Things just kept piling up. It cost a lot when the twins were born. They were six weeks premature and had some breathing problems at first, and their hospital care was more than our insurance plan covered. We needed a whole lot more stuff to look after them at home, too, plus all those diapers and things...''

"I can imagine it would be pretty brutal," Jackie said. "Raising four kids must be a huge expense."

"And then Cait needed some work on her teeth because her baby teeth weren't dropping out on time and her permanent teeth were starting to come in crooked. I tried to get Burkett to give me a dental plan but he wouldn't. He said he didn't want to set that kind of precedent. When our mortgage came up for renewal and the payments went up, I had to borrow ten thousand dollars from a finance company, just so we could stay afloat. The interest rate was horrendous. Right away they started dunning me for repayment and I couldn't find the money."

Jackie frowned, wishing she had her notebook with her. "Carly told me that when you left, you cleaned out all their bank accounts. You took nine thousand dollars in savings."

"Carly said that?"

"She was desperate. She didn't even have enough money to buy milk for the kids. I had to loan her a few hundred dollars."

"Oh, God, *Carly*..."

He began to sob, with deep shudders that racked his body. Jackie watched impassively, then got up and walked over to investigate a chipped enamel pot of coffee sitting on the back of the big woodstove.

There were a couple of mismatched mugs on the counter, but no sign of cream or sugar. She filled both mugs and carried one to Stevenson, still holding the gun in her left hand.

He took the coffee in both hands and glanced up at her, sniffling. "Sorry," he muttered. "This is just so damn..."

"Take your time." Jackie went back to the counter

to get her cup of coffee. She sat in her chair again and sipped the hot liquid, finding it pleasantly bracing in the chill of the cabin.

"That money we had," he began after a brief silence, "our nine thousand in savings, it was like the Holy Grail to Carly. She grew up poor, you know, and it was her security blanket. Poor kid, she always thought nothing bad could happen to us as long as we had almost ten thousand dollars in the bank. If I'd used that money to pay our debts, she'd have been terrified. I had to think of something else."

"Oh, I see. Something really comforting, like clearing out the bank accounts altogether and dropping out of sight?"

He flinched and avoided her eyes.

"In the White Wolf books," he went on reluctantly, "there was a holding account, kind of a slush fund. It was mostly profits earned on interest, dividends and foreign exchange, things that weren't directly related to sales of products and services. I filed incidental revenues in that account, and Burkett used it for personal things like gifts and holidays. The account was very fluid. I managed it myself and nobody ever checked my figures, not even my assistant."

"So you lifted a few thousand dollars to help you out of your troubles?" Jackie suggested.

He nodded miserably. "I did it twice so I could get the finance company off my back. At the time... always...I was honestly planning to pay back what I'd taken."

"How?"

"My father's been promising me and my sister some revenues from the sale of the family business when he retires next spring. I thought if I could just hang on till then, everything would be all right and nobody would have to know what I'd done, especially Carly. I was treating it like a loan, you see, even keeping track so I could pay fair interest on the money. But Burkett went through the books, and he caught my little efforts at creative accounting.''

He fell silent, staring gloomily out the window.

"And then he fired you," Jackie prompted. "And you took off because you couldn't bear to tell Carly.''

Suddenly she remembered that Burkett hadn't mentioned anything about theft, or firing John Stevenson. He'd said the man was always an exemplary employee, and nobody had any idea why he'd suddenly left his job.

It just didn't add up.

Stevenson shook himself and looked at her with a mirthless smile. "Hell, no," he said. "Burkett didn't fire me when he saw what I'd done. He gave me a raise.''

"Huh?''

"Oh, it all came clear pretty soon. He wanted me to do some more serious fiddling of the books, but on his behalf this time. And he had me by the…you-know-what.''

"What did he want you to do?''

"He's had a whole lot of mostly illegal contributions to finance his run in the primaries next spring.''

"What the politicians keep referring to as 'soft money'?''

"I guess so. Jason's a corrupt bastard, and his rich friends are trying to help him get to Congress where he can start returning favors. He needed to have that money buried deep in the business so when he went into the congressional race next spring, it'd look like he was spending his own money.''

"He was asking you to launder money?''

Stevenson nodded miserably. ''More than a million dollars. It's listed as coming into the various businesses through false jobs and accounts. Then it moves through the White Wolf corporate-tax structure and winds up in Burkett's political war chest. The whole process is as illegal as hell.''

"It certainly is. But you did it for him?''

"I started to. I couldn't bear to have him tell Carly about what I'd done, and maybe even have me charged with theft.''

"But you had enough against him that if he turned you in, you could have hurt him pretty badly, too,'' Jackie suggested.

"I know. When that dawned on me, I went and told him he'd better let up on me. I wanted him to let me repay the money in small monthly sums, and stop making me do all the illegal cash entries or I'd quit. I told him I'd go to the police and make a clean breast of everything before I'd keep doing this.''

"And then?''

"Then he brought Darla Drake into it.'' Stevenson glanced up at her.

Jackie's pulse began to race. She sipped coffee and gave him an encouraging nod.

"Burkett gave me an address and told me to go over to this condo to pick up some money that was being held for the cabinetmaker—that's one of Wolf Enterprise's companies. When I went inside, a woman was there, a beautiful blonde in a silk housecoat. I asked for the money but she just laughed at me and kept me standing in the doorway like an idiot. Then she took off her clothes and started wrapping herself all over me. Next thing I knew, there was a guy with a camera who came in from the other room, taking pictures.''

"So it was all a setup?'' Jackie asked. "You didn't even know Darla Drake?''

"I'd never seen her before in my life. But,'' he added, "I certainly knew the name when I heard it. She's Burkett's girlfriend.''

"Burkett's *girlfriend?*'' Jackie stared at him.

"Sure,'' Stevenson said bitterly. "She has a credit card, and she likes to use it. I used to pay her bills through the slush-fund account.''

Jackie said nothing. Stevenson was deep into his story by now.

"They got the pictures developed and Burkett called me into his office. He said if I didn't keep fiddling the books, he was going to show Carly and tell her I'd been cheating on her.''

"Nice guy,'' Jackie commented. "A real sweetie, isn't he?''

Stevenson gave her a fleeting, humorless smile. "I told him he was making a big mistake, that Carly and I had such a strong marriage, blackmail would never work. I said if he showed her those pictures, I'd just tell her everything he'd been doing to me, and then we'd go to the police.''

"What happened next?''

"I quit. I packed up my stuff and walked out, but I still couldn't bring myself to tell Carly what was going on. She'd have been so upset. Besides, I knew that wasn't the end of it. I had to get away from him somehow. I was right. Burkett called me the next day and told me I had to come back to work. He said I couldn't stop laundering the money and I'd better not go to the police because..."

Jackie watched a nerve tensing at the edge of his jaw. "Why not, John? What did he say?"

"He said he was going to hurt my wife and kids."

"Jesus, this guy plays rough," she muttered. "He doesn't look like the type."

"I know, he looks like the boy next door. But he's a real snake, and so is his wife."

"You think she knew about all this?"

"Norine? It was probably her idea."

"She even knew about Darla Drake?"

"I don't know," Stevenson said wearily. "Probably not. But once she found out about Darla, she wouldn't mind using her if she thought it might help their political ambitions."

Jackie nodded thoughtfully. "So you were in a pretty tight box," she said.

"It was impossible. All I could do was disappear. I had to drop off the face of the earth, and make it look like I'd run away, so he'd leave Carly and the kids alone. If he had any suspicion I was in contact with them, he'd grab them and use them as pawns against me. They were in real danger."

Jackie's eyes widened in sudden understanding. "That's why you cleaned out the bank accounts," she said. "You had to make it look like you were really gone."

"I had to leave Carly in desperate straits so everybody would believe I'd really run away and wasn't coming back. Before I left, I spent a week or so coming out here and laying in some supplies because I didn't know how long it was going to take."

"For what?" Jackie asked.

"For Darla to do what she was planning."

25

"What was that?" Jackie watched him suspiciously. "I thought you didn't even know Darla Drake."

"I didn't, not before that thing with the pictures. But she called me after that and told me she wanted to talk."

"But you didn't have an affair?"

"An affair? With Darla?" He looked up, clearly astonished. "I've never touched any woman but Carly in my life. Darla and I have no relationship at all."

Jackie noticed that he referred to the woman in the present tense, but she made no comment. This, after all, was not an unusual behavior pattern from somebody who'd killed on impulse and remained in denial.

"Darla and I have only one thing in common, you see," Stevenson told her. "We're both being screwed around by Jason Burkett. So we met a few times to make a plan."

"And what was the plan?"

"She's furious because he's been promising for years to leave his wife and marry her, but he never does. She's planning to confront them at their home and tell Norine all about her love affair with Burkett. Darla's strategy is that forcing the issue will split up their marriage and make him turn to her."

"Pretty gutsy strategy," Jackie mused aloud. "But how would that help you?"

"The scandal would destroy his political career. And if he can't run for Congress, I won't be useful to him anymore so there'll be no reason to threaten my family."

"Why would Darla want a man who was threatening your family?" Jackie asked.

"She's just crazy about Jason Burkett. I think she's convinced a lot of this political ambition comes from Norine. Darla believes Jason would be completely different if he could get away from that woman."

"A light begins to dawn," Jackie said. "So you and Darla…"

She raised her head suddenly, straining to listen. "Did you hear something just now?"

"Like what?"

"I don't know. Some branches snapping, and I thought I heard a voice."

"It must be one of your people outside," he said.

"I guess so."

But Jackie knew there were no police outside, nothing but miles of snow-covered isolation. Again she heard a faint sound beyond the cabin, and hoped it was just the wind.

Or did Stevenson have some reinforcements of his own out there, a group of thugs about to storm the cabin and overpower her?

She shifted nervously in the chair and gripped her weapon.

"So I made a deal with Darla," he was saying. "I was planning to drop out of sight even before she went over to Burkett's house. I needed somebody to bring me out to the cabin, and it couldn't be any of my friends because I didn't want them involved. Darla agreed to drive me. It took some convincing because she hates taking that little sports car out in the winter.''

''So Darla met you at the mall on Monday night. You left your van in the parking lot and she took you out to the cabin.''

''No, I drove to the cabin. Darla rode along, dropped me off and took the car back to the city. She promised to come and tell me as soon as she'd had her confrontation with the Burketts.''

Jackie nodded thoughtfully. This version of events certainly explained his fingerprints in Darla Drake's car.

But not that sad, bloody corpse in the little-girl slippers...

''She left me at the top of the hill because she was afraid to drive the road into the valley. I hiked down to the cabin after Darla promised she'd be back as soon as she could, once Jason's marriage and political career was ruined and he had bigger things than me to worry about.''

''But she didn't come back?''

''I haven't seen her since. In fact, I haven't seen a living soul except for you,'' Stevenson said, trying to smile. ''And believe it or not, I was almost happy when I spotted you out there with your binoculars.''

''What mood was Darla in that night when she brought you out here?'' Jackie asked.

''She was pretty wild. I was afraid for her. She's scared of Burkett, you know, and terrified of his wife, but she really loves the guy. Darla was determined it was going to be the night for this big showdown with them. I've wondered ever since just what happened when she got there.''

She never got there, Jackie thought.

On her way to her lover's house, Darla Drake jumped a curb, killing Jason Burkett's only child, then ran home to hide.

And apparently she forgot all about the man holed up in a cabin on the river....

"John," she said bluntly, watching his reaction, "what would you say if I told you Darla Drake was murdered a few days after she left you here?''

"Murdered?'' he looked up, stunned. "You're kidding me, right?''

"She was killed in her own home. Her wrists were slashed, but it wasn't a suicide.''

"But that's...'' Stevenson shook his head, looking dazed. "Who did it? Was it Burkett?''

"We don't know who did it, John," she told him quietly. "But there were two whiskey glasses at the murder scene, both recently used, and your fingerprints were on one of them.''

"My *fingerprints?* I was never even at the woman's house!''

"You said you were there the day the photographs were taken.''

"But...I just stood in the doorway. This is all so crazy. Why would you...''

"The other times when you talked to her, you didn't go to her house?''

"Never!'' he said passionately. "She'd call and arrange to meet at restaurants and coffee shops.''

Jackie watched his face, trying to determine if he was telling the truth, or if he was the most convincing liar she'd ever encountered.

No matter how much Stevenson protested his innocence, Jackie trusted Claire Welsh and her Ident department. The fingerprint evidence against this man was impossible to refute.

Suddenly a noise blasted the stillness, so loud it felt like an explosion. Glass sprayed from the front window of the cabin, littering the floor, and metal slugs peppered like hail against the outside walls.

"Hit the floor!" Jackie shouted, diving onto the rough planks. "Hurry! Crawl toward the bedrooms!"

She fell to her stomach on the floor and backed up crabwise, urging Stevenson to follow her lead, then wondering why she bothered.

If people were firing on this cabin, they had to be friends of the man, bent on rescuing him. She'd been duped by his sincerity, and now she was trapped.

But Stevenson didn't give the impression of a man about to be rescued. He looked as terrified as she felt, lying beside her at the entrance to the bedrooms, staring up at the shattered window.

"Why are they firing?" he asked. "Did you give them some kind of signal?"

She looked at him in confusion. His face was white, and his eyes looked enormous, almost childlike. His mouth quivered with fear.

"Oh, John," she muttered. "Each of us thinks the other has an army out there in the trees. And I'm afraid we're both wrong. Probably dead wrong," she added grimly.

"What's happening?" he whispered.

She reached out to grip his shoulder with her free hand. "Listen!" she hissed. "Are you telling me the truth about all this? The whole truth?"

He gave her a shaky nod. "I swear I am."

"Okay." She unlocked his cuffs. "Crawl back into that other bedroom." She jerked her head. "Get yourself sheltered behind the bed with as much protection as you can, but leave a clear sight line to the front window."

He moved hastily to obey. She edged closer to the fireplace on her knees and elbows, then leaped up and grabbed the rifle from its hooks, finding to her relief that it was loaded. Several boxes of ammunition stood on a wall shelf nearby.

Jackie grabbed the shells and sank to the floor again as another volley of shots rang out.

Whoever was outside had automatic weapons and were firing from at least two different vantage points. Those two alone would have enough firepower to level the cabin.

Inside, on the other hand, they were armed with a squirrel rifle and a handgun.

Pretty much typical, Jackie thought bitterly, of the difference in weaponry whenever police officers came up against bad guys bent on destruction.

She crawled past the bedroom and handed Stevenson the rifle and box of shells.

"Stay here," she told him. "Aim straight at the window. If anybody comes through, shoot him. I'll take the door."

Another deafening burst of gunfire hammered the front of the cabin. She slithered hastily into the adjoining bedroom and propped herself on her elbows behind the crude bed.

They heard some muffled noises, then the sound of steps mounting the veranda.

"Are you okay, John?" she called softly.

"I'm fine," he said. "You?"

"Ready for anything."

"I didn't kill her," he said in a muffled voice. "I didn't kill anybody."

"Okay, John. Let's not think about it right now. Let's just see if we can get out of here alive."

She swore under her breath when she heard the sound of an ax hammering at the front door. The wood creaked and splintered. In a moment the door would give way.

A shout came from outside and a bulky figure appeared suddenly in the shattered window. Stevenson's rifle cracked from the adjoining bedroom. The intruder screamed, then staggered backward and vanished.

"Good one, John!" she called.

Daylight began to appear through the slabs. With another whack and a shriek of metal, the slide bolt ripped away to leave the door hanging halfway open. Light and cold flooded in.

Jackie kept her eyes fixed grimly on the door, her gun braced on her left forearm. The ax head appeared, pushing the door wider open, but she held her fire.

A long moment passed. It was so intensely silent that she could hear the silvery chatter of magpies in the trees near the river.

She waited, conscious of her life passing in front of her eyes.

The desperate childhood years and her long struggle to become a police officer and then a detective. The slow growth of friendships, the lonely years before Paul came into her life, the fights and the tender loving they'd shared...

Suddenly the body of a man filled the open doorway. He held an assault rifle with a dangling ammu-

nition clip and he was spraying the cabin with gunfire.
The noise was horrific. Bullets ricocheted off the rock
fireplace, peppered the walls, zinged into the open
bedrooms and danced on the floor.

Jackie took aim and fired, and the noise stopped.
The man slumped forward into the room, sprawling.
Abruptly he changed from a monstrous avenger to an
ugly lump of flesh, slightly overweight in a pair of
tattered ski pants and a heavy knitted sweater.

Most of the back of his head was gone. Blood
flowed from the pulpy mass and spread across the
rough wooden floor.

Jackie tried to avert her eyes, but the smell of blood
filled the room along with a rank stench from the
man's bowels, loosened in death.

Bile rose sharply in her throat. She withdrew behind the bed and knelt to vomit, then raised the gun,
battling a wave of trembling weakness. She crept out
to the other room, avoiding the sticky flow of blood.

"John," she whispered hoarsely. "Are you all
right?"

"I'm fine."

"Cover me, okay? I'm going outside to see if
there's anybody else."

"I'm coming with you."

He appeared from the bedroom, clutching the rifle,
also looking shaken. Blood flowed from his upper
arm and drenched his shirtsleeve.

"Just a graze," he said when he saw Jackie looking
at the wound. "A stray bullet."

Together they edged toward the veranda, avoiding
the thing on the floor.

A man slumped against the veranda railing, bleeding from a wound in his abdomen. Another automatic

rifle lay discarded in the snow at the base of the steps. He slumped over, moaning and clutching himself.

Jackie turned the gun on him. "Are there any more?" she asked.

He whimpered.

She nudged him with her toe. "Tell me! Are there any more of you?"

"No, just two. Him and me." He rolled his eyes upward in a face that was ashen under a spotty beard. "I need help," he muttered between sobs. "I'm bleeding to death."

"Who sent you here?"

He shook his head.

"Who sent you?" Jackie repeated. She bent to grasp his hair and lifted his head so she could look directly into his face. "How did you find this place? Tell me, or we'll go away and forget about you."

"We been following you." His voice was thin and raspy. "Burkett told us you'd lead us to the other guy if we kept watching."

"You work for Jason Burkett?"

"Yeah," he muttered, then coughed. Blood spattered his upraised hands and he looked at them. "He wanted both of you dead."

She got up and turned aside. With a glance at Stevenson, she looked inside the cabin again at the body sprawled on the floor. After the fresh outdoor air, the stench was unbearable.

"Come on, John," she said dully. "Let's walk out of here and see if we can find their vehicle. My guess is it'll be a black sport-utility van. And if it is, we can probably use it to take this guy to the hospital."

He nodded, still gripping his rifle. They set off together, trudging side by side up the hill through the peaceful quiet of the falling snow.

Jackie filed her paperwork on the shooting and was extensively debriefed on all the events leading up to and including the gunfight at the cabin. Michelson reprimanded her privately for going to the cabin without backup, but agreed not to put a letter in her file when she explained that her intention had never been to go inside or engage the criminal, just to observe and report. Still, he ordered her not to come back to work until after Christmas, so she spent most of the week wandering aimlessly around her apartment.

She couldn't sleep more than a few hours a night. As soon as she closed her eyes, images of blood and noise came flooding into her mind. Nausea assailed her throughout the day and her appetite fled. Weight melted off her body, more than five pounds by the end of the week.

The details of their final confrontation at the cabin were kept out of the media, so even Adrienne didn't know much about her involvement. Karl Widmer suspected, though. He called and asked to meet with her, promising to keep their conversation off the record, but she declined.

Although she would have scorned such help in the past, Jackie went twice to the police psychologist for trauma counseling and found it helped a little to talk about what had happened. The psychologist, however, was also concerned about her physical condition and referred her to an internist for an overall examination.

Her appointment was the day before Christmas. She woke feeling sad and restless, made a breakfast that she didn't feel like eating, then wondered how to fill in the hour before she had to leave for the clinic.

On impulse she drove over to the Stevenson house.

She parked in the driveway, then walked up the freshly cleaned steps to the front door and rang the bell.

As so often happened, Emily answered the door and stood looking up at her. But instead of hanging on the doorknob and giving her one of those cold appraising stares, this time the little girl beamed happily and hugged Jackie's knees.

"Hey, Jackie's here!" she called, tugging at the visitor.

Jackie found herself in the living room, surrounded by people as she took off her coat and boots. Carly hurried in from the kitchen, accompanied by Caitlin and Rachel. Both children's faces were smeared with colored icing.

"We're making cookies for Santa!" Rachel said, jumping from one foot to another. "Christmas trees and angels and snowflakes."

Jackie smiled at Carly, who looked like a different person from the pale, desperate woman who'd first arrived at the police substation with her children a few weeks earlier.

Carly's face was flushed with happiness, her eyes bright. She reached out to touch Jackie's arm.

"How are you?" she murmured. "It's so nice to see you."

"I'm fine," Jackie said.

John appeared in the kitchen doorway, carrying Patrick who was dressed in a yellow terry-cloth sleeper and fuzzy socks, his hair damp from his bath.

Jackie smiled at them. "Hi, John. How's the arm?"

He lifted his free elbow, settling the baby more firmly into the crook of his other arm. "Getting better. It still hurts a lot, but there's no infection, the doctor says."

"Santa's coming tonight!" Emily shouted. "Daddy says he's coming down the chimney and bringing presents for everybody. Look, Jackie!"

Obediently Jackie examined the row of stockings hung by the fireplace. Her emotions, always distressingly close to the surface these days, threatened to overwhelm her again.

"I'll bet Santa's going to bring you nice things," she told the twins. "You've been good girls."

"Yes," Rachel agreed solemnly. "We really, really have."

The adults exchanged a smile.

"Caitlin," John told his oldest daughter, "take the twins into the kitchen and finish decorating the cookies, all right? Mommy and I want to talk with Jackie for a minute."

The children ran back into the kitchen, dancing and jostling each other with excitement. "Don't make a mess," their mother called automatically to the empty doorway.

But there was no conviction in her voice, and when she looked at Jackie her face was gentle and luminous with happiness.

The three adults sat in the living room by the decorated tree, next to the fireplace with its little row of stockings.

"Do you want to hold him?" John asked, pausing by Jackie's chair. "He's all cuddly now because it's just about nap time."

"Sure," Jackie said, startled.

John settled the little boy into her arms and she leaned back, holding him. Patrick smelled of baby powder and clean damp hair. He snuggled against her shoulder and blinked up at her gravely, a tiny thumb jammed into his mouth.

Jackie smiled down at him, then bent to kiss the top of his head.

She looked up at the couple sitting opposite her. "Jason Burkett's made a full statement," she said. "My partner's handling the investigation now, so I wasn't at the station when they interrogated Burkett. But I went down yesterday for a couple of hours to listen to the tape recording."

"So he admitted everything?" Stevenson asked.

"Pretty much the way you told me." Jackie glanced at Carly, then back at the man siting next to her in his faded jeans and college sweatshirt.

"Carly knows everything now," John said quietly. "I should have told her right from the beginning. We've already paid back the money I took from the company, and I have an interview next week for a job with a trucking firm out in the Valley."

Carly reached over and squeezed his hand, giving him a look of tenderness. Jackie knew there were no more problems in the Stevenson household on this snowy Christmas Eve.

"Well," she said, "he described your little fling at embezzlement, how he caught you at it, then used the fact to pressure you into laundering illegal campaign contributions. When you tried to back out, he trapped you into that nude scene with Darla Drake and hoped he could use the photos to blackmail you."

The baby's eyes dropped shut, his eyelashes dark and soft against his plump cheeks.

"By now," Jackie added, "that financial stuff all seems pretty much like a side issue. There'll be no political career for Jason Burkett."

"He talked about Darla?" John asked.

"He actually seemed relieved to tell the police what happened. He said as soon as Angela was killed and the police described the vehicle that hit her, he suspected it was probably Darla because she'd been threatening to come to his house and cause trouble. So he told Norine all about their relationship, and that's when the Burketts quit cooperating with police investigators. They didn't want Darla caught, knowing she'd talk and the whole scandal would surface."

Carly shook her head in disbelief. "Even after their little girl was killed, they were still thinking about their political career?"

"They were completely motivated by politics," Jackie said grimly. "That's why he killed Darla. She called him, distraught over the hit-and-run accident, and threatened again to go public about their relationship, so he knew he had to silence her. He doesn't seem to feel any remorse," she added. "His reasoning is apparently that she killed Angela, so she deserved to die."

"But how did my fingerprints get there?" Stevenson asked. "I was never at her house except for that time when they took the pictures."

"That was Norine's idea," Jackie said. "I guess she'd seen it on a television show. When Burkett had a drink with you the week before you took off, he put your glass in his pocket after you left the bar, planning to frame you for some sort of crime. He was really excited when he had the chance to plant that glass at an actual murder scene. That way, if you said anything against him, it would be discounted because you'd look like you were just trying to lie your way out of trouble.''

John and Carly exchanged a horrified glance.

''He got so slick,'' Jackie said, ''that he even called the Prairie Club on Tuesday and asked for Darla, reasoning that if we discovered their connection, this call would establish his innocence by making it look like he had no idea the woman was dead.''

''And did he say anything about…'' John looked at the baby, now drowsing in Jackie's arms. ''Did he admit anything about those threats to my kids?''

''He talked quite freely about that. The Burketts were both terrified when you quit your job, then dropped out of sight. As a loose cannon, you were a huge danger to their political ambitions. They decided the kids were the best means to flush you out of hiding, because Jason never really believed you'd take off and abandon Carly. He and Norine figured if they could grab one of the kids, you'd be upset enough to come forward where they could get at you and silence you.''

Carly shuddered and looked down at her hands, twisted together in her lap.

''But the attempt to drive me off the road while the twins were in the van…that must have been Norine herself,'' Jackie said. ''She was apparently following me, hoping I'd lead her to you.''

John reached out and took his wife's hand, gripping it tightly. ''Has Norine confessed to her part in all this?'' he asked.

Jackie shook her head. ''She denies everything. Norine claims she didn't have a clue what her husband was up to, and that she was so overwhelmed with grief over her daughter's death, she didn't know what was happening in their household. She even told my partner she had no idea Jason could be so ruthless."

"Does anybody believe her?"

"No, but I still think she'll get away with it. One of the thugs they hired is dead. The other one's going to survive, but he doesn't have anything incriminating to say about Norine. It's Jason's word against hers as to what she knew and when, and he's already quit talking about her. He says he won't testify against her, even if he could cut a deal. I think the poor guy still loves her."

"But Norine's not capable of loving anybody," Carly said.

"That's probably true. Norine Burkett is a bundle of ambition inside a stainless-steel casing. I predict," Jackie added, "that after Jason's gone to prison, she'll find some other guy on the way up and attach herself to him. She might make it to the White House yet."

The young couple shook their heads and sat quietly holding hands.

"She's not like your wife," Jackie said to John. "Carly never stopped believing in you, no matter what happened."

John Stevenson reached over without embarrassment and stroked his wife's cheek, smiling into her eyes.

Carly smiled back, then got up to take the sleeping baby.

"Would you like some eggnog, Jackie? Or maybe a decorated cookie?" she asked with a rueful grimace toward the noisy kitchen.

Jackie got to her feet and reached for her coat and

boots. "Maybe another time, okay? I have an appointment downtown in a little while."

John followed her to the door and surprised her with a fierce hug. "Thanks, Jackie," he whispered. "Thanks for everything."

She protested and drew away, embarrassed.

But as she walked down to her car, she remembered the row of little stockings on the hearth, the children's laughter and the sleeping baby in her arms, and felt almost unbearably lonely.

26

Almost two hours later Jackie left the doctor's office with a handful of pamphlets on proper diet and vitamin supplements.

She got into her car, drove to the edge of the parking lot and sat hesitantly at the street entrance, wondering where to go.

The world had changed since her arrival at the clinic. Though it was midday, the clouds had massed and closed in overhead, creating an illusion of nightfall. The city beneath was like a golden globe suspended in the winter stillness, shimmering brightly with colored lights and tinsel.

Snow continued to drift down, so gently that each flake was visible, enchanting in its delicate symmetry. There was a feeling of stillness and peace, of families safely enclosed within their houses, shutting out the rest of the world.

Finally Jackie drove south under the freeway and headed for the upscale neighborhood where Adrienne and Harlan lived.

She entered the house, stamping snow from her boots while Adrienne hugged her joyously.

"What a nice surprise, Jackie! I've been worried about you all week but I knew you had things to do, so I didn't want to intrude. How are you?"

Jackie looked into her friend's concerned face. "I'm okay, Rennie. It gave me a nasty shock, that whole incident. But I'm getting over it now."

"Well, when you feel better," Adrienne said, hanging Jackie's coat in the closet, "you can tell me all about it, or as much as you're allowed to say. In the meantime, come have some shortbread cookies."

Jackie followed her friend into the cozy family room and settled onto a leather couch next to Adrienne's Christmas tree. She pulled her legs up under her and looked around with a sigh of pleasure.

"I went over to visit the Stevensons for a few minutes this morning," she said.

Adrienne brightened. "How are they?"

"Happy as a bunch of little clams." Jackie told her friend about the decorated cookies, the little row of stockings by the fireplace and Carly's shining face.

Adrienne smiled dreamily at the flames on the hearth. "I'm so glad, Jackie," she said. "Just so glad. I love that family."

"Where are Harlan and Alex?" Jackie asked.

"They went out to do some very late Christmas shopping." Adrienne chuckled, filling tumblers with eggnog from the bar fridge. "That man always leaves his shopping till the last minute, then has to go out in a panic and try to find something."

"Well, at least he has Alex to help." Jackie examined her friend with new interest. "Hey, you're actually showing, Rennie," she said. "In fact, that's quite a bump you've got there."

Adrienne patted her abdomen contentedly. "I'm more than five months pregnant. By now, this little person not only moves every day, it does the backstroke."

"No kidding?" Jackie grinned, picturing the tiny swimmer.

"Have you decided what you're doing for Christmas tomorrow, Jackie? I don't want you to be all alone in that apartment. Not after what you've just been through."

Jackie moved restlessly on the couch. She picked up a needlepoint cushion and toyed with it, wrapping the strands of silken fringe around her fingers. At the moment, it was impossible for her to meet her friend's eyes.

"You're so pale," Adrienne went on, "and I'm sure you're thinner. Have you seen a doctor, Jackie?"

"I went to a trauma counselor a couple of times," Jackie said in a low voice. "We talked about the job and the..." She paused, then took a deep breath. "But we talked about a lot of other stuff, too, that had nothing to do with police work."

"Like what?"

"My childhood, my grandmother and the way I feel about my life...fear of commitment, all that sort of thing."

"Was it helpful?"

Jackie turned the cushion over and smoothed the velvet surface, spreading the nap back and forth. "It was okay. I never thought I'd get much out of talking to a shrink, but he was a pretty smart guy."

"I'm glad they provided you with some help. It's the least they can do."

Adrienne picked up a length of delicate crochet work and began to ply the hook. It flashed in and out of the creamy lace like a silver dart, catching flares of color from the Christmas tree.

"But this shrink," Jackie said, "he apparently

thinks I'm not as healthy as I should be, so he sent me to a doctor for a physical. I just went this morning and had a lot of tests."

Her voice went suddenly hoarse, alerting Adrienne, who looked up in alarm.

"Jackie," she whispered, the hook suspended above her crochet work. "Are you all right?"

Jackie got up and moved across the room to touch one of the ornaments on the tree, nerving herself to say the words aloud. "Well, it seems I'm—" She stopped midsentence.

"What?" Adrienne came and stood next to her, slipping an arm around her shoulders.

Jackie turned and stood in her friend's embrace, burying her face in Adrienne's shoulder.

"I'm pregnant, Rennie," she whispered. "The doctor says I'm three months pregnant."

Adrienne stood back, gaping at her with an expression of shock so profound that it was almost funny. Her face turned pink and she began to laugh, hugging Jackie in delight.

"That's wonderful news, Jackie! Oh, God, it's just so wonderful!"

Jackie stood unmoving in her friend's embrace.

Adrienne drew away again, gave her a shrewd glance and led her back to the couch, settling close beside her.

"*Is* it wonderful, Jackie?" she asked quietly. "How do you feel about this?"

Jackie shook her head, searching for words.

"When the doctor told me, I felt nothing at all, just total denial. I actually said that to him. 'Look, you've got to be kidding, this is all a mistake.' Even after he showed me the tests and convinced me it was true, I couldn't really feel anything. It never seemed real until just now, when I said it out loud to you."

"So how does it feel now? Do you...want the baby?" Adrienne asked.

"Want the baby?" Jackie turned to her, feeling dazed. "Of course I want the baby! This baby..." She touched her abdomen, still flat and taut under the cotton shirt and jeans. "The baby is...me and Paul. It's the most amazing..."

Tears filled her eyes and began to trickle down her cheeks. Without thinking, she wiped them on her shirtsleeve.

Adrienne smiled and supplied a couple of tissues from her pocket. Jackie seized them gratefully to blow her nose.

"Will you tell Paul?" Adrienne asked.

"As soon as I can," Jackie said. "It's his child as much as mine, and he has a right to know everything that's happening."

"So that means you're going to give in to his ultimatum and move to the ranch?"

Jackie shook her head, staring at the tree. "Nothing's really changed. In fact, back when Paul and I were fighting about commitment, I was already pregnant. The only thing that's different now is I know about the baby, that's all."

Adrienne patted her hand gently.

"But I grew up without a father," Jackie went on, "and I know how much it can screw a kid up." She frowned. "So is it my responsibility to give in and marry Paul even though I'm not ready, just because we've made a baby together?"

"That's up to you, sweetie. It's nobody's choice but yours."

Jackie nodded. As they talked, she was beginning to feel a little stronger, more in control of this devastating miracle that had somehow invaded her body.

She looked down at her hands, twisting them together nervously.

"At times like this, Rennie, I always start to hear my grandmother's voice inside my head," she said in a low voice. "I've never told anybody about it, except for the shrink."

"What does your grandmother's voice say to you?" Adrienne asked.

"She tells me I'm not good enough, not capable enough, that I'm sure to mess up, and whatever I decide to do it's going to be the wrong choice."

"Oh, for God's sake!" Adrienne said with an outraged indignant tone that, under other circumstances, would probably have made Jackie laugh. "What absolute, utter nonsense."

"Is it, Rennie?"

"Of course it is." Adrienne raised her hand and ticked items off on her fingers. "You're the best friend I've ever had, Jackie. You're also the most physically courageous woman I know. And you have so much generosity…you do good things for all kinds of people you meet during your job. I'm sure nobody even knows how much you help others. And you're going to be the best mother there ever was, no matter what kind of household arrangement you decide on. So to hell with your grandmother and her constant disapproval."

Jackie looked at her friend. "You really believe all that, Rennie?"

"With my whole heart and soul." Adrienne smiled. "When's your baby due?"

"June." As she spoke, Jackie felt a sudden little glow of excitement that trickled all through her body like a bright river. "As near as the doctor could figure, the baby's due in early June."

"What a lovely time to be born. Our babies will be just a couple of months apart."

Jackie got up and wandered toward the closet. "I need to..." she said vaguely. "Adrienne, I'm sorry, but I need to go now."

"Where?" Adrienne asked, looking worried. "Why don't you just stay and spend the day with us? The others will be home soon and we'll make popcorn and have a nice cozy Christmas Eve dinner."

"I want to go and tell Paul about the baby," Jackie said.

Adrienne got up instantly and went to fetch her visitor's coat.

"Well, *that*," she said solemnly, "is a different matter altogether. A far better plan than anything I could have suggested. But you be sure to drive carefully, you hear?"

Jackie put on her outerwear and boots, then paused in the doorway to hug her friend. "Merry Christmas, Rennie," she whispered. "I really love you."

"Here, what's all this?" Adrienne drew away, shaking her head. "Impending motherhood is making you all soppy." She brushed at her eyes. "Now *go*, before you get me started, too."

Jackie headed north toward the freeway. On impulse she stopped at a little hardware store and bought an artificial tree, some lights and an assortment of ornaments. Then she turned west and drove out of the city, wondering what was happening to her.

She'd never set up and decorated a Christmas tree in her whole life.

But then, Paul probably hadn't, either. It was something they'd have to muddle through together.

There would be so many adjustments ahead of them now, all kinds of bitter fights and awkward compromises, so much to learn.

In fact, this was the biggest challenge Jackie had ever faced in her whole troubled and difficult life. But for the first time, she wasn't frightened by what lay ahead.

She felt a huge relief, like a stone rolling away from her heart, when she realized what had caused her bizarre weepiness and irrational bursts of emotion over the past couple of months. The confusion, sickness and mood swings hadn't been due to some awful change in her personality.

They were simply a part of being pregnant.

Gram's mocking image and that voice whispering in her ear were gone too, magically vanished. In their place was a baby, nestled close to her heart, resting securely at the very core of her being.

To her astonishment, Jackie realized she already loved this unseen tiny person with a fierce passion. And she knew beyond a shadow of a doubt that she would be able to care for her baby.

Nothing Gram said could ever discourage her, nor could Paul's demands sway her resolve.

Jackie Kaminsky was having a baby, and she was going to be a good mother.

"I'm going to be a good mother," she whispered, then said it aloud, shouting to the western sky where the snowfall was increasing and the prairie spread white and silent all around her.

She turned onto the road leading to Paul's ranch and was surprised by a flood of joy so intense her body could scarcely contain the rich tide of happiness.

Soon she was able to see the sprawl of individual buildings and finally the lonely ranch house, dark and silent against the fading twilight.

Paul was trudging across the yard toward the house, carrying a metal pail. His broad shoulders were hunched and he looked small and lonely in all that vast landscape.

Jackie pulled into the ranch yard with her load of Christmas decorations piled high in the back of the little car. He caught sight of her and stood for a moment, staring in amazement. Then he tossed the pail aside and began to run toward her, clumsy in his winter boots.

Jackie scrambled from the car and flung herself into his arms, laughing.

"Merry Christmas," she whispered.

"Darling!" He was kissing her, his mouth moving hungrily over her face and eyelids. "Jackie, sweetheart..."

He felt so wonderful in her arms, so completely satisfying. Reluctantly she pulled away from him. "Can we go inside and talk for a minute, Paul?"

"Sure." He released her at once and followed her to the house, where they both stopped in the back porch to take off their winter coats and boots.

Inside the kitchen Jackie switched on the electric kettle. "I think I'll make myself a cup of soup," she said. "I'm starving."

"Jackie, I heard about what happened out in that cabin. Are you all right?"

"I'm getting better, but it was pretty awful."

"I was really worried about you." Paul crossed the kitchen and sat at the table. "A few days ago I called the office and Brian told me you were taking the week off work."

She tore open an envelope of dried soup mix and emptied it into a mug. "But you didn't call me?"

"I didn't want to put pressure on you."

Jackie turned to face him. "Well, I kept hoping you'd call," she said.

His face lit with disbelieving happiness.

"Don't misunderstand me," she said hastily. "I'm still not ready to move out here with you, Paul. But I want to see if we can work something out, because it's so damn hard to live without you. And because…"

She fell silent, her heart pounding.

"What?" he said, watching her intently. "What were you going to say?"

She took a deep breath. "I'm pregnant. I just found out this morning."

He stared at her, clearly thunderstruck. "You're *pregnant?*"

"Three months. The baby's due in June."

He got up and strode across the room to take her in his arms. "Jackie," he whispered against her hair. "Sweetheart, what are you telling me?"

"I'm telling you that you're going to be a daddy," she murmured against his chest. "How does it feel?"

His arms tightened. "It feels wonderful. A bit of a shock, I'll admit, but damn wonderful."

"Oh, Paul," she whispered, burrowing into his embrace. "It *is* wonderful, isn't it?"

He stood back for a moment to study her face

gravely. "So I'm going to be a father, but not a husband?"

"Give me just a little more time," she begged. "Please, Paul, let me work through this at my own pace. I don't want to live without you, and I don't want to raise a baby without a father. But I can't face the idea of marriage right now."

She could see the conflicting emotions on his face, and the battle that he was waging with himself. At last he gathered her into his arms again.

"Hell, who cares about the future?" he said. "You're here right now, and we're going to have a baby. I can be happy with that."

"I love you, Paul."

His lips began to move over her face again, warm and seeking. "Will you stay with me tonight?"

"I have to," she said.

"You do? Why?"

"Because I brought a Christmas tree," she murmured against his throat. "Do you know anything about setting one up and putting the lights on and stuff?"

"Not a damn thing." He began to kiss her again.

"Oh, Paul," she said, her voice breaking. "There are so many things we'll have to learn. We need to..." But he was kissing her mouth now and she couldn't speak.

Jackie sighed in bliss and gave herself up to the luxury of his embrace. There would be time later, in the lighted glow of their tree, to talk about the things they still needed to settle between them.

It was twilight on Christmas Eve, and they had all the time in the world.

*Turn the page for a preview
of Jackie Kaminsky's next exciting case*

FOURTH HORSEMAN

by

Margot Dalton

coming September 1999

only from

_ Fourth Horseman _

"So how big do you want this flower bed to be?" Paul asked her.

"Just a few more feet to the left, where the edge lines up with the sidewalk. But you don't have to finish it all today, Paul. I can dig the rest myself if you get most of the sod out."

"I don't think shovelling is a good thing for you to be doing right now." His eyes rested thoughtfully on her swollen abdomen.

"I've never lived in a house before," she said to change the topic. "Did you know that, Paul? First I lived in Gram's dumpy apartment, then..." She poked at the grass again. "Then a couple of fun-filled years in juvenile detention, then the police academy while I was in training. And I've always lived in apartments during my service."

"You've lived in my house sometimes," Paul said, digging without expression. "But I guess that was never long enough to classify as a life-style." He tossed a clump of sod onto the wheelbarrow. "Those were more like visits, weren't they, Jackie?"

He leaned on the shovel and watched her gravely.

"Is this what it takes to make you happy?" he said at last. "A little house with a brick fireplace and some flower beds...is that really going to do it for you?"

He didn't seem to be challenging her, just expressing interest. She took a deep breath and pressed one hand against her abdomen where the baby turned and kicked lustily. Then she looked around at the surrounding neighborhood. "Some of these people have lived here for seventy years. That's the kind of security I want to have. And I want it for the baby, too. I need to feel that sense of things continuing, of permanence and stability. My life has been so..."

"What's this?" he muttered, frowning as he jabbed at the loosened dirt.

"Paul?"

He looked up briefly. "Sorry, I didn't mean to interrupt."

"What are you looking at down there?"

"Well, I wanted to dig a little deeper to see what kind of soil bed you were going to have for your garden, but I'm coming onto something..."

"What is it?" She leaned forward.

He prodded experimentally with the shovel. "It feels like...I'm not sure."

"A treasure chest?" she asked hopefully.

"I'm afraid not. More likely a buried pet. That's what I'd guess, anyway. It feels like a bundle of bones wrapped in some kind of plastic tarp."

Jackie stared at the loosened soil and the narrow pit he'd excavated. Suddenly she felt a stirring of uneasiness in her stomach, accompanied by a cold chill of fear.

"Whatever it is," she said sharply, "I don't want it in the middle of my flower bed."

He poked the tip of his shovel along the trench, then frowned. "What the hell?" he muttered.

Jackie heaved herself erect and walked across the

freshly dug sod to peer into the furrow. At the bottom of the trench, partially exposed in the dark soil, was a blue plastic tarpaulin. The rotting fabric was riddled with holes from which frayed threads bristled, and had been wrapped tightly around something that formed a faded cocoon about five or six feet long.

Paul and Jackie exchanged a glance. "You know what?" she muttered. "It looks like…"

"It sure does," he said when she fell silent. "So what should we do now, Jackie? You're the expert in situations like this."

She knelt awkwardly over the bulk of her abdomen, reaching out to touch the brittle fabric. "There's no reason to suspect it's human remains," she said. "Any number of things could be wrapped in a bundle this size."

"Like what? A dead Russian wolfhound?"

Jackie found a loose edge of fabric and tugged gently, then with more force. Bits of the old tarp frayed and pulled apart in her hands.

"It's all stuck to itself," she muttered.

"Why?" Paul knelt beside her, staring into the pit. "Could somebody have glued it?"

"Not necessarily," she told him. "Decaying bodily fluids would also cause the plastic to stick and fuse together like this. But I can't smell anything at all, so if there's a body in here, it's been buried a good long time."

"Well," Paul said grimly, "that's comforting, isn't it?"

He reached into a small pouch at his belt and took out a black-handled case knife, flicking it open to reveal a shining blade.

"Here," he said, handing it to Jackie.

She took the knife, then hesitated. "Technically we shouldn't be doing this. We should call Ident and get them out here to take some pictures before we…"

"Come on," Paul said, touching her shoulder. "I think you're overreacting. You've been on the police force in Spokane for ten years, right?"

She nodded.

"And in that time, have you ever heard of a murder in this neighborhood besides Maribel Lewis, or anybody going missing?"

She shook her head.

"So the chances of this being a human body are pretty remote. More likely what's under this tarp is somebody's pet dog."

"You're probably right," she said reluctantly.

"Of course I am. So let's see what it is before we have police cars all over the place and wind up terrifying the neighbors. Do you want me to cut the tarp open?"

"No, I'll do it, just in case there might be some kind of question later."

Paul grinned. "Always a cop, even off-duty."

Jackie ignored him, placing the knife carefully into the chrysalis of faded blue plastic and slicing downward for a couple of feet. After she got it started, the blade moved easily.

She set the knife aside, grasped the cut edges of the plastic and pulled them open, then gasped.

A human skull grinned at her from the shadows. It was darkly stained, with bits of dirt and small roots lodged in the eye sockets.

A stale, fetid gush of air came from within the blue wrappings and vanished on the afternoon breeze. Apart from that, there was no smell of decay.

Paul knelt and pressed close to her, staring in fascination at the skull. "What's that stuff?" he asked, pointing. "It looks like dried grass or something."

"Probably hair," Jackie muttered. "Human hair will survive a long time underground, after all the body fluids and tissues are gone. It even outlasts cartilage."

She nerved herself to pull the plastic wrapping aside and looked more closely.

The skeleton was mostly bare and clean, a jumble of bones within its torn cocoon. Here and there she saw traces of a mottled, papery substance that could be the remnants of clothing.

She tried to think clearly, to remember the procedure for cases like this. But as she studied the clutter of bones, horror began to mount in her brain, screaming at her and making her dizzy.

"Jesus, Paul," she murmured, turning to lean against him.

"Jackie?" he asked. "What is it?"

She choked and swallowed a sob.

"Jackie, you're shaking." He put his arms around her and moved closer on his knees to hold her awkwardly.

She sniffled and took herself in hand, pulling away from him to swipe an arm across her damp face.

"Look," she told him, pointing. "Look there."

Amid the jumble of bones was a small, rounded object. Jackie turned it over with a shaking forefinger.

Paul gasped, then went pale beneath his tan. The little globe was a baby's skull.

He clutched Jackie's arm so tightly that it hurt. "It's a baby," he muttered. "And somebody made a hole in its head."

Jackie shook her head, still gripped by irrational, shuddering terror. She touched the place where her own baby kicked placidly in its safe, watery world.

"That's not an injury," she said. "It's a fontanelle. What people call the 'soft spot.'" She glanced briefly at Paul. "This was a newborn baby."

He settled back on his heels, looking at the two grinning skulls. "Maybe it was a natural death. She could have died in childbirth."

"She could have," Jackie said grimly. "But she damned sure didn't bury herself in the backyard."